"You're the lying scum of the earth, Sarah Parker,

"or whatever your name is. I've hanged nobler souls than you, and I won't have my nieces and nephews growing up under your influence. I won't have my sister—*ouch!*" Donovan snarled as the stinging alcohol penetrated raw flesh.

Sarah had never realized words could hurt so much. Inwardly she recoiled as if he had struck her, but nothing showed in her face. Whatever happened, she could not let him see how deeply he had wounded her. She could not give him the satisfaction, or the power.

Gulping back tears, she forced her features into an icy mask. "I'll not have you telling me where I can or can't make my home," she declared coldly. "Do your worst, Donovan. It won't make any difference. I can be stubborn as a mule, and I'm not going anywhere."

"Then you're a fool…!"

Dear Reader,

Elizabeth Lane's *Lydia* is the touching story of a former Union spy who moves to Colorado and falls in love with the brother of a man who died as a result of her actions. We hope you enjoy this moving Western from the author of *MacKenna's Promise*, which *Romantic Times* described as "...a richly passionate story sure to warm every reader's heart."

Sparks fly when a rogue knight who is running from his past rescues a strong-willed noblewoman who is running from her future in Susan Paul's *The Heiress Bride*. Don't miss this lively medieval romance, which is the second book in the author's Bride Trilogy.

Love and loyalty clash in *Devil's Dare* by Laurie Grant, a fast-paced Western about a sweet-talking cowboy and a straitlaced preacher's daughter whom he mistakes for a soiled dove.

The Gambler's Heart is the third book in Gayle Wilson's Heart Trilogy. This passionate Regency features a war-scarred French gambler who acquires a wife as payment for a debt, and must learn to accept her love for him.

Whatever your taste in reading, we hope that Harlequin Historicals will keep you coming back for more. Please keep a lookout for all four titles, available wherever Harlequin books are sold.

Sincerely,

Tracy Farrell
Senior Editor

Please address questions and book requests to:
Harlequin Reader Service
U.S.: 3010 Walden Ave., P.O. Box 1325, Buffalo, NY 14269
Canadian: P.O. Box 609, Fort Erie, Ont. L2A 5X3

ELIZABETH LANE
Lydia

Harlequin Books

TORONTO • NEW YORK • LONDON
AMSTERDAM • PARIS • SYDNEY • HAMBURG
STOCKHOLM • ATHENS • TOKYO • MILAN
MADRID • WARSAW • BUDAPEST • AUCKLAND

ISBN 0-373-28902-2

LYDIA

Books by Elizabeth Lane

Harlequin Historicals

Wind River #28
Birds of Passage #92
Moonfire #150
MacKenna's Promise #216
Lydia #302

ELIZABETH LANE

has traveled extensively in Latin America, Europe and China, and enjoys bringing these exotic locales to life on the printed page, but she also finds her home state of Utah and other areas of the American West to be fascinating sources for historical romance. Elizabeth loves such diverse activities as hiking and playing the piano, not to mention her latest hobby— belly dancing.

For Adam

Chapter One

Miner's Gulch, Colorado Territory
March 19, 1868

Donovan Cole had never felt more helpless in his life.

Not that he'd ever been a man to shrink from a tough situation. He had faced charging Yankees at Bull Run and Antietam. He had nursed fever and dug graves in the wretched Union prison at Camp Douglas, Illinois. And only last summer, as sheriff of Kiowa County, Kansas, he had brought in the murdering Slater brothers with the help of just one scared young deputy.

But this was different, and the very thought of what he was about to do made his hands shake with fear. Never, even in his wildest dreams, had Donovan imagined himself delivering a baby.

Crossing the cluttered cabin, he lifted the faded quilt that separated his sister's double bed from the living area. "You doing all right, Varina?" he asked, striving to hide his gnawing anxiety.

"Fair." The anguished whisper rose from the bulging mound of bedclothes. "But it won't be long now, I can tell. If Annie doesn't get back soon with the midwife—"

Varina's words ended in a gasp as another contraction seized her swollen body. Donovan reached for his sister's hands and clasped them tight. Varina's work-worn nails clawed into his palms as she twisted in agony. She would not cry out if she could help it, he knew. Her two younger children, Katy, six, and Samuel, a stoic four, sat huddled on the puncheon bench next to the cookstove. The sounds of their mother's travail would frighten and upset them.

Donovan had sent eight-year-old Annie posthaste down the gulch for the midwife when Varina's pains began in earnest. But that had been more than two hours ago, and in the interim it had begun to snow—the big, wet, feathery flakes of a spring blizzard. Annie could be anywhere, but he dared not leave Varina to go looking for her. He could only pray that the plucky child would be safe.

Donovan cursed silently as he stroked his sister's hands. He cursed the snow and the unplanned early onset of Varina's labor. He cursed Varina's gold-chasing husband, Charlie Sutton, and the fool's dream that had lured him to this miserable place. He cursed the mine cave-in, five weeks ago, that had left Varina widowed with three young children and another on the way.

Donovan had received the news about Charlie by letter. He had taken leave from his sheriff's job, planning to fetch his sister and her children back to Kansas. Only on his arrival in Miner's Gulch had he learned that Varina was in no condition to travel. And only then had he discovered her abject living conditions.

The first sight of the isolated, one-room hovel had wrenched Donovan's stomach. Ten years ago, Varina had been a belle, with dancing hazel eyes and flame red hair. She'd been raised to a gracious plantation life, pampered by slaves and courted by some of the finest young bloods in Virginia. Seeing her brought to *this* was almost more than he could stand. If flighty Charlie Sutton had been here to answer for how he'd done by her, Donovan would have given him the whipping of his life.

The contraction had passed. Varina lay exhausted on the sweat-soaked pillows, her lashes pale against paler cheeks. Leaving her for a moment, Donovan crossed the cabin and stepped out onto the rickety front porch. He needed a little time alone to think about what came next.

Snow swirled around him, blurring the ghost white trunks of the aspens that stood around the cabin. Even when he strained his eyes, Donovan could see no more than a stone's throw into the icy mountain twilight. What if young Annie had gotten lost out there? What if she'd fallen off a precipice or run afoul of a marauding cougar?

A wave of panic swept over him. "Annie!" he shouted, cupping his mouth with his hands. "Annie!"

The only answer was his own voice, echoing off the rocky cliffs. He was overreacting, Donovan admonished himself. Annie had grown up in Miner's Gulch. She could find her way blindfolded. Most likely, she'd simply had trouble locating the midwife in town—yes, that could be it. Or maybe the wretched female was too busy to come right away, and Annie was having to wait for her.

Donovan had met the midwife briefly on her last visit to check Varina. He had not been impressed. She was a spinsterly creature with pince-nez spectacles, skinned-back hair, and a Yankee's crackling, brittle speech—an odd presence in a town where nearly everyone had come from the South. When introduced to Donovan, she had not even raised her face to meet his eyes. She'd turned away so fast, in fact, that he'd scarcely gotten a decent look at her.

All the same, something about the woman had plucked a familiar chord in him. It was almost as if he'd seen her somewhere before. Try as he might, however, Donovan could not place her. He was imagining things, he'd concluded at last. Such an unsettling Yankee female would not have escaped his memory in the first place.

What had the children called her? Miss Sarah—that was it. Miss Sarah Parker. And when she wasn't delivering babies, they said, she ran a school in the rooms she rented above the general store. Oh, he knew the type. A Bible-toting, hymn-singing do-gooder. She probably wore long woolen underwear that scratched—on purpose.

Donovan glared into the snow-speckled darkness, swearing under his breath. If Miss Sarah Parker did not get here soon, he would have to deliver Varina's baby himself. He could manage a normal, easy birth, he supposed. But Lord, what if things didn't go as they should? How would he know what to do?

Lamplight from the open doorway flooded the porch as little Katy's voice shattered his thoughts. "Uncle Donovan, Mama needs you! She says to come right away!"

The baby! Donovan lunged back into the cabin, fighting paroxysms of cold fear. Why did it have to be now? What if he did something wrong? The infant could die. So could Varina.

"Sit with your brother and keep him quiet," he ordered the wide-eyed Katy. "Tell me if you hear anyone coming."

He stepped behind the quilt to see Varina writhing in the bed, her back arched in agony. "It's . . . time," she gasped. "I need Sarah—"

"Sarah's not here yet. You'll have to make do with me for now." Donovan leaned over her, praying silently for strength. "Tell me what to do, Varina."

"There's a bundle in that reed chest . . . right on top. Get it. . . ."

Fumbling in his haste, Donovan cleared the clutter from the top of the chest and raised the lid. The bundle was there, as she'd said. With shaking hands, he unrolled it on the foot of the bed. Inside were some threadbare cloths stiff from laundering, a string, a small, sharp kitchen knife, and a pint of cheap whiskey in a flat, brown bottle. He could imagine the purpose of the cloths. And the knife and string, he supposed, were for cutting and tying the birth cord. But what the devil was he supposed to do with the whiskey? Wash with it? Force it down his sister? Take a swig himself?

"Hurry—" Varina's hands clawed the patchwork coverlet. How did she find the strength to keep from screaming? Donovan wondered as he jerked back the bedclothes and, with effort, spread the clean cloths under the lower part of her twisting body. He would have sent the two children outside to wait on the porch, but in this damnable snowstorm—

"Donovan—" Varina caught his arm, her fingers digging into his flesh. "It's...coming!"

Sweat broke out like rain over Donovan's body. It was almost over, he reassured himself. Minutes from now, Varina would be nestling her newborn child in her arms, and he would be looking on in pride and joy, wondering why he'd been so scared.

Heart racing, he seized her hands. "Hold on tight!" he rasped. "Hold on and push for all you're worth!"

Varina's fingers taloned on his knuckles. Donovan could feel the strain in her, feel the excruciating effort as she struggled to give birth. Her face was a contorted mask in the yellow lamplight. The cords along her neck stood out like ropes.

"That's it!" Donovan urged as if he were prodding a faltering horse. "Come on, you can do it!"

"No—" Varina fell back on the pillow with an exhausted sob. "I can't," she whimpered softly, her head rolling from side to side. "Something's...wrong."

"What—?"

"I don't know—my other babies were easy—" She gasped as the next pain ripped through her tired body. Again she arched and struggled, battling vainly to push her child into the world.

Sick with fear, Donovan stroked her hands. Women died this way, he reminded himself. If he didn't do the right thing, and do it quickly, he would lose both Varina and her child.

But what *was* the right thing? He'd had no experience in birthing, not even with the animals on the plantation. An old slave named Abner had taken care of such matters. What he wouldn't give now for Abner's capable, dark hands, or for the quiet presence of Abner's wife, Vashti, who'd attended the slave women. Donovan felt as helpless as a child. And he was the only hope Varina had.

Damnation, where was that midwife?

Donovan bent over his sister and brushed the wet hair back from her care-lined forehead. He remembered how close they'd been in their growing-up years—he and Varina and their younger brother, Virgil. Virgil had died in Donovan's arms at Antietam. By all that was holy, he could not lose Varina, too!

"Tell me what to do," he pleaded, his throat so raw he could barely speak.

"Check for the head...." Her voice was a whisper, frighteningly weak. "If you don't find it...if the baby's lying wrong...you'll have to turn it."

"All right. Lie still." Donovan's stomach clenched into a cold ball as he imagined what he was about to do—the awful pain his fumbling hands would inflict on Varina, the risk to her fragile, unborn infant. Steeling himself, he reached for the hem of her flannel nightdress.

His quaking fingers could not even grasp the cloth.

"Donovan—?" She was waiting, her fists balled against the pain. But Donovan was paralyzed by his own dread. He could not move.

Racked with self-disgust, he wrenched himself away from the bedside. "I'll be right back," he growled. "Rest a minute if you can—and try not to push." Donovan shoved past the quilt and strode across the cabin. He groped for the door, then stumbled out onto the porch. His ribs heaved as he gulped the fresh, cold air.

He had to go back in there and help Varina. If he didn't, she and her child would die. But he was so afraid of hurting her, afraid of doing some terrible harm to the baby—

Snowflakes danced around him, diamond white against the darkness. They swirled down in infinite spirals from the murky sky as Donovan raised his eyes to heaven.

"Lord," he murmured, "I've tried not to trouble you much over the years. But right now I need your help. I have two lives to save, and I can't do the job alone." He paused self-consciously, cleared his throat and forced himself to continue. "You understand, it's not for myself I'm asking. I don't deserve any favors, least of all from you. But Varina, she's a good woman who's never done a lick of harm in her life. And she's got three fatherless little ones to raise—four, counting the baby—"

Donovan broke off in frustration. God could count, he reminded himself. As for the rest, he'd be better off inside, helping Varina, than standing out here stalling like a coward.

He cast one final, desperate glance into the snow-specked heavens. *"Please,"* he muttered. "Just—"

The sound of hoofbeats riveted his thoughts. He could hear them pounding up the gulch trail, moving rapidly closer. As Donovan's eyes probed the snowy darkness, a big dun mule burst out of the aspens and into the clearing.

Two dark shapes, one of them very small, clung to the mule's back. As the animal wheeled to a stop, Annie sprang to the ground and dashed toward the cabin. "Uncle Donovan, I brought Miss Sarah! Is Ma all right?"

"She's fine," Donovan lied. "Go on in and take care of Katy and Samuel. I'll see to the mule."

He loped off the porch and across the yard, to where Miss Sarah Parker was climbing down from the saddle, a canvas satchel clutched beneath her dark wool cloak. Relief jellied Donovan's knees. At that instant, he could have swept the spinsterly Miss Sarah into his arms, plucked off her pince-nez glasses, and kissed her full on her prim mouth.

"It's about time!" was all he could say.

"Sorry." She tossed him the reins. "I just finished delivering Minnie Hawkins down on Panner Creek. I couldn't get here any sooner. How is Varina?"

"Bad. The baby's not coming the way it should. I hope to heaven you haven't gotten here too late."

Miss Sarah swung resolutely toward the porch, her boots
crunching the new-fallen snow. Her plain, dark skirt
swished against her legs as she turned with one foot on the
rickety bottom step.

"Put Nebuchadnezzar in the shed and give him some
oats," she ordered crisply. "Then wash up and come inside. I expect I'll be needing your help."

She strode into the cabin. As he led the mule toward the
shed, Donovan heard her instructing Annie to take the
younger children to the cabin of old Ike Ordway, their
nearest neighbor down the gulch. By the time he'd stabled
the stubborn beast, they were on their way, trooping past
him in the sad little coats Varina had pieced from old blanket scraps.

Donovan dipped water from the porch bucket and used
a sliver of lye soap to lather his hands. He worked the suds
carefully around his fingers, shivering as the wind penetrated his worn flannel shirt. Everything was going to be all
right, he tried to reassure himself. The midwife was here.
She would know what to do.

All the same, he'd have felt better if the woman had been
older—say, a stalwart matron of forty who looked as if
she'd borne a half-dozen children of her own.

Washing done, he entered the cabin to find Sarah Parker
standing by the stove with her back to the door, rolling up
the sleeves of her gray shirtwaist. Strangely, the first
thought that flashed through his mind was how attractive
she appeared from behind. The lamplight melted on the coil
of her glossy brown hair where it lay low on the nape of her
neck. And even her drab clothes could not hide the elegant
set of her shoulders or the grace of a slender torso that
curved from hand-span waist to sensually rounded
haunches.

Donovan stared at her, galvanized once more by that
feeling he could not even name—as if the sight of her had
forged a dark link to some secret memory buried in the
depths of his mind. *What was it...?*

A frenzied moan from Varina burst the unfinished thought like a bubble. Sarah Parker turned and frowned at Donovan, as if she'd known all along that he was there.

"I just finished checking her. It looks like a breech birth."

Donovan nodded his understanding, mouth grimly set to hide his fear. "Then I guess you'll have to turn the baby. Can you do it?"

"I...hope so." Her gray eyes were pools of anxiety behind the pince-nez spectacles. Her fingers quivered as they fumbled with the cuff of her left sleeve. Midwife or not, she wasn't offering him much reassurance.

"Have you done anything like this before?" Donovan probed.

"I've never had to." She had turned her back on him again. "This is only my seventeenth baby. But I know how. I've read about it."

"*Read* about it! Good Lord, woman—"

"Would you rather do it yourself, Mr. Cole?" Her Yankee voice crackled like splintering ice.

Donovan surrendered with a ragged sigh. "All right. What can I do to help?"

"Come on." With an abrupt swish of petticoats, she strode behind the quilt, where Varina sprawled damp, tearful and exhausted on the rumpled sheets. Donovan's heart contracted at the sight of her. His questions about Sarah Parker evaporated as he knelt to take his sister's hand.

Sarah had taken a tin of greasy salve out of her satchel and was rubbing the stuff on her hands. "How long ago was the last pain, Varina?"

"Three...maybe four minutes." Varina's tired voice was so faint that Donovan could barely hear.

"We'll wait for the next one to pass. Then I'll try and turn the baby." Sarah hesitated, then continued. "It will hurt. I'll be as gentle as I can, but—"

"I know," Varina whispered. "It's all right. Do what you have to. And Sarah—"

"Yes?"

"If it's a question of saving me or the child...I want this baby to live."

"Hush!" As Sarah leaned over to squeeze Varina's hand, Donovan caught the glint of tears in her eyes. "Don't talk that way, Varina Sutton! You're going to be just fine, and so is your baby!"

Varina did not answer. Donovan watched the contraction take his sister. He watched it seize her swollen body in its cruel talons, squeezing and twisting until he wanted to scream for her.

"Get ready." Sarah shot him a hard glance through her round glass spectacles. "As soon as the pain eases, you hold her. Keep her as still as you can."

Donovan nodded, his throat too constricted to speak. He clasped Varina's hands, noticing how weak her grip was. She was nearing the end of her strength.

Varina's fingers began to relax as the pain diminished. Donovan could feel Sarah's presence in the tiny enclosure. He could sense the exquisite tension in her as she waited, drawing into herself like a cat preparing to spring.

"Now!" she exclaimed, shifting her position to the foot of the bed.

Donovan clasped his sister in his arms and held her with all his strength. Varina's nightdress, draped between her raised knees, blessedly screened Sarah from his view. But he could imagine what she was doing. He could feel every move she made in the agonized spasms that racked Varina's body. And once more, silently this time, he prayed.

Seconds oozed past like drops of blood. Varina's raw, anguished breathing rose to a gasp as she bit back the pain.

"It's all right, Varina." Sarah spoke with effort from the foot of the bed. "It—it won't be much longer now. I'm going to count to three, and when I do, you're to scream for all you're worth! Do you understand?"

"The . . . children," Varina murmured weakly.

"They've gone to Mr. Ordway's. They won't hear you." Sarah's shadow danced on the wall as she raised the lantern and set it on the washstand, then repositioned herself over the bed. "When I count three, now. One . . . two . . . three!"

Varina screamed. She screamed with the pent-up agony of hours. She screamed for Charlie, crushed in the mine. She screamed for Virgil, shattered by mortar fire at Antietam. She screamed for her own lost girlhood, and for the grace of a life that had vanished with the war's first shot.

Donovan squeezed tears from his eyes as her anguish knifed through him. If Varina survived this, he vowed, he would do anything to see her happy. He would work his fingers to the bone, risk anything to provide her with the comforts that footloose Charlie Sutton had never managed. Varina and her children were his only living kin. He would see that they never wanted for anything. He would—

"It's done!" Sarah gasped. "Varina—the baby's turned! Now—quickly, when the next pain comes—push! Push with all your might!"

Varina's next contraction came on the heels of Sarah's words. Shifting his position, Donovan cradled his sister's shoulders with one arm. Her frenzied fingers gripped his free hand as she bore down.

"Push . . . push . . ."

Donovan could hear the midwife urging as Varina gasped and strained. The two women were working together now, battling for the baby's life. Donovan could not see Sarah, but he could sense her agitation. He could hear the ragged little sobs of her breathing as she echoed Varina's effort. "*Push* . . . oh, yes, *yes!*"

Varina went limp in his arms as the new life slid out into the world. Donovan heard the sound of a sharp slap; then, miraculously, a thin, mewling cry.

"Oh!" Sarah's voice was husky with awe. "Oh, Varina, it's a boy! You have a beautiful little son!"

Varina stirred, moaning softly.

"Did you hear?" Donovan's own eyes were damp. His arm tightened around his sister's shoulders. "You've got a boy! Listen to him squall!"

Varina lay still for a moment, then rallied. "Let me see him," she whispered. "Give him to me, Sarah—"

"As soon as I cut the cord and wrap him up." Sarah fumbled with the knife and string behind the veil of Varina's nightdress. A moment later she straightened into full view, a tiny, squirming bundle in her arms.

"Here's your new son, Varina!" she exclaimed, her face glowing.

As she bent over the bed, Donovan noticed that the pince-nez glasses had dropped off her nose and were dangling from a cord pinned to her shirtwaist. Her eyes were a luminous silver gray, framed by thick, lustrous lashes. Tendrils of light brown hair had escaped their tight bun. They framed her sweat-jeweled face in damp, curling wisps. Her mouth, curved in a tender smile, was as softly inviting as a ripe peach.

Again, that sense of recognition stabbed Donovan's memory, this time with a force that made him reel. What the devil was going on here? He could have sworn on a stack of Bibles that he'd never seen Sarah Parker outside Miner's Gulch. And yet—

"Give me my boy!" Varina gathered the pucker-faced infant into her trembling arms. "I've got a name for him already. Charles Donovan Sutton—for his father and his uncle."

"That's fine, Varina." Distracted once more, Donovan gave her shoulder a gentle squeeze. He didn't relish the thought of his own name being coupled with mutton-headed Charlie's, but if that was what his sister wanted—

"We won't be needing you anymore, Mr. Cole." Sarah's crisp voice broke into his thoughts. She'd replaced her spectacles, Donovan noted, and tucked the loose tendrils of hair behind her ears. "If you'll be so kind as to leave us, I'll wash Varina and get her settled."

"I'll be on the porch if you need me." He edged around the blanket, leaving Sarah to her bustling, Yankee efficiency. Four long strides carried him across the too-warm cabin and out onto the snow-dusted porch. Latching the door behind him, Donovan sagged against the frame, limp kneed with relief. One hand raked his dark chestnut hair and eased down to massage the tension-knotted muscles at the back of his neck.

It was over. The baby was here, and Varina was all right. For this, he owed his thanks to the coldly capable Miss Sarah Parker, whoever she was. If she had not arrived in time—

He shuddered away the thought as he stared out into the falling snow. There was no use fretting over what might have happened, he reminded himself. Sarah had come. She had readily done what he himself had been afraid to do. *She'd read a book*—that's what she'd told him. A book! Good Lord, the woman had steel-wire nerves, and ice in her veins!

Sarah.

Enveloped by whirling snowflakes, he stepped off the porch and wandered into the dooryard. Her face shimmered before his eyes—the tender face he'd glimpsed as she bent over Varina with the child in her arms. Something about that face haunted him. What was it?

He was imagining things, that was all. He had never set eyes on Miss Sarah Parker until three days ago, when she'd come to check on Varina.

Damnation, what was it, then?

Unbidden, his mind had begun to drift. Through the blur of snow, he glimpsed the blazing lights of a grand ballroom and heard the faint, lilting strains of a quadrille. He saw gray uniforms with golden epaulets, the flash and swirl of a mauve skirt, a lace-mitted hand on his brother Virgil's sleeve . . .

And that face. That beautiful, laughing, sensual face—
a ghost's face now, Donovan reminded himself. A face he
had almost succeeded in forgetting.

Behind him, he heard Sarah Parker come out onto the
porch and close the door behind her. "I'm leaving now,"
she said softly. "Varina's resting with the baby. There's
some broth warming on the stove—" She broke off hesitantly as Donovan turned and started back toward her; then
she plunged ahead, a note of agitation straining her voice.

"I'll send the children back when I pass the Ordway
cabin. They'll be all right. It's not far, and Annie knows the
way. Don't let them trouble their mother too much. Varina
needs her . . . rest."

He had stopped a scant pace from where she stood. She
blinked up at him through the snow-blurred lenses of her
spectacles, her parted lips petal soft in the silvery light.

"I have to go," she said, turning away. "The storm's
getting worse."

"Wait." Donovan caught her elbow, spinning her back
toward him. He had meant only to thank her and go inside, but now he stood rooted to the spot, unable to tear his
eyes from her face.

The resemblance was coincidental, that was all, Donovan told himself. With so many people in the world, some
of them were bound to look alike. All the same, seeing
those features on a straitlaced Yankee spinster was like being gut-kicked by a ghost. His senses reeled as he struggled
with the bittersweet memories, the unanswered questions.

Leave it be, reason cautioned him. *Let her go before you
make a fool of yourself.* But it was easier said than done.
Donovan stared into Sarah's face, battling long-buried
urges that were too powerful to resist.

She cleared her throat nervously. "You won't have to
worry about taking care of the baby. Annie knows enough
to—"

Her words ended in a gasp as Donovan lifted the spectacles from her nose and let them drop to her breast.

Sarah twisted wildly away, averting her face as if she were disfigured. What was wrong with the woman? Donovan wondered. Why was she so afraid of having a man look at her? Didn't Sarah Parker know how pretty she was? Didn't she realize what a beauty she would be without those old-maid lenses and that skinned-back hair?

Somebody ought to tell her, he thought. Hell, somebody ought to *show* her.

Driven by some demon he could neither understand nor control, he gripped her arm harder, forcing her back toward him. "Let me look at you, Sarah," he rasped. "Let me see you as you were meant to be seen!"

"Let me go!" She was struggling now, in obvious panic. A gentleman would do as she demanded, Donovan reminded himself. But he'd left off being a gentleman somewhere between Camp Douglas and Kiowa County. Besides, the situation had already gone beyond propriety. Whatever it took, he vowed, he would see it through.

Catching her jaw with his hand, he wrenched her face upward. "Blast it, I'm not going to hurt you," he muttered. "Just hold still and trust me!"

Her only reply was a sharp kick in the shins. Clenching his teeth, Donovan held on to her. His fingers found the coiled knot of her hair and began to fumble with the pins. His pulse leapt as the silken cascade tumbled loose over his hand.

"Donovan! No!"

With a sharp cry, she wrenched herself away from him. Her own momentum flung her against the kindling pile. She stumbled over her skirt, then caught her balance and whirled back to face him, half-crouched, like a catamount at bay.

Donovan, she had called him. Back in the cabin, Sarah Parker had addressed him as Mr. Cole.

Bewildered, Donovan backed away a step. "Now listen," he began, "I didn't mean to—"

He broke off at the full sight of her face—the tousled curls framing high, elegant cheekbones, the stormy eyes, the wide, sensual mouth. And suddenly the face had a name—a name that blazed like hellfire across Donovan's mind.

Lydia.

He stared at her, too dumbfounded to speak. This was impossible, he told himself. Lydia Taggart was dead. Her own Negro servants had shown him her grave when he'd come back to give her Virgil's ring. They'd told him how a mortar shell had struck the house during Grant's assault on Richmond, exploding in her bedroom. He had placed the thin, gold circlet on her headstone and walked away.

Lydia.

A sense of betrayal stole over him, replacing disbelief and darkening his emotions. Whatever was going on here, he swore, he would get to the bottom of it if it took all night.

Fist clenched, he took a step toward her. "Lady," he growled, "you've got some tall explaining to do!"

But even as he spoke, she darted up with a little cry and sprinted for the shed. Donovan heard the mule snort as she flung herself onto its back. Numb with shock, he watched her come flying outside, wheel her mount and disappear like a phantom into the snowy blackness of night.

For a long moment he stared after her, snowflakes clustering on his unshaven cheeks. Then, with the sound of hoofbeats ringing down the gulch, he forced himself to stir. Like a sleepwalker, he turned and walked slowly back toward the cabin. His footsteps, crunching snow, echoed the rhythm of his thoughts.

Lydia. Lydia Taggart. Alive. And a Yankee.

Chapter Two

Sarah unsaddled her mule and left it munching hay in Amos Satterlee's barn behind the store. Calmly, as if the whole town might be watching, she mounted the snow-swept back stairs to her rooms, twisted the key in the lock and stepped inside.

Only when the door was securely bolted behind her did she surrender to panic. Her pulse, which she'd kept under control by sheer force of will, exploded into a ripping gallop. Beads of sweat broke out on her ash-pale forehead. She sagged against the wall, her knees too weak to support her weight.

She should have known it would happen—that sooner or later, even here, someone would recognize her. Most of the Southerners in Miner's Gulch, including the Suttons, had arrived before the war, in the '59 gold rush. Sarah had felt relatively safe among them. Then, just last week, she'd stopped by the Sutton cabin to check on Varina and had run smack into big Donovan Cole. Only then had she realized, to her horror, that Varina was Donovan and Virgil's sister.

She would never have gone back to the cabin if Varina had not needed her so desperately. But how could she have ignored little Annie's pleas, or her own awareness that Varina might die without skilled help? She had placed Christian duty above her own safety. Now she would have to deal with the consequences.

Sarah sank onto one of the split-log benches that she used in her makeshift classroom. By now, she realized, Donovan would have figured out everything. Even back in Richmond, where he and Virgil had frequented the parties she gave, he had seemed distant and untrusting. Now—yes, he would know. And what he didn't know, he would guess. Donovan was no fool.

But would he understand? No, of course not. She could not expect *any* Southerner, least of all Donovan, to grasp the motives behind what she had done during the war.

And even if he did understand, she could never expect him to forgive her. Not Donovan Cole.

Sarah pressed shaking hands to her ice-cold face. Dear heaven, what had happened tonight? Why had Donovan been so insistent on getting close to her? Why had she let him? There'd been nothing between the two of them in Richmond. It was Virgil who had courted her. Sweet, eager Captain Virgil Cole, who'd held back nothing from her—including Robert E. Lee's plan to push north into Pennsylvania.

She'd learned later that Virgil had died at Antietam, and that Donovan had been taken prisoner. For that, and other uncounted tragedies, she would never escape her own blame. The servants who'd acted as her couriers had relayed Lee's strategy to the North. The resulting alarm had galvanized Union forces, triggering the bloodiest day of the entire war.

Sarah had only done her duty. But that knowledge did little to ease the nightmares that racked her sleep.

Wild with agitation, she sprang to her feet and raced into the bedroom. Her battered leather portmanteau lay under the secondhand brass bed. She wrenched it out and, slapping off the dust, flung it open on the patchwork coverlet. Her quivering hands fumbled in dresser drawers, jerking out underclothes, toiletries, small treasures—

Stop!

Sarah forced herself to stand perfectly still and take deep, measured breaths. Running wasn't the answer, she reminded herself. She'd done it once before, three years ago in Missouri, when someone recognized her on the street. Now it had happened again. The odds were, it would happen almost anywhere she took refuge.

And Sarah had reason to stay. Miner's Gulch had become her home. She'd made friends here. She'd delivered sixteen—no, seventeen—babies, nursed the town through measles and scarlet fever epidemics, and taught nearly a score of children to read and cipher. To leave now, with so much more to be done—

No, she could not even think of it. It was time to face up to the past. It was time to take a stand.

Against Donovan Cole.

She sank onto the bed, cheeks flaming anew at the memory of Donovan's nearness—his iron-hard grip on her shoulders, his fingers loosening her hair, tangling roughly in its falling cascade. She'd been half-afraid he was going to kiss her. If he had, Sarah realized, she would have been lost. That kiss would have seared away her prim mask—and her own response would have betrayed the good woman she'd worked so hard to become.

Sarah's fist slammed into the pillow. Of all the men in the world, why did it have to be Donovan Cole? Damn him! Oh, *damn* him!

And damn her own foolish heart.

There could be no more hiding from the truth. Back in Richmond, even while she was charming secrets out of Virgil Cole, it had been Donovan who had haunted her dreams. Brooding, aloof Donovan, who never gave her so much as a smile.

And that, she realized with a shudder, had been all to the good. She could never have played Donovan as she had so many other men. He was too strong for that, and too astute. Sooner or later, she would have found herself at his mercy.

As for tonight—but tonight counted for nothing. Donovan might have been fleetingly attracted to Sarah Parker. But he had never even liked Lydia Taggart. Once the full truth dawned on him, he would despise her.

And Donovan was not one to let bygones be bygones—Sarah knew him that well, at least. As sure as sunrise, he would seek her out and confront her. When that happened, she would need all her strength. Otherwise, his anger would destroy her.

By morning, the storm had passed. Donovan stepped out of the cabin into a world transformed by white magic. Snowflakes glittered on budding aspens and frosted the dark green stands of lodgepole pine. On the high horizon, diamond-crowned peaks glistened against the clear spring sky. It was beautiful, Donovan admitted grudgingly as he strode off the porch and into the yard. Whatever else one could say about this godforsaken spot, at least it favored the eye.

Flexing his arms, he wrenched the ax blade loose from its chopping block and laid into the uncut logs with a fury that sent chips flying. He had spent a sleepless night tossing on his pallet in the loft. And it wasn't just the cries of his new nephew that had kept him awake. Every time he'd closed his eyes, it had been *her* face he saw—Lydia, or Sarah, or whatever her accursed name was.

His head ached from asking questions, then weighing his own answers. Who was Sarah Parker? Was she really Lydia Taggart, or had it been the other way around? Why would she fake her own death, then hide out in a place like Miner's Gulch? Why had she panicked when he recognized her?

The conclusions, as they slid inexorably into place, had sickened him. The war—yes, it had to be the war. The charming young Widow Taggart had appeared in Richmond at the war's beginning, then conveniently "died" at its end. The servants who'd recounted her death—yes, of course, they'd been her collaborators all along. And the young officers who'd frequented her parlor, Virgil among them, had been her innocent dupes.

Lydia.

His mind ejaculated her name with every blow of the ax. He should have known she was a Yankee spy. Maybe if he had, he could have saved Virgil. He could have saved himself two years in the hell of Camp Douglas.

His mind drifted back to Richmond, in those early days of the war—to Lydia Taggart, with her fine, big house, her money, and her knack for throwing the liveliest soirees in town. Lydia herself had been a dazzler, always gay and laughing, always surrounded by a bevy of young officers. Even Donovan had not been immune to her charms. But she was Virgil's girl, and so he had kept his distance.

If only he hadn't. He might have seen through her deadly masquerade before it was too late.

The cabin door swung open. Annie and her little red-haired sister, Katy, came trooping down the front steps, bundled into their ugly patchwork coats. They waved to Donovan as they trudged across the dooryard toward the gulch trail.

"Wait a minute, where are you two going?" Donovan lowered his ax. One hand reached back to massage his complaining back muscles.

"We're going to school," chirped freckle-faced Annie. "We always go to school on weekdays."

"At Miss Sarah's?" Donovan's voice dripped contempt.

"Uh-huh. Miss Sarah says that girls who learn to read and write can become anything they want to. I'm already in the second reader, and Katy's—"

"Go on back in the house," Donovan growled. "You're not going anywhere today. Your mother's bound to need your help."

Annie's chin lifted. Her grip tightened on her sister's mittened hand. "We already offered to stay. But Ma says she'll manage just fine. School's important. She doesn't want us to miss it. Not even today.''

Donovan sighed. "All right, then, go on. But be careful in the snow. Don't slip and fall."

The warning went unheeded as the two little girls scampered across the clearing and disappeared among the trees. Donovan gazed after them, storm clouds seething in his mind. What would Varina say, he wondered, if she knew her daughters were being schooled by a Yankee spy?

Maybe it was time he told her.

After chucking the ax soundly into the block, he swung back up the steps and into the cabin. He found Varina sitting up in bed, her newborn son slumbering in the crook of her arm. Her hair was mussed from sleep and her eyes were ringed with tired shadows, but her smile was as serene as a Madonna's.

"I keep thinking how Charlie would have enjoyed this little mite," she murmured. "I'll admit to his not having been much of a provider, but he loved his children, Donovan." She glanced fondly at four-year-old Samuel, curled like a puppy near her feet. "I only hope they'll be able to remember that."

Donovan sank onto a stool, his heart aching for her. "As soon as you're well enough to travel, I'm taking all of you back to Kansas," he said. "You'll have a proper house. The girls will wear proper clothes and go to a proper school, and as soon as the boys are old enough—"

"No." There was a thread of steel in Varina's soft voice. Donovan stared at her, shocked into silence.

"I'm not leaving Miner's Gulch," she said. "This claim was Charlie's dream, and now it's mine. I know you mean well, but I won't go back to Kansas and live off anyone's charity—not even my own brother's."

Donovan chewed his lip in a slow boil of frustration. How could he have forgotten how stubborn his sister could be? "Damnation, Varina, *look* at this place!" he exploded. "The slaves on White Oaks lived better than this!"

"White Oaks is gone, Donovan. And we're no better than anybody else these days—if, indeed, we ever were."

"Varina—"

"No, listen to me," she said. "I've got a business proposition for you."

Donovan groaned, guessing what that proposition might be. "If you're expecting me to stay and work Charlie's claim—"

"It's *my* claim now. Mine and the children's. But we can't work it alone. For your help, I'd be willing to give you half of any profits we make. Charlie always said the mine would pay off. He was so close to finding gold when he—"

"Don't, Varina." Donovan knew he was being cruel, but it had to be said. "Charlie was chasing a phantom. Everybody knows the gold veins in these parts played out years ago. And even if they hadn't, I'm not a miner. I'm a lawman."

"For how long?" Varina's free hand reached out to clasp his forearm. "How much time will you have before you cross some young hothead and he shoots you in the back? I just buried Charlie. I don't want to bury you, too."

Donovan battled the urge to grind his teeth. This discussion was not going as he'd planned. He'd come inside aiming to unmask Sarah Parker for what she was. Instead, Varina'd gotten the bit in her teeth, and now she was running away with it.

"I've made a home here," she was saying. "You could, too. You could build your own cabin right on this land if you wanted. Why, you could even court yourself a good woman and have some young ones to grow up alongside mine—"

"Blast it, Varina, don't you go planning my life!"

"And why not? If the planning was left to the men, this world would be a sorry place. And don't you tell me a pretty girl can't turn your head. I noticed the way you were eyeing Sarah Parker last night—"

"You were in no condition to notice anything." Donovan's controlled voice belied the emotion that flamed under his skin.

"I noticed enough." Varina's finger traced the curve of her baby's tiny, shell-perfect ear. "Sarah would be a right handsome woman if she hid those little round glasses and let her hair fluff out around her face. But pretty or not, she's got what truly matters—a good, kind heart."

Donovan's throat jerked as he swallowed an angry outburst. Varina wasn't strong yet, he reminded himself. It wouldn't hurt to wait a day or two before bringing down a woman who was clearly her friend.

He took a deep breath and forced himself to be calm. "You see everybody as good, Varina," he said quietly. "What do you really know about this Sarah Parker?"

Varina's arm tightened around her sleeping infant. "I know that this baby and I might not be alive if Sarah hadn't been here last night. I know that when Charlie was killed, she was the first one here to help wash him and lay him out. And I know that she gives my girls book learning—more and better than I could give them myself. What else is there to know about her? Sarah's as close to being a real angel as anybody I ever met."

Donovan felt as if he were choking. Unable to sit any longer, he erupted off the stool, strode to the cabin's single, small window and glared out at the pristine snow.

"But she's a Yankee—"

"The war's over, Donovan."

"But what do you know about her past? Where did she come from? What the devil would she be doing in a place like this?"

"If it's all that important, why don't you ask her?" Varina sighed wearily. "Now, will you forgive me if I go back to sleep? It'll be a day or two before I'm up to much—"

"I'm sorry." Donovan bent and brushed a contrite kiss across his sister's pale forehead. "I shouldn't have unsettled you so."

Varina inched her sore body down into the quilts and resettled the baby against her shoulder. "Promise me something," she said, already drifting off.

"For you, anything."

"Don't refuse my offer right away. Take a few days to mull it over. Look at the town. Think about the life you could have here."

"Varina—"

"Think about it. That's all I'm asking...." Her voice floated wispily away from him as she closed her eyes. Within seconds, she was asleep, the baby snuggled alongside her ribs and Samuel curled at her feet.

Donovan sighed as he rehung the quilt around the bed to shield them from drafts. When it came to muleheadedness, no one could match Varina. He'd learned that much years ago, when he'd tried to talk her out of marrying Charlie Sutton. Now, when he only wanted to help, he had run headlong into that very same stubborn streak.

Varina, he realized, would never agree to leave Miner's Gulch. She would cling to this land until her life slowly rotted away. Her girls would marry worthless dreamers like their father; and as for young Samuel and little Charles Donovan, there'd be no future for them here. They would break themselves in the search for gold or end up on the wrong side of the law.

No! Donovan could not let such things happen to his only living kinfolk. Building his own life in a forsaken hole like Miner's Gulch was out of the question. But he could stay here for a few weeks at least, long enough to make some badly needed improvements on the cabin, and maybe hire a good man to work Varina's claim. Then, when he got back to Kansas, he could open a bank account for the education of his nieces and nephews. He owed that much to his parents' memory. He owed it to Virgil's.

And—Donovan's jaw clenched as he remembered—he owed something else to Virgil's memory, as well. He stalked out onto the porch and glowered down the slope in the direction of the town, where, at this very moment, the most treacherous woman he'd ever known was schooling his nieces.

Even if he could forgive Lydia Taggart, he could not condone her presence here. Not when she was exerting such a strong influence on Varina and on her innocent young daughters. He could just imagine the lessons Annie and Katy would learn as they grew up under her tutelage—how to flirt, how to deceive, how to betray...

Whatever it took, he vowed, he would get Lydia, or Sarah, or whatever the devil her real name was, out of Miner's Gulch.

Striding out into the yard, he wrenched the ax from the chopping block and resumed his frenzied assault on the logs. Every blow called back another memory—Lydia, glancing up at him over the rim of her wineglass, her silver eyes meeting his, then darting swiftly back to Virgil; Lydia, laughing like a little girl as Virgil pushed her in the backyard swing; Lydia, waltzing around the ballroom floor, skirts swirling like a froth of peony petals below the tiny stem of her waist.

If she had not been Virgil's girl...

Donovan slammed the ax into the sweet-smelling pine. Chips as white as a woman's skin flew around him as he drove the blade home again and again.

He would get rid of her, he swore. Whatever it took, he would see her gone.

Whatever it took.

Miner's Gulch had sprouted amid the gold boom of the late 1850s. In its heyday, the population had soared to nearly a thousand, but most of the people were gone now. Less than two hundred souls remained, clinging to the played-out claims that dotted the slopes of the steep ravine. Of those who hung on, a few still dreamed of finding that elusive strike. Most, however, had long since given up. They stayed because they were too poor to pull up roots and start over, or because they had no other place to go.

Donovan walked the two-mile trail that meandered down the slope between Varina's place and the main part of town. By now it was midday. Warmed by the sun, the snow was melting fast. Water dripped from the bare aspen branches, turning the pathway to slush beneath his boots. Not that Donovan was paying much attention. His mind was black with thoughts of the coming confrontation with Sarah Parker.

Over and over, he ground out each phrase of what he would say to her and how he would say it. He would be calm, he resolved, but he would give the woman no quarter. And heaven help her if she tried to charm her way around him. A granite boulder would be more easily softened than his heart.

As the trees opened up, Donovan could see the town below him—a ramshackle spatter of wooden buildings, sprouting from the land like ugly, reddish toadstools. Hastily built on shallow foundations, they tilted rakishly along both sides of the muddy street. Many of them were boarded up, or had been pillaged for their glass windows. Even the places that were still occupied looked as if they would buckle in a heavy wind.

Pity Varina was so set on staying here, Donovan mused as he rounded the last bend in the trail. Otherwise, Sarah Parker would be welcome to this miserable town. She could set herself up as its queen, for all he cared, with a gold-plated spittoon for a throne. She could—

But he was getting emotional, Donovan cautioned himself, and that would not do. He had resolved to remain cold and implacable. His plan was to state his terms in a way that the woman could not possibly misunderstand, then leave her to make the only sensible decision. He had no wish to be cruel. He only wanted her gone.

He walked faster, steeling his emotions against the hot rage that boiled up inside him every time he thought of her. Laughing, lying Lydia, the very essence of treachery. Even last night—

But last night counted for nothing. It was prim, shy Sarah Parker who had attracted him. A phantom. A stage role—no more real than Lydia Taggart herself had been.

He broke into a sweat as the question penetrated his mind. Who *was* this woman? Was she Lydia Taggart? Was she Sarah Parker?

Or was she someone he did not even know?

He had reached the outskirts of town. Slowing his pace to a deliberate walk, he tried to calm himself by studying each building he passed. The two-story hotel had been boarded up for years, its faded green paint peeling like a bad sunburn. The assay office, too, was closed, but Varina had mentioned that Satterlee, the storekeeper, did assay work at the rare times it was needed. The barbershop was open only on Wednesdays and Saturdays, and the barber, a Mr. Watson, doubled as official undertaker and set an occasional broken limb. Sarah Parker doctored the few women and children.

Even the sheriff's office was empty, except for dust and pack rats. There seemed to be no laws worth breaking in this town, nor anyone who cared one way or the other.

The street was a quagmire of slush and mud. In front of the saloon, stepping boards had been laid from the hitching rail to the door. The saloon, in fact, was the only establishment in Miner's Gulch that still appeared to be thriving. Even at midday, idlers were meandering in, drawn by the lure of whiskey, the tuneless tinkle of the piano, and the shopworn women who lounged in the overhead rooms, framed like jaded portraits in the second-story windows.

Donovan avoided raising his eyes as he passed. Ordinarily, he didn't mind the company of whores. Some of them possessed a warmth and honesty that he found lacking in so-called decent women. But this town was his sister's home, and people were bound to talk. Neither he nor Varina needed that kind of trouble. Besides, right now, he had a very different kind of whore on his mind.

Satterlee's General Store was two doors down from the saloon. Three upstairs windows, curtained to eye level with flour sacking, faced the street. Donovan risked a tentative upward glance, hoping for some indication that Sarah was there, but he could see little more than the reflected glare of the bright spring sky. Swiftly he turned away. It wouldn't do at all for her to look down and see him standing in the street, gazing up at her windows.

He was wondering what to do next when a motley gaggle of children came trooping around the store through the alley that led to the back. Seeing his two nieces among them, Donovan realized that Sarah had just dismissed school.

He felt something tighten in his chest. Yes, she would be there. This was as good a chance as he was going to get.

"Uncle Donovan!" Little Katy had spotted him and was weaving through the crowd of children, dragging her big sister by the hand. "What are you doing here? Did you come to walk home with us?"

Donovan sighed. Fishing in his pocket, he dug out a palmful of small change. "Here," he growled, giving the coins to Annie. "Go on into the store and buy some peppermint sticks for yourselves and Samuel. Then start for home. I'll catch up when I've finished my business here in town."

"Thank you." Annie counted the money carefully while Katy danced around her like a pup anticipating a bone. She tugged her sister toward the front of the store, splashing mud with her small, prancing boots.

Donovan waited until they'd gone inside. Then, taking a deep breath, he turned and strode deliberately down the alley, toward the back stairs.

For the past three years he'd tried to believe that the war was really over. But he'd been wrong. There was one battle left to fight. He would fight it here and now.

Chapter Three

Sarah was wiping sums off the blackboard when she heard the sharp, heavy rap at the door. She knew at once who was there and why he had come.

For an instant she stood frozen, her heart in her throat. Every well-honed survival instinct screamed at her to leave the bolt in place and hide until he went away. But it would do no good, she realized. Donovan had seen the children leaving. He knew she was here, and he was quite capable of forcing his way inside.

The knock sounded again, louder this time, and even more insistent. Sarah willed her feet to move toward the sound. She had been expecting Donovan. And she had already made up her mind not to run away.

Once more she heard the angry thud of his big, rawboned knuckles on the wood, and his voice, chilling her with its cold contempt. "I know you're in there, Lydia. And unless you want a scene this town will talk about for the next decade, you'd better open that door!"

Lydia.

Sarah's ribs strained against the rigid stays of her corset. Her breath came in shallow gasps as she paused before the door, marshaling her courage. One hand rose instinctively to check her pince-nez spectacles. They were in place, perched firmly on the bridge of her nose. She hesitated, then deliberately removed them and laid them on one of the benches. The glasses were part of her masquerade—stage props, fitted with flat lenses that had no effect on her vision. It was time to put them aside. As far as Donovan was concerned, at least, the masquerade was over.

Donovan's anger seemed to emanate through the heavy door planks. Sarah fumbled with the bolt, her icy fingers betraying her panic. In the course of the war, she had braved enough dangerous situations to fill a whole shelf full of dime novels. But never before, until now, had she faced the blistering rage of a man like Donovan Cole.

Steeling her resolve, she tugged at the door. It swung inward with an ominous groan of its weather-dampened hinges.

Donovan's towering bulk filled the frame. His presence crackled like the air before a thunderstorm as he stepped over the threshold and closed the door behind him. Suddenly everything else in the room seemed small.

Sarah's throat was as dry as field cotton on an August afternoon. Fighting the impulse to run, she forced herself to stand straight and proud. He loomed above her—as he loomed above nearly everyone—his eyes searing in their unspoken indictment.

"Hello, Lydia." His voice was thin with contempt.

Sarah spoke calmly, as if she were reciting lines from a play. "My name isn't Lydia. It's Sarah. Sarah Parker Buckley."

The emotion that flickered across his face could have been anger, dismay or disbelief. "They told me you were dead. I saw your grave."

"Lydia Taggart is dead. If you saw a grave, it was hers."

His hand shot out and seized her upper arm, his fingers almost crushing bone in their powerful clasp. "No more riddles, Sarah, or Lydia, or whatever the hell your name is! I want answers. I want the truth about everything that happened. And once it's out, I want you packed up and gone."

Sarah glared up into the granite fury of his eyes. "You're hurting me," she whispered.

His grip eased slightly, but he did not release her. "I've never done physical harm to a woman in my life," he growled. "But heaven help me, if some things don't get cleared up fast, I'll shake you till your teeth fall out of your lying little head!"

"Let me go." Sarah thrust out her chin in regal defiance, like Antigone, or perhaps Medea. Her theatrical training had served her well, she assured herself. Donovan could not possibly know that she was quivering like jelly inside.

"You'll talk?"

She felt the hesitation in his fingers, the reluctance to trust her enough to let go. "I'll answer any questions you want to ask me," Sarah replied coldly. "But you might as well know right now, I have no intention of leaving Miner's Gulch."

"We'll see." His hand dropped from her arm. The pressure of his grip lingered, burning like a brand into her flesh.

"Sit down," she said.

"I'll stand." His gaze had left her. Sarah watched his restless eyes as he surveyed the makeshift classroom that doubled as her living quarters. Puncheon benches, arranged in rows with the lowest in front, took up most of the floor space. A desk in one corner was piled with slates and battered readers. A potbellied stove, with a narrow counter along the nearby wall, provided for simple cooking. The door that led to her bedchamber was closed.

Silence chilled the room as he strode to the window. For what seemed like a very long time, he stood staring down at the street. From behind him, Sarah's eyes traced the rigid contours of his shoulders through the sweat-stained leather vest and faded flannel shirt. Her gaze lingered on the flat, chestnut curls at the back of his sunburned neck. She tried not to remember how it had felt to be touched by him. She tried not to feel anything at all.

Abruptly he turned on her. "Damnation, I don't understand any of it!" he exploded. "Not then, and not now! I
don't even know where to begin!"

Sarah glanced down at her clasped hands, then willed
herself to raise her face and meet his condemning eyes.
"Neither do I," she said with forced calm. "Except that I
didn't mean for any of this to happen."

"You took up spying for the fun of it, I suppose." His
bitter voice ripped into her.

"Don't—" she murmured, but he was as implacable as
a millstone. Biting back hurt, she stumbled on. "At first, I
believed that what I was doing was noble and right. I didn't
realize how the consequences would just keep going on and
on, like ripples when you toss a pebble into a lake—"

"Virgil's dead. He was killed at Antietam."

"I know."

"*Do* you, now?" Donovan retorted savagely. "Did you
feel anything for him? Anything at all?"

Sarah fought back a rush of bitter tears. She would not
let him see her cry, she vowed. That would only feed his
rage. And she would not tell him about the dreams—the
nightmares of anguish, fear and guilt that time had done
little to ease.

"You *used* my brother! Virgil loved you. He trusted you.
And all that time—"

"There was a war on. I did what I had to!" For all her
efforts to be calm, Sarah felt her own anger rising. She had
hoped for understanding, even some kind of resolution.
But it was clear that Donovan's only intent was to hurt her.

His face, thrusting close to hers now, was dark with fury.
"How many others did you use the same way? How many
men died because of what you—"

Sarah's hand flashed out and struck the side of his jaw.
The slap echoed like a gunshot in the quiet room.

Shocked into silence, he stared at her. Sarah had half
expected him to hit her back—that's what Reginald Buckley, her long-dead husband, would have done. But Dono-

van did not move. Only a subtle twitch at the corner of his mouth betrayed any sign of emotion in him.

Seconds crawled past as they faced each other, bristling like two hostile animals thrown into the same cage. Sarah could hear the harsh rasp of his breathing in the tense stillness. Her own heart was a drum in her ears. Her body felt feverish.

His eyes—dark green with flecks of fiery amber—drilled into hers. His face—not a truly handsome face, but strong, blunt and oddly sensual—was frozen into a determined mask, inches from her own.

Sarah's nipples had shrunk to hard, brown raisins beneath her camisole. A poignant ache trickled downward from her chest to her thighs. She wished he would do something—grab her, curse her, stalk out of the room—anything but stand there like a stone, shattering her with his wintry fury.

With painful effort, she found her voice. "I think you'd better leave now," she whispered.

"No—" A shudder went through him as he cleared the huskiness from his throat. "Not until I find out what I came to learn."

Sarah took a step backward, widening the perilous distance between them. Fighting for self-control, she willed her thundering pulse to be still.

"I agreed to answer your questions, Donovan," she declared firmly. "I did not agree to stand here and submit to your bullying!"

With a small sound that was somewhere between a groan and a snarl, he turned back to face the window. His shoulders rose and fell with the force of his harsh breathing as he stared outside at the glaring sky.

"Who are you?" He spoke without looking at her, his voice harsh with emotion.

Sarah gazed at his rigid back. "My name is Sarah Parker Buckley," she said in a tightly modulated voice. "But I have been many women. Juliet...Ophelia...Portia... Beatrice...Lady Macbeth..."

"And Lydia Taggart! Lord, an actress!" His fist crashed against the window frame. "And I suppose that sweet Southern voice was as false as the rest of you!"

"I was born and raised in New Bedford, Massachusetts." Sarah recited the words as if she were reading a script. "At sixteen, I eloped with Mr. Reginald Buckley, an actor and a Southerner—"

"Of the Savannah Buckleys?" The question snapped reflexively out of Donovan, an empty echo of a social order that no longer existed.

"I believe so, although I can't be sure. Both Mr. Buckley and I were...estranged from our families. He taught me to perform with him. Shakespeare, mostly. We spent a number of years touring in the South."

"And where is your Mr. Buckley now?"

"Dead. He passed away a few months before the war began." No need to explain how, Sarah resolved. The fact that Reginald had been stabbed in a brawl over a saucy little Natchez whore was no longer of any consequence.

"An actress! Damnation, I should have seen through you! I should have guessed!" He spun back to face her, eyes blazing. "And this is your latest role, I suppose. Sanctified Sarah, the Angel of Miner's Gulch!"

His words slashed her, but Sarah masked her pain with ice. "What you *suppose* is of no importance. I'm doing what I can to make peace with myself, and for that I will not apologize—not to you or to anyone in this town!"

His chest quivered in a visible effort to contain his anger. "Does my sister have any idea who—*what*—you were?"

"No. But even if she did, I think Varina would be fair. Unlike you, she tends to look for the good in people."

"In your kind of woman, she'd have to look damned deep to find any! We're beholden to you for last night, but even that won't make up for what you did. It won't buy back Virgil's life."

Sarah withered inside as his words struck her. Donovan had suffered a deep loss, she reminded herself. She could not blame him for being bitter. Even so, anger was her only defense against him.

"That's enough!" she snapped. "I told you I wouldn't stand for your bullying! Ask your questions and be done with it!" She glanced at the battered pendulum clock that hung on the far wall of the room. "You have five minutes before I start screaming for help."

"Screaming?" He glared at her skeptically. "You'd really do that?"

"I've got friends in this town, and as you already know, I'm an accomplished actress." Sarah punctuated her declaration with a defiant thrust of her chin. "Now, I'd say you've used up about twenty-five seconds. What else do you want to ask me?"

Donovan rumbled his exasperation. Turning away again, as if he could not even bear to look at her, he stared emptily through the window. The next question seemed to explode out of the darkest pit of his soul.

"*Why?* How could you have done it?"

"You fought for what you believed in. So did I." Sarah spoke softly, addressing the rigid silhouette of his back. "I had seen the evils of slavery in the South, and I welcomed the chance to strike a blow against it."

"And that was your only reason?" Donovan's voice reflected bitter incredulity. "So now it's Saint Sarah of the Slaves! Life for you is just one noble cause after the other, isn't it?"

"Stop that!" Sarah would have slapped him again if he'd been standing close enough. "I'm trying my best to tell you the truth, Donovan, but you're not making it easy."

She paused, hoping, perhaps, for a word of apology from him. But it was not to be. Donovan's resentful silence lay cold as winter in the room, broken only by the slow, rhythmic tick of the clock. Taking a sharp breath, Sarah plunged ahead.

"No, it wasn't my only reason. My husband was dead. My family had disowned me. I had no money, no work, no home. The chance to live in Richmond as an agent for the Union was the only—"

Donovan had turned around. Sarah's voice dried up in her throat as she saw his face.

"So it was a blasted *convenience!*" he rasped. "The chance to lie and betray under comfortable circumstances. The house, the servants, the parties—you lived as well as any so-called lady in Richmond! Compared to you, those women down there at the saloon are rank amateurs!"

"No!" Sarah reeled as her defenses crumbled. She had tried to be honest with Donovan, but what was the use when he wouldn't even listen? How could she tell him what it had really been like for her? How could she tell him about the guilt-racked nights, the terrible dreams?

Seizing the advantage, he waded into the fray with renewed fury. "Virgil died in my arms, did you know that? He made me promise I'd return to Richmond and give you the ring he was saving for your wedding. The last word he spoke was your so-called name—*Lydia.*"

Donovan took a step toward Sarah. She fought the instinct to back away as he loomed above her, a tower of smoldering rage. "Did you love my brother, Sarah Parker?" he asked in a low, hoarse voice. "In your lying, mercenary heart, did you care for him even a little?"

Sarah forced herself to meet the raw hatred in his eyes. She was trembling inside, but she would not lie, she resolved. She was through with lying forever.

"Virgil was as fine and gentle a young man as I've ever known," she answered softly. "I was fond of him. But I couldn't allow myself to love him. I was not in a position to love anyone."

Donovan wheeled away from her with a snort of disgust. "That's all I want to know." He glanced up at the clock. "I see my time is up, so I'll be taking my leave."

He strode to the door. Sarah stood like a pillar, her impassive face masking the shambles he'd made of her emotions. Never, in all her life, had anyone spoken to her with such contempt. And to have it be Donovan—

"One thing more." He had paused in the open doorway, one hand gripping the frame. "I want you out of this town, away from my sister and her family. Be gone within one week, and I'll keep quiet about your past. Otherwise, the whole gulch is going to know what you did. And I'll wager there are people here who won't take kindly to it."

Sarah drew herself up with an air that would have done credit to Queen Victoria. "Do your worst, then, Mr. Cole," she said crisply. "But your allowing me the week won't make any difference. Miner's Gulch is my home. No matter what you might say or do, I have no intention of leaving."

Surprise flickered across Donovan's face, but he was quick to recover. "Then heaven help you, Sarah Parker Buckley!" he snapped. "At least you can't say I didn't give you fair warning. Remember that after it's too late to change your mind!"

Sarah did not reply. She stood like stone as Donovan turned his back on her and stalked outside, slamming the door brusquely behind him.

Only when the echo of his boots on the wooden stairs had died away did Sarah allow herself to react. Her throat constricted as if squeezed by an invisible fist. Her knees went liquid. She sank onto a bench, her heart pounding a tattoo of fear against her ribs.

It was not too late, she reminded herself. Donovan had given her a week to be gone. She could take her time—invent some pretty story about a new position or an unexpected inheritance back East. She could pack at her leisure and hire a wagon to drive her to Central City, where she could catch the stage for Denver.

And then what? Another masquerade someplace else, with more lies and the inevitable discovery? A retreat to the safety of New England, where nothing could follow her except those black, tormenting dreams?

No, Sarah concluded, gulping back her fear. Running was not the answer. She had worked too hard at building a life here, with the Southern children she taught and the Southern women who had come to depend on her. In recent months, she'd even experienced some nights of restful sleep, when the nightmares did not come.

Her only hope of peace lay here, helping the people she had betrayed—and had come to love.

Resolutely she rose, brushed the chalk dust from her skirt and began tidying up the classroom for tomorrow's lessons. She would go on as if nothing had happened—as if Donovan Cole had never come to her with his threats. She would show him what Sarah Parker was made of. She would show them all.

Squaring her shoulders, she chalked the new sums across the board in an order that began with the simplest problems and progressed to the most complex. Maybe nothing would happen, she speculated, trying to be cheerful. Maybe Donovan's threat to expose her had been an empty bluff.

But no, she knew better. Donovan was no bluffer. He was as blunt and honest as nature itself. Whatever intent he stated, he would carry out as surely as winter followed autumn.

The chalk slipped from her fingers and dropped to the floor, shattering as it struck. Sarah let the pieces lie where they had fallen. She clutched at her arms, trembling as if an icy wind had blown into the room.

Walking to the window, she gazed down at the passersby in the muddy street. The people of Miner's Gulch were her friends now, but the war had touched almost all of them. Many had lost friends and relatives. More than a few had lost property. They had forgiven her for being a Yankee, but how could they forgive her for being a spy?

If she'd been caught back in Richmond, she would have been tried and summarily hanged. What would happen to her here, in an angry little town with no law?

Closing her eyes, Sarah pressed her forehead against the rough-sawed frame of the window. Only moments ago she had convinced herself she was strong enough to face the past. But now she felt her courage slipping away, leaving her weak, frightened, and more alone than she had ever been in her life.

Donovan's long-legged strides ate up the ground. Mud spattered beneath his boots as he drove his energy into putting as much distance as possible between himself and Sarah Parker Buckley.

She had not even denied it, he fumed as he stalked past the boarded-up assayer's office. She had played Juliet, she said, and Ophelia, and Lady Macbeth—and oh, yes, Lydia Taggart, the belle of Richmond! Lord, she'd almost seemed proud of it! She'd admitted to everything, even the part about not loving Virgil.

Donovan fed the fire of his anger as he mounted the trail. Sarah Parker was a woman without a conscience. She deserved to be ridden out of town on a timber. She deserved to be tarred and feathered, even hanged. Back in Richmond, in fact, she *would* have been hanged. The gallows had been standard punishment for spies during the war.

Donovan's breath eased out in a ragged sigh. In truth, he had no stomach for that sort of violence, especially where females were concerned. That was why he'd allowed Sarah time to make a clean getaway. Some people might not view it as right, letting her go like that. But surely it was what Virgil, in his gentle, forgiving way, would have wanted.

As for Sarah, she might be stubborn, but she was no fool. Given a few days to think things over, she was bound

to take the sensible way out. There'd be no need to go
through the ugliness of exposing her past.

But if she refused to leave on her own—Donovan's jaw
clenched with the force of his resolve. He would do whatever it took to get Sarah out of Miner's Gulch. And if that
meant laying her treachery bare to the whole town—

His breath stopped for an instant as he remembered the
sight of her face, tilting toward him like a proud flower. His
mind retraced the quietly defiant eyes, the determined
thrust of her dimpled chin, the silkily parted lips that
seemed to be made for a man's kiss...

Damn her! Lydia Taggart was still working her cursed
magic, and he had already learned that he was not immune. If he wavered, even for an instant, he would be vulnerable. He could not afford to let that happen.

He walked faster, charging up the trail as if the devil were
pursuing him with the most enticing bundle of torments
ever devised. He would stay away from Sarah, he resolved. Varina's cabin needed plenty of work, more than
enough work to keep him busy for the rest of the week. He
would return to town only when the time limit was up. By
then, if she had any sense, the woman would be gone.

But if she chose to remain—yes, he would be strong
enough to make her pay. Sarah Parker Buckley would get
no second chance.

Ahead, through the screen of aspens, Donovan could see
the bright, bobbing patches of his nieces' coats. Anxious
for the distraction of their company, he lengthened his
stride to catch up. A smile tugged his lips as he remembered the coins he'd given them to buy peppermint sticks at
the store. Varina, he knew, didn't have the money for such
indulgences, but all youngsters deserved a treat now and
then. He could only hope that, in the days ahead, Varina's
staunch independence would allow him to provide more
than candy.

As he came abreast of the girls, Katy glanced up at him
with a hesitant smile. Annie, however, seemed to avoid his

eyes. Donovan swiftly saw why. Against her coat, she clutched a ten-pound sack of flour. They had not bought candy at all.

"Please don't be mad, Uncle Donovan," Annie said in a firm little voice that echoed her mother's. "We like candy. We like it a lot. But we *need* this flour. Ma's bin is almost empty, and I have to make bread this afternoon."

Donovan swallowed the sudden tightness in his throat. "That's fine, Annie," he said, feeling frustrated and foolish. "But you should have told me you needed flour. I'd have bought a big sack of it, and some candy, too."

"Oh, no!" Annie protested. "You're our guest! Ma said we weren't to ask you for anything!"

"In that case, I need to have a talk with your mother." Donovan cursed Varina's pride. The idea that her family was on the brink of starvation, and the woman would not even ask her own brother for help—

But anger wouldn't accomplish anything, he reminded himself. He had to find some other way to aid Varina. Something she would not reject as charity.

There was the mine—she had offered him a partnership. But the thought of grubbing away his days on Charlie Sutton's worthless diggings was enough to crush his soul.

There had to be another answer, another possibility, lurking just out of reach. Something in the land, perhaps, or even in himself. He would give the matter some serious consideration. In the next few days, when he wasn't working on the cabin, he would investigate Varina's mining claim and the terrain surrounding it. He would keep himself fully occupied, leaving no room in his thoughts for the likes of Sarah Parker Buckley.

But even as he made his plans, Sarah's image burst into his mind. His face blazed, recalling the sting of her slap on his skin. His body quivered with the memory of last night— her body straining against him, the silken feel of her hair, tumbling over his hand. Something clenched inside him—

a hunger so raw and fierce that it almost buckled his knees. He stumbled, damning his own weakness.

"Hurry, Uncle Donovan! We're almost home!" Annie called, and Donovan suddenly realized that the girls had left him behind. He hurried to catch up, breathing hard to clear his mind. He was thirty-six years old, he reminded himself, old enough to know that the woman who called herself Sarah Parker was pure poison. She'd deceived trusting friends and neighbors in Richmond. She'd betrayed Virgil, who had loved her with all the passion of his youth. And for all her virtuous demeanor here in Miner's Gulch, Donovan knew better than to believe she'd changed. Beneath Sarah's prim facade, Lydia Taggart was alive and well. She was his enemy. He would see her vanquished once and for all.

The Crimson Belle Saloon had seen better days. Its porches sagged where the unseasoned lumber had warped. Its paint, once a brazen red, was weathered and peeling. The men who drifted in and out of the double doors tended to have a whipped look, as if any spirit they'd ever possessed had been beaten away by the hard years. Even the piano sounded tired.

Not that Sarah was listening. The piano's tinny, thunking tone had filled her ears for so many seasons that she scarcely heard it anymore. Besides, this evening her mind was on other matters.

Lifting her skirts above the mud, she rounded the corner of the saloon and slipped through the shadows toward the back entrance. Her free hand clutched the canvas valise that served as her medical kit. Her spectacles were in place once more, perched firmly on her narrow nose.

The rear of the Crimson Belle was expressly designed for discreet comings and goings. A cluster of bushy blue spruce trees screened the entry, which opened into a dim hallway with a narrow, inside staircase leading to the second floor. The door at the top of the stairs was locked, but Sarah's

knock—three precise taps, a pause, then two more—
touched off a scurry of footsteps on the other side. The bolt
rattled and, seconds later, the door swung inward to reveal
a frowsy blond woman in a faded mauve silk wrapper. Her
husky shoulders sagged as Sarah stepped out of the shadows.

"*Ach,* thank goodness it is you!" She spoke in a rough
cello voice, heavily accented with German. "Marie is
worse—the coughing, the blood—"

"Take me to her, Greta." Sarah clutched her valise and
followed the woman down the carpeted hallway, her eyes
avoiding the closed door that indicated one of the girls had
a customer. She had long since lost count of her visits to
these rooms above the saloon, but all the same, she never
quite got used to things here. The lamps in the hallway cast
a hellish glow through their rose glass chimneys. The air
swam with incense, its sickly-sweet aroma mingling with
tobacco smoke. From downstairs, the muffled tinkle of the
piano did not quite drown out the lustful grunts and
whimpers that emanated through the walls of the locked
room.

"Here." Greta opened the second-to-last door to reveal,
in the dimly lit space, a thin, dark figure lying on a wide
bed. Sarah walked slowly toward her, weighted by a sense
of helplessness. She could deliver babies, apply poultices
and administer concoctions of whiskey, quinine and cam-
phor, but in this case, there was nothing she could do.
Marie, tragically young and no longer pretty, was dying of
consumption.

Marie's weightless hand fluttered like a leaf on the
stained brocade coverlet as Sarah approached. "Thank you
for coming," she whispered. "I wanted the chance to tell
you before—" She broke off, overcome by a spasm of
tearing coughs. The kerchief that Greta pressed to Marie's
mouth came away flecked with blood.

"Don't try to talk," Sarah murmured, her eyes welling
with emotion. "Just rest. I brought more of that chamo-

mile tea you like. The girls can brew it for you—'' She fumbled in her valise for the packet, her vision blurred by tears. Marie belonged in a hospital, with real doctors and nurses, or in some warm, dry climate where her lungs could heal. Here, in this wretched place, there was no hope for her.

"She ain't slept all day. Ain't done nothin' but cough, poor lamb." Another woman, near forty, with gentle eyes and garishly dyed red hair, had stepped out of the shadows to take the chamomile. "I'll start some water. Maybe this'll soothe her some."

"Thank you," Sarah said softly. "You've been good to her, Faye."

"We got to do for each other. Ain't nobody else'll do it for us—'ceptin' you, o' course, Miss Sarah. You been a real angel to us all."

"Ach, ja," Greta agreed. "But listen, we been fighting with that bastard Smitty again. He says that if Marie is too sick to work the customers, he can't afford to give her room and board."

"Not again!" Sarah sighed wearily, remembering the confrontations she'd had with the Crimson Belle's miserly owner. Smitty treated his girls like livestock, with no regard for their welfare. They'd lived in the most abject dread of him until last year, when Sarah had stepped in. Conditions were somewhat better now, but the old man's curmudgeonly heart was as hard as ever.

Sadly Sarah gazed down at Marie's pale face. It was Marie, she recalled, who had triggered her first visit to these upstairs rooms. The poor girl had miscarried and was near death when a desperate Faye had come pounding on Sarah's door in the middle of the night. Sarah had saved Marie's life that time. But there was nothing she could do now. She had no skill, no potion, to turn back the ravages of consumption.

Marie's skin was so transparent that the delicate blue tracery of her veins showed through at the temples. Her cheeks flamed like two garish red carnations against the white oval of her face. Her eyes had sunk into hollows. It wasn't fair, Sarah reflected bitterly. Marie was sweet and kind and had never willed harm to anyone. She should have had a different life—a home, children, the love of a good man. Now, even the brief, sad life she'd had was nearly over.

"I could take her to my place," Sarah said. "At least Smitty would leave her in peace there."

"Nein," Greta interjected swiftly. "With Marie in your room, how could you have the children come for their lessons? And what would their mamas say? You would have to close your little school."

"We can handle Smitty. Don't you worry none 'bout that," Faye added. "We done like you said—told the ol' buzzard none of us would work 'less'n he let Marie stay. He'll come 'round. Ain't got much choice. He won't get no new girls comin' to a town like this 'un."

Sarah sighed wearily, one hand brushing back Marie's dark, damp hair. "Give her as much of the tea as she'll take. At this point, there's not much else you can do. I'll be around to see her again tomorrow night."

"No need your takin' so many chances, Miss Sarah," Faye said. "You know what some of the ladies in this town would say if they ever saw you comin' in here."

Sarah nodded, knowing Faye was right. There were women in Miner's Gulch, self-styled social leaders like Mrs. Eudora Cahill, who would brand her an instant pariah if they knew she associated with Smitty's girls. In the days ahead their support would be more important than ever. But right now Marie needed her. And even in the face of wisdom, one did not turn one's back on a friend.

She leaned over, clasped Marie's fleshless hand and felt the tightening of the frail fingers. "I'll be back tomorrow," she whispered. "Meanwhile, you get some sleep. Try to have some beautiful dreams—" The words died as emotion choked her throat. Tears flooded her eyes as she turned away from the bed and left the room.

The night breeze blew cold on Sarah's damp face as she made her way home through the alley. Thoughts of Marie mingled with the memory of Donovan's threat, churning like a maelstrom in her mind. There was nothing she could do for Marie. And there was very little she could do about Donovan. Another man might be charmed or cajoled into changing his mind. But not Donovan Cole. He was too bitter, too determined, too cocksure that she would turn tail and run.

She could not let him win.

Whatever happened, Sarah resolved, she would not let Donovan see her fear. Until he played his ace against her, she would behave as if nothing had happened. She would hold her head high and go about her usual business.

Sarah's heart lurched with the sudden realization that her usual business would include looking in on Varina. She always followed up her deliveries with visits to the new mothers. If she did not come, Varina would wonder why.

Unless Donovan had already told her.

Sarah's pulse skipped erratically as she mounted the back stairs of Satterlee's store. Every impulse screamed at her to run—to fling her essentials into a bag, saddle her mule and ride for her life.

But running was out of the question. Miner's Gulch was her home. If she did not take a stand here and now, no place on earth would ever be home to her again.

The schoolroom was dark with familiar shadows; warm, still, from the embers that glowed in the potbellied stove. Locking the door behind her, Sarah paused at the threshold of her bedroom. Her eyes lingered affectionately on the squat log benches, the slates piled haphazardly in a far corner, the rows of sums and minuses chalked neatly across the blackboard. Not much of a kingdom. But it was hers. She had built it, carved it out of nothing, with pluck and patience as her only tools.

It was good, she reassured herself as she hung up her cloak, opened the bedroom door and lit the brass lamp on the dresser. She had made herself useful here. She had made a difference in people's lives.

Could it be? Had her father had been wrong, after all?

Her hands moved to the high muslin collar of her shirt-waist, fingers unfastening the buttons with practiced skill until the prim garment fell open in front. Sarah slipped her arms out of the sleeves and hung it with her other things on the row of hooks that served in place of a wardrobe. She could not afford to be careless with her clothes. They had to last.

With a weary sigh, she raised her arms and began plucking away the pins that held her hair in its tight bun. The silky locks tumbled loose, bringing back a sudden stab of memory. Donovan—his fingers tangling in her hair, eyes probing hers, dark and hot, seething with unanswered questions...

Turning, she caught a glimpse of herself in the cracked mirror—arms lifted, cheeks flushed, lips damply parted. She froze, staring at her own image. One hand quivered upward to touch her cheek.

She had almost succeeded in forgetting that she was pretty.

Seized by a sudden wild compulsion, she curved her mouth into a smile, inclining her head, arching the fine, dark wings of her brows. The image in the glass assumed a subtle sensuality, an air of unmistakable invitation.

Lydia.

Sarah's arms dropped to her sides as the sound of laughter echoed and faded in her mind. Was this what Donovan had wanted when he'd ripped the pins from her hair? Deep inside, without his even knowing, was it really *Lydia* he had wanted to see?

Driven by dark emotions, she raised her arms again, tightening the fabric of the worn chemise against her breasts. Her hands lifted and spread the satin wealth of her hair. Her eyelids lowered coquettishly.

"You're no good, Sarah Jane Parker!" Her minister father's voice rumbled like a tempest out of the past. *"Wasting your time playacting! Prancing and posing like a strumpet! Vanity is the devil's tool, Sarah! Mark my words! Remember them when you're burning in hell!"*

Sarah spun away from the mirror, hands quivering where they pressed her cold face. She'd gotten word from a cousin after the war that her father had died of apoplexy in New Bedford. In the eight long years since she'd run off with Reginald Buckley, he had not once spoken her name.

Sometimes at night, when the wind howled high in the Colorado pines, his voice echoed in her dreams, its thunder blending with the roar of cannon fire, the screams of horses and the groans of the wounded.

"You can't hide from the sight of God, Sarah Jane! Wherever you go, his wrath will find you, and in the end, you will burn for your sins! The devil will seize you and carry you down, and burn you forever in hell!"

Sarah blew out the lamp and finished undressing in the dark. She tugged her flannel nightgown over her head and buttoned it to her throat with trembling fingers. Moonlight made a window-square on the patchwork quilt as she crawled between the sheets and lay rigid, eyes wide open in the darkness.

Strange, how some things never seemed to change. As a little girl, she had lain awake at night, listening to the creaks and groans of the old frame house, waiting for the devil to come and snatch her from her bed. Twenty years later, she still jumped at shadows, her fear so deep that it defied every effort to reason it away.

When would it come, the moment of reckoning when the fire would exact its toll?

Impatient, Sarah turned over and punched her pillow. She had problems enough in the here and now, she reminded herself. The devil might be biding his time, but

Donovan Cole was not. Donovan was not a patient man. His revenge would be swift and without mercy.

Unless she could think of a way to beat him at his own game.

Restless now, she flopped onto her side, feet jerking at the tightly tucked quilts. There had to be an answer—there was always an answer.

All she had to do was find it.

Sleep was impossible. Sarah rolled out of bed, flung on her robe and strode to the window. The tick of the school-room clock echoed in the silence as she gazed through the tattered curtain at the black clusters of pine and the moon-lit peaks beyond.

There was always an answer. Maybe not an easy answer. Maybe not the answer one would ask for. But an answer all the same.

She shivered beneath the worn flannel robe, hands clutching her arms as she racked her brain and searched her heart. It was there, she knew, if only—

The solution fell into place like a thunderclap.

Sarah's breath caught as she examined it—an idea so simple that she could scarcely believe she hadn't thought of it sooner.

Simple. And terrifying. Her hands began to tremble as she weighed the risks, the ramifications. No, she did not have the courage. There had to be a different way, something easier.

She waited, cold and alone in the darkness, but when no other answer came, Sarah knew what she must do. She had spent years running, assuming one role, then casting it off for another, losing herself in lies.

It was time to stop running once and for all.

Chapter Four

Hammer blows echoed down the gulch, ringing like gunshots on the chilly morning air. Sarah could hear them a good half mile before she reached the Sutton place. Her throat knotted in dread at the sound. She had hoped Donovan would be elsewhere when she came to check on Varina and the baby. Alas, that was not to be.

She reined in the mule, half-tempted to turn back. But no, that would be the cowardly way. As a midwife and friend, she had duties to perform. If Varina's volatile brother chose to interfere, she would simply have to put him in his place.

Sarah adjusted her spectacles, plumbing the well of her own courage as the mule picked its way up the slippery trail. She had lived so long with danger that it had become a natural part of her existence. But Donovan Cole was more than dangerous. His was a rage that burned all the way to her heart. Every time he looked at her, his eyes blazed through her prim facade to the lying, faithless hellion she had struggled so hard to put behind her. To Lydia.

As long as she lived in Donovan's eyes, in his memory and in his hatred, Lydia Taggart would never die.

As the trees thinned, she could make out Varina's tiny log cabin. She could see Donovan just below roof level, straddling a massive crossbeam on the frame of what appeared to be an add-on room. The mine timbers he had salvaged for the purpose were heavy and awkward. Hammer blows echoed off the canyon walls as he whaled away at a stubborn nail.

A wry smile tightened Sarah's lips. One thing, at least, was clear: Donovan Cole was no carpenter.

Donovan was so intent on his task that he had yet to notice Sarah's approach. Despite the crisp air, he had flung off his shirt. Muscles rippled beneath his taut, golden skin. His bare torso all but steamed as he laid into the work with a fury so black that Sarah hesitated, her amusement darkening into fear.

The mule snorted and shook its shaggy winter hide as she reined up alongside the porch. Only then did Donovan pause in his hammering to glare down at her. The contempt in his eyes froze her to the quick of her soul.

"I've come to see Varina and her new son," she declared, thrusting out her chin.

"Varina's fine," he growled. "So's the baby. We don't need your kind looking in on us."

"That's not for you to say, Donovan." Sarah swung out of the saddle, her medical bag clutched under her cloak. "When I hear it from your sister, that's when I'll leave." She turned and strode determinedly toward the porch.

"That's far enough." Donovan's sharp voice caught her like a blade between the shoulders. "Lady, if you don't want one hell of a scene—"

"Miss Sarah!" Katy came bounding out onto the porch, her carrot-colored pigtails dancing. "I can do carries and borrows now! Uncle Donovan helped me last night! Come on in, and I'll show you!"

"That's wonderful, Katy." Sarah accepted the chapped little hand and mounted the steps, avoiding Donovan's seething gaze. How much had he told his sister? she wondered. Varina had been one of her staunchest friends here in Miner's Gulch. But then, Varina had known nothing about her past.

Sarah stepped into the dimly lit cabin, braced for an on-slaught of hostility. Varina may have gone West before the war, but its tragedy had touched her all the same. Like Donovan, she had lost a family home and a much-loved young brother. Who could blame her for hating the woman who'd had a hand in it all?

"Come on, Miss Sarah!" Katy tugged eagerly at her hand. "You can see little Charlie first! Then I'll show you my carries and borrows!"

Little by little, Sarah's eyes adjusted to the shadows. She could see Annie washing dishes at the counter, with Sam-uel clumsily drying them. In the darkest corner, Varina was sitting up in bed, nursing the baby. Sarah's breath caught.

Varina was smiling.

"Sarah!" She reached out, beckoning with her free arm. "I was hoping you'd come today! Little Charlie and I are doing fine, as you can see. But I'm afraid I didn't get a chance to thank you properly the other night. Come here!"

Sarah put down her medical kit and moved slowly to-ward the bed, tears stinging her eyes.

Donovan hadn't told her. He hadn't told any of them.

"Here—" Varina seized her shoulder, drawing her close in a loving embrace that almost shattered Sarah's heart. "We owe you our lives, the two of us. I know I can never repay you, but if you ever need—"

"It's all right, Varina!" Sarah squeezed the words out of her aching throat. "Seeing you like this, with your family, is repayment enough. I could never ask for more."

"All the same—" Varina drew Sarah down until their gazes met on the same level. Her eyes were the same color as her brother's, except that where Donovan's shot icy sparks, Varina's eyes glowed with the purest kindness Sarah had ever known.

Her grip tightened on Sarah's arm. "All the same, Sarah, I want you to know that Varina Sutton is your friend for life. If ever you need anything from me, just ask, and—"

"Varina, I was only doing my Christian duty! It's all right!" Sarah felt as if she were choking. She should tell her now, she thought. Tell her this minute and get it over with.

But no, it wouldn't do. Not in this quiet moment with the children so near. Not with little Katy tugging at her skirt and Annie looking back over her shoulder with big, serious eyes. Varina would know soon enough.

The baby whimpered, squirmed and spat out his mother's nipple, providing a welcome distraction. A tender smile wreathed Varina's face. "It appears the little mite's had enough. You can hold him now, if you like. But you'd best lay this cloth on your shoulder. He tends to spit after he's eaten."

Putting aside her cloak, Sarah draped the cloth over her shirtwaist and gathered the tiny, squirming bundle into her arms.

"Oh!" she whispered, snuggling the baby close as the sweet, milky aura enfolded her. "Oh, he's beautiful!"

For Sarah, holding new infants never lost its wonder. She loved their softness, the incredible lightness of their little bodies, their tiny, puckered faces and clasping fingers. What would it be like to cradle a baby of her own? Would it ever happen?

But she could not even think about such a miracle, Sarah reminded herself. She was twenty-eight years old, a woman whose past would haunt her to the end of her days. No honorable man would ask for her hand in marriage. The best she could hope for was a lifetime of cuddling other women's babies and teaching other women's children.

Varina's son stirred in her arms and opened round indigo eyes to gaze up at her. Sarah brushed a finger across the velvet scalp, teasing the delicate fuzz that showed promise of growing in fiery red like Varina's hair and Katy's.

And Virgil's.

With cooing whispers, she lifted the infant to curl against her shoulder. Her hand gently patted the tiny back until she was rewarded by a wet little baby belch.

Varina chuckled. "I declare, Sarah Parker, you need babies of your own! You'd make a wonderful mother!"

"I seem to have my hands full just now," Sarah murmured, muffling her words against the baby's satin cheek.

"Listen, Sarah." Varina's voice dropped to a conspiratorial whisper. "I should probably just be quiet and let nature take its course, but I've never been one to keep a thing to myself." She leaned close to Sarah's ear. "My brother hasn't been the same since you were up here the other night. He's been as restless as a tomcat under a full moon. Now, I know Donovan pretty well, and I'd say he's taken a real shine to you!"

Sarah lowered her face, struggling to hide the hot rush of dismay that flooded her cheeks. From outside, Donovan's furious hammer blows punctuated the pounding of her own heart. For all her stage experience, she found herself tongue-tied.

"Varina, I—"

"You what? He likes you. I can tell."

"No." Sarah shook her head, writhing inside. "You're wrong, Varina. I'm not Donovan's kind of woman at all."

"Nonsense! You don't know how many ladies have tried to trap that man over the years! Pretty ones! Wealthy ones! None of them seemed quite right. But you, Sarah, you're different. You have an inner beauty that shines through your face. If you'd only show some interest in—"

Varina's words were shattered by the crash of splintering wood and falling timbers against the outer wall. The sound galvanized both women. They stared at each other in alarm.

"Here—" Sarah thrust the baby back into Varina's arms. "You stay put. I'll go see what's happened."

Sarah gathered up her skirts and raced outside with the three children at her heels. The sight that met their eyes as they rounded the corner of the cabin stopped her heart cold.

Donovan was lying on the ground beneath a tumble of heavy beams. Lying as still as death.

"Stay where you are!" she ordered the children. "Annie, run back inside and get my medical kit. Don't tell your mother what's happened. Not till we know—"

Annie was gone like a streak. Katy had begun to whimper. "Miss Sarah... is Uncle Donovan dead like my pa?"

"Dead? Don't be a little goose, Katy!" Sarah threw her full strength against the topmost beam, straining her tight corset stays as she swung the heavy end around and rolled it to one side. She had to hurry. She had to get the weight off Donovan's chest before it crushed the breath out of him.

"Don't let him be dead, Miss Sarah!" Katy whined.

"Be still and hold on to Samuel!" Sarah wrestled frantically with the next timber. She could see Donovan's face now, white and still, the eyes closed. A small gash at his hairline was oozing blood.

No—with Virgil long since buried and Charlie Sutton not two months gone, they couldn't lose Donovan, too. It would destroy Varina and her little ones. She had to get him free, had to save him... please... please...

Donovan's head moved slightly. He groaned.

Sarah froze. As her heart began to beat again, she remembered the frightened children looking on. "Katy, Samuel, it's all right!" she gasped, heaving the last timber aside. "He's breathing! He's alive! Tell Annie to hurry!"

She flung herself to the ground beside Donovan. He was alive, yes. But how badly was he hurt? He could have broken bones. He could have head injuries. He could—

He groaned again as she placed a trembling hand on his chest. His skin was wind chilled, but his heart throbbed steadily against her palm. Sarah was dimly aware of Annie thrusting her medical bag into reach. Willing her emotions to freeze, she snatched it up and rummaged inside for the vial of smelling salts.

The big, stubborn fool! What business did he have trying to frame a cabin alone when he obviously knew nothing about it? He could have been killed. He could have—

Sarah's hands shook as she yanked out the stopper and waved the vial a finger's breadth from his nostrils. Donovan's face twitched. A shudder rippled his long, muscular body. His eyelids fluttered. Sarah held her breath as he opened his eyes and looked up at her.

For the space of a heartbeat his gaze held hers—warm and open, as if he saw into her soul and understood everything. But the bond was as fleeting as a moonbeam. His mind was clearing now. As he recognized her, his eyes glazed over with hatred.

"What the devil—?" He thrashed against her, struggling to sit up.

"Don't try to move!" Sarah ordered in a frigid voice. "You could be hurt."

"Blast it, I'm not—" His words ended in a grunt of pain as he collapsed back onto the ground.

"What is it? Your ribs? Keep still a minute." Her fingertips slid over his sun-burnished flesh as she fought to detach her feelings, to make believe this was just another injured man she was touching, and not Donovan Cole.

But try as she might, Sarah could not close her mind to the manliness of his body—the finely sculpted curve of arm and shoulder, the splendor of his broadly muscled torso, the shadow of coarsely curling chestnut hair that trickled along the midline of his flat, tan belly to disappear in—

Stop it! Sarah tore her eyes away from the distinctly male bulge that rose below his belt line. There was no part of a man she hadn't seen before, she reminded herself bitterly. Donovan would be no different from Reginald Buckley, or from anyone else, for that matter.

He flinched visibly, biting back a yelp of pain as Sarah's fingers probed along his left side.

"Hurts there, does it?" She paused, studiously avoiding Donovan's eyes.

His sharp exhalation answered her question.

"Nothing feels broken, but you may have a cracked rib or two. How about your legs? Your arms?" Sarah tried to sound disinterested, as if it didn't matter one way or the other. She was conscious of the three children, huddled in a worried little cluster, watching and waiting.

"My legs and arms are fine!" he groused. "Annie, Katy, you take Samuel and go back in the house! This isn't a blasted sideshow!"

"They're just concerned about you," Sarah murmured as the youngsters scattered for the porch. "And you can hardly blame them, after what happened to their father."

"Oh, damnation, don't I know it?" Donovan sat up gingerly, blood dripping down his temple to mingle with the rough, reddish whiskers on his unshaven jaw. "I'd give anything if they'd just pull up stakes and go back to Kansas with me. But Varina's as stubborn as that mule of yours. This was Charlie's land, and now it's hers. She won't budge an inch."

"Varina's the finest woman I know. But you're right, she can be stubborn. Hold still, now, while I clean up that gash on your head. Then we'll see to your ribs." Sarah fished a pint of cheap whiskey and a clean wad of cotton wool out of her bag. "This'll sting some."

He held himself rigid, wincing as she dabbed away the blood. "This doesn't change anything, you know," he muttered through clenched teeth.

"I didn't expect it to."

"You've still got till Monday night to be gone from Miner's Gulch. Otherwise, I spill your treachery to the whole town."

"Save your bluster, Donovan." Sarah balled another wad of cotton wool and saturated it with the whiskey, hoping he wouldn't notice her quivering hands. "I told you I wasn't leaving. I meant it."

His green eyes, inches from her own, narrowed like a puma's. "If you're gambling on the chance that I'll back off, forget it. You're the lying scum of the earth, Sarah Parker Buckley, or whatever your name is. I've hanged nobler souls than you, and I won't have my nieces and nephews growing up under your influence. I won't have my sister—*ouch!*" Donovan snarled as the stinging alcohol penetrated raw flesh.

Sarah had never realized words could hurt so much. Inwardly she recoiled as if he had struck her, but nothing showed in her face. Whatever happened, she could not let him see how deeply he had wounded her. She could not give him the satisfaction or the power.

Gulping back tears, she forced her features into an icy mask. "I'll not have you telling me where I can or can't make my home," she declared coldly. "Do your worst, Donovan. It won't make any difference. I can be just as stubborn as your sister, and I'm not going anywhere."

"Then you're a fool." He stared sullenly past her shoulder as she applied a plaster to the cut. Her hands trembled where they touched his face. More than anything, she wanted to be done with this ordeal, to be back in the security of her little schoolroom with the door bolted behind her. But there would be no security anywhere for her, she realized. Not now.

"How much experience have you had framing a cabin?" she asked, breaking the weight of his silence.

Donovan's jaw twitched, but he did not reply.

"A fortnight ago, I delivered Jemima Hanks down in the creek bottoms. Lanny Hanks, her husband, is an able carpenter. He needs work." Sarah paused to retrieve the roll of muslin stripping she used for bellybands. "Raise your arms, now, and I'll bind your ribs. Framing's not a job for a lone man—not even one who knows what he's doing."

"Save your do-gooder advice for somebody else. I should have seen through you back in Richmond." Donovan's voice was a lash, but he did raise his arms, giving silent consent for Sarah to wrap the muslin around his bruised rib cage.

Sarah bent to the task, steeling herself against his nearness. Donovan held himself rigid, his whole frame radiating unspoken fury. Along his ribs, the flesh had already begun to discolor. The bruises would be painful for a long time to come.

"This wrapping will help, but you're going to be sore. I'd advise you to take it easy for a few days." She bent close to pass the binding around his back, swallowing a gasp as one tightly puckered nipple brushed her cheek. Donovan's was a soldier's body, hard, disciplined and nicked with the marks of battle. The track of a rifle ball creased his lean left flank. His right shoulder was pocked with shrapnel scars. They lay creamy white against his golden skin, oddly, compellingly beautiful.

Donovan's lips tightened as the muslin passed around his ribs. His silence seethed, emanating ice-cold fury.

I should have seen through you back in Richmond.

The words echoed in Sarah's ears as she struggled with the wrapping, bending close again to circle his rigid back. The memory that flashed through her mind was scalding in its pain.

Richmond...music...a waltz. Her peony pink gown afloat in the midst of the swirling ballroom. Golden epaulets blazing in the lamplight. Her lace-mitted hand, resting on the fine gray wool of Virgil's tunic...

And Donovan, his face glimpsed through the shadows beyond Virgil's shoulder, his mouth set in a hard line, his expression guarded and cautious, veiling his emotions.

Almost by chance their eyes had met—and in that blistering instant, it was as if their naked gazes had penetrated each other's souls, leaving no secrets unseen. So searing was the connection that Sarah had gasped and torn her eyes away from him. For days afterward she had lived in fear, certain that he had detected her masquerade. Only now did she realize he had not. It was something else she had glimpsed that night. Something deeper.

Oh, Donovan, if only we'd been born different people, you and I. If only we'd come together in a less dangerous time...

Sarah's hands had slowed in their task. Sensing his impatience, she hurried to finish. The children had not reappeared. Varina, Sarah realized to her chagrin, was probably keeping them inside the cabin to further her misguided matchmaking efforts.

"Leave the wrapping in place for the next few days, at least," she said, snipping off the end and fashioning a square knot. "Promise me, too, you'll get some help with that framing. You'll never manage it alone, especially with cracked ribs."

"Promise?" His wry chuckle carried the bitterness of a January wind. "I owe you no kind of promise, *Miss Sarah* Parker. It amazes me, in fact, that your lying lips can even speak the word."

"Stop it!" Sarah jerked away from him, quivering with the fury of her frayed patience. "I can't change who I am, Donovan Cole, not even for you, and I'm through apologizing for it! You gave me an ultimatum, and I gave you my answer! As far as I'm concerned, there's nothing more to say between us!"

"Nothing more to say." He watched her through slitted eyes as she fumbled for the scattered contents of her medical kit—the scissors, the roll of stripping, the whiskey.

"Nothing more to say, Miss Sarah, except this—"

Donovan's hand flashed out like the strike of a rattler, fingers locking on to her wrist. His powerful arm wrenched her hand behind her back, the motion pinning her against his chest.

Too startled to fight, Sarah stared up into his hard green eyes. His face was chiseled granite, his breath a harsh rasp in his throat.

"Back in Richmond, I treated you like a lady because you were my brother's sweetheart!" he raged. "If I'd known the truth, I would have unmasked you then and there, Sarah Parker Buckley! I would have stormed your room and bedded you like the false-hearted little trollop you were—and are!"

Sarah's outraged gasp was lost against the brutal impact of his lips. There was no tenderness in Donovan's kiss, and certainly no trace of affection. His roughness wrenched her head backward, bowing her body hard against his naked chest. His contemptuous tongue invaded her mouth, probing, pillaging, challenging her to resist.

Head spinning, Sarah struggled in the vise of his arms. Oh, she knew what Donovan was after. He was intent on proving the truth of his own terrible words—proving to her and to himself that behind Sarah's virtuous mask, Lydia Taggart still lived and breathed.

He was wrong. He had to be wrong. She had to show him.

She willed herself to go rigid against him, but this was Donovan. *Donovan*—and she had been alone too long. Her body was as pliant as tallow in his arms. Through the thin shirtwaist, her breasts had molded to the solid contours of his chest. Her lips were softening under the fire of his kiss. His tongue was a flame in her mouth, its heat rippling downward in sweet, hot waves. Sarah could feel her hips twisting against him, feel her whole being igniting like gunpowder...

No! The last vestige of reason screamed in her head. This man hated her. He was bent on her destruction. Give in to him now, and there was no hope for her.

With all her strength, Sarah shoved her arms against him. Donovan gasped at the sudden pressure on his rib cage. His grip loosened. Sarah tumbled away to sprawl in the spring mud, her skirts askew, her hair falling loose, her mouth damp and swollen from his bruising kiss.

Donovan had collapsed against the timbers. His face was twisted in pain. His eyes flickered, half angry, half amused. Watching him, Sarah had just one wish—to be gone. She struggled to rise, stepped on her own petticoat and toppled headlong to the ground again.

For the space of a long breath she lay there, her face blazing as Donovan's sardonic laughter filled her ears. He thought he had won, she realized. But he was wrong. By this time tomorrow he would know exactly how wrong he had been.

She clawed her way to a defiant crouch, facing him now like a wounded animal at bay. "You—you bullying bastard!" she hissed.

His mouth twisted in a bitter smile. "Sanctimonious Sarah, the Angel of Miner's Gulch," he drawled. "What a joke! Strip away that self-righteous window dressing, and you haven't changed a whit. Lydia Taggart is alive and well...and I just had the dubious pleasure of renewing our acquaintance."

Sarah struggled to her feet, battling the urge to fly at him like an enraged wildcat. "Don't think you can trifle with me, Donovan! I've got friends in this town, and I'm stronger than you know!"

"We'll see about that." His expression did not change as Sarah snatched up her medical bag and strode furiously toward her mule. In her muddy, disheveled state, she could not think of going back inside the cabin—not to see Katy's carries and borrows, not even to retrieve the cloak she had left on a kitchen chair. The cold spring breeze buffeted her skirts, chilling her through the thin shirtwaist as she swung into the saddle.

Donovan had pulled himself to his feet. Catching Sarah's eye, he raised his hand in a mocking salute. The insolent gesture snapped the final thread of her hard-won self-control.

"I should have just let you lie there!" she sputtered, jabbing her heels into the mule's shaggy flanks. *"I should have let you die!"*

Jerking the reins, she wheeled the mule and bolted for the trees. A gust of wind caught her tousled hair, whipping it loose to stream behind her like a banner. Her spectacles dangled forgotten from the silver brooch on her shirtwaist. Tears blinded her eyes—tears she could not afford to let Donovan see.

She clung to the saddle, grateful for the mule's sure feet as they lurched down the trail. Donovan's mocking kiss burned her lips and seared her memory. He had all but undone her, she realized. Another instant in his arms and her defenses would have shattered.

At close quarters, she was no match for him. He was too bitter; she was too vulnerable. Her only hope, Sarah knew, lay in keeping her distance—that, and fighting him with the one sure weapon that lay within her reach.

The truth.

Chilled, now that his rage was spent, Donovan shivered in the raw spring wind. His lips stung with the memory of kissing Sarah. His cracked ribs burned like a jab from the devil's own pitchfork.

Reaching for his flannel shirt, he slipped his arms awkwardly into the sleeves. As his numbed fingers worked the buttons, Sarah's parting epithet rang in his ears.

I should have let you die!

His fingers brushed the ridge of the muslin bandage. It was true that Sarah had probably saved his life. A minute more under the crushing weight of those timbers, and the breath would have been squeezed from his body. She had saved him, just as she'd saved Varina and the baby.

But it wasn't enough.

Donovan rubbed his burning mouth with the back of his hand, wiping away the taste of her deceitful lips. His jaw tightened as he forced himself to remember what she had done.

As Lydia Taggart, Sarah Parker Buckley had plotted against her friends and neighbors in Richmond—people who had welcomed and accepted her. She had used trusting young men like Virgil to betray the Confederacy. Her lying ways had killed Virgil as surely as if she'd fired the mortar shell that shattered his body. And Virgil was only one man. Who could say how many other lives her treachery had cost the South?

No, Donovan told himself, whatever good Sarah had done here in Miner's Gulch, it wasn't enough. It didn't balance the scales. It couldn't buy back Virgil's life.

He exhaled painfully as the mule's iron-shod hooves echoed down the gulch. Kissing Sarah had been a damn fool thing to do, he reflected. He'd started out with the idea of keeping things clean and businesslike between them. All he'd wanted was to get her out of Miner's Gulch, away from his kinfolk. Then something in him had gone haywire.

Why couldn't he have left well enough alone? What was it about the woman that turned him into a raving lunatic every time she came within shouting distance?

I should have let you die!

And she should have, Donovan realized as Sarah's bitter words flashed through his memory like summer lightning. He had told no one about her past, not even Varina. If he had died, her black secret would have died with him.

She must have known it. Sarah was no fool. Another minute's delay in moving the timbers, that's all it would have taken. His death would have been a tragic accident, with Varina and the children as witnesses. No jury on earth would have found her guilty.

Yet, she had chosen to save him.

Donovan's cracked ribs screamed as he picked up the hammer and slammed it against a stump. Sarah Parker Buckley possessed all the maddening qualities of a good woman—and her goodness was driving him crazy. She was sucking away at his resistance like a blasted leech.

Was that what had driven him to kiss her? Was it the idea that it was easier to punish a bad woman than a good one—easier to punish Lydia Taggart than saintly Sarah?

The wind had freshened, bringing the scent of another storm. Donovan glowered at the encroaching clouds, cursing under his breath. Why did everything in life have to be so hellishly complicated? Why couldn't Sarah have been a man—someone he could simply challenge to a gunfight or thrash to a bloody pulp? Why did she have to be so beautiful, so soft, so full of courage?

"Uncle Donovan?" Katy's forlorn little voice shattered his reverie. He turned to see her standing alone on the porch, clutching her slate.

"Where's Miss Sarah, Uncle Donovan? I wanted her to come in and see my carries and borrows."

"Uh—Miss Sarah had to leave in a hurry." Donovan squirmed under her innocent scrutiny. "She said to tell you she was sorry," he added, hating the lie but seeing no other way out.

"But I was all ready to show her." Katy's small head drooped. The sight of her tugged at Donovan's heart. Annie was the bright sister, the capable, responsible one. And young Samuel was the best natured of Varina's brood. But it was lively, loving little Katy who had truly won him.

He lifted her chin with a solicitous finger. She and her sister deserved toys and fun and pretty dresses, he thought, not ragged clothes, hard work and a miserable shack in the mountains with no father to look after them.

"Hey, where's that smile?" he cajoled her.

"It's hiding!" Katy clutched her slate to her chest. "I want Miss Sarah to come back!"

Donovan sighed, wincing at the pain in his ribs. "You'll see Miss Sarah at school," he said. "You can show her your carries and borrows there."

"But it's Saturday!" Katy pouted. "And tomorrow is Sunday. That's two whole days!"

"Don't worry about it." Donovan mounted the rickety steps to the porch. "You'll still know how to carry and borrow on Monday."

"But it won't be the same!" Katy flounced into the cabin with an impatient little huff. Reluctantly Donovan followed her. Varina was bound to ask him what had happened outside and why Sarah had bolted. He would have to have a good story ready. The truth would not do at all.

He would be glad when the lying was done, he thought. Things would be better when Sarah was gone. And she would go—Donovan had no doubt of that. Her declaration that she would stay was nothing but a bluff.

Mentally he ticked off the days in his mind. Time was running out for Sarah Parker Buckley. He had given her a week to get out of Miner's Gulch. On Monday, at sundown, her time would be up.

Monday night. And tomorrow was Sunday. Soon—very soon—the battle would be over.

Chapter Five

Church services in Miner's Gulch were a plain affair. A traveling preacher came through town every two or three months to perform marriages and christenings. The rest of the time, the little flock stumbled along on its own.

Over the years, a simple, nonsectarian worship routine had evolved. Each Sunday morning at ten o'clock, the congregation gathered in the weather-beaten church across from Smitty's saloon. They opened the meeting with an unaccompanied hymn and a prayer, followed by a reading from the scriptures. The rest of the time was set aside for anyone who felt moved by the spirit to rise and speak. At the end of an hour—sooner, if no one had much to say—the meeting ended with another prayer.

Most people looked forward to the weekly service. It marked a break in the gulch's plodding pace. It gave isolated neighbors a chance to get together, to exchange greetings, news and gossip. It lent unity to a town so disordered that there was no local government, no law enforcement, no court and no usable jail.

Sarah seldom missed the Sunday meeting—not that she could honestly claim to enjoy it. Setting foot in a church—any church—brought back the memory of her girlhood in New Bedford, a girlhood spent cringing in the family pew while her father spewed fire and brimstone from the pulpit, his words scourging her rebellious young soul like a cat-o'-nine-tails.

The Sunday atmosphere in Miner's Gulch was much gentler. But even here Sarah could not walk through the doors of the drab little church without feeling the sting of that old guilt, and with it, the overpowering sense that she was not worthy to be there.

All the same, she went. It was a way to keep in touch with people. A way to belong. Perhaps the only way, she reflected as she twisted her hair into a tight knot and jabbed in the pins with a force that made her wince. The face in her mirror was pale and tired, red eyed from a sleepless night. Raw tension quivered through every nerve and sinew of her body. Her fingers shook as she buttoned the high collar over her throat and added the plain silver brooch that had belonged to her mother.

She felt as if she were dressing for her own execution.

From up the street, a single discordant clang of the church bell quivered on the morning air. The sound went through Sarah like a shock.

It was time.

Hastily she caught up her tiny leather-bound hymnal and the gray merino shawl she wore on Sundays when the weather wasn't too bad. She pulled the shawl tightly about her shoulders, needing its soft warmth on a day when little else could offer her comfort. At the door she paused to let her gaze drift over the small, crude schoolroom. Her eyes lingered affectionately on the worn log benches, the slates, the blackboard with Monday's sums already chalked across it in a precise line.

Her own little world. Until this very moment, Sarah had not realized how much she loved it.

The church bell had begun to clang in earnest, its brassy tone resonating up and down the gulch, summoning the faithful and disturbing slackers like the girls above Smitty's, who were no doubt trying to sleep off a hard Saturday night's work. As Sarah plucked her key from its hook and turned to go, she remembered the dying Marie. It was time she paid the poor young woman another visit—tonight, perhaps, if she was able.

Tonight.

Would her world still exist by tonight? Would *she?*

The morning air stung her cheeks as she opened the door. Its sudden coldness slammed home the memory of Donovan's kiss, of struggling in his powerful arms, lashed by the bitter spring wind. Even now, when she remembered the wild, angry roughness of his mouth on hers, Sarah's face blazed like a torch.

She had battled all night to erase Donovan's image from her mind, as she might rub yesterday's sums from the blackboard. But her efforts had come to nothing. The memory of his unshaven face, his hard, angry eyes, his bronze skin cool against her palms, was as wrenchingly vivid as ever.

Oh, Sarah knew men, and she was no fool. Donovan felt nothing for her but contempt. Even his kiss had been an act of rage, an overt move to control and punish her. And she had almost let him. He would never know how close she had come to flinging away everything she'd fought so hard to become.

Would Donovan be in church this morning? Surely not, she reassured herself as she locked the door behind her and made her way down the stairs. Varina, still bedridden, would need his help at the cabin. In any case, Donovan had never impressed Sarah as a churchgoing man, which was just as well. What she had resolved to do this morning would be difficult enough without him. With Donovan there, with his eyes on her . . . but Sarah did not even want to think about that possibility.

Yesterday's storm had melted to a gritty slush that had refrozen overnight, leaving a quagmire of icy mud. Wary for her freshly polished boots, Sarah picked her way across the morass of ruts and puddles. Out of the corner of her eye, she could see Mrs. Eudora Cahill bustling up the church steps on the arm of her husband, Sam, trailed by their two gangly teenage daughters. As the town's one-time banker, Sam Cahill had made enough money to retire when the gold veins played out, but not enough to leave the dying boomtown and set himself up in Denver or Central City. Even so, the Cahills owned the most imposing house in Miner's Gulch. Eudora Cahill functioned as the town's self-appointed social leader and arbiter of taste. Where she led, other women tended to follow.

And that, Sarah told herself, could be of life-or-death importance this morning. Up to now, she had managed to stay on Eudora's good side. But Eudora Cahill, like most of the townspeople, was a Southerner. She could not count on Eudora's support, nor on anyone else's, Sarah realized. After today, she could depend on no one but herself.

She was halfway across the street, lifting her skirts to clear an ice-rimmed puddle, when she saw him—Donovan Cole, scrubbed, slicked and dressed in his Sunday best, striding around the far side of the church with Annie and Katy dancing along on either side of him.

Sarah's heart plummeted like a stone. An icy wetness penetrated her boot as she stepped squarely into the puddle.

Not Donovan! Please, anyone but Donovan! Anytime but this morning!

Sarah battled the urge to turn tail and slink back to her room. Neither Donovan nor the girls had glanced in her direction. Maybe it wasn't too late. She could pretend to be ill—yes, for that matter, she was feeling a bit ill already.

Sarah hesitated, poised for flight, then brought herself up short. Where was her courage? Where was her resolve, her determination to end the lies once and for all?

She could not lose heart. Not now.

Donovan and his nieces were mounting the steps, their backs toward her. Thrusting out her chin, Sarah marched toward the church. Her boots crunched a determined rhythm through the half-frozen mud. Her throat quivered with a martial melody, hummed in cadence with her stride. Her lips moved subtly, forming words under her breath.

She had reached the foot of the steps before she realized, to her chagrin, that she was singing "The Battle Hymn of the Republic."

Donovan moved down the crowded aisle, Annie holding his right hand, Katy clutching his left. The small church was filling up fast, and the seating appeared to be on a first-come-first-served basis. Annie spotted an opening for three at the far end of a pew. Tugging Donovan's wrist, she led him along the gauntlet of knees, petticoats, boots and canes, into a space so cramped that when he sat down, his long legs folded against his chest like a carpenter's rule.

Making himself as comfortable as his rangy frame would allow, Donovan settled back with a sigh. He could not remember when he'd last set foot inside a church, but Varina had insisted he go and take the girls. For the sake of peace, Donovan had given in. There was no way an hour of hymn singing and Bible thumping could be any worse than arguing with Varina Cole Sutton. What the hell, maybe it would even do him some good.

His gaze wandered idly around the shabby meeting hall, picking out a familiar face here and there—the shopkeeper and his wife; the one-armed Shiloh veteran who managed the livery stable; gray-headed Widow Harley, who ran a boardinghouse for gentlemen across from Satterlee's store.

He did not see Sarah Parker. Not that he'd expected to. After yesterday, Donovan would've wagered a month's pay that Sarah would not have the nerve to show up here. He had her on the run, he calculated. She was probably at home packing her trunk this very minute.

He had no regrets for what he'd done. Sarah was a spy and a liar. She deserved to be strung up from the tallest tree in the gulch. All the same, he had been more than fair with the woman. Because she'd saved Varina and the baby, he was giving her a chance to run. But that was all. Sarah would end up very sorry if she called his bluff. Donovan Cole was a man who only bluffed at poker.

Yes, he'd handled the whole dirty business with skill and tact, Donovan congratulated himself—except for yesterday, when he'd seized Sarah in his arms and kissed her till his blood blazed like pine pitch. That was something he hadn't planned, something he was still at a loss to explain, even to himself.

Only half-aware, he rippled his tongue along the sensitive inner rim of his lower lip. His flesh tingled with the memory of Sarah's sweet mouth, its silken moistness melting to his heat, opening to the hungry invasion of his tongue. His nipples shrank beneath his shirt as he recalled the touch of her hands on his bare skin, the firm points of her breasts crushed hard against him through the thin fabric of her blouse. The sudden tightness in his loins was so painful that—

Blast it, Cole, you're in church!

Annie nudged his arm with her open hymnal. Widow Harley had taken her place at the front of the congregation, her rawboned arm poised to lead the hymn. Wrenching his mind back to the here and now, Donovan accepted a corner of the songbook and balanced it on two fingers. As the somber tones of "Rock of Ages" swelled to the rafters, he added his untrained baritone to the other voices.

A smile teased his lips as he caught Katy's loud, off-key soprano on his right, piping, "Rock the pages, clever me, let me hi-i-ide myself in tea..."

Perversely tempted to join her, he glanced around for any sign of disapproving eyes. That was when he glimpsed Sarah, slipping into the far end of the pew behind him.

Donovan's throat went dry. She was as primly done up as he'd ever seen her—her lips set in a determined line, her hair pulled severely back from her pale face, her collar buttoned all the way to her jaw and fastened with a tarnished silver brooch. The pince-nez spectacles perched firmly on her nose.

He watched her sit down, remembering her fire as she twisted in his arms.

Who are you today, Sarah? Who were you yesterday? Which one of you is real?

She sat with downcast eyes, her lips barely mouthing the words of the hymn. She looked tired, even ill, he thought. The clothes, hair and glasses might be part of her act, but the shadows beneath her bloodshot eyes were genuine.

An unexpected jab of worry needled Donovan's conscience. If Sarah's condition was his doing...but then, why should he care? The woman was his sworn enemy. She had wronged him, wronged his family, wronged the South, far beyond the point of restitution. Any suffering on her part was no more than she deserved.

He tore his gaze away from Sarah as the hymn ended. It wouldn't do, after all, to have people catch him looking at her. Someone might get the wrong idea, and he was already having enough trouble with Varina on that account. He would be smart to set a good example for his nieces and pay attention to the rest of the service.

He forced himself to listen to every word of the customary scriptural reading, an obscure and depressing passage from Ecclesiastes, quoted by a dim-sighted old man who kept squinting at the page and clearing his throat. Donovan battled the temptation to pull out his pocket watch and check the time. Varina had told him the meeting would probably end around eleven. How far off could that blessed hour possibly be?

Sarah's presence burned into his back as his own words returned to haunt him.

If I'd known the truth...I would have stormed your room and bedded you like the false-hearted little trollop you were—and are.

Where had those words come from? Had he meant them—he, who had never plotted violence against a woman in his life? In the depths of his unspoken heart, had he wanted Lydia Taggart that badly?

With a resounding amen, the reading ended. Donovan knew that the time remaining would be left open to the congregation. He strove to keep his mind on Widow Harley's account of a Comanche attack in the fifties, and on the elderly scripture-reader's revelation that he'd once seen a vision of the son he lost at Gettysburg. From the slack faces around him, Donovan gathered that everyone else had heard the stories before. They were new to him, however, and he made an honest effort to pay attention.

But listening wasn't easy. Not with the long-buried fantasies that kept creeping into his mind, tormenting him with the devil's own fire.

Lydia... soft in the Virginia moonlight, her hair fanned like rippled silk on the pillow, the aroma of jasmine warm on her skin... his hand cupping her breast through the gossamer lace of her nightgown, molding the rose-tipped perfection to the curve of his palm, taking time to tease the nipple to a puckered raspberry, salty sweet to the taste... her hands clasping him close then, fingers raking his hair, urging his head downward along the flat curve of her belly, thighs parting, musk-scented secrets opening to his tongue like the quivering petals of a flower...

"I've never spoken to all of you as a congregation before."

Sarah's hard-edged Yankee voice jerked Donovan back to reality. She was standing half in the aisle, her white-knuckled hands clutching the back of the pew for support. Her face was pale, her posture rigid, taut with strain.

No! Donovan stared at her, seized by a black premonition of what she was about to do. Suddenly, inexplicably, he wanted to stop her, to shout her down, to grab her and drag her from the church before it was too late. But there was nothing he could do. He sat frozen to the bench, fists clenched in a paroxysm of helplessness as Sarah cleared her throat and continued.

"In the years since I first came to Miner's Gulch, you have honored me with your friendship and your... trust."

Her voice wavered. She gazed down at her hands. For an instant, Donovan hoped she might come to her senses and stop, but it was not to be. Raising her head and taking a deep breath, Sarah plunged toward the precipice.

"I've tried to be worthy of that trust, that friendship. I've tried to be a good neighbor... tried to make myself of use. I've delivered your babies, schooled your children—" Her breath caught in a little gasp as she struggled for self-control. "I've tried. But when someone is living a lie, nothing else matters. Nothing else counts enough to make up the difference."

Again Sarah paused to collect her thoughts. The meeting's drowsy atmosphere had evaporated. Every head was turned, every eye riveted on the slender figure who stood alone in the aisle, a beam of light from the window falling on her tightly bound hair.

Donovan felt Katy nudge his arm. "What's happening, Uncle Donovan?" she asked. "What's Miss Sarah talking about?"

"Hush!" A frowning matron in the next row spared Donovan the task of silencing his niece. "Be still and listen, child!"

Sarah's face was so pale that Donovan feared—or perhaps hoped—she would faint. He had not expected this of her. He had not asked it, nor even wanted it. He had only wanted the woman out of Miner's Gulch. Now she was about to destroy herself, and he was powerless to stop her.

She roused herself at last. Squaring her jaw, she plucked the pince-nez spectacles from her nose and let them drop, to dangle unneeded from their thin black cord. Her voice, when she spoke, was neither Sarah Parker's brusque Yankee twang nor Lydia Taggart's languorous Southern purr. It was the rich, cultured voice of a professional actress—a voice with the strength to penetrate the upper balcony of a theater, a voice with the subtlety to curl around a man's heart. The sound of it thrilled Donovan to the quick.

"I've lied to you long enough," she declared to the gaping townspeople. "It's time to open the book of my life and set the record straight. When you've heard my story..." She drew a tremulous breath. "When you know everything, I leave it to you, my friends and neighbors, to sit as my judges. I can only ask for your understanding... and your forgiveness."

A rustle, like the sound of wind through a Kansas wheat field, passed through the congregation. In Miner's Gulch, Sarah Parker had clearly lived above reproach. The idea that this saintly but mysterious young woman had something to hide created a stir of the most delicious anticipation. These were decent people, Donovan reminded himself. But they were human. All too human.

They would crucify her.

"I spent most of last night wondering where to begin," Sarah continued, plunging relentlessly toward her doom. "In order for you to understand everything, I suppose I should start at the beginning. I was raised in New Bedford, Massachusetts. My father was a preacher—which church no longer matters. He loved me in his way, I suppose, but he was strict, and I was rebellious. At sixteen, I eloped with a traveling actor, a Mr. Reginald Buckley from Savannah."

An audible buzz rippled through the little church, a murmur of surprise and speculation. Donovan felt a dark tightening in his gut. Sarah's first revelation was merely scandalous. How would the people of Miner's Gulch react to the rest of her story? There was no call to even wonder.

"Mr. Buckley taught me his profession," she continued as crisply as if she had memorized the lines. "We performed together for nearly six years, mostly in the South. I grew to love the warmth and graciousness of the Southern people. But there was one thing I could not abide, and that was slavery!"

There—she had touched a nerve. Most of the listeners had been too poor to own slaves before the war. But the idea was a point of bitterness all the same. Donovan could feel the rising tide of hostility in the little chapel. He could hear the murmurs, sense the clenching of fists and quickening of pulses. Sarah was already in danger.

Suddenly he knew what he had to do.

"I've heard enough!" He sprang to his feet with a force that tumbled poor Annie into the lap of the woman on her right. "We won't have a blasted abolitionist living in this town and teaching our children!" he thundered. "Pack your trunks and be out of Miner's Gulch by sundown, Miss Sarah Parker, or else—"

"Sit down and be quiet, Mr. Cole."

Sarah's voice rang out in the shocked silence of the little church, its queenly tone riveting even the frantic Donovan. She stood alone and erect, an imperious figure now, in her prim white shirtwaist and dark blue skirt. What role was she playing now? Donovan wondered. Was she Medea? Antigone? Joan of Arc?

Her calm gray eyes drilled into Donovan's like rifle bullets. "I know what you're trying to do," she said. "But it won't work. I told you Miner's Gulch was my home, and I intend to remain—at least until these good people have heard everything I came to say."

Donovan felt a sharp tug at the tail of his coat. "Siddown!" a male voice hissed behind him. "Let the little lady have her say!"

"Yes!" a woman chorused. "We want to hear everything!"

Swearing under his breath, Donovan crumpled in defeat. He had done his best to save Sarah Parker's miserable life. But as he had long since learned, there was no point in saving someone hell-bent on self-destruction.

He sagged into his seat, glaring at her in impotent rage. Why had he even bothered? Why should he care? Let the stubborn little fool hang herself! Heaven knows, she deserved it!

Sarah stood quietly, waiting for the uproar to fade. Only when the chapel was as silent as the grave itself did she take up her story.

"Many of you have seen what I saw. Children sold away from their mothers. Men scarred and broken under the lash. Women living as concubines to their masters... I never got over the horror of it. And I vowed that if I were ever offered the chance to fight such an evil, I would not turn away."

Some members of the congregation listened with downcast eyes. She was good, Donovan conceded. The slaves on White Oaks had been decently treated, but he knew of other plantations where blacks had been shamefully abused. Sarah's eloquent voice brought back every wretched sight he had ever witnessed, and he knew she was having the same effect on others within her hearing.

"My chance came just before the war," she continued, plunging ahead with an abandon that made Donovan reel. "My husband had died. I found myself alone in Washington, in desperate straits. I had no money. No employment. My family had disowned me when I ran off with Mr. Buckley, and there was no hope of going back to them. That was when President Lincoln's first secretary of war, Mr. Simon Cameron, summoned me to his office."

The chapel was deathly still, except for the wail of a baby, who was rapidly hustled outside, and the intermittent coughing of the old man who had read the scriptures. The sense of anticipation darkened as the listeners strained in their seats. This, they'd begun to realize, was not the simple confession of a woman gone astray. What Sarah Parker had done went beyond the bounds of ordinary sin. It was something that had touched them all.

Sick with fear for her, Donovan watched helplessly as Sarah squared her shoulders and went on speaking. "Mr. Cameron offered me a new name and a new life, in Richmond, Virginia, working as a secret agent for the United

States government. Out of duty and necessity, I had no choice but to accept."

The explosion of a mortar shell could scarcely have had more impact on the little congregation. People sat frozen in shocked disbelief, eyes staring, jaws gone slack, as Sarah's words sank in. Donovan drew his nieces protectively close, expecting a riot to break out in the next instant. But he had underestimated Sarah Parker's theatrical talents. She held them in thrall with her voice, with her eyes, as the fatal flow of words continued.

"In Richmond, there was a woman with secret abolitionist sympathies who had died and left her property to the cause. Posing as her widowed niece, I was set up in her fine house. I was supplied with servants, with beautiful clothes, and enough money to give the most lavish parties in town. Music...the best food, the best wines...the gayest conversation. At the beginning of the war, when spirits were high, there was no livelier place in all of Richmond."

The cadence of Sarah's voice had slowed and softened, taking on a throaty sweetness that clawed at Donovan's heart. He stared at her, transfixed. Had anyone else noticed the change? The coquettish tilt of her small, cleft chin? The subtle arch of her torso that thrust her breasts into saucy little points beneath the prim shirtwaist? Or was his mind playing tricks on him?

He tried to blink the vision away—but no, what he saw was real. She was doing it on purpose, and her witchery was directed right at him.

Forget the drab clothes. Forget the pale face and skinned-back hair. The woman who stood before Donovan now was Lydia Taggart.

Their eyes met with an impact that flashed like flint igniting tinder. For an excruciating instant, their gazes locked—his astonished and angry, hers blazing defiance. Then, with a self-possession that made Donovan grind his teeth, she turned away from him, back to her riveted au-

dience. Once more, Lydia's honeyed voice took up the
thread of her story.

"My home became a gathering place for young officers
of the Confederacy. They were free with their talk, especially when their tongues were loosened by a bit of Ma-
deira or peach brandy. Learning military secrets was little
more than a matter of listening and remembering."

A shudder, slight but unmistakable, passed through
Sarah's slim body. Only then did Donovan realize how
deeply she drew on her own courage. "I did my work well,"
she said softly. "For nearly four years, I gathered information and relayed it through the lines to the Union army."

The chapel was a powder magazine, primed to explode
at the touch of a spark. Donovan could feel the tension
rising, the long-suppressed rage of a proud people shamed
by defeat—the lost sons, fathers and brothers, the homes
and fortunes gone up in smoke.

Sarah was throwing herself on their mercy. But mercy
was not what she would find. Donovan could see it in the
eyes of the congregation. He could see it in the tightened
fists, the clenched jaws. They were bitter enough to kill her.
And some of them were capable of doing exactly that.

Was this what he'd wanted when he'd threatened Sarah?
His sister's neighbors thrown into mob violence? A helpless—albeit guilty—female, destroyed at their hands, in an
act that would haunt them to the end of their days?

Damn the woman! Why had she done such a crazy fool
thing? Why couldn't she have simply packed up and left
town?

Sarah had fallen silent and was staring down at her fingers. Lydia Taggart had vanished. The self-possessed actress had vanished. Now, when Donovan looked at her, he
saw only Sarah Parker, thin and pale and vulnerable,
standing alone in a sea of anger.

He was sick with fear for her. But then, he'd done all he
could, he reminded himself. He had tried to get her out of
this mess, and Sarah had adamantly refused his help.

The crowd was stirring now, muttering like a swarm of riled-up hornets. Without Sarah's story to hold them at bay, they were losing control. Donovan circled each of his nieces with a protecting arm. Annie was as rigid as ice. Katy was trembling. They were too young to understand what Sarah had done, but they sensed the darkness that had invaded their worship house. They felt the danger around them. They felt the rage, the fear.

It was MacIntyre, the one-armed ex-corporal who ran the livery stable, who touched off the powder keg. Reeling to his feet, he staggered into the aisle and shook his single gnarled fist in Sarah's face.

"You lyin' Yankee bitch, you owe me an arm!" he rasped. "We oughta string you up here and now!"

Hoots of approval rang out in the chapel. The crowd was boiling, surging with pent-up fury. People were jumping to their feet. Another instant and they would all be out of their seats, swarming over Sarah like a pack of wolves.

Sarah had backed up against the end of a pew. She stood tall, her chin lifted in proud defiance. Donovan felt a prickle of grudging admiration. Seldom, even in battle, had he witnessed such cool courage. The woman's veins had to be pumping ice water.

Half hesitating, she turned toward him. For the space of a heartbeat, their eyes met. Only then did Donovan glimpse the flash of stark terror in their depths. Sarah had bared her soul to the neighbors she'd served. She had gambled on their forgiveness, and she had lost. Her plight tore at his heart. Suddenly something in him snapped.

"Hold it right there!" Donovan was on his feet, barreling his way into the aisle. He was not armed, of course, but his broad shoulders and towering bulk defied any man to lay a hand on the woman beside him. Most of the townspeople knew he was a lawman, as well. They hung back, MacIntyre with them, waiting to see what would happen next.

"Listen to me!" Donovan glowered beneath his thick eyebrows. "I suffered more than most of you in the war. The Yankees burned my family's plantation! I lost a brother at Antietam and rotted away nearly two years at Camp Douglas! But that doesn't entitle me to lynch a helpless woman, no matter what she might have done! When the war ended three years ago, the president declared an amnesty! Stringing up former spies is against the law these days!"

Donovan glared at the congregation. As he waited out their anger, he could feel the sweat drops beading his temples and trickling between his shoulder blades. He was right about the law. But no jury in the land would convict a churchful of embittered Southerners for lynching a self-confessed Yankee spy.

Willing himself to stay calm, he glanced up and down the pews, focusing a hard, direct gaze on each face. A retired U.S. marshal in Dodge had taught Donovan the trick as a means of controlling unruly crowds. Although he'd never had occasion to use it until now, the method seemed to work. Little by little, Donovan felt the frenzy easing. His eyes met downcast faces as people settled back into their seats.

"That's better," he rumbled, surveying the chapel. "Now, I don't know about the rest of you, but me, I'm still curious. I'd like to know how Miss Sarah here managed after the war. I'd like to know how the devil she ended up in a godforsaken place like Miner's Gulch, playing Yankee nursemaid to a bunch of washed-up Southerners who have every reason to hate her guts."

He glanced pointedly at Sarah, who stood rooted at his elbow, her body frozen in an attitude of determination.

"As for you, Miss Sarah Parker, I'm prepared to offer you a bargain. You tell us the rest of your story, and I'll promise to see that you walk out of this chapel in one piece. All right?"

Sarah nodded, her throat twitching as she swallowed her fear. Her eyes were like a fawn's, huge and wary in her pale, thin face. Donovan backed away a few steps and sat down. He had done all that could be expected. Now she was on her own. It was up to Miss Sarah Parker to talk her way out of this mess.

Her hands clenched nervously, fingers bunching the fabric of her skirt. She looked small and scared and vulnerable, Donovan thought. Was this an act, too? Was there any part of this woman that was real?

Her voice rose thinly, like a child's, in the silence. "I was still in Richmond when the city fell to Grant. Luckily for me, the general knew who I was. He even gave me an escort to Washington. My servants stayed behind and staged the death of the woman I had been. . . ." Her eyes flickered toward Donovan. "I was told they'd even made a grave for her, with a fine headstone . . . in the parish cemetery."

Sarah's words faltered. For a moment, Donovan feared she would break down and cry. Then she rallied and, with a tremulous little half smile, took up her story like a piece of knitting she had dropped and retrieved.

"Many people must have felt lost after the war. For me, it was almost as if I no longer existed. I was dead in Richmond, and dead to my family in New Bedford. The theater—perhaps the one setting where I might have found a home—was closed to me as well, out of the fear that someone might recognize me onstage.

"The government had granted me a small pension, so at least I was able to live. But the day came when I knew I had to decide who—and what—I would be for the rest of my life.

"I tried making a new start in St. Louis, but even there, I lived in constant fear of discovery. Worse—infinitely worse—I was haunted by memories of my years in Richmond, of the good people, the kind neighbors I had known and betrayed. The awful nightmares—I still have them, the nightmares—"

This time Sarah did break. Her shoulders sagged like an abandoned marionette's. She buried her face in her palms, her body quivering with silent sobs.

Donovan watched her with a cynical eye. "Bravo, Sarah," he muttered under his breath. "We could set you up on a stage over at Smitty's, and you could give nightly performances!"

He glanced around at the congregation. They were leaning forward in rapt attention. Good Lord, she'd done it again! She had them!

Slowly Sarah lowered her hands. Her face, splotched with red now, was plain, almost ugly in the harsh light that struck her from an upper window.

"Someone—someone I met by happenstance—told me about Miner's Gulch—told me about the people here. I knew this place was the answer to my prayers. A chance to find a life, to serve, to forget myself—"

A single violent sob racked Sarah's body. Donovan could feel her battling for strength, and for an instant, he, too, was with her, pulling for her to win. But no—he brought himself up with a mental slap. Sarah Parker had the devilish gift of making a man believe anything she chose to put into his head. He could not afford to be taken in by her wiles, least of all now, with the future of Varina's family at stake.

Fighting for composure, Sarah forced herself to go on speaking.

"All I'm asking from you is a chance. A chance to stay and try to make up for what I've done. A chance to be your neighbor and friend, to find my own peace—"

She bowed her head in silence. Donovan expected her to say more, but no words came. Sarah had finished speaking. She stood like a prisoner on trial, her fate in the hands of the jury.

In the small chapel, tension crackled like the leaden clouds of an oncoming storm. No one moved. No one spoke. Every eye was fixed on Sarah as they waited.

Chapter Six

Sarah stood drained and trembling, one hand gripping the end of the pew. Her heart pounded erratically in her ears. Her stomach felt as if it were about to reject her breakfast—except that she'd been too nervous to eat that morning.

Her eyes were fixed on the floor, but she could feel the congregation staring at her, its judgment hanging like a sword above her head. It was done, she told herself. The truth was out at last.

But at what cost?

Donovan's square-toed brown boots jutted into a corner of her vision from where he sat at the end of the next pew. If she glanced that way, she knew she would meet his eyes, but she could not bear the thought of what she would see there. Twice that morning he had leapt to her rescue. But he would not be her champion again. She could feel the wall he was building against her as he remembered Richmond, remembered Antietam, remembered Virgil dying in his arms.

The only sound in the chapel was the leaden tick of the meetinghouse clock. She counted the beats, slowing her jerky breaths to match their cadence. Thanks to Donovan, she no longer feared for her life. But could the people of Miner's Gulch find it in their hearts to forgive her? Could they weigh her past against the neighborly service she had given, with an added measure of understanding to tip the scales?

Sarah stood with her head bowed, praying for a miracle.

At last someone stirred. That someone was Eudora Cahill. She rose imperiously to her feet, smoothed her skirts and, with a summoning nod to her husband and two daughters, glided out of the pew like a steamboat leaving port.

Sarah held her breath as Eudora paraded up the aisle, her plump chin thrusting ahead of her stride. Eudora's reaction was critical. It would set the example for the rest of the town.

Only last winter, Sarah remembered, she had nursed the entire Cahill household through a bout of influenza. Eudora had thanked her profusely. But would the woman remember that now? Would it be enough?

The distance between them was closing. Sarah stood her ground, hoping desperately for some gesture of acceptance. As Eudora came abreast of her, Sarah raised her eyes and forced herself to look directly into the woman's face.

What she saw there froze her heart.

Eudora Cahill's expression was as rigid as a granite slab. Her cold, blue eyes looked straight ahead, as if Sarah Parker did not even exist.

A half-spoken plea died on Sarah's lips. It was already too late. Eudora had passed her without so much as a nod. Now her daughters, both of whom Sarah had schooled, were doing the same. Even the easygoing Sam Cahill knew better than to defy his formidable wife. He crept past Sarah, his eyes carefully averted.

Another couple had risen near the front of the chapel. Sarah recognized them as Mattie and Roy Ormes. They had a young baby she'd delivered last fall and a little boy who attended her classes above the store. But Mattie had lost a father and brother at Chancellorsville. She followed Eudora's example and led her family past Sarah without so much as a glance.

Sarah's worst fears had come true. The Southerners of Miner's Gulch had forgiven her being a Yankee. But they could not forgive her for being a spy.

Widow Harley was next, followed by the Fieldings, the Camps and the Gordons. Sarah stood like stone as each family passed her in icy indifference. Behind her stoic facade, her spirit twisted and withered. Hanging would have been a kinder fate, she mused bitterly. At least the ordeal would have been swift to end.

Slowly the chapel emptied, the customary hymn and closing prayer forgotten as the congregation filed out. Sarah watched them go—mothers she had saved, babies she had birthed, children she had taught to read and cipher... and the men who had always tipped their hats and addressed her respectfully as "Ma'am" or "Miss Sarah." Now, those who acknowledged her at all cast looks of such contempt that they might as well have spat in her face.

At last she stood alone. There was no one left—no one except Donovan and the two little girls, who hung close to their uncle, glancing up at Sarah with frightened, puzzled eyes.

Donovan had been seated in a nearby pew. Now he rose to his feet, his muscular height looming darkly above her. When Sarah gathered the courage to look up at him, she saw that his face wore the same mask as the others—contemptuous and coldly angry. His eyes were as as hard as jasper. But then, what else could she have expected? He had even more reason to hate her than the others did.

Sarah's heart shuddered and sank.

He cleared his throat, an awkward sound, startlingly human in the silence of the church. "I'll hire a wagon and driver to take you as far as Central City," he said coldly. "After that, you're on your own."

"Save your money, Mr. Cole." Sarah's voice wavered, then rose steel-edged from the pit of her humiliation. "If there's one thing I won't be needing, it's a ride out of here.

I told you I was staying in Miner's Gulch, and I meant it.
This is my home.''

Something flickered in Donovan's eyes, only to vanish
like the flash of a trout fin in a deep green lake. "Then
you're an even bigger fool than I thought!" he growled.
"And I won't protect you from your folly! I only hope you
live long enough to change your mind!"

Flinging the words at her, he turned away, caught up his
nieces with either hand and stalked out of the church. Annie's bewildered gaze darted frantically back over her small,
sturdy shoulder. Then the doors closed behind them, and
Sarah was alone.

For a long moment she stood where they had left her, her
emotions frozen against an anguish that was too painful to
bear. Then, little by little, the thaw began. She pictured her
little classroom, the benches empty, the slates untouched.
She pictured the women who had been her friends—fine,
strong women like Eudora and Mattie and Varina, who
would turn their backs now when they saw her coming.
And the babies—so tiny and soft and perfect. Would she
ever be summoned to deliver a baby again?

The Angel of Miner's Gulch—that was what Donovan
had so mockingly called her. Sarah's knees weakened as the
irony of his words sank home. She had been so smug, so
satisfied with the pitiful service she had rendered here. She
had truly believed this poor, backward town needed her.

Needed her. What a joke. The need had been hers—to
serve, to belong. The people had indulged her need. They
had tolerated her interference and her odd Yankee ways.
They had allowed her to live among them, to be of use.
Only now that it was too late did Sarah realize the worth of
what they had given her.

In the days ahead, Miner's Gulch would get along fine
without her services. The parents would school their children at home. The women would aid each other, as women
had done since the beginning of time. Miss Sarah Parker
would scarcely be missed, let alone needed.

But what would she do? What would she do without the children, the women, the babies?

What would she do without her town?

The somber cadence of the old pendulum clock filled the empty church. For the space of a dozen ticks, Sarah stood needle straight, willing herself to be strong. But the effort was too much for her. Slowly her chest crumpled. Her face dropped to her hands as her shoulders quaked with savage, tearless sobs.

Up the slope from the Ordway place, the trail forked like a rattlesnake's tongue. The lower branch cut another half mile through the aspens to Varina's cabin. The upper one, Donovan had been told, followed the ridge to some long-abandoned mining claims along the crest.

After setting his nieces on the path for home, Donovan had turned up the steep, rugged ridge trail. He could not go back to the cabin and face Varina. Not while he was so churned up inside. He needed some settling-down time and some good, hard walking to work off steam and collect his thoughts.

So far, however, the strenuous trek wasn't helping. He had covered a good three-quarters of a mile at a pace that left his body dripping sweat beneath his leather coat. He had cursed and muttered most of the way, struggling to purge his spirit and regain his sense of purpose. Even so, when he closed his eyes, all he could see was Sarah.

He cursed again, remembering the woman's maddening display of courage and brutal, reckless honesty. In all his life, Donovan had never seen a performance like it. He had planned to be discreet, to give her a chance to leave quietly without exposing her past. But Sarah had more than called his bluff. She had wrenched the truth from him and made it her own.

She had left him powerless.

Donovan's boots spat mud as he forged his way through the pines to mount the ridge top. Oh, Sarah would pay. He was sure of that. The people of Miner's Gulch had already turned their backs on her. Sooner or later they would force her to leave.

Wasn't that what he had wanted all along? To see her shamed? To see lying Lydia Taggart brought to her knees?

Donovan stripped off his coat, his cracked ribs screaming as he flung it over his shoulder. The breeze was icy through the dampness of his shirt. He let it chill his skin— as if its coolness could quench the fever that raged like a forest fire inside him.

Sarah's mouth, soft-blown satin, damp where his tongue probed, and sweet as the heart of a rose. Her body melting to his heat, stirring with the promise of hidden hungers . . .

Cursing the image away, Donovan kicked at a stone, sending the melon-size rock bounding down the slope to crash into the trees. The impact set off an explosion of crows. The big, black birds scattered in a squawking flurry, spreading their wings to soar free against the clear spring sky. Snow-crested peaks glittered in the sun. Their serene beauty mocked Donovan's anger.

With a long sigh, he yielded to their spell and sank down on a lichen-covered outcrop. A piñon jay scolded him from the branch of a pine, to disappear in a brilliant indigo flash as Donovan turned his head. The air sang with the smells of spring, the whisper of the wind and the gurgle of melting snow.

A little ways up the ridge, Donovan could seen the tailings from the old mines—shallow affairs, shoveled out in an effort to find the source of the gold that sparkled in the mountain streams. He thought of the backbreaking labor that had gone into those diggings, the dreams that had dwindled and died when the gold veins played out. There was plenty of gold left, someone had told him. But it existed in minute granules, locked into hunks of solid white quartz like the ones that littered the mountainside.

Mildly curious, Donovan peeled back a tuft of moss from the rock where he was sitting. The clean stone glittered with tiny gold flecks. Hell, he could be sitting on a fortune right now—except for one problem. There was no way to separate the blasted gold from the rock. That was why Miner's Gulch had died.

Donovan gazed out over the rugged mountains, his thoughts drifting gloomily from the dying town to poor, dead Charlie Sutton; from Varina's bleak outlook to his own. Back in Kansas, nothing waited for him but a lonely room in a boardinghouse and a grim, dirty job. Packing a gun for the rest of his life was a joyless prospect. He had seen too many men shot and hanged, and he was sick of death. Worse, even, was the loneliness. But there wasn't much cure for that. Sharing a life as dangerous as his was more than a man could ask of any woman.

Maybe he ought to take Varina's advice and turn in his badge. But what could he do here? Mining Charlie's worthless claim would be a fate worse than prison. And he sure as hell was no builder. He'd proven that much to Sarah Parker back at the cabin. Maybe he ought to look up that carpenter she had mentioned, the one she said needed work. It was pretty clear he'd never get that spare room built on his own.

Sarah.

Donovan swore as he realized how his thoughts had circled back to her. She was always breaking in where she had no business, always getting in his way. Blast it, when was he going to put her out of his mind?

Stretching his long legs, he eased himself to his feet. It was time he was getting back, he told himself. Being up here alone wasn't doing him any good. Besides, it was anybody's guess what kind of mixed-up story his nieces had told their mother by now. The sooner he arrived to straighten things out, the better.

The little girls had peppered him with questions all the way back from town. But he hadn't felt like talking about their precious Miss Sarah. His answers had been mostly evasions, the sort of thing Varina would never settle for.

She would demand the whole truth, and she would get it, he promised himself. She would hear the whole miserable story, from beginning to end.

He moved swiftly down the trail, knees held loose to ease the jarring on his ribs. His mind churned as he pieced together the thread of what he would tell his sister.

He would be patient and gentle, he promised himself. Varina, he knew, would take it hard. Sarah Parker had been her friend. But Varina was a Southerner and a Cole. In the end, Donovan had no doubt where her loyalties would lie.

He reached the fork in the trail where he had parted company with Katy and Annie. As he turned toward the cabin, he glimpsed a lean female figure in a cloak, striding toward him through the budding aspens.

For the space of a heartbeat, he thought it might be Sarah, and his heart leapt into his throat. But no, it was someone else. It was one of the women he'd seen in church. Yes, she had also hiked up the gulch to see Varina a couple of days after the baby came. Donovan remembered her well now. Mattie, that was her name. Mattie Ormes.

He hailed her as she came closer, but Mattie did not even look at him. Her freckled young face was a study in grim outrage, the mouth set in a thin line. Her dark gabardine skirt switched like the tail of an angry cat as she stalked down the path, leaving Donovan no alternative except to move aside, tip his hat and let her pass.

What in blazes was going on?

Donovan's long legs ate up the distance to the cabin. He burst into the clearing expecting some kind of trouble, but nothing there seemed amiss. Samuel was on the porch, playing an imaginary game with a pile of wood chips. Katy was in the front yard, gathering more wood for the stove. The savory aroma of hot rabbit stew wafted out through the half-open doorway.

"Varina—" He burst inside to see his sister in the rocker with the baby, a quilt bundled around her legs. Her pale lips parted as she saw him, but she did not speak.

Donovan took a deep breath, forcing himself to be calm. "I just passed Mattie Ormes charging down the mountain like a runaway freight wagon," he said. "Would you care to tell me about it?"

"You were in church this morning. I think you already know." Varina's voice was uncharacteristically cold.

"About Sarah."

"Yes, about Sarah, and how shabbily she was treated, even by you! After all she's done here, and the courage she showed today—why, I'm ashamed of the whole town!"

"Varina—" The name emerged as a groan as Donovan sank onto the foot of the bed.

The rockers of the old chair—the one decent piece of furniture Varina owned—creaked on the rough-sawed floor. "The war's over, Donovan. It's too late to change the past. Why can't people just accept that and leave well enough alone?"

He stared at her, incredulous. "Is that what you said to Mattie?"

Varina bent to adjust the baby's wrappings, taking her time to tuck the ragged blanket tight around the tiny feet. Fuming with ill-concealed impatience, Donovan watched the calm movements of her work-worn fingers. She didn't understand, he reminded himself. She would feel differently when she knew the whole story.

"I know Mattie lost kinfolk in the war," Varina said gently. "A lot of us did. But hate is like poison, don't you see? Sooner or later, the bitterness has to end so we can heal and go on. As far as I'm concerned, that time is long overdue."

Donovan's fist slammed onto the bed, its impact crushing the straw in the thin mattress. "Damnation, Varina, when you get a notion in your head, you're like a mule with blinders on! There are things you don't understand—things you still don't know about Sarah Parker—"

"And now I suppose you're going to tell me, whether I like it or not." Her fingertip teased the sleeping baby's fine russet hair into a curl. "All right, Donovan, I'm prepared to indulge you. I'll listen."

Her gaze shifted to the front of the cabin. Donovan became aware of Annie, who stood wide-eyed at the stove, stirring the stew with a long-handled wooden spoon.

"That stew should be about done, dear," Varina said. "Slide the pot off the heat and go on outside for a while. Your uncle Donovan thinks he needs to talk to me."

She settled back into the rocker, the baby's face a crinkled pink blossom against the drab ecru flannel of Varina's wrapper. Donovan seethed as he waited for Annie to leave. The thoughts he'd organized so masterfully on his walk had scattered like thistledown. He struggled to catch and rearrange them as the curious child dragged her feet out the door.

"Close it, honey," Varina called softly.

The latch engaged with a reluctant click, leaving them alone. Varina waited, her green eyes sharp and guarded as Donovan took a deep breath.

"What do you know about Sarah Parker?" he asked her.

Varina's gaze was direct and defiant. "I know that Sarah is kind and brave and honest—and that during the war she fought for what she believed in."

"You also know the woman was a spy. Say it, Varina. Don't play these damned evasive games with me."

"All right. She was a spy. And you shot Yankees. Who's to judge which was worse?"

Donovan ground his teeth, then, remembering his resolve to be patient with her, he exhaled his frustration, backed off and started over.

"There's more," he said in a low voice. "There's a lot you don't know."

"I'm not sure I want to hear it." Her pale-lashed eyes searched Donovan's face. "But then, I suppose that's too much to ask, isn't it?"

"Varina, you've got to understand—" He made a half start at the thing. Then, too agitated to sit, he sprang to his feet and began pacing the rough boards.

"I knew Sarah Parker in Richmond. Only she wasn't Sarah then. She was someone else—someone you wouldn't even know. Last week, when she stopped by to check on you, I didn't even recognize her. But the night your little Charlie was born—"

"Wait!" Varina stared at him, bewildered. "You knew all this time? And you didn't tell me?"

"I tried. But Sarah had just saved your life. You weren't ready to listen, let alone believe what you heard."

Varina's pale forehead furrowed in thought. "You knew Sarah in Richmond. And you didn't tell me... Donovan, you were in love with her, weren't you?"

His breath caught as the words slammed into him. "Now listen, Varina—"

"No, you listen! I've known you all my life, Donovan Cole, and nothing else could explain the way you've been behaving! You were in love with her. And I'll wager anything you're *still* in love with her—"

"That's enough, Varina!" Donovan exploded. "Blast it, once you get an idea in your head, you're like a runaway horse with the bit in your teeth! Sarah wasn't my sweetheart back in Richmond. She was Virgil's."

"Virgil's?" Varina's eyes rounded as the revelation dawned on her. "Sarah was Virgil's sweetheart? She was *Lydia?*"

This time it was Donovan's turn to be dumbfounded. He stared at his sister, too stunned to respond.

"The chest," Varina said swiftly. "In the very bottom, under Charlie's old suit, there's a bundle of letters. Get them out for me."

Donovan hesitated, knowing suddenly what Varina wanted him to see. It made sense that Virgil would have written to her during the war. It made sense that he would have told her about Lydia. But to read his words again, to open up the old wounds—even the thought of it was more than he could stand.

Varina's infant son slumbered in her arms, his lashes pure gold against peach-petal cheeks. He would look like Virgil when he grew older, Donovan reflected. Even now, he had the same fiery hair and delicate skin, the same impetuously thrusting jaw. Maybe he would even have Virgil's eager, passionate nature.

No, damn it, he could not read what Virgil had written. The anguish, the sense of loss he had kept at bay for so long would sweep in and destroy him.

Varina was waiting, the baby cradled tenderly in the crook of her arm. Something in her eyes both moved and frightened him. "Please, Donovan," she whispered.

Steeling himself against the pain, Donovan bent over the battered reed chest and raised the lid.

The letters were where Varina had said they would be, bundled together and tied with a dirty string, which, Donovan supposed, was all his sister had. They fell onto the bed when he loosened the knot—a couple dozen letters in all. A few, though not many, were addressed in his own large, blocky hand. Seeing how Varina had prized them, he was sorry he had not written more.

Another letter, the only one of its kind, was scrawled in a delicate, wavering script that Donovan recognized as their mother's. His throat tightened as he realized it had been penned a week before her death. Putting it swiftly aside, he rummaged through the rest of the pile and separated the six or seven missives he recognized as Virgil's. Even the sight of that awkward, grammar school penmanship tightened a knot of bitterness in his chest. He remembered kneeling in the cemetery to fulfill Virgil's dying wish, placing the sad little gold ring on the grave marked *Lydia Rawson Taggart*...

"Find Virgil's last letter," Varina said softly. "Open it and read it to me."

"Varina, I don't think—" he began, but then he saw in her face that arguing would only waste time. Bracing himself against a flood of bittersweet memories, Donovan found the last posted envelope and slipped out a single, faded sheet, covered with writing on both sides. The creases, he noticed, were worn limp from repeated unfolding.

Dreading the pain, he hesitated again. "Read it," Varina prodded him. "I want to hear you read it out loud."

Donovan swallowed the raw lump in his throat. His shaking hand blurred the writing on the page.

"Don't worry," she added more gently, "it's not a very long letter."

Clearing his throat, Donovan forced himself to begin.

"Dearest Varina,

I don't have much time tonight. It's late and we're marching out at dawn. It looks like I may get to see some action at last. As a member of General Lee's personal staff, I've spent most of my time in Richmond, or at least behind the lines. But the general's promised me that's likely to change this time out. Donovan's fought a half-dozen skirmishes with the Yanks already. He tells me it's pure hell, with not a shred of glory to it, and that if I've got any brains, I'll just keep my head down and stay alive. But I don't feel that way at all. A man's not quite a man, I say, until he's been baptized by fire. I'm more than anxious to do my part for the honor of our family and the South.

"Damned, impetuous young fool!" Donovan wiped his stinging eyes with the back of his hand. "I tried to tell him how ugly it all was, and how senseless, but he wouldn't believe me. I don't know that he ever did, not even when he was lying there with his guts shot out. Virgil died believing it was the noblest thing he could have done!"

"Go on," Varina said gently.

Donovan blinked his eyes clear, steadied the page and moved to the next paragraph.

"But that's not the real reason I'm writing. I wanted to send you some good news. Today I went to a jeweler's shop and bought a dainty little gold wedding band. When this campaign is over, I plan to come back to Richmond, show it to the sweetest lady in Virginia, and ask her—to be my bride."

The words stuck in Donovan's throat. He coughed awkwardly, seized by a sudden emotion so dark it had no name. Reading the rest of Virgil's letter, he knew, would be unremitting torture. But Varina was waiting, and it was easier to go on than to explain stopping.

"I haven't told you about Lydia before. Not only is she an angel, she's the most beautiful woman in Richmond. I still can't believe she would single me out from a city full of dashing officers. Donovan, I sense, doesn't quite approve of our relationship. That may be because Lydia is a widow and a few seasons wiser than I am. But what do such things matter when two people are in love? And I am in love, Varina. Meeting Lydia has been the happiest event of my life. If I die tomorrow, just knowing that she loved me will have been enough to—

"No more!" Donovan flung the letter down on the coverlet, too agitated to continue. "You're not putting me through any more of this! Not without an explanation!"

"I'm sorry. I only wanted you to understand."

"What's to understand?"

Varina clutched the baby against her, her face pale but determined. "The letter—the one you were reading—arrived the same day as the news of Virgil's death. You can't know how I clung to it—to every word of it—so grateful that Virgil had a sweetheart, that he'd known something of love in his poor, short life. And I vowed, for Virgil's sake, that if I ever met his Lydia, no matter what the circumstances, I would embrace her as a sister."

"Varina!" Donovan exploded. "Don't you see what was happening? She was using Virgil! She didn't love him at all!"

"How can you be sure of that?" Varina's controlled voice could not mask her clashing emotions.

"She told me herself—Sarah did. Not one week ago. She explained that she'd been fond of Virgil, but that in her position, she couldn't allow herself to love any man."

"She was fond of him." Varina's flat voice bore a stubborn refusal to see the truth.

"Virgil was on Lee's staff. He was young and trusting. He was the perfect target. Don't try to defend her, Varina."

"But Virgil never knew the truth. He died happy, Donovan, thinking his Lydia loved him."

"He died *hideously!* I know! I was there!" Donovan reeled with the impact of the memory. Blood...blood everywhere, soaking the proud gray uniform. The shattered organs, the labored breaths, the racking coughs, and finally the mercy of death clouding Virgil's clear, young eyes.

Donovan faced his sister, his gaze riveting hers. "I'll never know how much information that woman charmed out of Virgil, or how decisive it was in the awful pounding we took that day. But I can't forget who Sarah Parker was, and I can't forgive her for what she did. No matter how much good she's done here, Varina, *I can't forgive her!*"

Jerking away from her stricken face, Donovan bolted blindly for the door. Escape—that was the one thing he wanted now. The demons of Virgil's death were all around him—the pain, the horror, the burden of his own guilt. No matter how fast, no matter how far he ran, he knew he would never be free. But he had to try. That, or lose his mind.

He was stumbling across the yard now, past the startled eyes of the three children. The trees were ahead of him, and the rocky slope, jutting upward toward the ridge and beyond, where the jagged peaks scraped the sky.

Clouds were scudding in from the west, the first harbingers of a spring storm. From beyond the peaks, thunder rippled like a distant drumroll, but Donovan paid it no heed. His memory was trapped in the damp chill of a September night, with Lee's troops camped behind the protecting ridge above Antietam Creek, while Yankee shell fire blazed against the ink black sky.

They had sought each other out, he and Virgil. As the darkness flashed around them, they crouched in a sheltered hollow, talking away their fears.

For a time, things had gone well enough. The old brotherly closeness, all too rare of late, had returned to enfold them in its warmth. They had relaxed and reminisced, savoring each other's company for what could be the last time. Then Virgil had fished the gold ring out of his pocket and announced his plan to propose to Lydia Taggart.

Donovan had countered with a barrage of frantic advice. Lydia was too knowing, he'd argued, too worldly for a twenty-year-old innocent like Virgil. As for love, the boy would be well-advised to let his blood cool. He was suffering from a bad case of infatuation, that was all. It would pass, and he would be the wiser for it.

"Let Lydia go her way, Virgil," he had counseled. "I know her kind. In the end, she'll only break your heart."

Virgil's youthful temper had flared like tinder. In his anger, he had lashed out at Donovan.

"You've never approved of Lydia and me! I've always wondered why, but now I know! You want her for yourself!"

"Now, Virgil—"

"Don't deny it! I've seen the way you look at her! You're in love with her, too!"

"Be sensible, boy!" Donovan had seized his brother's arm, but Virgil had wrenched away from him and lunged to his feet.

"I'm no boy!" he flared. "And you keep away from me, Donovan Cole! From this moment on, you're no brother of mine!"

He had plunged out of the hollow and started to run— not back toward the camp, but uphill, onto the exposed ridge.

"Virgil!" Donovan had yelled desperately. "Virgil, get back down here!" But his words were lost in a hellish blast of fire and sound that seized Virgil's slim, young body and flung it, shattered and bleeding, almost at Donovan's feet.

Virgil... Virgil...

Donovan was running hard now, his lungs burning in the thin Colorado air. Thunder echoed behind him, indistinguishable now from the roar in his mind.

Virgil...

Upward he plunged, heedless of the rocks that twisted his ankles and the brambles that clawed his skin. Even when the rain began to fall, he paid it no heed. He was running now, through the foggy bottomland of Antietam. He was running toward the enemy, no longer caring whether he lived or died.

Chapter Seven

Sarah lifted the edge of the sheet. Drained beyond tears, she drew it upward to cover the lifeless face of Marie Cecile LeClerq. "It's over," she murmured to the hovering Faye. "She's at peace now."

Heartrending sobs rose from a dim corner of the room, where the distraught Greta hunched in a maroon velvet armchair, giving full vent to her grief. Faye wiped her eyes with a yellowed lace hankie. Her garish vermilion curls hung lank and untended around her tired face.

"I hope there's a heaven for whores," she said. "Marie was one of the sweetest little gals I ever knew. She deserves to be someplace nice."

"I'm sure she is." Sarah smoothed the sheet, fussing needlessly with the hem. "You and the other girls were good to her, Faye. At least Marie died among people who cared about her." She forced herself to turn away from the bed. "I'll go downstairs and tell Smitty she's gone. It shouldn't take more than a few minutes. After that, I'll be back up to help you lay her out."

She turned, only to be blocked by Faye's cushiony bulk. "Ain't no need for your goin' down there, Miss Sarah. Smitty'll find out soon enough, the old buzzard. An' we can take care of fixin' up poor Marie ourselves. You go on home, now. You been sittin' with her most o' the day. You look plumb tuckered out."

"Faye's right, Miss Sarah, you mustn't go downstairs." The sable-skinned woman who'd spoken from the doorway was a few years younger than Faye and Greta. Her sultry features were marred by a thumb-size chocolate birthmark that lay along the left side of her nose. She was from an island off New Orleans, and her father had sailed with Jean Lafitte. Her name was Zoe.

"I was down there 'bout half an hour ago," she said. "There's a whole lot of talk goin' on about what happened at the church this mornin'. Not good talk, if you get my meanin'. You'd best stay out of sight, Miss Sarah. This town's a dangerous place for you right now."

"You're welcome to hide out right here till things blow over," Faye interjected. "What you done in the war don't make no difference to us. By our book, you're still the finest lady in the whole Colorado Territory."

"Thank you," Sarah murmured, touched by the irony of it—that only these outcast women remained her friends. "But I can't put you to that kind of trouble—"

"You mean Smitty?" Fay snorted. "Hell, that skinny old rattlesnake don't even have to know you're here! We could—"

"No, it's not that," Sarah countered, realizing the truth of her words only as she spoke. "I can't depend on anyone, not even you, to protect me. I've got to face up to the people in this town. They have to know that I'm not afraid to defend what's mine!"

She glanced back toward the bed, where Marie's emaciated form barely raised the coverlet. The air in the stuffy room smelled of rose water and death. It pressed around her, suddenly too warm, too close.

"You don't look real pert, Miss Sarah." Zoe was beside her, gently supporting her arm. "Why don't you come with me and lie down. Nobody's usin' my bed just now."

"I'm all right," Sarah protested, ignoring her own rubbery knees. "Here, someone fetch me some water and a

comb—and choose one of Marie's pretty dresses from the
wardrobe. She would have wanted to look nice—''

"Child, you'll be on the floor in another minute!" Faye
had her other arm now and was guiding her firmly out of
the room. "What you need is some fresh air and rest. Greta
and Zoe and me, we can do for Marie. We even pooled our
change and bought the poor lamb a casket last week. It's
down in the cellar right now, ready and waitin'...."

Too tired to argue, Sarah allowed Faye to steer her down
the hallway toward the back entrance. She was numb to the
marrow of her bones, as if Marie's death, on the heels of
her own ordeal in church that morning, had drained her of
all feeling.

"You go on home and rest, honey." Faye paused at the
door that opened at the foot of the back stairs. "Been
rainin' cats and dogs all afternoon, so you ought to be safe
in your room. Ain't nobody riled up enough to bother you
in weather like this." She opened the door a crack and
squinted out at the dark, drizzling sky. "I reckon we'll be
buryin' Marie in the mornin'. That is, if the undertaker can
get his rig through the mud."

"I'll be there," Sarah murmured.

"Don't be a fool, child." Faye spun Sarah toward her,
gripping both her arms. "You're in enough trouble already. Showin' up at a whore's funeral can't help but make
things look worse. You stay away, hear? Marie will understand, poor lamb. So will the rest of us. Now you get on
home, afore you topple right over."

Glancing out to make sure the coast was clear, she thrust
the passive Sarah outside and closed the door behind her.

The fresh, cold air startled Sarah back to her senses. She
stood under the eaves for a moment, gathering her meager
strength for the sprint across the alley. Rain poured off the
roof, forming a drab, gray curtain where it fell. The day-
light was fading fast. Soon it would be night, she realized
with a shock. In the thickly curtained room, tending to
Marie, she had lost all sense of time.

She plunged into the downpour, her mind flashing back to the cloak she'd left at Varina's cabin. By now, Donovan would have told his sister everything. Varina, once the most steadfast of her friends, would be as bitter and hateful as the others. The loss pierced Sarah like a shaft of ice.

She had reached the foot of her own stairway when a sudden fear knifed her soul.

Her classroom.

She had been absent all afternoon. There would have been plenty of time for someone to break in and wreak total havoc. Everything could be destroyed.

Heart in her throat, she gripped the railing and mounted the rain-slicked wooden stairs. The door at the top was closed—she could see that much, at least. But what would she find inside? Utter destruction, or worse, someone waiting to finish the job on *her?*

Stop it! Sarah admonished herself as she climbed higher. In her struggle to make Miner's Gulch her home, her one real enemy was fear. Conquer that, and there was nothing mere mortals could do to defeat her. She would be invincible!

Brave thoughts. Sarah filled her head with them, pumping herself full of courage. All the same, by the time she reached the top step, her heart was jumping against her rib cage like a trapped rabbit. Her hand shook as she fumbled for the key. That was when she noticed a bundle, wrapped in tattered oilcloth, stuffed into a corner between the threshold and the door.

The rain was coming down hard. Catching up the bundle, she thrust the key into the lock and turned it. As the door creaked inward, she squeezed her eyes shut, afraid of what she might see. Her hands clutched the bundle against her chest. Its thickness muffled her heartbeats.

Holding her breath, Sarah stepped across the threshold and willed her eyes to open.

The little classroom lay peacefully untouched in the slanting gray light. Her anxious gaze found nothing amiss.

Her ears caught no sound except the measured tick of the clock, the patter of raindrops on the glass, and the strained gasp of her own breathing.

Forcing herself to relax, she locked the door behind her, carried the bundle into the bedroom and put a match to the lamp. The warm, yellow glow confirmed that she was safely alone.

She sat down on the edge of the bed, half-afraid to open the mysterious package in her lap. The dash through the rain had soaked her to the skin. Shivering in the drafty, unheated room, she plucked at the string that held the bundle together. The water-swollen knots were stubborn, her fingers numb with cold. After a few seconds of effort, Sarah's teeth were chattering like Spanish castanets.

This would not do, she resolved, laying the bundle aside and unbuttoning her wet shirtwaist. At a time like this, the last thing she needed was a bad chill. When she was dry and warm, then she would open the package.

Trembling with cold, she peeled off her clothes, pausing to hang each damp piece where it would have a chance to dry by morning. Her white cotton nightdress lay rolled under her pillow. Sarah tugged it over her head. The fabric was soft, light and dry against her bare skin. She flung her warm blue flannel wrapper over it and cinched in the tie at the waist. Only then, sitting cross-legged on the coverlet with her bare feet tucked under her for warmth, did she take up the bundle again.

This time the knots yielded more readily. The worn oil-cloth fell aside to reveal her own carefully folded wool cloak, the one she had left at Varina's cabin when she'd fled Donovan's bitter embrace. Even now, when she remembered that moment and the feel of his rough, angry mouth, Sarah's face flamed like a torch. She should never have let him get so close. She should never have let him know how vulnerable she was.

She thought of him again, in church that very morning, leaping to his feet to protect a woman he despised. Dear

Donovan was as forthright as she was secretive, as passionate as she was self-contained.

What would it be like to be loved by such a man?

Forcing the thought aside, she lifted the cloak in her hands. Who could have left it? she wondered. Had Varina sent it down the mountain with Annie? Or could it have been—

A faint crackle, deep in the folded cloth, scattered Sarah's thoughts. When she shook the cloak, a single sheet of paper tumbled loose, fluttered to the floor, and, blown by a stray air gust, skittered under the bed.

With a little huff of impatience, Sarah clambered down to retrieve it. She was crouched awkwardly on the floorboards, just reaching under the edge of the coverlet, when a loud knock at the door stopped her breath like a hard jab to the ribs.

Sarah froze, her pulse slamming. She knew that knock well. She had heard it before, less than a week ago.

Donovan.

Again it came—an impatient staccato series of raps like the fire-burst of a Gatling gun. He would not go away, she knew. He had seen her light—maybe even been watching for it. He would know she was here.

"I'm coming!" she called, forcing the words from a throat that was ropy with tension. Whatever Donovan had to say to her, Sarah knew it would not be pleasant.

She scrambled to her feet, legs tangling in the loose, thin fabric of her nightgown. Tendrils of hair had escaped their confining pins to dangle around her face in dark, wet strings. A glance in the mirror showed shadow-rimmed eyes, red with exhaustion. She looked awful. But what did her appearance matter? She could not be sure why Donovan was outside her door, but one thing was certain. He had not come courting.

The rain was pelting down even harder than before. It lashed against the dark windows, beating a wild tattoo on the glass as Sarah crossed the schoolroom. Oh, she knew what to expect from Donovan Cole. More threats. More demands. But he would not intimidate her. She would be stone in the face of his bluster, steel against his determination to see her gone.

Jerking her wrapper sash tight, Sarah strode resolutely toward the door. Her shaking hands released the latch. She stepped back into the schoolroom as the hinges creaked inward.

Donovan's dark bulk loomed in the doorframe. He was hatless, coatless, his hair and clothes drizzling rain. A prickle of concern softened Sarah's resolve, but it swiftly vanished, washed away by fear as a flash of lightning illuminated his face.

His rigid mouth and grimly set jaw were off-putting enough. But it was Donovan's eyes that struck Sarah with cold terror. They lay like hell pits below the dripping crags of his eyebrows, their expression as savage and desperate as a wounded timber wolf's.

He looked like a man gone mad.

Braced in the doorway, Donovan stared down at Sarah. She looked delicate, almost fragile, he thought. The white lace collar of her nightgown was bunched at her throat, framing her fine, pale features like a moonflower in the darkness. Her shadowed eyes gleamed large and soft. Her moist, satiny lips were as full as a child's.

The Angel of Miner's Gulch! Looking at her, a man could almost believe it. He could almost forget what a treacherous little liar she was!

"What do you want, Donovan?" Her voice was a strained whisper. Was she afraid of him? He hoped to hell the answer was yes. He wanted her to be afraid. He wanted her to be sorry when he told her exactly how Virgil had died.

"I want to talk," he growled. "Let me in, and don't worry about your reputation or your precious virtue! Your standing in this town couldn't get any lower than it already is! As for whatever's left of your honor, Sarah Parker, I wouldn't lay a hand on your sanctified hide! Not even if you begged me!''

Sarah gasped as the impact of his words sank in. He was braced for her to slap him. Instead, she spun behind the door and shoved it hard in his face. The door would have slammed shut, but Donovan deftly blocked it with his foot, then countered with his own greater weight to push his way inside.

He expected to find Sarah sputtering like a doused barn owl. Instead, his eyes met a calm, icy glare. "I think the reputation that's at stake here is your own," she said, turning away from him and walking toward the window.

Donovan followed her with his eyes, trying not to notice the way her shapely little buttocks flowed beneath the tightly belted robe. That wasn't why he'd come, he reminded himself angrily. What he needed from Sarah tonight had nothing to do with sex.

"You're wet and chilled," she said in a voice that would have frostbitten the devil's own ears. "I can brew some fresh coffee, if you'd like."

"Save it," Donovan muttered, locking the door behind him. Hot coffee would have been heaven right now, but he wanted nothing that would ease his temper. He wanted to hang on to his misery, his frustration, his rage until he had finished with the woman.

"Sit down!" he ordered roughly.

"I'll stand, thank you." Sarah remained where she was, gazing calmly through the curtains at the rain-swept darkness outside.

Donovan stood fuming in the pale shaft of lantern light that fell through the open bedroom door. His hair, clothes and boots puddled water on the floor. He had been wandering for hours in the wild mountain storm, tormented to a frenzy by the memory of Virgil's death. He had run, climbed, plunged through the lashing darkness, fleeing demons that would not let him rest. Only when he was near dead from exhaustion, had the idea come to him that Sarah was his one hope. He had to confront her, had to get everything out in the open. Once and for all, he had to purge himself of Lydia Taggart.

"You said you wanted to talk." Her voice was guardedly expressionless. "Frankly, Donovan, I don't think we've much left to say to each other. By now, the whole town knows my secret. Your threats won't work—not that they ever did."

"I didn't come to make threats." He glared at her across the graduated rows of log benches. "I want you to tell me about you and Virgil. What you did together. How much he told you. The best and the worst. I want to know it all."

"Why?" She spoke defiantly, her upthrust features gleaming in the dim glow of the lamp.

"Because you killed him, Sarah. You killed my brother as surely as if you'd fired the mortar shell that blew his guts out."

He glimpsed the pain that flashed across her face before she turned away. "Say what you like," she whispered. "Say whatever you believe. That doesn't mean I have to accept it, or that I have to tell you anything at all." She shuddered with visible anguish, her back ramrod straight as she stared out the window, then spun abruptly to face him.

"Virgil was under orders not to reveal Lee's plans. No one forced him to disobey those orders, Donovan. Your brother betrayed the Confederacy of his own free will!"

"The young fool was smitten out of his mind!" Donovan snarled, slamming his shin on a bench in his blind anger. "Damn it—how was he to know the woman he loved would turn the information over to the Yankees?"

"I didn't force him to tell me. I never forced a man to tell me anything."

"No?" Donovan reeled under a rising tide of white-hot fury. "Then how did you get what you wanted? Did you sleep with them? Did you sleep with my innocent, young brother, Sarah Parker?"

"I did not!" The words exploded out of her. "I didn't sleep with any of them—not even Virgil! Would to God I had! At least things might have been more honest that way! At least I might have sent them off with something to remember!"

She stood quivering in the darkness, bursting with her own bitter memories. "Virgil was only one of them! I never kept a count, but there were many, Donovan—so many that it would shock you if you knew! Earnest, eager young men, ready to tell me anything for a kiss and a promise! None of them came back...not one!"

She stood a half-dozen paces from him, framed by the blackness of the window. Donovan moved toward her like a sleepwalker, not knowing in his own befuddled mind whether he wanted to strike her or seize her in his arms. But it made no difference. Another step, and her tormented eyes stopped him like a bullet.

"I see their faces in my dreams," she whispered. "Their fair, young faces. I see them dying. I see their hands. Their torn bodies..."

She turned, drifting away from him, into the shadowed corner of the room. "I think of their families, people who loved and needed them. And I know it's too late—that's the worst hell of all, Donovan. Nothing I do can bring them back. Ever."

Donovan refused to be moved. "A pretty speech, coming from you," he commented sarcastically.

Abruptly she spun back to face him. The bitter smile that teased her lips was Lydia's. Completely Lydia's.

"Of all the dashing, young officers I knew in Richmond, only one came home alive," she said. "Strangely enough, he was the one I couldn't seem to fool, the one who was never quite taken in by Lydia Taggart."

Donovan stared at her as the realization dawned that she was talking about him. The irony of her words was an awl between his ribs. *Never quite taken in*— Lord, if only the woman had known about his tortured nights, imagining her

in Virgil's embrace as he ached to have her in his own. And
the fantasies—fantasies to make a libertine blush! Her
lovely, naked body, liquid satin in his arms, his to explore,
to tease, to possess—

Damn! Damn! Damn!

Donovan cursed the involuntary surge of heat to his
loins. Lydia Taggart had been the devil's own daughter even
then, he reminded himself. But even if he'd had the chance
to make love to her, he would never have betrayed Robert
E. Lee and the Army of the Confederacy. Such a lapse
would have been unthinkable.

"Your charms would never have worked on me," he declared gruffly, grateful that the boast was at least partly
true.

"I know." Her voice was like the whisper of raw silk in
the darkness. "I stayed away from you, Donovan—as far
away as I was able—because I couldn't trust myself with
you. I could never be certain that I wouldn't let my guard
down, that you wouldn't see right through me."

Sarah's face was moon pale, reflecting the dim glow of
lamplight from the bedroom. Tendrils of hair had escaped
her bun to hang in wet strings around her face. She looked
damp and exhausted, he thought. All the same, her eyes
and voice were Lydia's, as were her words—drawing him
closer to the precipice.

"You told me you didn't love Virgil." The words rasped
in his throat. "You said you couldn't allow yourself to love
anyone."

Her eyes were luminous in the shadows. "Yes," she said
slowly. "So I did. But you weren't like the others, Donovan. If I could have loved anyone at all . . . it would have
been you."

Something stirred and broke inside Donovan—something aching and lonely and too long held back. He took a
step toward her, then hesitated, violently torn. This woman
had betrayed all that he held dear, he reminded himself. She
was his sworn enemy till the end of time.

He caught her in his arms.

Sarah's resistance was no more than a cobweb. With a little sob of release, she crumpled against him. Her lips rose to meet the hard hunger of Donovan's kiss. Her arms circled his neck, fingers raking his hair as he crushed her close. Her lips parted, tongue darting to meet his in wanton, searing abandon.

Donovan staggered under a rush of physical sensation. She was sweet as summertime in his arms, and more desirable than he had imagined in his wildest dreams. The warm, musky scent of her sang in his head until he was drunk with it—out of his mind and out of control.

Her uncorseted spine arched at the pressure of his hand. She was naked under the robe and gown, he realized, the awareness flaming his vitals. Where her hips pressed his, Donovan's manhood rose hot and hard. She knew—hell, she had to know—the woman was no innocent virgin. She knew, and she did not pull away. Donovan reeled with the staggering awareness that she wanted him as much as he wanted her—that she had wanted him from the beginning.

The bedroom—it lay tantalizingly close, the glow of the lantern casting a golden path across the schoolroom floor. Seizing the moment, Donovan caught her up in his arms. A shudder went through her body, but she made no sound as he carried her toward the soft, warm light. Her arms clung to his neck; her hair curled damply in the hollow of his throat. He could feel her trembling against his heart.

Sarah's simple bedroom was so small that there was scarcely room for the two of them to enter. Donovan kissed her again, deeply, dizzyingly, the fire in his blood burning away all reason. The room, the whole world, seemed to be spinning in his head until nothing made sense. Nothing mattered except possessing this woman who had haunted his dreams for years.

As he lowered her to the coverlet, his hands caught the tangled knot of her hair and pulled it loose from the pins. The glorious satin cascade tumbled loose on the pillow.

Donovan buried his face in its damp, fragrant waves. His mouth found the sweet, white curve of her neck, the moist hollow of her throat, the open neck of her nightgown...

"Donovan—" she gasped as his lips brushed the pulsing swell of her breast. "Donovan, we—"

"Hush!" he whispered, stopping her words with hard, urgent kisses. "This is what we both want...you know it...I know it. We were born for this, you and I...."

Lightning flashed blue through the thin lace curtains. A boom of thunder shook the room like cannon fire as Donovan's fingers found the sash of her robe and jerked at the knot. The robe fell open to reveal a white nightdress, gossamer sheer to his senses.

The feel of her through the soft, light fabric was erotic beyond belief. Donovan's palm brushed the tip of her breast through the gauzy cotton. Her nipple hardened at his touch, sending shudders of response through her body. Her hands clasped his head, drawing him down to the ripe satin globes. Half-delirious, he licked her nipples through the cloth, laving, nibbling, sucking. She writhed beneath his touch, her body pleading for fulfillment.

Remembering the desire of his old, forbidden fantasy, Donovan allowed his mouth to graze downward along the long, flat curve of her belly. She was satin heat through the wispy gown, her muscles shimmering at his touch, her breath coming in helpless little gasps as he slid the hem up her legs, up her slim, taut thighs to expose the delicate nest of light brown curls at their joining. Her sweet, musky aroma swam like brandy in his senses. He was drunk with her nearness, mad beyond reason with his own aroused need.

Senses reeling, Donovan bent to the heart of that wild, womanly aroma and flicked a tentative tongue along the moist, silken cleft.

"Donovan don't—" she gasped, but her willing body, opening like a flower to his touch, made lies of her words.

"Lie still," he whispered, the delicious curls brushing his lips. "Lie still and let me love you, Lydia...."

She went rigid as ice beneath him.

"What the—?" Donovan drew back, bewildered, but only for an instant. Sarah's eyes and the cold fury in her voice told him exactly what he had done.

"Leave me alone!" she rasped, scrambling away from him to crouch at the far corner of the bed. "I'm not Lydia! I was *never* Lydia! You fell in love with a stage role, Donovan, a phantom! Lydia Taggart doesn't exist!"

Dazed, Donovan stumbled backward against the wall. Even now, she was beautiful, with her nightgown fallen off one creamy shoulder, her glorious hair tumbled in her face, her eyes blazing defiant fury. But she had spoken the truth, he realized as his reason returned. She wasn't Lydia. She was Sarah Parker, a woman he barely knew. And they had both come close to making a calamitous mistake.

"Get out of here, Donovan Cole!" She hurled the words like acid in his face. "Never come near me again! You do, and so help me... I'll get a gun and I'll shoot you!"

"Sarah, I never—" Donovan struggled to form the right words, then realized there was nothing he could say to justify himself—and nothing he could do except leave.

Burning with humiliation, he backed toward the door. Sarah had shrunk against the wall, one hand groping toward the dresser for something—a hairbrush, a drinking cup, anything she could throw in his direction. She was as wild as a cornered lynx, and as dangerous.

Donovan flung her a final, regretful glance, then wheeled and strode across the schoolroom to the outside door. She would not call him back, he knew. And even if she did, he would not come. The woman could go or stay, he told himself as he stepped out into the rain. She could hang herself, for all he cared.

Reaching back, he closed the door firmly behind him. The wind was icy through his wet clothes, the rain half-turned to driving sleet. In the heat of his shame, Donovan scarcely felt the cold. He only knew that he could never face Sarah Parker again. Whatever happened next, he was through with her. For good.

Sarah heard the shutting of the door. He had not exactly slammed it, but the sound carried a note of absolute finality. She knew that she would not see Donovan again—not if either of them could avoid it.

For the space of several long breaths, she sat huddled forlornly on the bed, her knees clutched to her chest, her body burning with rage and shame.

Why had she done it? Dear heaven, what had possessed her to tell Donovan how she felt about him? How could she have let him get so close, when she knew his first kiss would shatter her resistance like fine crystal?

Lydia.

Sarah closed her eyes as Lydia's mocking laughter echoed in her head. Lying, wanton Lydia. Even Donovan had been taken in by her false charm. Even Donovan had wanted her.

Sarah's fist slammed into the pillow, scattering feathers through the loose seams. She had spent the past three years running away from Lydia Taggart. Here in Miner's Gulch, she had almost succeeded, or so she thought. But no, even here, the past had caught up with her. The past in the person of Donovan Cole.

Taking a deep breath, she uncurled her legs and willed herself to slide off the bed and stand up. Her knees were jelly. Her body quivered with the fading tingle of Donovan's passionate mouth. Her face, as confirmed by an accidental glance in the mirror, was still flushed with a warm radiance, the eyes luminous and strangely alive.

We were born for this, you and I....

Sarah pressed her hands to her hot cheeks as Donovan's words, mocking now, rang in her memory. *No, Donovan,* she thought bitterly, *you and I were not born to be lovers. We were born to be mortal enemies all of our lives. Why else*

*would fate have placed us on earth in such terrible times—
I in the North, and you in the South?*

But this would not do, Sarah brought herself up sharply.
Any more of such thoughts, and she would be wallowing in
self-pity, the last thing she needed at a time like this. The
past was Lydia Taggart. The past was Donovan Cole. But
she was through looking back. From now on, she would
live in the present. She would look only toward the future.

She would survive.

In a furious burst of energy Sarah flung on her robe,
jerked the sash tight, and began frantically straightening the
room, as if to remove any sign that Donovan had been
there. She fluffed the pillow, jerked the coverlet tight on the
bed, then seized the schoolroom mop and wiped away every
one of his big, muddy boot prints.

She flung herself into the work with the vigor of desperation and the frenzied strength of fear. The whole town
would hate her now. Except for the girls above Smitty's, no
one, not Donovan, not even Varina, would be her friend.
The days ahead would be fraught with loneliness and terror. She would need to be stronger than she had ever been
in her life.

Only as she was hanging up her cloak did Sarah remember the paper that had fallen out of the bundle. It had
blown under the bed, she recalled now. She had been about
to reach for it when Donovan came pounding on her door.

Crouching low, she stretched an arm into the dark re-
cess. The paper was there, crisp beneath her fingers as she
drew it out into the lamplight.

It was a letter, she saw at once. A letter, written in a cultured but slightly unsteady feminine hand.

My dearest Sarah,
Donovan has told me everything. I cannot profess to
understand all that happened in Richmond. I only
know that it is my Christian duty to forgive you, and I

do so with open arms. The war is over. For me, at least, your goodness has wiped out any past wrongs.

Virgil wrote me about his "Lydia." I confess that I have longed to meet the young woman who made my brother's last days so happy. What a surprise to learn that I have known her all this time, as my own dear friend.

Know this, Sarah. Even though the whole town may turn against you, you have my pledge of undying friendship, support and gratitude. I owe you my life, and the life of my precious baby. Whatever you might have done in the past, and whatever may happen in the future, I will never turn my back on you.

> With all my love,
> Varina

Sarah stared at the letter, emotions washing over her like the waves of a flood. No—Varina could not take this burden on herself. When Donovan left—as he surely would—Varina would be alone on the mountain, with four young children. She would need this town and the friendship of the people in it.

But Varina had made her choice. She had chosen with her heart. She had chosen with all the goodness and truth that was in her. And whatever happened, Sarah vowed, Varina Cole Sutton would not stand alone. Her needs would not go unmet. She would have one friend—a friend who would die, if need be, for her and her children.

Sarah read the letter again. Her hands began to tremble. The ink on the page splattered and blurred as, at long last, her tears began to fall.

Chapter Eight

Donovan had picked up the long, open freight wagon at the livery stable before dawn. Now, at first light, he guided the plodding team down the main street of Miner's Gulch, headed for the road to Central City.

The new day was no more than a promise, a pearly glow that silvered the snowcapped peaks to the east. Donovan drove slowly, savoring the silence. After the past week, the need to buy lumber for Varina's new room had come as a heaven-sent deliverance. He could not have endured another day of the clamorous tension at the cabin.

Eudora Cahill, along with other women of her stripe, had been up the gulch almost every day, threatening, demanding, imploring Varina to change her mind about Sarah Parker. True to her nature, Varina had not budged an inch. Before long, Donovan feared, his sister would be as much a pariah as Sarah herself.

As for Sarah—Donovan risked an upward glance at her window as the wagon passed Satterlee's store. The glass panes were dark, with no sign of life behind them.

He had not seen Sarah since that wild night when she had banished him from her quarters. But she was there, all right. Donovan knew because Varina still sent Annie and Katy trooping down the gulch every day to attend her school. The two little girls were Sarah's only pupils.

Mud plopped from the hooves of the four big draft bays
as the wagon creaked past the empty church. At least
there'd been no violence against Sarah. In fact, Sarah's
punishment bore more of a resemblance to an Amish-style
shunning than to anything else Donovan could think of.
Except for the intractable Varina, most of the townspeople
were behaving as if Sarah Parker did not exist.

And what did it matter? Donovan asked himself angrily. He had washed his hands of the woman for good. If
she was fool enough to stay in Miner's Gulch, so be it. He
had not asked her to parade her past before the whole town,
and he could not be responsible for the way people treated
her.

All the same, Donovan could not quell a prickle of worry
as he remembered his conversation with MacIntyre that
morning. The hulking war veteran had met him at the livery stable to help hitch up the hired team and wagon. A
ruddy-faced bear of a man, he appeared to have just gotten out of bed. His thinning, dishwater hair stood on end.
Greasy leather suspenders held up his trousers over faded
gray long johns.

Donovan had averted his eyes from the sleeve that dangled like an empty sock below the right shoulder. Still, he
could not help being impressed by the way MacIntyre handled the horses and the heavy harness tack. His huge left
hand was quick and dexterous, the arm as massive as an
average man's thigh.

MacIntyre had noticed Donovan watching him. "Don't
do too bad for a one-armed freak, now, do I?" he growled.
"Imagine what I could be with two good 'uns, like you
got."

Donovan had nodded slowly, thinking the better of a reply. He had no desire to set MacIntyre off. He only wanted
to get the wagon hitched and be on his way.

"Lost more'n an arm at Shiloh," MacIntyre had groused
as he bent to tighten a bellyband. "Lost a cousin and my
best friend, too. And when I finally got home, my bride

took one look at me an' lit out with a stinkin' whiskey drummer. Wanted a whole man, she said, not a cripple."

"I'm sorry." Donovan adjusted the fit of a padded collar around one horse's powerful neck.

"Not that I blame her none. I ain't too purty lookin' without a shirt. Only woman'll have me now is the likes of Smitty's girls. But then, they'll have any man what's got the money. That Zoe, now, she ain't too bad. Ever try her?"

"Can't say as I have." Donovan mounted the wagon seat, anxious to be on his way. MacIntyre made a final check of the harness, then turned to squint up at Donovan, the flare of the lantern making a devilish mask of his bewhiskered face. "'Course the real whore, now, is that 'un livin' over the store—that high-an'-mighty Miss Sarah, as she calls herself. Woman like that don't belong in a town with decent folk. I say she oughta be tarred an' feathered an' rid out on a rail! An' if you don't agree with me, Cole, you ain't no son o' the South!"

Donovan had shot him a brief scowl as he caught up the reins. "No son of the South would wish that kind of harm on any woman. Give Sarah Parker a little time, MacIntyre. She'll leave on her own. You'll see."

MacIntyre had muttered something under his breath and spat in the mud. "Far as I'm concerned, her time's about run out. I say, people in this town oughta git together and do somethin'!"

"Talk to me about it when I get back from Central City." Impatient to be off, Donovan had brought the reins down hard on the withers of the huge bays. The wagon had jerked and rolled out of the livery stable yard, leaving MacIntyre standing in the mud, vilifying Sarah's name to the fading stars.

Remembering the scene now, Donovan forced himself to shrug off a foreboding chill. MacIntyre was all talk, he reassured himself. As for the rest of the people in Miner's Gulch, they seemed like a decent lot, certainly not the kind to harm a helpless female. Sarah would be safe enough until he got back into town tomorrow night.

Not that Donovan really gave a damn. He had washed his hands of Sarah Parker. She had brought her present trouble down on her own head. Whatever happened to the woman now was no longer his concern.

No longer his concern. Donovan hoisted the words like a banner in his mind, ignoring the heat that flooded his body when he remembered the feel of her through the gauzy nightdress—the silky, molten sensuality that, even now, jellied his legs with desire.

Blast it, he'd been out of his mind that night, a panting, lust-drunk maniac with his brain in his crotch! As for his calling her *Lydia*—Donovan reddened at the remembered humiliation, his face flushing hot in the cool dawn air. In that single instant, he had betrayed everything—his brother, his principles, his own sense of integrity. He had thrown it all away.

Seething with agitation, he steered the team around Pete Ainsworth, who had collapsed drunk in the road outside Smitty's. Donovan had had a bellyful of this town, he told himself. It was as if the cursed place had poisoned him. In all his life, he had never felt more befuddled, less sure of himself.

Sarah had almost told him she loved him.

But no, that wasn't right. She didn't love him now. She had loved him—or could have loved him—in that other life, as a woman who no longer existed.

No longer existed . . . except that when he had taken her in his arms, it had been Lydia who had returned his kiss, Lydia whose body had molded so passionately to his. And in his muddled state, he had all but committed the ultimate betrayal.

Donovan was still asking himself why. Liquor might have given him an excuse, but he hadn't touched a drop that night. Rain chilled and exhausted, he had climbed Sarah's back stairs seeking answers about Virgil. But he had not found answers. He had only found more questions.

Sarah was not his concern, he reminded himself again, this time more forcefully. He could not afford to make her his concern, not when their every encounter left him more exposed and vulnerable. Donovan resolved to put her out of his mind for the duration of this trip. Maybe that would give him a head start on putting her out of his mind for good.

The main street buildings were thinning out now. He passed the hovels that sprawled along the creek bottom, and the gingerbread-trimmed Cahill house that perched atop a bluff and had its own well, or so he'd been told. A bitter smile flickered across Donovan's face as he remembered Eudora's imperious demands and Varina's calm refusals. Eudora Cahill might be the town's self-styled social leader, but Varina Cole Sutton, poor though she might be, was also a force to be reckoned with.

Dear, stubborn, impossible Varina, who was more true to herself than anyone he had ever known.

Donovan's shoulders slumped as he realized how tense things had become between himself and his sister over the past few days. Varina clearly considered him one with the enemy camp. He knew she kept in touch with Sarah through the girls, but the nature of their communications was secret. Donovan had never known Varina to keep anything from him in her life. He was surprised at how much it hurt.

For the sake of peace, however, he had tried to stay out of her way. Thanks to Lanny Hanks, the able young carpenter Sarah had recommended, the new room on the cabin was rising fast, so fast that the two of them had already worked themselves out of the mill-sawed lumber they'd salvaged from Charlie's mine.

Donovan had leapt at the excuse to go and buy more. He planned to stay the night in Central City, pick up the lumber in the morning and arrive back in Miner's Gulch before dark.

The first ray of sunlight slanted between the peaks, setting off an explosion of bird songs. The sky was clear, promising fine, warm weather. Donovan's spirits lifted as a blue jay sassed him from the limb of an overhanging pine.

He would enjoy the journey, he resolved. He would explore Central City, buy himself a bath and a good dinner, and maybe play some seven-card draw if there was a decent game to be found. For the next forty-eight hours, he would do his best to forget there had ever been such a person as Lydia Taggart.

Maybe then, he might even be able to forget Sarah Parker.

Toward afternoon, the sky began to darken. Sarah stood at the window of her schoolroom, watching the clouds roll in over the peaks. She was glad she'd sent Annie and Katy home early. As long as they didn't dawdle, the two little girls would make it up the gulch well ahead of the storm.

She was more worried about Donovan.

She had watched him drive past at dawn, shrinking back from the glass, heart pounding, as he raised his eyes. What if he had seen her? What if she had stood there in full view and met his gaze with her own? Would it have made any difference?

Sarah toyed with the question, then swiftly dashed her own hopes. This was no time to be foolish.

Turning wearily away from the window, she began rubbing the sums from the smudged blackboard. Even the most fleeting contact between Donovan and herself would cause more pain than she ever wanted to feel again in her life. She had to keep away from him. Her own survival depended on it.

Annie had confirmed that her uncle was on his way to Central City. The girls, in fact, kept their teacher fully apprised of the goings-on at Varina's cabin. She knew that

Varina's loyalty was costing Donovan's sister the friendship of almost every woman in the gulch. Sarah had even sent a letter by way of Annie, begging Varina to change her stand before it was too late. But Varina remained, stubbornly, her steadfast friend.

Drawn to the window again, Sarah stared out at the darkening sky. Under the best conditions, the ten-hour wagon ride to Central City was punishing. When rain turned the powder-fine dust to slimy mud, it could be treacherous, as well, especially where the road edged deep ravines. Donovan had left town at dawn, but the storm could catch him miles from his destination, with the most dangerous part of the road ahead.

Restless beyond endurance, she threw herself into tidying the already neat classroom, scrubbing the board, sweeping up the chalk dust, arranging the benches into perfect geometric rows. From outside, a rumble of thunder shook the windowpanes. The image of Donovan in the open wagon, on the slippery road, flashed like lightning through her mind.

He would be all right, Sarah reassured herself. Donovan had survived war and prison camp, not to mention three years as a Kansas lawman. He was strong enough to withstand a storm, and smart enough to seek shelter if the going got too hard.

But what if something *did* go wrong?

How would Varina manage? How would her children, who clearly adored their big, brusque uncle, ever survive his loss?

Sarah walked to the window again, parted the curtains and stared at the sky through the rain-splattered glass. Varina and her children were Donovan's only living kin. Their relationship had been close when he'd first arrived in Miner's Gulch—Sarah knew that much from listening to the girls. But her own presence here had put them in conflict, brother against sister. Blood against blood.

Sarah laid her forehead against the cool glass and closed her eyes. Did she have the right to set a family at odds for the sake of her own wishes? Did her desire to stay in Miner's Gulch justify alienating Varina from her friends and neighbors?

Wandering away from the window, she sank dejectedly onto a bench. It was no good, she realized. For Varina's sake, and for her children's sake, she had no choice except to leave this town as soon as possible.

Thunder filled her ears as the storm burst full force over Miner's Gulch. She would stay until the storm passed and the road dried, Sarah resolved. She would stay until Donovan returned to watch over Varina and her little ones. Then she would pack her trunk, hire a rig and go.

A bitter smile flickered across Sarah's lips as the irony struck her. She had vowed to stay in Miner's Gulch at any cost. In her determination, she had stood up to Donovan's wrath. She had stood up to the ill will of the whole town.

But she could not stand against Varina's impassioned friendship.

Six miles short of Central City, the wagon skidded on a mud-slimed downhill curve. Donovan swore as the rear end fishtailed like a whore's bustle and slid off the main track, to crash against a hog-size boulder. The sickening crunch he heard could only be the sound of a splintered wheel.

Donovan climbed down from the seat, rain streaming off his hat and making rivers down his oilskin poncho. His language purpled the air, especially when he discovered that MacIntyre had neglected to attach a spare wheel to the wagon box.

All afternoon, he'd been dreaming of a hot bath, a sumptuous meal and a warm, dry bed. But he could not leave the horses to stand all night in the icy rain. Either he would have to unhitch the entire team and drive it the rest of the way, or ride one horse bareback into town, pick up a new wheel and come back for the whole rig. Right now, with rain chilling him to the bone, neither idea had much appeal.

Donovan was standing by the roadside, muttering under his breath and weighing his choices, when a buckboard with a two-horse team pulled out of a side road and came splashing toward him through the mud. Donovan's first impulse was to reach for the loaded rifle he'd stowed under the seat. But no, it was all right. The driver was hailing him now, his manner open and friendly.

"Whoa, there!" The stranger halted alongside him. He was wearing a black hat and slicker of the kind common to sailors, an odd sight in these parts. Beneath the sloping brim, his square, robust face was framed by dark side-whiskers.

"Looks as if thee've run afoul of some bad luck, sorr." In a country where a man's speech marked him as friend or foe, the stranger's accent was like nothing Donovan had ever heard. Not Cockney or proper British. Not Scotch or Irish, and certainly not American.

But this was no time for fine dithering. Not with the wagon pitched half on its side, the horses wild-eyed and snorting, and rain pouring down in solid gray sheets.

"Bad luck?" Donovan nodded slowly. "Yes, I guess you might say that."

"Wheel, I see." Brown eyes, sharp as a robin's, surveyed the wrecked wagon. "Where be the spare?"

"Ask the idiot who rented me the damned rig!"

"No need t' get sour, me son." The stranger was already climbing down from the buckboard. He was not a large man, but there was a wiry vitality about him that spoke of strength and competence. "I've got a wheel right 'ere that should fit."

Donovan blinked through the curtain of rain that cascaded from his hat brim. "I'll buy it off you. How much will you take for it?"

"Oh, 'tisn't mine to sell. This be a company wagon. But I'll give 'ee the loan o' the wheel long enough to get the rig into town. Come on, I've got tools in the back. I'll 'elp thee make the switch."

"Only if you'll allow me to buy you dinner at the hotel tonight."

"Dinner? Aye, that I will." The stranger's grin flashed beneath the odd black hat. Then, without another word, he swung around the back of the buckboard and began rummaging in the tool chest that was there.

Only then did Donovan notice the rain-blurred red lettering, freshly painted on the side of the wagon box. Pausing to wipe away the water drops, he took in the words at a swift glance—Boston and Colorado Smelter, Ltd.

Donovan was still digesting what he'd read when the stranger came hustling back around the buckboard, armed with two hammers, a wedge and a crowbar. "Don't just stand there," he said with a grin. "Let's change that wheel and get ourselves down the mountain to that 'ot, tasty dinner thee promised!"

Sarah had gone to bed early. She lay there in the darkness, listening to the hollow patter of the rain and feeling lonelier than she had ever felt in her life.

The hours of the day had crawled by at the pace of a prison sentence, with nowhere to go, no one to visit and no one who professed to need her. She had tried cleaning, mending, reading, writing in her journal. In her loneliness, she had even considered a backdoor visit to Smitty's, until she remembered that the girls were busiest in bad weather, when the men tended to cluster in the saloon.

As darkness fell, she had lit the lamp and begun rummaging through her clothes, books and other meager possessions, sorting things into piles for packing or discarding. Her good woolen skirt and Sunday shawl she would give to Varina, who needed them badly. The books she would leave behind for whoever took over her little school. Beyond those things, there was little left except for underclothes and toiletries. Fine, it would make sense for her to travel light.

Where would she go? Sarah mused now as she lay sleepless beneath the quilts. Maybe California would be a good starting-over place. Or even Canada. She didn't care, as long as she never ran into Donovan Cole again.

A sudden knocking at the door startled Sarah out of her reverie. No, this would not be Donovan, pounding on the planks, demanding entry. This was a frantic series of raps, spurred by fear. Someone was in trouble.

Tossing aside the quilts, she flung on her robe and raced along the back of the schoolroom. Her fingers fumbled in the darkness, struggling with the latch. When she finally swung the door open, the young man on the other side almost tumbled onto the floor.

"Miss Sarah!" It was Myles Smithers, who lived in the creek bottoms with his young wife and four-year-old boy. He was drenched from the rain and wild-eyed with fear.

"It's Betsy Mae, Miss Sarah! Her water's broke and her pains've started. She's hurtin' bad, and I don't know what to do for her. You got t' come! Now!"

Sarah's muzzy brain snapped into focus. Betsy Mae Smithers wasn't due for nearly another month. If she was in labor now, something could be seriously wrong.

"Go saddle my mule!" she ordered the trembling Myles. "By the time you have him back here, I'll be ready to go!"

As Myles darted off into the black rain, Sarah raced back to the bedroom, threw off her nightgown and began flinging on her clothes. She was deeply worried about Betsy Mae, but all the same, it was gratifying to be needed again.

Myles had brought his own scrawny pinto horse. He was mounted and waiting at the bottom of the stairs when Sarah, dressed, cloaked and clutching her black medical bag, emerged from the door and hurried down the stairs. Her sturdy mule stood alongside them, rain cascading down its patient sides.

"Creek was goin' up fast when I crossed it," Myles said. "Lord, I hope we can get back. Betsy Mae and little Eli's all by theirselves down there."

"Come on." Sarah vaulted expertly into the saddle and dug her pointed boot toes into the mule's flanks. The Smithers place wasn't far—a couple of miles, at most. But fording the creek, easy enough for most of the year, could be perilous when the stream was swollen with spring run-off. Add the storm, and the crossing could be a nightmare. Worse, if the creek overflowed its banks, nearby homes, including the Smithers cabin, would be flooded.

The white rump of Myles's horse flashed like a beacon as Sarah followed him through the dark rain. As they wound their way through the aspens along the creek bank, she could see the muddy current, swirling so high that it lapped at the mule's shod hooves. The water would be deep here, well over her head. Even at the ford, it would be deep enough to drown in.

A brief image of Donovan, toiling through the rain, flickered through her mind. But no, he would be all right. He was probably in Central City right now, enjoying a drink and flirting with some pretty saloon girl. Not that it mattered one way or the other. What Donovan did was his own business.

"This way!" Myles's horse lurched down the bank, and Sarah realized they had come to the ford. A chill of dread passed through her as the mule plunged into the swirling water. She clung to its sturdy neck, recalling the time when, as a child, she had fallen into an icy river and nearly drowned. That feeling of sick, cold panic returned now as the current sucked at her skirts, threatening to drag her out of the saddle and sweep her downstream. She worked her boots free of the stirrups and lifted her feet in an effort to keep dry.

The mule's sure hooves found bottom and moved steadily ahead. Everything was all right, Sarah reassured herself. A few more seconds and they would be climbing up the opposite bank. If only Betsy Mae would—

"Look out!" Myles's warning cry caught Sarah off guard. She glanced upstream to see a huge, gnarled stump sweeping down on her like a hellish black monster.

There was no time to get out of the way. The stump crashed into the mule's side, knocking the animal off-balance. Sarah flew headlong out of the saddle. Her scream was cut off by the muddy water. It filled her mouth and nose as she clawed her way upward.

"Miss Sarah!" She could hear Myles yelling as she broke the surface. His voice echoed in the darkness, and she realized she had already been carried some distance downstream.

Coughing and spitting water, Sarah fought to stay afloat as the flood swept her along. Her cloak was a waterlogged weight—somehow she got free of it. But even then, the current was too much for her. Chilled and exhausted, she could feel herself going down.

"Miss Sarah..." Myles's voice was faint, almost dreamlike now. Sarah drifted, resisting halfheartedly as the silky water closed over her head. An odd sense of sweetness stole into her benumbed mind.

Donovan, she thought. *Donovan...*

Yes...it was as if his arms were around her, as if she had come home, safe and warm at last....

Suddenly her hand touched something solid. Something big, alive and thrashing in the water.

The mule!

Shocked back to her senses, Sarah grabbed for the struggling beast. Her fingers clutched at the shaggy coat. They caught and held as she worked her frantic way along the saddle to clasp the straining neck. Her touch seemed to calm the mule. Its massive body heaved as it righted itself, feet suddenly finding bottom. Seconds later, it was plunging out of the water, dragging the exhausted Sarah with it.

"Miss Sarah, you all right?" Myles, on foot now, was sliding down the bank. "Mercy, I thought you was drowned for sure! Come on quick! We got to get to Betsy Mae!"

Hair and clothes streaming, Sarah crawled the rest of the way into the saddle. Her canvas valise was gone, washed away somewhere down the creek. Trying to find it would be hopeless. She would just have to make do without the precious medical supplies inside.

"Hurry!" Myles was urging Sarah on, fear making him heedless of her own condition. "I jist hope Betsy Mae's all right. An' little Eli. The poor mite must be scared nigh on t' death, 'specially if the water's started comin' in...."

Sarah gave the mule its head, trusting the wise beast to follow the horse. Willows, newly leafed, whipped her face as they galloped through the damp bottoms, splashing through ponds and puddles. Icy wind fingers plucked at her soaked clothes, numbing her flesh to the bone.

She sagged with relief as her eyes caught a faint glow through the trees. The cabin. It didn't appear to be flooded yet, but the water was coming up fast.

Sarah took charge. "You get a shovel and shore up the low spots," she ordered Myles as they reached the cabin and tumbled off their mounts. "I'll go in and see to your wife. Go on, now, there's nothing you can do in there."

She slogged through the mud toward the cabin door, which yielded at a push. The flickering lamplight revealed a white-faced little boy, huddled in a corner of the room while his mother writhed helplessly on the bed.

"Betsy Mae!" Sarah leaned over the laboring young woman. "It's all right, dear! I've come to take care of you!"

"Sarah!" The small, callused hands reached out to grip Sarah's arm. "I was afraid you wouldn't come, after what we done to you in church! You're a angel of mercy for sure!"

"Hush! Lie still if you can, and I'll check you." Sarah turned to the little boy, who was staring at her with huge, frightened eyes. "Get your coat on, Eli. Go out on the stoop and wait under the eaves till your papa sees you. All right?"

The child hesitated, then ran to fetch his ragged little coat, which hung on a nail beside the door.

"Stay on the stoop and keep dry, now." Sarah rolled up her sleeves, forcing her own chattering teeth to keep still. She had never felt colder, wetter or more exhausted in her life. But her own needs would have to wait. Right now, she had a patient to take care of.

"Button me, Miss Sarah." Eli stood in his coat, clasping the open front. Sarah tried to look cheerful as she bent to help him.

"Don't worry, sweetheart. Your mama will be fine. And soon you'll have a new little brother or sister to play with. Would you like that?"

Eli's lower lip quivered. "I'm scared, Miss Sarah."

Sarah caught him close for an instant. *I'm scared, too,* she thought. *I've only delivered seventeen babies and read a couple of books, and I'm not even sure what's wrong here, or what to do about it.*

"Go and wait for your papa, Eli," she said. "And while you're waiting, say a little prayer for your mama. Will you do that for me?"

Eli nodded gravely, then spun out of Sarah's arms and scampered out the door.

Sarah turned back toward the bed. Her body was chilling. She was weary to the point of collapse, but she could not think about that now. She could not think about tomorrow, or even about Donovan. In the hours ahead, her whole mind and strength would have to be focused on saving Betsy Mae and her child. Nothing else could be allowed to matter.

The beefsteak at the Golden Plume was as tough as boot leather, the gravy like congealed glue over watery mashed potatoes. Donovan had scarcely noticed. His plate sat almost untouched as he stared across the table at his newfound friend, Jamie Trenoweth from Cornwall. "Tell me more about this new smelter," he said.

"So that caught thee fancy, did it?" Jamie shoveled another forkful of potatoes into his mouth. He was about Donovan's age, with swarthy skin, twinkling brown eyes, and an appetite matched only by his boundless energy.

Jamie Trenoweth was a hard-rock miner, one of many such men who'd come over from England in the past few months with skills honed in Cornish tin mines, skills now being used to blast gold-bearing quartz out of Colorado mountainsides.

But the mill, the new gold-refining mill built in nearby Black Hawk, that was what had stirred Donovan's imagination to a fever pitch. According to Jamie, its massive machinery could pound the resistant quartz to powder, making it possible to extract the gold by smelting.

"Blimey, wot's to tell, laddie?" Jamie spoke between vigorous bites. "'Twas your American Mr. Hill bought the model in Swansea, me 'ome town, and built 'is own in Black Hawk. H'it's been runnin' nigh onto four months now."

"And it really works?" Donovan's mind was seeing the glittery quartz that abounded on the old claims at Miner's Gulch, including Charlie Sutton's. "It can really get the gold out of solid rock?"

"Works on gold just like on tin." Jamie motioned to a passing waitress. "I'll 'ave another 'elpin' of these scrumptious potatoes, me beauty!" He bent to sawing another slice off the stubborn beef. "Now, sorr, if me wife was alive, I'd have her cook thee a real Cornish meat pasty! Always made 'em for me lunch, she did, bless 'er."

"Your wife?" Donovan asked politely, his mind still on the gold smelter.

"Aye, lad. She died two years ago, she and our three little ones, all of a fever in the same week. Finest woman wot e'er drew breath. I've ne'er found another to take 'er place."

"I'm sorry," Donovan said. "Truly sorry." He picked up his knife, made several attempts to cut the rubbery steak and finally abandoned the effort as hopeless.

"An' thee, me 'andsome. Thee've a wife? Or a sweetheart?"

For some absurd reason, the picture that flashed through Donovan's mind was of Sarah, standing in the lamplight of the cabin, disheveled and glowing as she cradled Varina's newborn son. He held the image for an instant, then blinked it determinedly away.

"No," he said. "No wife. No sweetheart."

"Pity." Jamie forked up more potatoes. "'Tis a woman's sweetness that makes life truly worth the trials."

"Tell me more about the smelter." Donovan forced a change of subject. "Where does the ore come from?"

"Gregory Gulch, mostly. 'Tis close by an' not far to 'aul the rock. But mind 'ee, the smelter's of a goodly size. 'Twas built to 'andle ore from all these parts, once there be enough miners what can blast 'ard rock. 'Tis a dangerous job. A mon's got t' know what 'e's doin', or 'e gets blown sky-'igh."

"And you?" Donovan asked. "I take it you know good ore when you find it."

"Aye, that I do. Worked enough of it. Truth be, when I come over 'ere, 'twas with the 'ope of findin' me own claim an' workin' it. 'Ad too many years of bein' a company mon."

"But hard-rock mining's not like placer. From what I know of it, there's no way a man can work hard rock alone. It takes capital and a crew of men to work a strike."

"True, me son. But find thee a good claim, and the rest follows like magic!" The wiry Cornishman took a bite of inedible steak, chewing with relish. "There be always them what's got money to invest, and them what's got strong backs and a need for the wages."

Jamie bent to eating in earnest. Donovan, however, had given up on his meal. He leaned back in his chair to survey the crowded dining room, with its vermilion walls, gilt-painted moldings and motley clientele. Through a long, open archway, he could see into the smoke-hazed bar, where the town's rougher element was lined up for glasses of cheap Tennessee lightning.

He was giving the drinkers a cursory glance when one of them, a hulk of a man in a grease-stained canvas coat, turned toward a companion. The move gave Donovan a full view of his flat-nosed profile.

Another ghost.

Donovan blinked, certain his eyes were deceiving him. But there was no mistaking Corporal Simeon Dooley, a brawler and troublemaker from the start, who'd served in Donovan's Virginia regiment. The strange thing was, he had seen Dooley fall at Antietam, with a hole in his chest that would have dispatched a buffalo bull. Donovan had assumed he was dead. Now, here he was, drinking and laughing at a bar in Central City, Colorado Territory.

First Lydia Taggart. Now Dooley.

Donovan toyed briefly with the idea of calling out to him. But no, he'd never gotten along with the man. As a soldier, the big corporal had been surly, insubordinate, lazy and constantly picking fights. From the looks of him, he did not appear to have changed.

Shrugging Dooley out of his thoughts, Donovan turned back to Jamie Trenoweth, who was wiping his plate with a hunk of sourdough biscuit.

"When's your next day off?" he asked the Cornishman.

"I get Sundays. But the boss 'e's good to let me take other days when I ask ahead."

"Think about paying a visit to Miner's Gulch," Donovan said. "There's something there I'd like to show you."

Betsy Mae's newborn girl was little more than matchstick bones—a small, scrawny stick of a thing with a gnomish face and a mop of light brown hair. But she squalled lustily against Sarah's damp shoulder, her rose-bud mouth groping for nourishment.

Sarah stole a few more seconds to cuddle her close, savoring her kittenlike smallness, her tiny, clutching hands and her wonderful new-baby smell. Then, with a sigh, she turned back to the exhausted Betsy Mae.

"There's not much to this young lady. But what there is seems healthy, and she's certainly got good, strong lungs. Are you up to feeding her?"

"Here, give her over." Betsy Mae held out her arms with a weary smile. "I can't believe she's really here, after the time we had. I don't know what we'd have done without you, Sarah."

Sarah handed over the tiny mite with a twinge of separation pain that had become all too familiar. Babies were so precious. But they were never hers to keep.

Betsy Mae opened her nightgown and offered one swollen breast to the wriggling infant. With knowing skill, she let her nipple tease the silky lips. Instinctively the tiny mouth clamped on and began to suck. The small, bundled body quivered contentedly as the warm nourishment began to flow.

Sarah sagged against the rough log wall, her clothes still wet from last night's rain. Only now that her hands were empty did she realize how tired she was. And how cold. Fatigue lay like ice in her marrow, so heavy and draining that she could barely stand. She had to get home, she realized dimly. She had to get out of her soaked clothes and into a warm bed.

A deep snore rose from a bedroll on the floor, where Myles and his son had fallen into slumber after the birth. The baby's noisy little sucks were the only other sound in the cabin.

"You look all done in, Sarah," Betsy Mae said softly. "Go on home and get some rest. We'll be fine here. I can wake Myles if I need anything."

Sarah nodded, lacking even the strength to speak. Her cloak had washed away in the flood, and this poor family had no wrap to lend her. She could only hope the rain had stopped and the creek had gone down.

She slipped out of the door and found her mule under the lean-to, munching a wisp of hay. Marshaling her strength, Sarah crawled into the saddle, gave the beast his head and collapsed over the sturdy neck. She could doze a little now. For all his mulish ways, Nebuchadnezzar could always be trusted to find the path home.

The sky was leaden with morning clouds. The rain had stopped, but the newly leafed aspens drooped with moisture that drenched Sarah's hair and clothes as they brushed past. The droplets fell like ice on her fevered skin. She was too tired to think, too tired to care.

An abrupt lurch and the sound of a running creek told her they were crossing the ford. Sarah clung to the mule's neck, her feet dragging listlessly in the ripples. If she fell, she knew she would drown. She did not have the strength to swim.

The mule plunged up the opposite bank and headed for the main road. The next thing Sarah remembered, they were standing outside the stable, with the hungry beast nickering to be led to his stall.

Exhausted as she was, Sarah forced herself to remove the saddle and bridle, rub down the mule and give him a bucket of oats to munch. Nebuchadnezzar had saved her life in last night's flood. It was the least she could do for him.

That accomplished, she staggered out of the stable. The sky was the color of unpolished pewter, pale in the east where the sun would soon be up. The birds had already awakened. Their songs, which Sarah usually loved, screeched a menacing cacophony in her ears. Her skin burned like fire in the morning chill.

The stairway to her rooms loomed above her like the side of a mountain. Seizing the rail, she dragged herself upward. The earth seemed to be spinning below. She could not look down.

At last she gained the door. Somehow she got it unlocked, got it open and locked again behind her. Reeling across the classroom like a drunkard, she reached the bedroom.

A black cloud seemed to swirl around her, closing in as her fingers fumbled for the top button of her shirtwaist. Head spinning, she tugged helplessly at the wet fabric. One button popped its thread and bounced to the floor.

That was the last thing Sarah remembered as she spun forward into darkness.

Chapter Nine

Waltzing couples whirled in a ghostly ballroom, their faces concealed by exquisite masks fashioned of jewels, fur and feathers. The music was dark and sensual. Its passionate rhythm pulsed like a heartbeat through Sarah's veins as she dipped and spun.

Donovan's hand cradled the small of her back. From behind a golden lion's mask, his eyes blazed their emerald fire into hers, their tender heat all but melting the clothes from her body.

She was a bird in his arms, her mask a bird's, its vibrant colors echoing the purple, magenta and crimson plumes that adorned her gown. Her skirt swirled and floated as they moved together in a world all their own, the other dancers no more than a rainbow blur around them.

Where her hand lay on his shoulder, she could feel the heat of his body. She could feel the desire that tightened his muscles at her touch, and she burned for him. Achingly, wantonly, in a way, she supposed, that no decent woman should want a man, Sarah wanted Donovan Cole.

She smiled up at him, her chin tilting coquettishly. His lips moved in response beneath the mask, forming words without sound. *I love you, Lydia,* they said.

The sentiment knifed through her with the pain of cold steel, but Sarah kept her silence, kept her smile. The mask was Lydia. For as long as she wore it, Donovan was hers.

The music faded; the dancers melted into mist. She and Donovan were alone under the open stars. Flinging aside his own golden mask, he swept her into his arms. His searing kiss sent wet-hot waves rippling downward through her body. She moaned in a frenzy of yearning. Her fingers raked his hair as she pulled his head down to the pulsing cleft between her breasts.

He doesn't love you, a voice cried out inside her head. *It's the mask he loves, you fool, only the mask. . . .*

But the warning turned to smoke in the heat of Sarah's desire. She trembled as he arched her backward onto a bed of fragrant, scarlet blossoms. Their clothes fell away as if by magic—all but the glorious feathered mask. A furtive touch reassured her it was still in place.

Donovan leaned above her, his nakedness beautiful in the starlight. Sarah touched him in wonder. Her fingers reached up to brush the virile tangle of hair that spread between his nipples; they traced its downward trail along his hard, flat belly to where it curled luxuriantly around the marbled shaft of his manhood. He moaned as she stroked him, guiding him gently toward the aching center of her need.

It would happen now, she told herself. Donovan would love her, and the mask would no longer matter.

He tensed, poised to thrust, then hesitated. His hand moved swiftly to sweep the mask from her face. She cried out as he stared down at her. Her dismayed eyes saw his expression harden, saw him draw back . . .

Sarah awoke with a start.

She was lying fully dressed across the foot of her bed, her damp clothes clammy against her fevered skin. She struggled to sit up, only to collapse dizzily onto the coverlet. She was ill, she realized. As ill as she had ever been in her healthy, young life.

She remembered staggering home in the early light of dawn. Now, through her window, the sky was a deep indigo, the color of evening. Sarah groaned as the clock in the

schoolroom struck eight. Unbelievably she had slept for
nearly fourteen hours in her water-soaked clothes.

Gritting her teeth against the dizziness, she pushed herself to a sitting position once more. Her throat was raw.
Her chest felt as if it had been encased in tight iron bands.
She had to get up, she realized foggily. She had to get some
hot liquids into her body. She had to get out of her wet
clothes and into her dry, warm bed.

Gripping a bedpost, she swung herself to her feet. The
room swam around her as she inched along the wall. If she
could get far enough to light the stove, she would use the
water in the kettle to make some good, hot tea.

She had rounded the doorway into the classroom when
her ears caught shouts from the street below. The windowpanes flickered red, reflecting flame from somewhere outside.

Fire. Sarah's heart contracted in sudden dread. Even after rain, a blaze could make swift work of the old wooden
structures that sprawled up and down Miner's Gulch. Forgetting how sick she was, she reeled across the room to a
front window, parted the curtains and peered down at the
street.

She had expected to see a burning building, with the
townspeople forming up to pass buckets from the creek.
What she saw instead was a single bonfire, piled high with
scrap wood, blazing squarely in front of the store.

A dark premonition stole over Sarah as she noticed the
three men clustered tensely around the flames, orange light
dancing on their soot-blackened faces. If they were trying
to disguise themselves, it was a pathetic attempt. Even from
the window, she had no trouble recognizing any of them.
MacIntyre, the one-armed livery stable owner stood close
to the blaze, using a long stick to stir something in a big iron
pot. And the spidery figure next to him—that would be
Pete Ainsworth, who spent most of his time drinking at
Smitty's. A little farther off, the squat man holding what
looked like two pillows would be—

Dear heaven.

Sarah staggered back from the window, knees buckling as the realization hit her.

Feathers. Tar and feathers. Meant for her.

Her heart slammed into a panic-stricken gallop, pumping adrenaline through her fever-racked body. A quick look out her bedroom window confirmed that she had no hope of getting away. Three more men stood at the foot of the stairway, cutting off her escape.

Tar and feathers. She had seen the horror of it once, in Vicksburg, where townspeople had caught a traveling medicine drummer cheating his customers. His body had been stripped, slathered with blistering hot tar, then doused with a bag of feathers, after which the poor miscreant was carried out of town on a rail and left by the roadside. Sarah had seen him weeks later in another town, his skin hideously scabbed from burns, his hair, what was left of it, still matted with tar. She had never forgotten the sight.

Nerves screaming, she darted back and forth like a cornered mouse, searching for a place to hide. The bed, the wall, the floor—there was nowhere a grown woman could conceal herself. And she knew the men would be coming for her soon—as soon as the tar was melted.

The door! In a frenzied burst of activity, she began shoving benches across the floor to make a barricade. But it was no use. The heavy tread of boots on the stairway told her that her pathetic efforts were already too late.

Wood splintered as the door swung inward with a sickening crash. The three dark figures who lurched into the schoolroom reeked hellishly of smoke, tar and cheap whiskey. White-rimmed eyes glittered in their soot-smeared faces.

"Come on out, you goddamned Yankee bitch," one of them snarled. "We know you're in here, and we ain't leavin' without you!"

Paralyzed with terror, Sarah crouched beneath her desk as the big, dirty boots tromped closer. Her teeth chattered with the chills that racked her fevered body. The room swam dizzyingly in her head, and she knew she was on the verge of fainting. Maybe it would be a mercy if she did.

One of the creatures stomped into her bedroom. Sarah could hear him rummaging through her things, snorting like an animal. "Hey, look a' this! So this is what a Yankee spy wears under them fancy skirts. Lace britches!"

Chortling, the other two stampeded into the bedroom. As Sarah heard their lusty hoots, she suddenly realized the classroom was empty, its door dangling open on shattered hinges.

Reeling with fever, she slid out from under the desk and stumbled to her feet. She had seconds, at most, to make it outside. And what then? Could she reach the barn? The trees? Her friends above Smitty's? Could she even manage her way down the stairs?

Sarah's legs wobbled like a newborn calf's. She staggered across the schoolroom, praying under her breath as the darkness swam around her. From her bedroom came the sound of slamming drawers and drunken laughter. Any second now, the three men would burst out and see her. Then she would truly be lost.

The door—she reached it and collapsed against the broken frame. She couldn't stop. She had to keep moving, she lashed herself as she stumbled out into the cool night air.

The stairs fell away below her like the edge of a deep ravine. Clinging to the rail, she ventured one step downward, then two more...

"Thar she is, the lyin' Yankee slut!"

The shout from behind her flung Sarah into a panic. She plunged down the next half-dozen steps. Then her out-of-control legs tangled in her skirts, and she pitched forward, sliding headfirst to the mud-slicked bottom of the stairs.

They were on her like a pack of dogs. Rough hands clamped her arms and dragged her, gasping and clawing, across the muddy ground into the alley. Ahead in the street, Sarah could see the leaping flames of the bonfire. Gathering her strength, she began to scream. Surely someone would hear her, someone would come—

A blow from the flat of a big, sooty palm exploded in her head. Shocked into silence, Sarah sagged against the hands that gripped her limbs. A sob broke from her lips as the sickening realization hit her.

No one would fly to her rescue. No one would dare. Not even the women at Smitty's, her staunch and courageous friends, would be foolish enough to defy this drunken, raging mob and turn its anger on themselves. She was alone in her peril. Utterly and completely alone.

Even Donovan . . .

"Yankee bitch!" It was MacIntyre who loomed above her now, his eyes glittering yellow in the firelight. "You owe me an arm, Yankee bitch! You owe Ainsworth a brother an' O'Rourke a flour mill! You owe us all, an' it's time t' pay!"

She moaned feebly as the men flung her to the ground. How many hidden eyes were watching? she wondered. How many eyes, from the saloon, from the store, from the shadowed porches? How many people stood in silent consent, waiting to see her punishment?

Sarah gasped with pain as MacIntyre's single, powerful hand locked into her hair and pulled, wrenching it loose from its remaining pins so that in one motion he held its unbound length in his fist.

A knife blade flashed before Sarah's horrified eyes. Glancing toward it, MacIntyre nodded.

"Cut it!" he rasped.

Donovan had planned on arriving in Miner's Gulch before sundown. However, he had taken extra time that morning to ride out to Black Hawk and see the new smelter. The delay had cost him a good two hours, but the time had been well spent. He had driven home bursting with plans— for Varina and her family, for the dying town, and maybe even for himself.

He was still in high spirits as he rounded the last mountain curve before the long, sloping descent into the gulch. Jamie Trenoweth had agreed to come up on his next day off to examine Varina's claim. If the gold-bearing quartz was as rich as Donovan hoped, his sister would never be poor again.

The night was diamond clear, the air cool and fresh with the smell of wet earth. Above the peaks, the full moon lay like a ripe, golden peach. Donovan inhaled deeply, his weariness a pleasant weight in his bones. The rough bed in Varina's loft would feel good tonight.

A faint whiff of smoke drifted on the air, teasing at Donovan's nostrils. At first nothing unusual registered in his mind. There could always be campfires along the road or cook fires in the outlying cabins. On a cool spring evening, a passerby could expect a whiff of smoke here and there.

But no, he suddenly realized. This smoke had an odd scent about it, greasy, acrid and heavy, almost as if someone was melting...tar.

Sarah!

With a shout, he whacked the reins down hard on the rumps of the four big bays. The wagon lurched ahead, wooden frame groaning as it careened around the bend. Ahead lay the road that sloped downward to the foot of the gulch—two miles, maybe less, but it might as well be a hundred. The sickening odor of tar, growing stronger by the second, told him he could already be too late.

Frantic now, Donovan pressed the horses to a full gallop down the moonlit roadway. With one hand, he steadied the reins. With the other, he fumbled under the seat for the rifle.

Strands of Sarah's silky brown hair littered the trampled mud around the fire. Bending at the knee, MacIntyre scooped up a handful of curls and tossed them into the flames. "That was the easy part, girlie. Now you're gonna see what we really do t' Yankee whores in these parts!"

Faint with shock and fever, Sarah lay collapsed at his feet. There was no more need for the men to hold her. She was too weak to fight or escape.

Deliberately, MacIntyre turned his back on her to stir the pot of black tar that simmered on the coals. Its sickening heat swam in the air, almost making Sarah retch. People had died from tarrings, she recalled. Maybe they were the lucky ones. Maybe she would be fortunate enough to pass out before the pain got too bad, and never awaken again.

"Tar's ready," MacIntyre announced. "Strip the bitch! We want t' put this black honey where it'll hurt the most!"

"No—" Sarah protested weakly as unfeeling hands tore away her skirt and shirtwaist, ripping them in the process. "Please, no—" She could feel them jerking away her petticoats, exposing her drawers. She writhed and twisted in a pitiful attempt to cover herself. "You're decent men, not monsters. You've got wives and daughters. How can you—?"

MacIntyre's hand struck her face in a jaw-wrenching slap. "Shut up, Yankee spy! We're gonna—"

He stiffened at the sound of a rifle shot, and the clatter of a heavy wagon thundering up the street from the bottoms. One of the men dropped his grip on Sarah's leg.

"Oh, hell," he groaned, "it's that damned Cole!"

Sarah heard a voice shouting something. Then her whole world went black.

Standing in the wagon box, Donovan leveled the rifle at the small cluster of men. "First one of you bastards makes a move, I'll give it to him where it hurts!" he shouted.

Six blackened faces gazed up at him, eyes shifting uneasily under the fury of his glare. He'd underestimated MacIntyre and his cronies, Donovan reflected bitterly. They were cowards to a man, but with enough liquor in their guts, they'd at least proven themselves capable of ganging up on a helpless female.

Sarah lay crumpled in the mud, firelight flickering on her pale, bare limbs. Aside from the awful thing they'd done to her hair, she didn't appear physically hurt. But then, the worst hurts didn't always show.

"You ought to be ashamed of yourselves!" he snapped. "This whole town ought to be ashamed! The law of the land says that Sarah Parker has a right to go free! Who are you to set yourselves above that law? A bunch of liquored-up, no-good—"

"You ain't sheriff in this town, Cole!" It was MacIntyre who spoke. "We got a right to avenge our own! Ain't no law what can take that away from us!"

"Then take this as law!" Donovan's hands tightened on the rifle. "I'll see to it that Sarah Parker leaves this town. I'll even take her to Central City and put her on a stage myself. But meanwhile, any man who lays a hand on her will answer for it—to me!"

He glanced down at Sarah, who was moaning softly, her eyes still closed. Donovan's heart twisted, but his face betrayed nothing. "Ainsworth, Thomas—you two, pick her up and get her back to her room! The rest of you buzzards, douse the fire and dump out that damned tar! You'll thank me in the morning when you wake up sober!" His voice dropped to a menacing snarl. "Now, move it!"

He leveled the gun, eyes glaring, as the men shuffled drunkenly to obey him. Two of them lifted the half-conscious Sarah to her feet, bracing her under the arms. The sight of her, shorn and barely clothed, grimy hands supporting her body, tore at Donovan's heart, but he dared not lower his weapon to go to her aid. He could only watch out of the corner of his eye as they dragged her toward the alley.

"Stop right there!" The thin male voice riveted everyone, including Donovan. He blinked incredulously as Amos

Satterlee, the balding storekeeper, stepped out of the shadows with a Colt .44 clutched in his trembling fist.

"You're not taking that woman upstairs," he declared, his strained voice cracking like a teenage boy's. "I'm sorry, Cole. As a Canadian, I've tried to stay out of this ridiculous dispute. But I've got a business to protect. After what happened here tonight, with *her* above my store, I'm liable to be burned out. I can't afford to let that happen."

"Oh, for hell's sake—" Donovan groaned his dismay. But even as he spoke, he knew the little storekeeper was right. Sarah's old rooms were no longer safe. It would be up to him to protect her until he could get her out of town.

His eyes shifted to Sarah, where she hung between her erstwhile captors. Her shorn head dangled limply to one side. Her closed eyes were sunk in dark shadows. She was in no condition to go anywhere, he realized.

"Give her a few hours to rest, Satterlee," he pleaded. "I'll stay with her myself to guard your property. By sunrise, I'll have her out of there, and your troubles will be over. You have my word on it."

The little man's eyes slid to one side, then the other. "I don't know if—"

"Damn it, Satterlee, *look* at the woman! She's been through hell! You can't just throw her out in the night!"

The storekeeper hesitated, then lowered the pistol cautiously. "All right. But I don't want any more trouble, Cole. This isn't my fight, understand?"

"I understand. Just keep these yahoos covered till I get her upstairs. That's all I'll ask of you."

Shouldering the rifle by its sling, he vaulted to the ground. Sarah had opened her eyes, but she scarcely seemed aware of him as he caught her in his arms and lifted her against his chest. Her underclothes were wet and muddy, her skin fearfully dry and burning with fever.

With Sarah in his arms, Donovan paused to cast a contemptuous glare at the men who huddled like whipped dogs around the smoking embers of the bonfire. Cowed and drunk, their victim gone, they weren't likely to cause more trouble tonight. MacIntyre would be occupied with putting up the team and wagon. The others would drift away to sleep off their lunacy.

Satterlee, the wretched little man, brandished his Colt with the bravado of a child holding a toy pistol. Damn them, Donovan thought. Damn them all.

Without a word, he turned and strode away, carrying Sarah into the alley.

"No...no, please—" Sarah cried out in her fevered sleep as her mind relived the horror. "Please don't—"

"Shh...be still and rest." Donovan sponged her hot face with a damp cloth, stroking gently downward along the curve of her throat. "You're safe, Sarah. I'm here. I won't let them hurt you again."

She whimpered in terror, her slender limbs twitching as she dreamed. Two hours had passed since he'd carried her up to her room, stripped away her muddy underclothes and tucked her, innocently naked, into her clean, dry bed. Except for the few minutes it had taken to repair the door, he had been with her constantly, bathing her face and forcing sips of tea between her fever-flushed lips. In all that time, even when her eyes fleetingly opened, Sarah had given no sign that she recognized him.

She had been sick before the bastards took her, he realized. Too sick to run or fight. Coupled with that, the fear and shock of her ordeal had all but pushed her over the edge.

Moonlight drifted through the small bedroom window, its platinum beams falling across her sleeping face. Donovan's heart contracted as his gaze lingered on the bruised cheek, the swollen lower lip and pain-shadowed eyes. Her once-glorious hair, pathetically shorn, curled damply around her face like a young boy's.

Donovan's finger traced one delicate lock where it lay along the curve of her cheek. This woman had posed as

Lydia Taggart, he reminded himself. She had used young men, his own brother among them, to betray the Confederacy. She had aided the force that destroyed his home, his family and their way of life.

Now he was looking upon his vengeance.

But he felt no satisfaction when he gazed at Sarah Parker. He felt only pity and rage, and a tenderness so deep that it shook him to the roots of his soul.

Sitting on the edge of the mattress, he lifted her head to coax a few more drops of tea into her dry mouth. She sputtered in semiconscious protest, choking a little on the warm liquid. Her eyelids flickered open, but again, her brief gaze was a stranger's, holding no sign of recognition.

Donovan lowered her head to the pillow and replaced the chipped cup on the dresser. Glancing around the tiny room, he cursed his own helplessness. Sarah needed a doctor. She needed medicine to bring down her fever and plenty of good, hot broth to build her strength. She needed long days of rest and care.

Here, in this bitter little town she had served so well, there was no help for her.

Distracted by worry, he dipped his fingers into the washbowl and stroked them along her burning cheek. If he could get her to Central City—but no, he realized, Sarah was too sick to be moved that far. The ten-hour ride in a jarring open wagon could kill her.

There was Varina. She would be more than willing to take Sarah in. But the little cabin would be the most useless of hiding places. Worse, for their help, Varina and her children could face the same kind of ugliness Donovan had witnessed tonight. No, the whole idea was out of the question.

Donovan's hand ruffled Sarah's hair, his fingers tangling in the damp silk of her curls. She moaned softly, stirring in response to his touch, but her gray eyes did not open.

Impulsively he bent and brushed his lips across the bridge of her nose. "What am I going to do with you, Sarah Parker?" he whispered, amazed at the surge of emotion that simple gesture aroused. "Why can't I just turn my back and leave you to your fate? My life would be so damned much simpler without you...."

His lips nuzzled her eyebrow and grazed the pale sunken moons of her closed eyelids. Her skin was as sweet as a child's, satin smooth, with its own innocently sensual aroma. Aching with tenderness, Donovan ventured lower to kiss her temple, her earlobe, the exquisite little crease at the corner of her mouth. How had this happened? he wondered dizzily. How had Sarah Parker, a woman he'd professed to hate, managed to enmesh herself so deeply in the roots of his soul?

"No..." She had begun to dream again, her limbs jerking in their imagined struggle.

"Sarah..." His lips pressed her cheek and brushed the softly opened flower of her mouth. "It's all right, Sarah. I'm here."

"No—" A quiver knifed through her body, and suddenly she was shaking all over, her teeth clattering in an agony of chills. Donovan glanced frantically around the room for something, a blanket, anything, to add warmth to the doubled quilt that covered her trembling body, but there was nothing. Even her cloak was gone from its hook on the wall.

In desperation, he kicked off his boots and trousers, lifted the sheet and, still clad in his long underwear, slid into bed beside her.

He had half expected her to resist, but she came to him like a frightened child, nestling into his warmth as he drew her close. Tiny whimpers of need rippled through her body as she found a haven in his arms.

Donovan gasped at the first press of her sharp little hipbones through the threadbare wool. Sarah did not know what she was doing, he reminded himself. She was delirious, out of her mind with fever.

He, unfortunately, was not. His male response was instantaneous, his awareness of it a cold stab of guilt. This was no time for lust, Donovan admonished himself. But his painfully aroused body wasn't listening. Sarah's fevered nakedness was a flame in his arms. Her trembling need tested him, teased him to the breaking point. He had wanted this woman for years, first as Lydia Taggart, now as Sarah Parker, and here he was in her bed. It would be so easy—

But what was he thinking? To take advantage of Sarah in her present condition would be nothing short of criminal. He wanted her, yes. But he wanted her healthy and awake, her passion real, her desire igniting like wildfire with his own.

And in view of the way Sarah felt about him, those circumstances would probably never come to be.

Resigning himself to the torture, he focused his energies on keeping her as warm as possible. With his arms, he turned her over and pulled her backside tightly into the curve where he lay. His legs entangled hers so strategically that even her toes were covered. Sarah lay cocooned in the heat of his tormented body.

Even then, she continued to chill. Her flesh was dry and fiery hot, her body racked by shivers. Her labored breathing told him of the congestion welling in her lungs.

Pneumonia.

Donovan's frantic mind leafed backward to the long months he'd spent in the wintry hell of Camp Douglas. With no medicines available, the prisoners had treated pneumonia with steam. Could he do that here, for Sarah?

She moaned as he slipped away from her and padded into the schoolroom to assess what was available. The stove was barely adequate, Sarah's iron kettle pitifully small. But there was a full rain barrel at the foot of the stairs and a stack of wood in a corner of the classroom. It was a start.

Within minutes, he had stoked up the fire, refilled the kettle, and rigged the classroom benches to form a makeshift tent frame around the stove. When a plume of steam arose from the boiling water, he draped Sarah's quilt over the framework and crawled underneath with her in his arms.

Time blurred into hours as Donovan staggered between feeding the fire, filling the kettle and crouching with Sarah under the steam-soaked blanket. Rivulets of sweat poured off his body as he held her, praying that the hot steam would ease her congested lungs.

He could feel the fever raging in her body, feel her struggle for life as she lay fighting for breath across his cramped knees. Her quieter moments gave other worries a chance to gnaw at his mind. What would he do if Mac-Intyre and his cohorts decided to pay them a return visit? And what about tomorrow? Could he buy more days from the wormy little storekeeper? Or would Satterlee hold him to his word and put Sarah out on the street?

By three in the morning, Donovan had run out of wood. As the last embers died in the stove, he carried Sarah back to the bedroom and gently dressed her in her dry gown and robe, which he'd discovered flung under the dresser. Her breathing had eased some, but she was still feverish, still drifting in and out of delirious sleep. Her head and limbs flopped like a rag doll's as he tugged the clothes over them.

By now Sarah's body seemed almost as familiar as his own. In the course of caring for her, he had come to know every lovely curve and hollow of her torso, every line of her lean-muscled legs, every subtle nuance of her face, with an intimacy almost as deep as if they had been lovers.

Later he would remember. And he would wonder how it might have been.

Reeling with exhaustion, he laid her on the bed, covered her with the sheet and stretched himself out beside her. He would allow himself a few hours' rest before morning. Then he would seek out the storekeeper and plead for more time, or pay for it in cash, if need be. The thought of dealing with Satterlee turned his stomach, but he could think of no other way to save Sarah's life.

Donovan was just drifting off when the creak of a wooden stair outside startled him into wakefulness. Blinking his head clear, he lunged for the rifle. His ears strained in the silent darkness. Just one person, he calculated as he listened to the cautious tread mounting the steps. Whoever it was, he would be ready.

The knock at the door was light, almost hesitant. Maybe it was Satterlee, snooping around to see if Sarah was gone yet. So much the better, Donovan groused as he cocked the rifle, then raised the latch with his free hand. Too bad he couldn't afford to let the spineless little bastard know exactly what he thought of him.

"Come in," he rasped, backing away a few steps.

The door swung open to reveal a woman standing in the moonlight—a big woman, rawboned and fleshy, with garishly dyed red hair. One of Smitty's girls, Donovan realized dimly as she stepped inside and closed the door behind her.

"Ain't no need to point that gun at me, mister. I only come to check on Miss Sarah."

The rifle sagged in Donovan's hands. "You—you're a friend of hers?"

The middle-aged whore shot him a contemptuous glance. "Miss Sarah's been a good friend to us all. Damned Smitty locked us up, so's we couldn't do nothin' when them sons o' bitches hauled her out in the street. But Zoe heard what happened later from one o' her reg'lars."

She paused to tighten the sash of her tattered silk wrapper, her hair and clothes exuding a rich aura that blended sweat, cigar smoke and cheap eau de cologne. "Faye Swenson's the name," she declared, extending a man-size hand. "An' I guess you'd be Mr. Donovan Cole."

Donovan accepted the woman's powerful handshake. "I'm glad you came," he murmured, tugging her toward the bedroom. "Sarah's not doing at all well. She's burning up with fever, and Satterlee wants her out of here by sunup."

Faye's muttered sentiment echoed Donovan's opinion of the storekeeper, but her breath caught in a gasp as she touched Sarah's cheek.

"Willow bark tea," she grunted. "It was Miss Sarah herself told me about it. Old Injun remedy. Best thing for fevers. But first we got to get this poor lamb out of here. From what Zoe heard, MacIntyre an' his pals might be cookin' up more devilry. We can't let them bastards find her."

"If you know of somewhere safe—"

"We got a spare room upstairs. Safest place in town, long as we can keep Smitty from knowin' about it." She glanced at Donovan with watery blue eyes. "She's a real angel, that Miss Sarah. Most folks don't know she was friends with the likes of us. But Greta and Zoe and me, there ain't nothin' we wouldn't do for her."

Donovan glanced down at Sarah's fitfully sleeping face. *The Angel of Miner's Gulch.* His own mocking words came back to haunt him now. Angel or devil—who was this woman?

"Best we move her now, afore it gets light," Faye was saying. "Then we'll need you to go down by the creek and strip some willows for the tea. Leave the bark by the back door—we'll find it all right."

Nodding his agreement, Donovan scooped up Sarah, sheet and all, and strode with her toward the door. She was weightless in his arms, her hot body as limp as death. His throat tightened with concern.

Faye had gone ahead to scout. Now she came creaking back up the stairs. "All clear—but hurry!" she whispered.

Donovan followed her across the alley, through the thicket of blue spruces, up the hidden back staircase and into the cloyingly scented darkness of the upper rooms.

Sarah hung in his arms, moaning softly as he shifted her position to accommodate the narrow hallway.

"Here—" Faye had lit a candle and opened a doorway at the far end of the hall. Donovan carried Sarah into a dim, tawdry room furnished with a wardrobe, a dresser and a stripped-down bed. He remembered, now, hearing that one of Smitty's girls had died of consumption. This, he realized, would be her room.

"Hold her another minute while I throw a clean sheet on the mattress," Faye said. "Then you'd best be off after that there bark. Sooner you can get some back to us, the better."

Donovan cradled Sarah against his chest, torn by a strange reluctance to let her go. He could only hope that Faye was right about the willow bark, and that she was as capable as she appeared. He could not bear the thought of Sarah spending the last hours of her life in such a godforsaken place.

Sarah moaned and stirred slightly, her head falling back against his sleeve. Looking into her lovely, ravaged face, Donovan was struck by the realization that he could never allow himself to see her again. His feelings for Sarah Parker were a betrayal of everything he had ever stood for—his family, his principles, his loyalty to the defeated South. For his sake and hers, they would have to remain apart. They would have to remain enemies. Otherwise, even under the best of circumstances, his bitterness would seep out and destroy her.

"One thing, Faye," he ventured as if the thought had just occurred to him. "Miss Sarah doesn't exactly have a high opinion of me. She might not take kindly to the idea of my having nursed her. I'd appreciate it if you didn't mention my part in this."

Faye's shrewd eyes, pale in the candlelight, flashed their understanding. "Don't worry, we won't say nothin' about it," she grunted. "Here, you can put her down now."

Donovan laid Sarah tenderly on the bed, battling the urge to bend down and kiss her soft lips. "Get well," he whispered. Then he forced himself to turn away. The darkness waited outside, and the creek, with its life-giving willows. There was no time to lose.

Chapter Ten

Sarah was aware of the scent even before she opened her eyes. She knew it at once—that pungent blend of smoke, perfume, incense and carnality that she had long since come to associate with the rooms above the Crimson Belle.

Her nostrils twitched as her limbs stirred sleepily. How weak she felt, as if every cell in her body had been drained of its substance. Even her eyelids seemed incapable of movement. It required the full concentration of her will-power just to raise them to the faint reddish light.

The light...

She gasped as she came awake to the dim glow of sunshine through threadbare velvet curtains. She was in Marie's familiar scarlet-walled room, in the very bed where Marie had died. Yes, there was the wardrobe on the far wall, the perfume bottles and rose glass lamp on the dressing table, the tarnished brass spittoon in the corner.

Only Sarah herself was out of place.

For a long moment she lay still, scarcely daring to breathe as the questions churned darkly in her mind. She had no memory of coming here, no recollection of what had brought her to this room. But one thing was certain. She needed answers. Now.

Straining with the effort, she worked an elbow under her body and managed to raise her head and shoulders. Her free hand moved instinctively to brush her long hair from her face.

Her hair.

Sarah clutched at her shorn head as the shock of memory slammed home like an explosion. The shattered door. The sickening odor of tar—

Panic surged through her ravaged body. This was a dream, one of her nightmares, that was all. But now she had to get up. She had to prepare her schoolroom for the day, the children would be coming—

Lurching out of bed, she took a single wobbly step, swayed, then crumpled to the faded Persian carpet with a helpless cry. The sound brought Greta pounding into the room.

"*Ach!* What are you doing out of bed? Lie down, before you make yourself sick all over again!"

Too dizzy to protest, Sarah allowed the plump, blond woman to boost her back into bed and tug the blankets up to her chin. She lay quivering with agitation as Greta's white hands, glittering with cheap rings, smoothed the sheet evenly over the top edge and tucked the edges neatly under the mattress. Sarah was warm, too warm. Her nightdress was sticky with sweat.

"Greta—" Her voice emerged as a rasp from her dry throat. "What's going on? Stop fussing and tell me!"

"*Ja,* I will tell you. But first some good, hot soup!"

"But I need to know everything—"

"No, first you eat. Then we talk." Greta bustled out of the room, her heavy footsteps creaking down the narrow hallway as Sarah sank back into the pillows. Yes, it was coming back now. She'd gone to deliver Betsy Mae's baby and fallen into the swollen creek. And she'd awakened later with a fever. That was when she'd seen the flames outside—

Sarah clenched her teeth as quivering spasms racked her body, leaving her breathless. It wasn't the fever this time. The sweat that soaked her nightgown told her plainly that the fever had broken. No, it was something else. Something so fearful that her memory would not let her open its doors more than a crack.

"Here you are!" Greta had come bustling back with a bowl of steaming chicken soup. "Now, eat. Build your strength, *meine kleine maus. Ach,* so ill you have been! For the first two days we feared you might not live!" She dipped a generous spoonful of the soup, blew on it and thrust the lip of the spoon between Sarah's dry, cracked lips.

"Greta—"

"Eat!"

The hot liquid shocked Sarah's mouth for an instant. Then, suddenly, it was as if she could not get enough. She sank back into the pillows with hungry compliance and, for the next few minutes, simply allowed Greta to spoon-feed her like a baby.

"Ja..." Greta's thickly rouged face creased in an approving smile. "That's right. The fever made you weak. You must eat, eat to grow strong again!"

Sarah closed her eyes as the warm nourishment curled pleasantly into her stomach. She could feel its strengthening heat radiating into her limbs. She could feel stirrings of life in a body that felt as if she had not eaten in days.

Days...

Sarah's eyes jerked open. "Greta, how long have I been here?"

"Five days. Eat."

"Five days!" She sat bolt upright, knocking the spoon from Greta's hand. It clattered to the floor as she seized the woman's fleshy, braceleted arm. "My classroom—my students—I have to get back—"

"Nein." Something flickered in Greta's face as she bent to pick up the spoon. "No more classroom for you. You cannot go back to that place. Ever."

"I don't understand—" Sarah kicked her legs over the edge of the bed in a frantic struggle to get up. But Greta's strong hand, shoving insistently against her sternum, was all it took to flatten her once more against the pillows.

"Listen to me, *liebchen*. You cannot go back to your little school. You cannot show yourself anyplace in this town."

"What—"

"The people—they think you went to Central City and got on the Denver stage. That's what they were told. It was the only way to keep you safe."

"But, my things—"

"Your things are packed in your trunk, in the storeroom." Greta bent closer, her voice a wine-saturated whisper. "In a few more days, when you are strong enough, then we will help you find a way to leave—at night, when no one will see."

"Oh—" A despairing moan escaped Sarah's lips as she sank back into the bedclothes and lay staring wretchedly at the ceiling, crushed by her own awareness.

She had wanted so desperately to redeem herself here in Miner's Gulch. She had tried so hard. But she had failed. The years of hope and backbreaking effort had come to nothing. Now, in the end, she would be forced to sneak out of town like a common fugitive.

Sarah had always detested self-pity. But now, weak and bewildered, she allowed the ugly emotion to seep into her system, allowed its black weight to drag her down. She had come so close to finding a life here. Then Donovan Cole had come storming into her world and made a shambles of it all. His unforgiving anger had stripped away her mask. His hatred had spread like an epidemic, and in the end...

Sarah's fingers crept furtively to her scalp, probing and exploring, as if to make certain the nightmare was real. Her hair would grow in time, she reminded herself. But it was hopeless to think she could ever put Richmond behind her. And even if she lived to be an old, old woman, nothing she did would atone for the sins of Lydia Taggart. Donovan Cole had seen to that.

Donovan.

His image flashed vividly before her, the acuteness of memory so sharp that she almost cried out. If only things had been different. But no, it wouldn't do to think of Donovan now. Donovan was her enemy. He had brought about her downfall. She had to accept the fact that she would never see him again.

Hardening herself to the challenge, Sarah erased his features from her mind—the luxuriant chestnut hair that curled at a touch, the smoldering green eyes, the stone-chiseled nose, cheeks and jaw, the passionate mouth that had caressed and cursed her. No more Donovan. Ever.

And no more wallowing in her own emotions! There were new questions now, bubbling to the surface in her seething, confused mind, demanding answers.

"Greta, how did I get here? Who brought me?"

"You don't remember?" Greta had turned to the pointless task of rearranging Marie's jumbled perfume bottles on the dresser.

"No." Sarah tottered on the edge of a black abyss. "I don't remember any of that part."

"What do you remember?"

"Waking up sick and seeing the fire. Smelling the tar. Trying to hide . . ." She had begun to shake again. "I know there's more. It's as if part of me doesn't want to remember."

"Then don't try." Greta bent over her to tuck the stray covers around Sarah's chin. "Rest and eat and keep warm, that's all you should do until you're stronger. Remembering is *verboten, ja?*"

"What do *you* remember?" Sarah persisted recklessly. "What did you see?"

Greta's massive breasts quivered with her shrug. "Nothing. Smitty was afraid we would try to help you. The old devil ordered the three of us to the wine cellar. He locked us up till it was over."

Sarah exhaled forcibly and tried to relax. Greta was right. Until she was stronger, the memory was best left alone. Why not just let it be?

But something was driving her, edging her beyond the point of risk. There were things she had to know.

"Someone must have talked, someone must have told you what happened," she said, dogging the evasive Greta.

"Enough!" Greta had clearly been pushed too far. She spun back toward the bed, scowling like a rouged mastiff. "The butchers chopped off your hair and tore away most of your clothes before—before they were stopped. You were not tarred—and, as far as we know, not raped—" She gathered up the bowl and spoon from the nightstand. "Rest, now. Close your eyes. And no more thinking about what happened. Not till you're stronger."

Drained of will for the moment, Sarah did her best to obey. Closing her eyes was easy. In fact it had become all she could do to keep them open. But shutting down her mind was impossible. She lay there pretending to sleep, her thoughts a whirlpool of disembodied faces, words and memories.

. . . before they were stopped.

Sarah's throat constricted sharply, trapping her breath as she struggled with the implications of what she had heard.

Who stopped them? Who brought me here? The questions shrieked to be heard and answered, but Sarah's tongue would not obey the urge to speak.

And that was just as well, because Greta had turned away and left the room.

The crescent moon lay like an abandoned bangle in the late-night sky. Against its wan light, the towering spruces loomed stark and black as Donovan stole down the alley toward the rear entrance of the Crimson Belle.

The door opened at his first light tap. Faye, wearing an old military coat over her tattered silk wrapper, slipped out to join him in the shadows.

"You brung the cash?" she whispered.

"It's right here." Donovan drew a sealed, brown envelope from under his jacket. "This should be enough to get her wherever she wants to go."

Faye hefted the envelope with a practiced hand. "Good thing she don't know it's from you, or she wouldn't take it."

"That's just why she mustn't know." Donovan bit back a surge of bitterness. He knew from earlier conversations with Faye that Sarah blamed him for her ordeal—and rightly so. It was his determination to see her gone that had triggered the whole hideous chain of events. In her eyes, he might as well have led the mob of drunken rowdies that had battered down her door and dragged her screaming into the street.

Now she despised him. But that was just as well, Donovan swiftly reminded himself. Let her hate him. Let her hatred take her away to someplace beyond the reach of his desire. That way, maybe they would both be safe.

"She still doesn't remember anything?" he asked.

"'Bout you takin' care of her?" Faye shook her frizzy, red hair. "We done like I promised you. Far as Miss Sarah knows, somebody comin' up the street scared the buggers off, an' she managed to git to our back door afore she keeled over."

Feeling the weight of the lie, Donovan nodded his assent. "How's she faring otherwise? When do you think she'll be strong enough to leave?"

"A few more days, I reckon. She's out of bed now, eatin' passable. An' she's gittin' mighty restless cooped up in that little room. 'Course, she knows she can't go nowhere on account of Smitty and the customers seein' her."

Faye's mannish voice had trailed off. Her eyes, Donovan suddenly realized, were no longer looking directly at him. Something, he sensed, was wrong.

"What is it, Faye?"

"I . . . don't rightly know," she answered in a voice muffled by emotion. "Miss Sarah looks pert enough, all right. But somethin' about her ain't the same. Ain't none of us up there can put a finger on it."

"What do you mean?" Donovan battled a sense of foreboding.

"You knowed her. You knowed what an angel she was, always ready to help out, not an enemy in this world—"

"That's changed?"

"Miss Sarah—she's like a different person now. She don't seem to care much about nobody or nothin'. Not that she's bad, mind you. But the angel in her is gone, Mr. Cole. It's almost like them dirty buzzards killed it!"

Donovan could not meet Faye's eyes. He stood looking past her into the black-shadowed trees, remembering how things had been when he'd first come to Miner's Gulch. Sarah had been happy then. The townspeople had accepted her. Her services had been valued and needed.

Then *he* had stepped in. Donovan Cole, so quick to judge, so determined to see justice carried out. And in his zeal, he had touched off the avalanche of hate that destroyed her.

The mocking, off-key notes of the piano twanged on the night air. From an upstairs window came the sound of a lusty snort and a shrill, feminine giggle. Faye stirred in the darkness.

"I got to go back in," she said wearily. "Smitty'll be lookin' for me. But don't you worry none about your money, Mr. Cole. I'll keep it safe for Miss Sarah."

"I know you will," Donovan murmured. "And thank you. You're a good woman, Faye Swenson."

She responded with a bitter chuckle. "Now that's one line I ain't heard much in my life. G'night, Mr. Cole."

With a swish of faded silk she was gone, leaving nothing behind her but the lingering aura of smoke, whiskey and cheap cologne, which was soon blown away on the night wind.

Thrusting his hands into his pockets, Donovan strode back up the alley toward the main street. Above Amos Satterlee's store, the windows were dark and empty. Mrs. Eudora Cahill had taken over Sarah's precious school, and the daily classes went on there as before. But no one lived in the rooms now. By night, the place was as bleak as Donovan's own spirit.

As he rounded the corner and tramped past the saloon, he kept his eyes focused on the ground. There was no sense in looking up at the windows and wondering about Sarah. She was gone from his life for good now; even though he felt like hell about it, he knew their separation was for the best.

Besides, he had other concerns on his mind. Jamie Trenoweth would be in town tomorrow, and Varina had insisted on inviting the doughty Cornishman to dinner. Afterward, the two men would spend time walking the boundaries of Varina's claim and collecting ore samples, which Jamie would take to the assayer in Central City.

Donovan had not told his sister the real purpose of Jamie's visit. If the ore was rich and the claim truly workable, Varina and her family could be secure for life. But the gold, like the rest of Charlie Sutton's dreams, might just as easily turn out to be a will-o'-the-wisp. Getting Varina's hopes up, only to have them dashed, would be a cruel blow to a woman who'd already seen a hundred times more disappointment than she deserved.

Donovan lengthened his stride as he passed the church, the tumbledown sheriff's office and the hardware store with its gaping holes where the windows had been pillaged for their glass. Miner's Gulch had been a flourishing town in the days of the old boom. It could prosper again if the rockbound ore proved rich enough for milling. People who'd held out for years on their spent placer claims could sell out to the big hard-rock operations and retire in comfort. There'd be new businesses, new people, money for street improvements, law enforcement, a telegraph office, even a real schoolhouse with a paid teacher.

But he was getting ahead of himself. He was starting to think like mutton-headed Charlie, who'd seen rainbows over every hill. The yellow-flecked quartz that littered Miner's Gulch could be worthless, for all he knew. What the hell, it probably *was* worthless—just like most of the people in this backward, dying town. If he had any sense, he would torch Varina's cabin and cart the family back to Kansas where they could have a safe, decent life.

Donovan had reached the top of the street where the trail up the mountain began. On the pretext of catching his breath, he paused to look back on the slumbering town— slumbering except for the gaudy lights of the Crimson Belle, which the avaricious Smitty would likely keep burning till the last customer had staggered out the door.

Even at a distance, the place was a tawdry beacon in the spring night, beckoning him where he could not go. He had put Sarah out of his heart and his life. To weaken, to see her again, would be like slashing a hornet's nest to release a swarm of pain that would never heal.

The sound of the piano, clunking out a tinny rendition of "Lorena," floated up the street on the dark wind, stirring images in Donovan's memory. Lydia, laughing behind her mauve lace fan; Sarah, holding Varina's newborn son to the lamplight. Lydia, flirting roguishly over a crystal wineglass; Sarah, bruised, shorn and feverish, clinging to him in the darkness like a terrified child.

Lydia.

Sarah.

Who was she now?

Donovan's pulse skipped erratically. He could go back— the lights were still on, and Faye would let him in. This time he would be completely honest with Sarah. He would open his heart, bare his emotions, and maybe this time she would understand. She could join him in Kansas, they could make a new start—

But he was pushing himself over the edge now. There was no hope for anything between Sarah and himself. The past was too close, too devastating for them both. Sarah did not want him. And even if she were willing, it would come to no good in the end. Once the first burst of passion faded, there would be nothing left between them but anger and distrust.

Swallowing the hardness in his throat, Donovan turned and strode up the trail as swiftly as his long legs would carry him. The small-leafed aspens whipped his face as he passed. His boots spat mud and gravel as he willed a wall to rear itself behind him—a wall to shut out the memory of her face, her voice and the baby-soft warmth of her flesh against his own.

A hundred yards shy of the cabin, he paused to calm himself. He could no longer see the lights or hear the piano, but he knew she was back there. He could almost feel her, alone in her sad little room above Smitty's with Lord knows what going on through the walls. It was no place for a woman like Sarah Parker.

He could only hope that soon she would be strong enough to fly away, leaving them both in peace. And he could only hope that one day, in some distant place, Sarah would find what she was looking for.

The wind from the peaks was sweet and cold. It rippled his hair back from his face, chilling the wetness in his eyes as he lingered facing the gulch.

Goodbye, Sarah, he thought. *Good luck and Godspeed.*

Sarah sat on the edge of the bed, facing the window and wishing for magic eyes to see through the velvet drapes to the sunlit day outside. The wine red darkness that cloaked her days had been bearable enough while she was too weak to do anything but eat and sleep. Now, however, with her strength returning, the little room had become an upstairs dungeon, and she its prisoner.

From the room next door, Greta's breathy afternoon
snores reverberated through the paper-thin wall. Sarah
willed her ears to block out the sound. The three women
had saved her life, she reminded herself, and they had been
more than kind to her. It wasn't their fault she'd begun to
pace and snap like a caged animal. It wasn't their fault that
her life had been reduced to counting the days, hours and
minutes until her release. But Sarah had been busy all her
life, until now. Here, in this dim little room, the long hours
of idleness had become slow torture, and she was beginning to crumble under the strain.

The isolation and the darkness were trying enough. But
it was the memories—lost times and faces, crowding in on
her mind with nothing to keep them at bay—that were
edging her toward the brink. Any unguarded moment
would be enough to summon her father, his black brows
knotted in a thunderous scowl. Or her mother, a pale
shadow who had never spoken her own mind. Or Reginald
Buckley, his hat rakishly tilted, his coffee-colored eyes
twinkling with cruel, secret jokes.

Sometimes it was Richmond that came back to haunt her.
Then she saw the stoic black faces of the servants who had
been her comrades. She saw Virgil and all the other spir-
ited young men who had marched off to die.

And she saw Donovan. Donovan most of all.

And almost anything was less painful than thinking
about Donovan.

Jerking at the sash of her robe, Sarah pushed herself to
her feet and began pacing the length of the mud-stained
Persian rug. Yesterday, without raising her voice above a
whisper, she had managed to recite all of Ophelia's lines
from *Hamlet*. Today she felt darker, more like Lady Macbeth, or perhaps Medea.

It was urgent that she leave, Sarah realized. She was far
from strong, but for everyone's sake, she needed to get out
of this place. Later, when Faye came in with her supper, she
would ask again. Maybe this time . . .

The gilded clock on the dresser caught her passing gaze. Twenty-five minutes to three, according to the little brass hands. Twenty-five minutes until the worst time of the day, when the children finished their classwork and came laughing and skipping up the street, directly under her window.

The discovery that Eudora Cahill had taken charge of her school had stung Sarah like a whiplash. She had tried to convince herself that it was for the best, that at least the children would continue to learn. But from Eudora! It was more than she could stand. And when her former students came trooping up the street after school, their familiar voices floating upward through the faded velvet curtains, Sarah's heart ached.

A distraction—that was what she needed today. For the first time, Sarah's restless gaze fell on the wardrobe that had held poor Marie's clothes. A bit of exploring would pass the time, she thought. Maybe it would even help take her mind off her students.

And Donovan.

The carved doors proved to be locked when she tugged the knobs, but a minute's rummaging in the dresser drawers produced the key. Sarah felt a refreshing prickle of interest as she turned it in the lock. Marie's slim, narrow-boned stature had been much like her own. If the clothes were still inside, maybe she could liven up her solitary theatrical performances with a costume or two.

The doors stuck for an instant, then swung open, releasing the poignant scent of Marie's cologne into the room. Lilac and gardenia—Sarah's throat tightened as the fragrance touched a freshet of bittersweet memories. Tears stung her eyes, and for the space of a heartbeat she resolved to close the doors again and walk away. But Marie was gone, she reminded herself. The clothes had no owner now. And it wasn't as if she planned to take any of the dresses. She was only going to borrow them.

Steeling herself, Sarah began sliding the padded hangers along the rod, examining one gown, then another. The dresses were in surprisingly good condition. Some of them were expensive, even lavish, with matching shoes tucked into tissue-lined boxes along the back of the wardrobe. Marie had been a beautiful girl before her illness, and it was evident that at least one of her admirers had been wealthy and generous.

On the wardrobe's overhead shelf, Sarah found an unlocked jewelry chest, but it contained only gaudy trinkets. If Marie had owned any valuable pieces, she had evidently pawned or sold them. That, or the box had been pillaged.

Feeling like a guilty invader, Sarah replaced the velvet-covered box on its shelf. The clothes were of more interest to her in any case, even the shoes, which looked as if they might fit her.

Almost before she knew it, she was pulling dresses out of the wardrobe and flinging them on the bed. In the open, they were even more elegant than she had guessed. Even as Lydia Taggart, she had not owned such lavish gowns.

Her favorite was fashioned of emerald green silk bombazine, edged with bands of matching velvet ribbon that converged in a cascade of ruffles down the back of the skirt. When Sarah stood before the mirror, clasping the dress to her shoulders, she saw that the color brought out the silver in her eyes and lent a subtle glow to her pale, thin face.

She hadn't really intended to try the dress on. But suddenly she found herself rummaging shamelessly through the drawers in search of underclothes and stockings, all of which she found clean and in good condition. The drawers, camisole and petticoat were of fine spun batiste, delicately made, soft as peach down against her skin.

Only when she was drawing the corset laces did Sarah realize how much weight she had lost. Her waist had always been slim. Now, with little more than a tug, it became hand-span size below the gaunt frame of her rib cage.

Her hipbones jutted beneath the gathered flare of the pet-ticoat—a stranger's body, almost, in a stranger's clothes.

The dress came next. Holding her breath, she lifted the rich green silk and worked it over her head. The sensuous fabric enfolded her, sliding like perfumed water over her skin, slipping down the curves of her body to settle effort-lessly into place.

As she reached behind her back to work the long row of buttons, Sarah realized her hands were trembling. Some-thing about the gown, about wearing it, was vaguely dis-turbing, like opening a door into an unfamiliar room.

Fully dressed now, she stepped hesitantly in front of the full-length mirror that was mounted on the inside of one wardrobe door. What she saw brought a startled gasp to her lips.

Sarah had acted out many roles in her stage career, and more than one role in the real world. She knew how to change her hair, her clothes, her makeup, her voice and gestures to fit any part she wished to play.

But reflected in the glass, framed by its cheap gilt bor-der, was a complete stranger, a woman she had never seen before in her life.

Heart skittering nervously, she ventured a step back-ward to survey the full effect. Zoe had taken a razor to Sarah's cropped hair to even its scraggly length. The tou-sled curls that remained outlined her face in elfin spikes, making her eyes look as large and luminous as a cat's.

The gown itself was cut daringly low at the neck, its tight-fitting bodice thrusting the tops of her breasts into plain view. From the shoulders, which were accented by velvet bows, the dress tapered downward to her impossibly tiny waist. The fit was so close, Sarah realized, that if she had tried on the dress before her illness, it would have been too tight.

But it wasn't the dress, or even the hair that had struck her so sharply. It was what she saw in her own face. She was as gaunt as a cougar after a hard winter, her mouth hard, her eyes wary, almost feral.

What had become of her? Sarah asked herself. Where was her softness? Where was her innocence? Her trust?

Repelled yet strangely intrigued, she leaned closer to the glass. What would Donovan think if he could see her now? she wondered. What would he say?

But what did it matter? She would never see Donovan again.

Detaching her emotions, she studied the effect of the gown. One thing was missing—jewelry. In Marie's velvet case, she had noticed a citrine pendant with matching ear-bobs, not valuable enough to have been pawned or taken, but elegant in their own glittery way. Fishing the baubles out of the box, she held them up to the mirror. Yes, they would do.

She had clasped the thin, gold chain around her throat and was threading the second ear-bob when the door opened and Faye came hurrying into the room.

"My stars, child!" she exclaimed, looking Sarah swiftly up and down. "You could take up whorin' and make enough money to buy this whole damned stiff-necked town!"

The old Sarah Parker might have blushed at such a plain-spoken comment. Now, however, Sarah's only reaction was to notice that Faye looked drawn and agitated.

"What is it?" she asked.

"Jist heard somethin'." Faye sank down on the edge of the bed. "Deputy feller's downstairs in the saloon. Says some galoots robbed the bank in Central City an' murdered a teller. Three of 'em. Buzzards took the old mountain road outa town, he says. The sheriff expects they'll double back and light out for Denver, but there's a chance they might be headed this way."

"He came alone?"

"Damn near killed his horse gittin' up the main road. The sheriff is formin' up a posse in Central City, but they'll be takin' the Denver road. Just in case they guessed wrong, the sheriff sent this purty young deputy feller up here to warn us. I guess he's hopin' to git a bunch of men together and form a second posse."

"In this town?" Sarah shook her head disparagingly. Miner's Gulch, with its scattered cabins and indifferent citizens, would be a frustrating place to try to raise a posse. She did not envy the deputy his job.

She turned and walked toward the window, the sensuous green silk rustling with each swing of her legs. "Let's just hope the robbers are headed someplace else," she said, fighting the temptation to part the curtains, peer outside and run the risk of being seen. "Where's the deputy now?"

"Still downstairs havin' a drink, I reckon. He come a long way, an' he's got a mighty big thirst. Sent Pete Ainsworth off to spread the word. Ainsworth!" Faye gave a derisive snort. "Little wart'll prob'ly stumble over a whiskey bottle an' that'll be the end of it! He shoulda—"

"Faye, be still a minute!" Sarah hissed. "I think I hear something!"

She pressed toward the window, ear to the curtain. From the hitching rail out front, the nervous whinny of a single horse—the deputy's, she calculated—quivered on the afternoon air.

Faye stirred restlessly. "That's just—"

"Shh!" Sarah strained harder against the glass. Her breath caught as she heard, faintly, a chorus of answering nickers from the direction of the overgrown trail that had once been the only road to Central City.

"Horses," she whispered. "It could be them. Get Greta and Zoe."

Faye lumbered to her feet. "I can wake Greta, all right. But Zoe's busy. Got a customer what won't take kindly to bein' interrupted."

"Interrupted for what?" Greta stood in the doorway, rubbing her kohl-smeared eyes. "*Donnerwetter*, can't a hardworking woman get any sleep? *Was ist denn los?*"

"Shut up and get over here," Faye snapped. "You can help Miss Sarah keep a lookout whilst I hightail it downstairs and warn that purty young deputy feller!" She strode toward the door, yanking Greta inside as she passed.

"Come on, Greta!" Sarah beckoned urgently. "Hurry! I need you to look outside and tell me what you see!"

Greta ambled across the carpet, muttering under her breath. Her eyebrows shot upward as she noticed Sarah's appearance.

"*Ach*—" she began, but Sarah's finger, pressing her lips, warned her into silence. While Sarah flattened herself against the side of the window, Greta obligingly parted the curtains and assumed a casual posture on the edge of the wide sill.

"I see three men on horseback, coming up the far end of the street," she said in a low voice. "Riding slow. Wearing guns. *Ach,* I don't like this. They look like bad men, 'specially the big one in front."

"Let me see—" Risking the chance, Sarah edged closer to the window, and carefully pushed aside the outer edge of the drape. Through the narrow crack of light, she could see the three riders, moving grimly closer. People in the street were edging quietly out of their way. Either Pete Ainsworth had already done his job, or they knew trouble when they saw it.

Faye had slipped back into the room. "Deputy says he'll be ready for the sons of bitches," she reported. "But 'less'n he can take 'em by surprise, the boy ain't got no chance a'tall. I tried to git him to light out the back an leave 'em be, but the young'un's got more pride than sense." She tugged at Greta's elbow. "You git outa that window, now, gal, and keep low! There's liable to be shootin'!"

Greta rolled inward, closing the drapes behind her as she sank to the floor. Sarah, however, remained where she was, peering intently out through the side of the curtain as the three riders grew larger in her vision. They were moving at a cautious pace now, but it was plain to see they'd been riding hard. Their horses were lathered and heaving. Their hats were jammed hard on their heads. The big man in the lead had a rifle slung across his saddle.

Fear formed a cold ball in Sarah's stomach as she watched them come. Why hadn't they kept to the road? she wondered. What would they want in this run-down little backwater of a town? Supplies? Shelter? A chance to do more devilry?

She thought of the callow young deputy who waited below, his courage braced with Smitty's rotgut whiskey. She could only pray that he'd rethought Faye's advice and crept out the back. No lone man would have a chance against these three. They looked to be seasoned fighters, ruthless, hard and desperate. The one big man alone would be too much for—

Sarah stifled a gasp as the realization struck her. The man in the lead—she knew him!

Her hand clutched the curtain as her mind leafed back through the years. Richmond—yes, she remembered now. He'd been an enlisted man, serving in the same Virginia regiment as Virgil and Donovan. A surly fellow, from the little she'd known of him. A drinker and a brawler who'd seemed at odds with the the whole world.

Unbidden, his name slipped into place. Dooley, it was. Corporal Simeon Dooley.

"Come on back and git down!" Faye tugged insistently at Sarah's skirt. "I seen gunfights in this place afore. Walls is so thin, the bullets whiz right through 'em! We'd best crawl behind the bed, afore things really git hot out there!"

"But there's got to be something we can do!" Sarah clung to her place, watching helplessly as the grim trio approached the saloon.

"Child, there ain't nothin' none of us can do 'cept git out of the way! Come on, now!"

"Wait—" Sarah froze, transfixed with sudden horror as the familiar sound reached her ears—the laughing, teasing babble of young voices, coming up the alley from the back of Satterlee's store.

"No," she whispered. "Please, God, no! The children!"

Chapter Eleven

Sarah could see her students now. They had come out of the alley and were fanning into the street, ignoring the three men on horseback who had pulled up even with the saloon and begun to dismount.

There was no time to think, only to act.

Pivoting like a whirlwind, Sarah seized the low wooden bench from its place in front of the dresser. Before Faye or Greta could stop her, she lunged for the window and, with all her strength, drove the bench's four legs into the panes. Glass shattered, exploding outward as the sash splintered loose from the frame.

"Children! Run!" she screamed into the cold, spring air. "Run for cover!"

Then all pandemonium broke loose.

The first shots exploded from inside the saloon as the green young deputy began firing wildly into the street. Scrambling for cover, the bank robbers returned a few cautious gunshots. The panic-stricken youngsters scattered like chickens, some racing back down the alley, some diving for the shelter of an abandoned wagon, some—a few of the younger ones—frozen in place, too terrified to move. Sarah gripped the frame of the broken window, her heart convulsing with each shot as she silently prayed that none of them would be hit.

Then, as suddenly as it had begun, the gunfire from the saloon stopped. Either the deputy had become aware of the children, or he had simply run out of bullets.

Simeon Dooley had wheeled out of range and dismounted at the first shot. He crouched behind his horse, taking no more than an instant to size up the situation as he shouted to his cohorts to hold their fire.

"Grab them damned kids!" he bellowed. "Move it! We're goin' in!"

The handful of smaller children who'd huddled together on the boardwalk were the most vulnerable. Saucer-eyed with fear, they submitted mutely as the gunmen rounded them up and marched them in a cluster toward the Crimson Belle's front entrance. Dooley, limping, had moved in close and stood flattened against the wall outside the open double doors, the cocked rifle clasped in one massive hand. The saddlebags from his horse were flung over one shoulder, and there was a dirty rag crudely knotted around his left thigh.

"Listen good in there!" he shouted. "We've collected a bunch of young'uns out here, and we're bringin' 'em inside! 'Less'n you want to see these kids hurt bad, you'd better throw your shootin' irons in the middle of the floor! All of 'em!"

A silence like the slow tick of death hung over the street. Then, from inside the saloon came the heavy, metallic clatter of guns hitting the worn plank floor.

"That all of 'em?" Dooley shouted into the stillness that followed.

"That's all, mister!" The answering voice was youthful and scared. "Let them young'uns go, now, and you can ride out of here in peace."

"Can we, now?" Dooley's laughter boomed up and down the street. "Looks to me like we got some talkin' to do first!"

"Come on inside, then," the shaky young voice called out. "Nobody's armed in here. Just please, mister, don't hurt them kids!"

Sarah clung to the open window, heedless of outside eyes, as the outlaws funneled the little band of children into the saloon. Dooley walked in their midst, the cocked rifle balanced loosely between his hands. As he disappeared into the doorway, the long gun barked once, then two times more.

The silenced that followed was as black as the grave.

Sarah turned away from the window, choking on her own horror. Greta was sobbing openly. Faye's complexion was putty gray beneath her rouge.

"We got to do somethin'," she gasped.

Sarah nodded, racking her shock-befuddled brain for some kind of logical plan. See to the children, that was the most urgent priority. After that—

But she could not think beyond the children. She could not carry out any kind of intelligent scheme until she knew whether they were safe, or even alive.

Crouching low in the clinging emerald silk gown, she drew the two women close. "Listen to me," she whispered. "I've got to be the one to go down there first. I know the big man, the leader, and I might be able to talk with him—"

"Ach, nein!" Greta interrupted. "He'll shoot you! He'll shoot us all!"

"Hush, now." Sarah gripped Greta's plump arm. "We can't think of our own safety. Not at a time like this, with those children downstairs! But I'm going to need your help."

"Tell us what to do." Faye's hands trembled, but her deep voice was resolute.

"Just this," Sarah hissed. "Whatever I say down there, whatever I tell those men, you back me up and go along with it as if it were true. Understand?"

"*Ja.*" Greta wiped her eyes. "And we tell Zoe to do the same."

Sarah had forgotten Zoe and her customer, but this was no time to worry about them. "I'm going downstairs now," she said. "Stay out of sight until I tell you it's safe. If you hear more shooting..." She paused, battling for composure. "I can't tell you what to do. But if anything happens to me, somebody's got to save those children!"

Grim-faced, Faye and Greta nodded in unison. Swiftly then, before her courage could fade, Sarah scrambled to her feet and hurried from the room.

The open stairway into the saloon descended from a secluded landing at the end of the upstairs hall. From the landing, it was possible to stand and look down on the main floor, hidden from eyes below.

Sarah held her breath as she stepped out of the upper hallway and paused at the top of the stairs. For the first few heartbeats, she stared straight ahead, steeling herself against what she was about to see. Slowly, by degrees, she forced her eyes to look down, down into the jaws of the nightmare.

The young deputy—at least Sarah assumed it was he—sprawled facedown on the floorboards a half-dozen paces from the front door, drilled point-blank through the chest.

Back of the bar, Smitty lay dead in a pool of his own blood. From behind wire-rimmed spectacles that were still in place, his lifeless eyes stared up at the crystal chandelier on the ceiling. In one open hand lay the tiny derringer he'd always kept hidden in his boot.

George, the black piano player, was still alive but bleeding badly from the shoulder. He lay curled against the foot of his instrument, grimacing as he tried to stop the wound with his handkerchief.

The children—Sarah's frantic gaze found them in a far corner, guarded by one of the desperadoes. She counted five of them, including Mattie Ormes's boy, Isaac, and—Sarah's heart contracted—Varina's little redheaded Katy.

None of them appeared to be hurt, thank heaven, but all of them were white with shock. They huddled together like driven lambs, some sniffling, but none daring to cry out loud.

Simeon Dooley sat alone at a poker table, facing the bar and sucking morosely at a bottle of whiskey. His rifle and saddlebags lay flat on the table in front of him. The third man was nowhere in sight.

For a long, awful moment, Sarah gazed out over the horror, willing herself to blot the dead bodies from her vision and see only the children. Closing her eyes, she took three long, deep breaths, an exercise she had always done before walking onstage. When she made her move, there could be no hesitation. There could be not a flicker of fear or she and the little ones would be lost.

Opening her eyes again, she fixed her face in a jaded smile and glided down the stairs. Sarah Parker was about to give the most dangerous performance of her life.

As she came into full view, Dooley glanced up and saw her. His hand darted to the rifle as his upper lip curled in an ugly snarl. "What the devil—?"

Sarah forced her smile to broaden. "Why, as I live and breathe!" she exclaimed gaily. "If it isn't Corporal Simeon Dooley!"

Dooley's jaw sagged. His eyes rounded in puzzled surprise as he found his voice again.

"Listen, lady, I don't—"

"You don't remember me?" Sarah's laughter jangled like Gypsy brass. "Why, Corporal, I'm disappointed—no, *crushed* that you could possibly forget!" She reached the bottom of the stairs and swaggered over to his table, where she stood with one outthrust hip, leering into Dooley's nervous face.

"It's Lydia, you big, bucking stallion! Lydia Taggart, and by the way, you owe me a bartender!"

Donovan balanced himself on the slope of the roof, one hand bracing the nail, the other swinging the hammer. He was finally becoming a fair carpenter. It had taken some mistakes and a few crushed fingers, but by now he could drive nails and miter corners with the best of them. Another couple of days, and the spare room on Varina's cabin would be finished.

Lanny Hanks, the young builder he'd hired, had taken another job in Central City last week. Thanks to what he'd learned, however, Donovan was managing fine on his own. His only aid had come from Jamie Trenoweth, who had spent half a day hammering shingles and helping cut a connecting doorway into the main part of the cabin.

Jamie's overnight visit had been a rousing success, Donovan reflected as he snubbed another shingle into line. Not only had Jamie looked over the claim and pronounced it "a promisin' sweet piece o' ground," but his presence had been like a spring tonic for the whole family.

The Cornishman had ridden up by muleback, bringing a bag of precious sugar for Varina and trinkets for each of the children. His stories over dinner had kept the whole family in stitches. By bedtime, the youngsters had been climbing all over his lap, clamoring to hear more.

The next morning, while Jamie mounted the roof to help with the shingles, Varina had baked up a tasty batch of sugar cookies and presented him with a sackful to take home.

Varina had looked pretty that day, Donovan recalled. She'd put on a fresh calico dress and a fresh apron, and tied back her curly hair with a band of thin, black velvet. Her cheeks had bloomed with the first flush of color he'd seen in her face since Charlie's death.

She would be in mourning for months to come, Donovan reminded himself. All the same, his sister was still a young woman, warm, loving and vibrant. If anyone on earth deserved a second chance at happiness—

But he was getting ahead of himself. After the roof was finished and the ore samples back from the assay office, after everything possible had been done to set up a secure future for Varina and her children, maybe then there'd be time to think about matchmaking.

Donovan paused in his hammering to move the pack of shingles along the roof peak. From the kitchen he could hear, faintly, the sound of Varina humming as she snuggled the baby with one arm and stirred a pot of beans with the other. Something tugged at his heart as he remembered the night Sarah Parker had risked exposure to come and deliver little Charlie. If Varina was singing now, if she stood on the threshold of a happy new life, he had Sarah to thank for it.

But he could not get started on Sarah now. He could not allow himself to sink into the morass of wanting her again. He had put her out of his life when he'd left her at the Crimson Belle. One of these nights—and Donovan did not even want to know when—she would be gone for good.

He was shifting up to the last row of shingles when a flash of bright color caught his eye through the aspens. That would be his nieces coming home from school, he reckoned. Sarah had always conducted class in the mornings. Eudora, however, preferred afternoons, and most days the girls barely got home in time to help with supper.

Resting on his knees, he watched the small red-orange patch bobbing closer. Before he left Miner's Gulch, he resolved, he would talk Varina into letting him buy new coats for the children. Those sad little piecework creations of hers weren't fit for—

Donovan went cold as the realization slammed into him. Only one of the girls was coming up the path, flying through the aspens like a panic-stricken squirrel.

Brown hair. It was Annie.

He was off the roof by the time she burst out of the trees. She was sobbing, her lungs so spent that she could only gasp as he caught her in his arms.

"What is it?" he said hoarsely, not wanting Varina to hear until he knew. "Where's your sister?"

Annie's eyes were almost swollen shut from crying. "They—they got her!"

"Who?" Donovan strained to keep from gripping her thin shoulders too roughly. "Slow down and breathe, Annie. Who's got her?"

"Men—bad men with guns! They got Katy and Isaac and Molly Sue and—" She broke into hiccuping sobs again.

He caught her close, feeling her small rabbit heart pounding through her ribs. A sick, cold fear had crept over him, paralyzing in its weight. He struggled to throw it off, to freeze his emotions until he could act.

"Speak slowly now," he said, bracing Annie at arm's length. "Tell me everything from the beginning."

Annie snuffed noisily, her bony little frame pushing against his hands. "We came out of the alley after school, and there were these three men. On horses. Then... everything happened so fast, Uncle Donovan. We heard a window breaking and a voice—a lady's—screaming for us all to run. Somebody started shooting. I ran—" She was shaking now, losing her hard-won control. "I thought Katy was with me. But she wasn't. And when—when I looked back, the men had her and Isaac and Molly and—"

Annie's small, spent body sagged in Donovan's arms as she dissolved in tears. "I should've grabbed her hand! I should've looked out for her—"

Donovan rubbed the sharp little shoulder blades, biting back his own anguish. He knew exactly what Annie was feeling. He hadn't looked out for Virgil, either.

"It can't be helped now, Annie," he murmured. "Tell me where the man took Katy and the others. I'll go after them and get them back. I promise."

"The men—they took them into Smitty's. There was shooting. I—I'm scared, Uncle Donovan. What if they killed her?"

"Hush!" Donovan gave her a quick, hard hug and let her go. "You've got to be a brave girl, now, and take care of your mother and Samuel and little Charlie while I'm gone, understand?''

Annie nodded mutely, biting her lip.

"Come on, now." They walked into the house, where Varina waited white-faced and silent, as if she already knew. Donovan climbed to the loft, tugged the hefty Griswold and Gunnison pistol from its hiding place under a pile of quilts, slid six bullets into the revolving cylinder and slapped the gun belt around his hips.

In the kitchen, Varina huddled with Annie and Samuel and the baby, holding them so tightly against her that her fingers furrowed into their flesh. Only her eyes spoke.

"Take care of each other," Donovan said, reaching for the door. "I'll be back with Katy. That's a promise."

He strode across the clearing, breaking into an uneven run at the edge of the trees. His mind churned over what he'd been told as he pounded down the zigzag trail. Bad men with guns, Annie had said. Probably on the run from the law. Probably holding the children hostage. He could only pray they would stay put in the saloon for a while. That would afford the best chance of getting the youngsters back safely.

The saloon.

Sarah.

Donovan's heart lurched into his throat as the realization sank home. Unless Sarah had left early, she would be there, at the mercy of the three desperadoes. And from what he knew of Sarah Parker, she would be a tigress defending her cubs. She would give her life, if need be, to protect the children.

He could see down the gulch now, where the moldering town sprawled in the hollows along the creeks that had once washed gold into pans and sluice boxes. The slanting afternoon sunlight glittered on people swarming to the main street, clustering in frightened knots before the saloon. No one would know what to do, he realized. There was no law in Miner's Gulch, no one with the skill to take on three desperate armed men and their precious little hostages.

No one but himself.

Donovan plunged down the trail, praying for time, praying that no one would get excited and start shooting. Praying for the children, and for Sarah.

Sarah's shaking knees would no longer support her weight. She had sunk casually onto the edge of a chair, where she sat with crossed legs, smiling across the table at Simeon Dooley.

"So what are you going to do now?" she asked with a toss of her cropped head. "Who's going to clean up this god-awful mess in my saloon? And what are these damned kids doing in here? I don't like kids. They make me nervous."

Her narrowed eyes slid sideways to the huddled children. Any one of them could call out to her, she realized. Any one of them could give her identity away, forcing her to scramble for a new, less believable story. But the children only clung to each other and stared. Either they did not recognize her or they were too frightened to speak up. The piano player, too, lay still, eyes closed, one hand pressing the kerchief to his bloodied shoulder.

"And what about old George over there?" she snapped, gesturing toward the wounded musician. "I can hire a new bartender anytime, but good piano players don't grow on trees! I want him taken care of!"

Dooley's finger toyed with the trigger of the rifle. Little by little, his puzzled smirk relaxed into an ugly grin. "Miss Lydia Taggart! Ain't you the uppity one! Hell, you was always uppity! A man what wasn't an officer could scarce get the time of day from you! But that didn't stop me from lookin'!"

"Look all you want, Corporal." Sarah recrossed her legs with an enticing swish of dark green silk. "But while you're looking, those two bodies will start smelling up the place.

My piano player will bleed to death, and those blasted kids will start yammering for their mamas. Is that what you want?''

Dooley did not answer. He was leaning back in his chair, his eyes measuring Sarah from head to toe. "You're skinnier than I remember," he growled. "And what the devil happened to your hair?"

"I got sick over the winter. You didn't answer my question."

Dooley made a sudden, snarling lunge toward her, like a bulldog on the end of a chain. "I don't reckon I got to answer nobody's questions, *Miss* Lydia! I just shot two men dead here, and another one back in Central City! There could be a posse on my tail, and I'm gonna need them kids for—*damn!*"

The big man had gone rigid, his eyes riveted on the stairs. Turning to follow his gaze, Sarah saw MacIntyre's bearish form lumbering down the steps. He was fastening his belt awkwardly with his single hand, swaying drunkenly from side to side as he walked.

Zoe's customer.

Looking down on the chaos below him, MacIntyre seemed to see only Sarah, where she sat at the table with Dooley, nerves screaming beneath her glassy mask. At the sight of her, his small, bloodshot eyes narrowed with hatred.

He took a stumbling step toward her. "So you finally found where you belong, you lyin' little Yank—"

A gunshot rang out from the shadows. MacIntyre reeled, spun and pitched forward on his face. As a sickening red stain blossomed over the back of his shirt, the third gunman, a dark, thin, nervous man holding a pistol, stepped calmly out from behind the bar.

"Who else you got up there, the whole damned U.S. Cavalry?" Dooley snarled.

"Just—my girls. Three of them." Sarah had strangled a scream when MacIntyre fell. Now she fought to keep her terror locked up inside her. "That was one of our customers your man just gunned down," she said. "Not exactly what I'd call good business, Mr. Dooley."

"How many back doors to this place?"

"Two." Sarah knew better than to lie when she could so easily be caught. "One off the kitchen. The other off the stairway going down the back."

Dooley nodded at the ferretlike gunman who slithered into the darkness to check out what she'd said. Sarah tried not to look at MacIntyre, who lay sprawled just a scant pace from her chair, alive, still, his breath wheezing in low, anguished gasps. She tried not to look at the children, who might recognize her if she paid them too much attention.

Instead, she focused her gaze on Simeon Dooley, who sat leaning back in his chair, studying her through pain-glazed eyes. One hand balanced the rifle on the edge of the table. The other rested on the saddlebags, which bulged suspiciously with what Sarah guessed to be loot from the robbery.

"What do you want, Simeon Dooley?" she asked. "If you came to this two-bit town looking for a little fun, you've gotten yourself off to one hell of a start."

Dooley neither moved nor answered. His attention seemed to be focused on some inner point of irritation, as if he had a burr in his soul.

"Look," Sarah persisted recklessly. "Tell me what you want, and I'll see that you get it. Just roll these bleeding bodies outside and send these pesky kids home. Then I'll be at your disposal. For a price, of course."

Dooley blanched at her audacity but did not argue the point. "I need a doc," he grunted. "Got hit in Central City. Bullet's deep. I don't aim to get blood poisoning, lose my leg."

"There's no doctor in Miner's Gulch. But I've pulled my share of bullets out of the customers here. You won't get any better help in these parts."

"I'll need vittles and three fresh horses."

"My girls and I can arrange that, as long as you've got the money to pay."

"And can you and your *girls* hold off a posse if it shows up?" Dooley pulled at the bottle, closing his eyes as the cheap whiskey burned down his throat. "Sorry, *Miss* Lydia Taggart, no dice on the young'uns. When it comes to bargaining, kids is worth a hell of a lot more'n whores."

He grimaced, twisting in his chair to ease the pressure on his wounded leg. "So bring 'em down here! Let's see what you got hidin' upstairs!"

"My girls won't do you any harm. Leave them be."

Dooley tilted back his head and gave a long, loud whistle. "Come on, you little bitches! I know you been up there listenin' to everything that's goin' on. Get down here, now!"

There was a stirring overhead. Sarah's throat clenched as Faye, Greta and Zoe filed meekly down the stairs. She could only hope they'd been listening closely and would back up what she'd told Dooley. If not, anything could happen now.

At the sight of them, Dooley threw back his head and roared with laughter. "Hells bells, how long you ladies been up here, anyway? Since the '59 boom? They got sixteen-year-old whores in Central City now!"

"Leave them alone, Corporal," Sarah said in a low voice. "They're loyal to me, and they do their jobs." She glanced at Zoe, who was hastily knotting her robe, then gave MacIntyre's ribs a contemptuous nudge with the toe of her green silk slipper.

"Why didn't you send that fool out the back way?" she snapped. "How could you let him come blundering down into this mess? Now look what's happened!"

Zoe's dark head drooped contritely. "I'm right sorry, Miz Lydia. We heard the shots, but we thought somebody was just funnin' around. He wanted to see what was goin' on, that's all."

A small weight lifted from the black center of Sarah's fear. It was all right. The girls had heard enough. They would play their parts.

She gave MacIntyre another poke with her shoe. "The big hulk's still alive," she said. "See what you can do for him, Zoe. Greta, you take care of George, over there. Faye, what've we got in the kitchen?"

"Cook's gone home. But there's a big pot o' beans on the stove. Maybe a couple loaves o' bread from yesterday."

Sarah nodded. Riding the wave of her fear, she turned back to Simeon Dooley and forced herself to meet his contemptuous gaze head-on. "Those brats'll start squalling if they don't get some supper," she said. "Your man can guard them just as well in the kitchen as in here."

She was half-afraid Dooley would resist, but she saw that his eyes were glazed with shock from the wound. She could push him a little, Sarah calculated, as long as she didn't push too hard.

"What can it hurt?" she wheedled artfully. "I don't want their empty little bellies on my conscience! If there's anything worse than kids, it's hungry kids!"

A spasm of pain flickered across his face. "That bullet's got to come out soon. After that, I'll need some time to rest up afore we pull out of here."

"I'm not touching you with hungry kids squalling in my ears. It makes me nervous, makes my hands shake. As soon as they're fed and settled someplace out of my sight, then we'll lay you out on the kitchen table and do the job."

"No tricks, Miss Lydia Taggart. I got no scruples about shootin' a woman. Or a young'un, either, for that matter."

"No tricks, Corporal," Sarah answered, knowing he meant it. Some men were mostly bluff and bluster. But Simeon Dooley was a mad dog, capable of anything. She might risk her own life, but she could not risk the children.

"Get on with it, then." He glanced toward Faye. "You, Red! Take them kids in the kitchen an' get 'em some vittles. Spade'll go with to guard the back door and make sure there ain't no funny business. Get along now!"

Dooley jerked his head toward the gunman, a stocky fellow with his hat pulled low, who was guarding the little clutch of frightened children. Sarah caught a glimpse of his face—young and brutish, the dull eyes reflecting a slowness of wit—as he turned to herd his small charges toward the kitchen. The other man, the dark, shadowy ferret, had not yet returned. Sarah imagined him prowling the rooms, checking the back stairs.

She lowered her face as the children filed silently past on Dooley's side of the table. It wouldn't do for one of them to recognize her and cry out. And it wouldn't do for them to see the terror in her eyes.

"Get me another bottle, Miss Lydia," Dooley rasped. "You and me's stayin' right here for the time bein', and I ain't lettin' you out of my sight!"

"Be my guest." Sarah forced a brazen smile, forced her unwilling legs to stand and move as she picked her way among shards of broken glass to retrieve more whiskey from the shelf behind the bar. She kept her gaze carefully averted from the grim spectacle of Smitty sprawled on the floor at the other end. One look, and her tenuous grip on self-control would shatter. She would not be able to stop herself from screaming.

The children were trudging single file into the kitchen. Last in line was Katy Sutton, her small, pinched face ghost white below her bright carrot hair. Sarah turned away from the bar and suddenly found herself looking straight into Katy's round ginger eyes.

The contact was as brief as a heartbeat. But Sarah could not miss the shock of recognition or the frantic questions that flashed in the little girl's stricken gaze. Katy knew. And soon the other children would know, too.

But would they understand? No, Sarah realized bleakly as the kitchen door closed behind them. They were too young. It would be too much to expect of them.

MacIntyre lay where Zoe had dragged him, moaning insensibly as she struggled to stop his bleeding. Alongside the piano, Greta had torn off George's shirt and was using strips of it to wrap his shoulder. With luck, Sarah calculated, Greta would be able to whisper a few words in the piano player's ear—enough, at least, to keep him quiet.

Sick with fear, she strolled back toward the table, lowered herself to the chair and slid the bottle across the varnished surface toward Dooley's waiting hand. "Drink up," she said, flashing a bitter smile. "It's on the house, Corporal!"

By the time Donovan reached the middle of town, a swarm of anxious people had clustered in the early twilight outside the Crimson Belle. A hysterical Eudora Cahill was being calmed by Satterlee, the storekeeper. Mattie Ormes and her husband clung together at the edge of the crowd. Some of the men had brought guns, but for the most part they held the weapons awkwardly, as if they were unsure of what to do with them.

The saloon's double doors were tightly closed, the barest flicker of lamplight showing through the cracks. There were no windows on the first floor, and those on the second were dark and silent.

"Ain't heard nothin' but one shot from in there since they took the kids inside," Widow Harley told Donovan when he asked her. "Pete Ainsworth's claimin' they robbed a bank in Central City. He says the fool posse went the other way, toward Denver. But then, who can hold with what a no-account like Ainsworth says?"

"Where's Ainsworth now?"

"Passed out in some ditch, I'd wager. Anyway, a posse the size of Tennessee couldn't guarantee to get them young'uns out safe. Them three fellers has got us all over a barrel, Mr. Cole.''

Donovan's gaze sifted through the milling crowd, hoping to spot someone who looked as if they might be in charge. Seeing no one suitable, he turned to the old woman again.

"I'm going to scout around back and see what I can find out," he said. "If any kind of posse shows up, can I count on you to tell them where I've gone?"

"That you can, young man."

"Wish me luck, then. And don't let any of those trigger-happy fools shoot me when I come out." Donovan slipped into the shadows without waiting for a reply. His senses sprang to full alert as he crept down the alley. Finding out whether the back door was guarded would be the first order of business. When he knew that, he could plan the next step.

The spruces that screened the back entrance rose thick and black against the twilight sky. Edging along the wall of the alley, Donovan slipped the big Griswold and Gunnison out of its holster, cocked the weapon and, with his free hand, reached low to work a pebble out of the mud. Tensing for action, he flung the small rock into the midst of the trees.

The pebble tumbled through the branches, bouncing and rustling until it struck ground. The silence that followed was broken only by the raucous scolding of an awakened squirrel.

Sweating now, Donovan eased closer. His fingers found another pebble and tossed it through the trees to strike the closed door.

The sharp thud echoed like a gunshot in the darkness as he waited, his nerves taut and tingling, his thumb riding the hammer of the pistol.

Nothing.

He flung another pebble, a smaller one, just to be sure. Then, when nothing happened, he crept close enough to try the door. To his surprise, he found it unlocked. When he turned the knob it swung inward on its well-greased hinges.

Reminding himself that he'd gotten in much too easily, Donovan checked behind the door. No one was there. Above him, the stairway rose open and empty in the garish mauve lamplight.

He took the stairs in long silent strides, spurred by the awareness that he was unsheltered here, open to gunfire from above or below. At the top he checked each of the rooms. All of them were empty, including the one where he had left Sarah. Donovan stood for an instant in its cool darkness, staring at the open, shattered window.

Breaking glass, Annie had said. *And a woman's voice, shouting for the children to run.*

But there was no trace of Sarah here. The room was in disarray, the dresser drawers pulled open, the contents of the wardrobe strewn on the bed. Fragments of glass glittered on the floor, reflecting the light from the hallway.

She was gone, Donovan surmised. She had taken her meager possessions and left in the night while he slept unaware in his solitary loft. She was gone, as he had so often wished her gone, from the town and from his life.

At least she would be safe, he reminded himself. With luck, she would be on the Denver stage by now, headed for a new life. Sarah was a tough woman. She would do all right for herself. But he would never see her again.

Turning his back on the pain, he slipped out into the hallway again, the pistol a cold weight in his hand. He had checked all the upstairs rooms and found them empty. Nothing remained but the stairs that led down into the saloon.

Silent as a mountain cat, he moved out onto the secluded landing. In the lamplight that flickered below, he could see the saloon keeper sprawled behind the bar and another man, a stranger, lying dead a few paces short of the front door.

He could see the round, empty tables, and one, near the bar, where a man and a woman sat together. The man was drinking, his massive shoulders hunched over the bottle. The woman sat leaning back in her chair, legs brazenly crossed to show her slender ankles. And she was laughing, laughing boisterously at something the man had said.

It was like looking down into a scene from hell.

Still hoping to see the children, Donovan inched closer. He recognized the man now. It was Simeon Dooley, the troublemaking ex-corporal he'd seen in Central City. But the woman—

Donovan's breath choked off as she turned her head, revealing her cropped hair and finely chiseled profile.

Sarah.

Donovan felt his insides caving in, as if he'd just been gut-kicked. He was not aware of having made a sound, but something made her stiffen, made her swivel in her chair and look straight in his direction.

His eyes caught the flash of her face in the lamplight and the glint of her jeweled ear-bobs. Then something crunched into the back of his head. The room exploded in sparks that swirled into blackness as he pitched forward and toppled down the stairs.

Chapter Twelve

The lamp was a blur of flame, its light a sickening rainbow before Donovan's eyes as he blinked himself awake. He was lying sideways on the floor, the pain in his head a dark, pulsing throb.

His muscles jerked in a reflexive effort to sit up. Only then did he discover that his hands and feet were bound with twiny ropes that burned into his flesh as he strained against them. His gun was gone, of course, and the belt with it. In a rage of confusion, he sagged back to the floor.

"So you're awake!" Dooley's flat-nosed bulldog face, grotesquely haloed by the lamp, leered down at him. "Remember me, Major? How could you forget, eh?" His laughter stank of chewing tobacco and cheap whiskey. "Looks like we got ourselves a little reunion goin'. Me and you and the proper Widow Taggart. Only she ain't quite so proper now. I wouldn't exactly call owning a bar and whorehouse a ladylike profession, would you, Lydia?"

Lydia.

The name slammed like a hammer blow to Donovan's aching head. Sarah, it seemed, was playing her own games. She was Lydia Taggart again, and she had taken advantage of Smitty's murder to claim the place as her own. That much was self-evident, but not her reasons.

"Where are the children?" he muttered.

"The kids ain't your problem, Major. In fact, if I was you, I'd be a lot more more worried about my own skin. You rode me damned hard in that regiment. And all the time I was diggin' trenches and standin' extra duty, I swore I'd get back at you one day. I swore I'd get you real good."

"You were always making trouble, Dooley. Any punishment you took, you brought on your own head."

One big ham of a hand shot down to clutch Donovan's shirt and jerk him off the floor. "You hear me good, Major! The war's over! Corporal Dooley's callin' the shots now, and it's gonna be the greatest pleasure of my life to watch you squirm before you die!"

"Dooley, you're out of your mind." It was Sarah who spoke. Only it wasn't Sarah's voice. It wasn't even Lydia Taggart's voice. It was the voice of a woman so jaded by life that she no longer seemed to care about things like decency or dignity.

"The major, here, is a lawman," she said. "A full-fledged sheriff out of Kiowa County, Kansas. If that posse catches up with you, he'll be worth more as a hostage than as a corpse."

Dooley let go of Donovan's shirt, releasing him to crash back to the floor. "Hell, who needs another hostage? I already got more kids an' whores than I know what to do with!"

Sarah got out of her chair and walked around to where Donovan could see her green high-heeled slippers below the hem of her skirt. He forced himself to lie still, without looking up at her.

"Kids are more trouble than they're worth," she said in a hard voice. "Let the little brats go. You won't need them now that you've got a real, live sheriff."

Dooley took a long pull on his whiskey bottle. "You sweet on this man, Lydia, honey?"

"Sweet on him?" Sarah's laugh was razor edged. "This high-handed bully did his best to run me out of town! If I weren't afraid of hanging for it, I'd shoot him myself!"

"Now, that could be an amusin' sight." Dooley chuckled under his breath. "But I can't say as I'd trust you that far, Lydia. Besides, shootin' would be too easy on the major here. Maybe I'll let him sweat while I take my time to think up some real entertainment."

He lifted his head and spoke to someone Donovan could not see. "Get the major into a chair and tie him good. I'll deal with him after this damned bullet's out."

Donovan's eyes darted to the dirty, makeshift bandage knotted around Dooley's thigh. Things were beginning to make sense now. Dooley had been shot during the robbery. He couldn't run far with a bullet in his leg, so he'd come through Miner's Gulch for help. The shootings, the children—they'd tumbled into the horror like rocks pulled into an avalanche. Even Sarah—

His thoughts exploded in a burst of nauseating pain as a pointed boot toe crunched into his ribs. Limp with the sudden shock, he had no power to struggle as two wiry arms hoisted him into a nearby chair.

"I wouldn't advise you to put up a fight, Major." Dooley grinned, covering Donovan with the rifle while the invisible hands retied his ropes to the chair. "Cherokee here's just waitin' for an excuse to do somethin' real nasty."

Cherokee. Donovan cursed under his breath as his vision cleared. He knew the cold-blooded half-breed well. In fact, he'd had him in his jail for murder once, and would have hanged him if a slippery lawyer hadn't gotten him off. It was an experience Donovan would never forget.

Cherokee was a man without a name or a soul, his tongue cut out in some long-ago incident that had spawned a hundred stories. He was as silent as snowfall and as vicious as a weasel.

Donovan could only glare helplessly as the half-breed ambled into full view and spat contemptuously on his boots. Fear was an icy ball in his stomach, not only for himself, but for the women and children. When it came to

cruelty, Cherokee possessed the chilling lust of a wolver-
ine. He had no compassion and no conscience.

Dooley threw back his head and laughed as Cherokee
turned away and moved toward the bar, his odd, cat-footed
gait making no sound on the weathered plank floor. While
the half-breed poured himself a drink, Donovan took advantage of his first chance to look around the saloon.

In the back corner, half-hidden by the piano, Greta and
Zoe were tending two wounded men. The black piano
player was sitting up, his back against the wall, eyes closed
with the pain of his bandaged shoulder. The other man—
Donovan shuddered as he recognized MacIntyre—lay flat
on the floor, his breath rasping in and out with a labored,
bubbling sound. Lung shot. Bad news. Donovan had seen
enough of them to know.

Raising his eyes, he forced himself to look directly at
Sarah. She was leaning back in her chair, facing Dooley,
one slim leg crossed over the other. Her fingers toyed in-
differently with an empty glass.

She would not look at him, Donovan knew. Not if she
could avoid it. After all, she had every reason to blame him
for this debacle. If he had not interfered, she would be safe
now. The children, too, would be safe, because, as their
teacher, she would have dismissed school hours before the
robbers appeared.

He studied her profile as she turned in her chair. She appeared drawn and painfully thin, her ordeal mirrored in the
violet shadows beneath her eyes. But even now, Donovan
was struck by her beauty, by the way her hair curled to the
shape of her head like an exquisite little cap, by the fine,
strong curve of her jaw and the swanlike grace of her neck.

But what the devil was the woman up to?

In that first instant, when he'd glimpsed her with Dooley,
he could have sworn she'd gone over to the outlaws to save
her own skin. Even her urgings to let the children go had
been so rough, so cynical that he could not be certain of her
motive. And looking at her now...no, he could not be sure.

He had seen Sarah's talent for playacting, and he knew how convincing she could be. But she had suffered terribly at the hands of people in this town. If she had changed, if she'd become hard and bitter, who could blame her?

Sarah, Lydia, or someone new? Who was she now?

Donovan forced his eyes away from her. No, he concluded, he could not allow himself to trust her. He would have to think and act for himself, to find his own way out of this mess.

Dooley flung his empty bottle against the bar, where it shattered with a crash. "Time to get this damned bullet out," he growled. "I hope the hell you're as good a doc as you say you are, Lydia, old girl, 'cause if anything goes wrong, you'll be a dead woman, understand?"

"It will hurt," Sarah said in a cold, flat voice. "You know that, don't you?"

"Hell, yes." He swung toward the dark man at the bar. "Cherokee! Get them damned kids out of the kitchen. And that old redheaded whore, too. Spade can guard 'em in here. After the bullet's out, we'll figger what to do with the high-an'-mighty Major Cole!"

Cherokee disappeared without a sound. A few seconds later, the five children came trooping out of the kitchen, shepherded by Faye and a squat, youngish gunman Donovan did not recognize.

"Uncle Donovan!"

Donovan's heart stopped as Katy broke from the line and ran to him. Her face was milk white below the red-orange tangle of her hair. Her eyes were swollen pink from weeping as she flung her arms around him.

"Go back, Katy!" he rasped under his breath. "Go back with the others, and do exactly as you're told!"

"But I want to stay with you! Why are you tied up, Uncle Donovan?"

"Go back, Katy!"

Stung by the vehemence in his voice, she flew with a little sob back to the cluster of children. The young gunman maneuvered them into the far corner of the room, Faye with them, and ordered them all to sit on the floor.

Crying openly now, Katy hurled herself into Faye's arms. "I want my uncle Donovan!" she sobbed. "I want him to take me home!"

As Faye soothed the distraught little girl, Simeon Dooley leaned back in his chair, taking in the scene with grim amusement.

"Uncle Donovan, eh?" An evil smile curled his upper lip over his teeth. "This could get interestin', Major. Mighty interestin' indeed."

Where would Smitty have kept forceps?

Sarah rummaged frantically through the kitchen drawers. Surely, she reasoned, a man who ran the only saloon in a town with no regular doctor would have a few emergency medical items on hand.

She could feel icy perspiration beading beneath her dress as she searched. Cherokee, as cold and silent as a snake, leaned against a counter and watched her, one finger testing the hammer of his Colt. He would welcome the excuse to kill her, she sensed. Or to kill Donovan, or even to kill one of the children. She could not allow him that excuse.

The table had been cleared and wiped, and a spare bedsheet torn into wrappings that were more or less clean. Dooley was in the saloon, waiting for word that she was ready. All that remained was for her to find the accursed—

Sarah's knees sagged with relief as her hand closed on a flannel-wrapped bundle in the back of a drawer. She unrolled it to find forceps in two different sizes, a scalpel, needles, thread, scissors, and a small bottle of alcohol.

"Have Mr. Dooley come in," she said. "As soon as these instruments are clean, we can start."

She was using tongs to lift the forceps and scalpel from the boiling water when Dooley hobbled into the kitchen and heaved his body onto the groaning table. He had drunk enough whiskey to put down a bull buffalo, Sarah observed, but he was still awake and alert. When the pain got bad, there would be no keeping him still.

"Go ahead! Get it over with!" he growled. "But I'm warnin' you now, lady, if you want to live through the next hour, no tricks. Cherokee here'd just as soon cut out your gizzard as look at you!"

Sarah forced herself to laugh as she tied a cotton apron over her green silk gown. "Why, I declare, Simeon Dooley, you sound as if you don't trust me!"

"Don't trust no female. Least of all when I got my britches down!" Dooley hooted at his own joke as Sarah approached the table, her instruments laid out on a pewter serving tray.

"All right, Corporal, let's have a look," she said, bracing herself against the revulsion of touching him. "First the bandage, then the pants."

She felt Dooley go rigid as she loosened the blood-soaked knot of the dirty rag that circled his thigh. He flinched as the fabric came stickily away to reveal the ugly purplish mass of the wound through the bullet-torn trousers and long johns.

"Bad?" The word seeped out of him.

"Bad. It's already started to fester. That bullet can't come out soon enough. But there's one problem."

"Problem?" Dooley's head came up.

"Even with the whiskey, you're feeling a lot of pain. And I'll need you perfectly still while I probe the wound. Somebody's got to hold you. One man, maybe even two."

"Cherokee—"

"Cherokee's not big enough. Neither is Spade. You outweigh either of them by at least a hundred pounds." Sarah paused, giving him time to arrive at the obvious conclusion. "You've got to untie Major Cole," she said. "He's the only one strong enough for the job."

Dooley made a choking sound. "Turn Cole loose? Hell, woman, you're crazy!"

"Not as crazy as you might think. The major won't dare try anything. Not while Spade's got a gun on that little carrottopped niece of his."

Sarah held her breath while Dooley deliberated. It wasn't that she'd lied to him. Probing for a bullet was an excruciating business. The pain would make Dooley a wild animal; she would need the strongest man she could find to hold him down.

And it wasn't that she planned to harm the burly ex-corporal. That would pose too much risk to the children. But she needed Donovan, Sarah realized. If nothing else, she needed him for herself. Whatever had happened between them in the past, she needed his strength beside her now or she would crumble and break under the strain.

Simeon Dooley sagged back onto the table, his eyes bloodshot from drink and fatigue. "No," he grunted, "I ain't untyin' no lawman. You're gonna have to do the job by yourself, lady. And Cherokee'll be keepin' his gun on you to make sure you do it proper!"

"All right, then." Sarah unbuckled his belt and slipped off his leather-sheathed knife. "Here." She thrust it between the big man's teeth. "Bite on this. Hard."

In a single motion she seized the waistband of Dooley's trousers and jerked them down to his knees. His teeth clenched on the knife as the matted fabric tore loose from his wound, but otherwise he held admirably still.

"Relax, now." She took the scissors and trimmed away a circle-cut of his long underwear around the ugly wound, then splashed the open area with whiskey to cleanse it. Next she picked up the forceps.

"Now!" she muttered, plunging the tips into the hole where the bullet had entered.

Dooley's breath was a long suck of pain. His leg jerked wildly, forcing Sarah to withdraw the forceps.

"If that bullet stays in, you'll die from blood poisoning," she said calmly.

Dooley swore under his breath. "All right. Get Cole!" He motioned to Cherokee. "But one wrong move, and Little Red's a goner. Make sure he knows that."

"He'll know." Sarah sagged against a cabinet, her legs gone limp beneath her, as the half-breed glided out of the room. She had to be strong, she reminded herself. She could not rest until the children were safe.

Donovan entered the kitchen, rubbing the circulation into his wrists. Sarah's throat went hard as their eyes met across the table. She saw the fear, the soul-chilling anger in his face. Couldn't he see through her mask? Didn't he understand what she was trying to do?

Maybe she had played her part too well.

Breaking away from his painful gaze, she glanced down at Dooley. "Hold him," she said in a flat voice. "Don't let that leg move until I'm finished."

Donovan nodded curtly. "Let me know when you're ready."

Sarah picked up the forceps. "Now!"

Donovan's weight braced Dooley's chest and legs as the probing began. She could feel the shock of pain that surged through the big man's body, but he bit hard on the leather-sheathed knife and did not cry out.

Perspiration trickled down Sarah's face as she dug for the bullet. It was deep, too deep for the smaller forceps to reach. Frustrated, she abandoned them for the larger pair. Dooley's rancid sweat smell made her stomach lurch. She was aware of Cherokee, leaning against a cabinet with the pistol cocked in his hand, waiting like a coiled rattler for the first excuse to strike.

Her head brushed Donovan's arm as she labored over the wound. She could feel the tension in him, the nerves frayed to the snapping point. If only he would give her some sign that he trusted her—a look, a touch. At least she would know they were on the same side.

But Donovan was making every effort to ignore her. Even when she looked straight at him, he stared coldly ahead as if she were invisible, or as if she were someone he had no wish to see.

Why couldn't Donovan have stayed away? she asked herself angrily. Why did he have to be here, complicating everything, including her own emotions? She hadn't asked him to risk his life! She hadn't asked him to come tumbling down the stairs, just when she was gaining some sense of control! And now—but what was the use? Donovan was here, and there was nothing to be done about it.

Forcing his presence to the back of her mind, Sarah bent to the task of finding a lead ball the size of her little fingertip in the purpled mass of Dooley's flesh. If she bungled it, if she slipped and punctured an artery—but no, she had to save the man. Dooley's death would unleash Spade and Cherokee on the children, on them all. Then anything could happen.

As she glanced up to wipe her perspiring face with her sleeve, she noticed that Donovan was bending close to Dooley's ear, his voice a rumbling whisper. Sarah strained to hear as she worked the probe deeper.

"Listen to me, Dooley, I've got a business proposition. But it's just for you, not those two hired freaks of yours."

Dooley's pain-glazed eyes rolled in Donovan's direction. His jaws tightened on the knife. He was in agony, but he was listening.

"I'm finished with the law," Donovan continued. "It's a dirty, rotten, thankless way to earn a living. But I've stumbled onto an idea. One that'll make that bank loot of yours look like pocket change—and I'm willing to take you on as a partner. For a price, of course."

Sarah's hand had fallen still. Catching herself, she swiftly resumed her work.

"Interested?" Donovan quirked a sardonic eyebrow.

Dooley could not answer. His body arched as the forceps touched lead. Grunts of pain exploded past the blade in his teeth.

"Hold him!" Sarah muttered. "I think I've got—"

The knife fell loose as Dooley screamed, an inhuman shriek that ripped out of him, tearing from the core of pain before he passed out and went limp in Donovan's arms.

Sarah stood gazing down at the misshapen lead ball that she gripped between the bloody points of the forceps. Her head felt weightless. Her legs quivered like a newborn colt's. She had done it.

Donovan had let Dooley fall back onto the table. He stepped away, his shoulders heaving from the strain, his eyes staring at the wall. Sarah knew she could not speak to him now. Not with Cherokee lurking so close. But she struggled to reach him with her thoughts.

Do something, Donovan ... look at me, touch my hand, anything to let me know ...

But she could feel her efforts meeting a wall of resistance. It was achingly clear that Donovan wanted nothing to do with her.

"Do you need help dressing the wound?" His voice was coldly guarded.

"No," Sarah murmured. "But unless he wakes up soon, I may need your help getting him off the table."

"He'll wake up in time for that."

"In that case, why don't you go see what you can do for George and MacIntyre?"

Donovan turned without a word and strode out of the kitchen. To Sarah's relief, Cherokee made no effort to stop him. It had become common understanding that as long as Spade held the children at gunpoint, Donovan Cole was as good as bound.

But things could not go on like this, Sarah reflected as she wiped away the blood, bathed the wound in disinfectant and bandaged Dooley's leg. The presence of the three desperadoes was a burning fuse, the inevitable explosion just a matter of time.

At first she'd hoped the resolution might be simpler. She'd hoped that once Dooley's wound was treated and enough supplies rounded up, the outlaws would be on their way. But Donovan's arrival had complicated everything. Dooley hated him, and, from the looks of it, so did Cherokee.

They would not leave until Donovan was dead.

Sarah's eyes shifted to the razor-edged scalpel where it lay on the bloodstained table edge, and she found herself wondering whether she had the strength to kill with it. One well-placed slash, and Dooley would die before even Cherokee could stop her.

But no, she could not commit the act, even for Donovan. She might risk her own life, but she could not risk the children. Somehow, she would have to find another plan.

Dooley was beginning to stir. His mouth twitched. A moan quivered deep in his chest. Very soon he would be awake.

Sarah leaned against a cabinet and closed her eyes for an instant, drawing on the empty well of her own strength. The ordeal was only beginning, she reminded herself. And she could not rest until it was over.

Simeon Dooley sprawled on a mattress that Donovan had lugged down from an upstairs room. The big ex-corporal was fully awake now, but in considerable pain—a pain whose edges he'd dulled with more whiskey than Donovan had ever seen a man swallow in his life. Aside from the stench, the drinking had done little more than worsen Dooley's grizzly bear disposition. It was anybody's guess when he would be ready to ride.

Things were settling down some in the saloon. Donovan had persuaded Dooley to let him drag the two dead men into a cool room off the kitchen, where they wouldn't upset the youngsters so. Greta had been sent outside to relay Dooley's demands for food, ammunition and fresh horses to the crowd that waited outside. Hopefully, the woman would have better sense than to come back.

Cherokee had spelled Spade on guarding the children. He lounged in a chair a stone's toss from the corner where they huddled, his steel-wire body tautly relaxed. Donovan studied him furtively through the slits of his narrowed eyes. Of the three outlaws, it was Cherokee he feared most. Simeon Dooley was a man of volcanic temper and rash judgment, dangerous but predictable. Spade appeared to be dull, mean and slow-witted, a follower of stronger men's orders. But Cherokee . . . his was a reptile's nature, cold and black and unfathomably silent. He could strike with a rattler's speed, and he killed without emotion or remorse.

Cherokee would not hesitate to kill a child.

Or a woman.

All evening, Donovan's eyes had avoided Sarah. He had told himself he mustn't trust her. The sad truth of it was, he couldn't even trust himself. As things stood, he didn't dare give her so much as an open glance. His emotions were too raw, too close to the surface. A single meeting of their eyes would betray everything he felt.

But now, cautiously, his gaze drifted around the saloon to seek her out. He found her kneeling on the floor in her bloodstained apron, helping Zoe dress MacIntyre's awful wound.

MacIntyre, whose hate had nearly destroyed her.

Donovan struggled to distance his feelings as his eyes followed the strong, sure motions of her hands. This was Lydia Taggart, he reminded himself. This was the woman who had coldly gathered information from smitten young officers and relayed it through the lines to Union troops. This was a woman who could lie and betray from behind myriad smiles and voices. She was the last person on earth he ought to trust.

Yet, as he watched Sarah nursing the unconscious MacIntyre, Donovan was struck only by her tenderness, her compassion, and the softly shining light of her courage.

Could he trust her?

Even as he asked himself the question, Donovan realized he had no choice. They were in this trap together, he and Sarah. They were fighting on the same side, for the same cause—to save the children. Whatever his plan, she would have to be part of it. He would have to take her into his confidence. Otherwise they would only find themselves working at cross-purposes.

A ripple of childish laughter, startling in its beauty, burst from the corner of the room. George, the wounded piano player, had volunteered to join the little ones and distract them with a few stories. He was doing his job almost too well, Donovan observed as Dooley, swearing under his breath, hurled an empty bottle toward the group.

"Shut them damned kids up!" he bellowed as the glass shattered harmlessly against a table leg. "Take 'em upstairs or somethin'! Let a man get some rest!"

Sarah glanced up from wrapping a bandage. "Take those little brats up to one of the bedrooms, Faye." Her voice cracked with weariness. "Haul in some extra pillows and blankets and see if you can get them to sleep. We could all use some peace and quiet around here!"

"Go with 'em, Cherokee!" Dooley snapped. "Where the hell is Spade?"

"Gettin' some beans in the kitchen," Faye said. "He told me he was hungry."

Dooley muttered a curse. "Damned fool boy's nothing but a walking belly! Go on, now! Get them kids upstairs!"

Donovan sat rock still as the children trooped past him. Katy's big ginger eyes darted in his direction, but she kept her head high, her small chin thrust bravely ahead. Aching with pride and fear, Donovan sent her a flicker of a smile. Right now, it was all he could do. One wrong move on his part, and Katy would be the first child to die.

Dooley watched the procession trail upstairs, Cherokee bringing up the rear. Only when they were gone did he beckon Donovan slyly over to where he lay.

"This proposition of yours—it better be as good as you say it is, Cole."

"It is." Donovan crouched beside the mattress, forcing himself to pace things slowly. He could bluff well enough when it came to poker, but this was a game he'd never played before, a game where the rules changed as you went along, and the stakes were life and death. The worst of it was, he didn't even know where his plan would lead. It was little more than a diversion, a way of buying time while he searched for a way out of this debacle.

Should he involve Sarah? The question flashed through his mind, but Donovan swiftly realized he had no choice. Sarah was here. She was part of this. There was no way he could *not* involve her.

"How much money have you got in those saddlebags?" he asked Dooley. "Four or five thousand? Ten? Fifteen?"

"I ain't took the time to count."

"No matter." Donovan took his time dangling the bait. "It's pocket change compared to what this would give you. And it's legal. You could go someplace else. Mexico, maybe, or South America. You could change your name and live like a king for the rest of your—"

"Quit stalling and tell me, damn you, Cole!"

"All right." He hesitated, then took the plunge. "But we've got to include my partner in this. Otherwise, it's not going to work."

"Your partner!" Dooley's face had purpled. "Who the devil—?"

Donovan glanced knowingly toward the far end of the room, where Sarah had collapsed in a chair, her shorn, tousled head drooping like a wilted chrysanthemum. She was exhausted, he realized. And now he was about to demand more of her.

"Lydia!" He stage-whispered the name over the distance. She glanced up as if he had struck her with a stone, her eyes wide and startled. "Get down here!" Donovan beckoned with his arm, praying she would understand and play along. "Come on, partner! You and I are about to negotiate some business!"

Chapter Thirteen

Sarah forced herself to rise from the chair and walk slowly toward the two men. Maybe she had fallen asleep—yes, that was it. She was having the strangest nightmare of her life, and it was getting stranger by the minute.

That, or Donovan Cole had lost his mind.

He was beckoning to her now, his expression as guileless as a schoolboy's as he swung a wooden chair away from a nearby table and motioned for her to sit. "Take it easy, partner," he muttered. "You look like you just fell off the back end of a wagon."

Sarah collapsed onto the hard chair, so frayed that even breathing seemed too much effort, let alone talking. She had hoped for some sign of trust from Donovan, but this high-handed summons, coming so abruptly, was more than she was prepared to deal with. How could she play along with his game when she didn't even know the rules?

"How's MacIntyre?" Donovan glanced up at her from the floor, where he had resettled himself near Dooley. His casual tone did not match the snapping tension in his eyes.

"It's too soon to tell. He's a big, tough man, but lung shots are always nasty, and he's lost a lot of blood." Sarah forced her mouth to form the answer, forced her fatigue-dulled mind back to full alertness as Donovan impaled her with his gaze. Whatever his plan, she had no choice except to go along with it. But until she understood her own role, she would have to feel her way from one moment to the next.

Dooley shot a contemptuous glance in MacIntyre's direction. "Huh! Cherokee don't usually miss shots like that. I shoulda finished the big son of a bitch off myself."

Sarah willed a cold chill to pass unseen beneath her careless mask. "Leave him be," she said. "We've had enough killing for one night."

She glanced back to where MacIntyre lay with his head in Zoe's lap. Dressing his wound, even touching him, had not been easy at first. Her whole being had revolted at the memory of that awful night. Her hands had trembled so violently that she could scarcely do the work. But as the minutes ticked by, she had come to see only the wounded body, only a person who needed her help.

"And how are you faring, Corporal?" She cast a jaded smile in Dooley's direction. "That bullet was so deep it missed shattering your thighbone by a finger's breadth. You're lucky it didn't hit an artery."

Simeon Dooley shot her an alcoholic glare. "Hurts like hell," he growled.

"And you, *partner*—" She nudged Donovan's leg with the toe of her shoe. "You said something about negotiating a little business with the corporal, here. Personally, I'd like to hear more. Go on, I'll just listen."

Donovan's eyes flashed a tentative warmth into hers, but only for an instant. The face he turned back to Dooley was a mask of indifference.

"As I was about to explain, Corporal, I've been Lydia's silent partner in this saloon for as long as she's owned it ... and in a few other things, as well."

Other things ... Sarah swallowed hard as Donovan's hand found the arch of her foot. His index finger stroked a simmering path around her silk-stockinged ankle, tracing the circle of each bone, then gliding lightly up the sensitive curve of her inner calf.

Her breath went ragged at his touch. Oh, she knew what he was doing. The sensual gesture was for show, nothing more. It was just an act, part of some elaborate ruse to befuddle Simeon Dooley. All the same, she could do nothing to quell the sensations that quivered up her leg, triggering surges of warm wetness from the intimate core of her body. Her mouth softened, lips parting in a soundless moan.

Even a man as drunk as Dooley could not have missed her response. "Hell, Lydia, I thought you said you didn't like him," he mumbled.

"So, I lied." Sarah affected a shrug and an easy laugh. "Let's hear what my silent partner has to say."

Donovan's hand had paused mercifully at Sarah's knee. For an agonizing moment it lingered. Then, withdrawing the torture, he turned back to where Dooley sprawled on the mattress. "All right, then." He spoke in a conspiratorial whisper. "Lydia and I bought this saloon last fall. The place was pretty run-down, but it was cheap, and I figured that when I quit the law in Kansas, I could always come back here and keep an eye on my widowed sister."

"So get to the point, Cole." Dooley upended his whiskey bottle to let the last drops trickle down his throat.

"Just this." Donovan edged closer, dropping his voice. "I learned something last week, something that could make this place worth a hundred times more than either of us ever dreamed, and I'm willing to let you in on it."

Dooley's small, pale eyes narrowed greedily. "This damn well better be good, Major. If you're pullin' my leg—"

"You'll know I'm not when you hear this. You were in Central City. You know about the new stamp mill."

"Yeah. So?"

"The ore around here's at least as good as what they're blasting out of Gregory Gulch for the mill. Once a hard-rock mining operation moves in, the folks who've hung on to their claims will be as rich as Croesus."

The tip of Sarah's breast brushed Donovan's hair as she leaned forward to hear. Casually she let her hand drop to his shoulder. It was part of their act, she reasoned, even as his muscles hardened in response to the contact, even as her own hand warmed to the unexpected pleasure of touching him. Danger crackled in the air like the prelude to a summer storm.

"An' you think they'll be spendin' their money in this two-bit saloon?" Dooley spat off the edge of the mattress. "Stop wastin' my time, Cole."

"All right, have it your way. Don't listen to the rest." Donovan twisted backward to glance up at Sarah, his eyes guarded, his hand resting lightly on her knee. "Come on, darlin'. It looks like we get to keep all those mining claims for ourselves."

Dooley's hand shot out to catch his arm. "Minin' claims? Hell, man, how many you got?"

"How many?" Donovan settled back onto his haunches. "I can't rightly say. I've never counted. Never even seen them, in fact. But Lydia has, haven't you, partner? Remember all those old claim transfers you wrote me about? The ones the miners had signed over to the former owner to pay their bar tabs when the town was going bust?" His hand tightened almost painfully on her knee. "Don't tell me you threw them away!"

Sarah scrambled for her wits, still unsure of what Donovan had pulled her into. "Oh—those papers! No, I knew they weren't worth much, but I wouldn't have thrown them out. Let me think—I haven't run across them in the office lately. I...uh...may have boxed them up with the other things and had Smitty put them in one of the storage rooms."

She paused for breath, her heart pounding. "They could be anywhere. And unfortunately, Corporal, I can't ask Smitty to help find them because he's one of the men you shot."

Dooley's string of oaths broke off abruptly. His head jerked up as Spade walked out of the kitchen, wiping his mouth on his shirtsleeve.

Spade had taken off his hat, giving Sarah her first full view of his face. What she saw there—the pudgy, almost babyish features, the lusterless eyes—only confirmed her first impression of a young man whose life had been nothing but brutality, first received, then learned to be inflicted on others. The lamplight swam around his head, its devilish halo glittering in Sarah's eyes as he moved. She needed to lie down, she realized groggily. She had pushed herself beyond the end of her strength.

With his gun holstered, hands in his pockets, Spade ambled over to where Zoe, still in her bloodstained dressing gown, knelt on the floor cradling MacIntyre's head in her lap. He stopped a pace away and stood there, his eyes roving openly over Zoe's pitch-black curls and voluptuously exposed body.

"Hey," he announced in a loud, nasal tone. "This 'un ain't too bad."

Zoe, acting with stoic dignity, did not even look up at him. When no one else responded, Spade spoke again.

"Them other two whores is old 'nough to be my ma, an' that Miss Lyddie's as skinny as a goldanged plucked pigeon. But this 'un ain't bad a'tall, an' I ain't had no woman in a good six weeks o' Sundays."

When he clapped a familiar hand on Zoe's shoulder, she twisted away. "Leave me alone, boy," she said in a low voice. "I got better things to do."

"An' I got a itch that's hot to be scratched!" He seized a fistful of hair, yanking her head upward. "C'mon, gal! Now!"

Zoe's hand lashed out like the paw of a lynx. Her long, pointed fingernails raked the back of Spade's wrist, leaving wet, red streaks on his skin. Spade yelped and went for his gun. "You bitchin' black slut—" He cocked the pistol and aimed it at Zoe's defiant head.

Sarah was up, flying toward them even before Donovan could stop her. She would have hurled herself against

Spade's trigger arm if Dooley's whiskey-laced voice had not grated into the tense silence.

"Oh, hell, Spade, leave the woman alone! You leave all them whores alone, or you'll end up with a knife in your fool back!" He eased up taller on the mattress, wincing as he shifted his bandaged leg. "Go on upstairs and see if Cherokee needs any help guardin' them kids. Go on, now, boy."

Sarah watched the pistol waver, then drop once more to the holster. She watched Spade turn away with a nasal whine and disappear up the stairs, his lower lip outthrust like a thwarted child's.

The room had begun to blur and shift. Sarah turned unsteadily and found herself staring into Zoe's dark-rimmed eyes. As she met the fear in their depths, they seemed to grow as large as lakes. The irises swirled with moon gold flashes around the bottomless black pits of the pupils. Those eyes were pulling her in, Sarah realized. She was floating, drifting helplessly in narrowing circles, down, down into the darkness.

A whimper shook her body as she crumpled to the floor.

Donovan moved like lightning. His arms caught Sarah where she fell and lifted her tenderly against his chest. Her small, cropped head lolled in the hollow of his shoulder, cheeks white below the darkness of her lashes. Her weight seemed no more than a bird's, her body more air than substance. For the first few seconds, he had hoped her fainting spell might be a ruse, but no, this time, he realized, Sarah was not acting.

And he realized something else, as well. Through the nightmare blur of the evening he had been studying her, weighing her actions on the pan-balance of his trust. He had watched as she joked with Dooley, snarled at the children and tended the wound of a man who hated her. He had pulled her into his own web of intrigue and seen her quick-witted response—and still he had held back, afraid of his own emotions. Only now had this last small act of hers—this dash into danger to save a woman many would judge as worthless—tipped the scales.

Only now did Donovan realize what an unforgiving, judgmental fool he had been.

"She's sick," he said, turning back to Dooley. "If I don't get her to bed for a while, she'll be no good to either of us."

Dooley muttered something under his breath, eyes squinting in an effort to bring the room into focus. "All right. But I'm not finished with you, Cole. I want you back down here in fifteen minutes. And no funny stuff. Cherokee don't care who he hurts, if you get my point."

"I do. And I'm not finished with you either, Dooley. Fifteen minutes." Donovan swung up the steps with his delicate burden. He could feel Sarah stirring against him, feel her erratic breath fluttering against the hollow of his throat. She was waking up, and he wanted her away from the horror of this room. He wanted her as safe as possible.

A sense of urgency stole over him as they rounded the top of the stairs. Every minute was a burning fuse, sputtering toward the inevitable explosion. Danger lurked in every tick of the clock, in every breath and heartbeat. There was no time to resolve the past or contemplate the future. For Sarah and himself, there was only here, only now.

She lay in his arms, infinitely precious now that he saw her with clear eyes. Her bravery, her tenderness, her unbending integrity glowed in her pale face. *The Angel of Miner's Gulch,* he had called her once, hurling the appellation like a curse. Only now did he realize how right—and how wrong—he had been. Sarah was as close to being an angel as anyone he had ever known.

He remembered his first sight of her as prim Sarah Parker, bustling around Varina's cabin in those ridiculous little pince-nez glasses. Even then he had loved her. Even after he'd recognized her as Lydia Taggart she had remained stubbornly in his heart. He had fought her, but the only real battle had been with his own pride.

Not that it did either of them any good, Donovan reminded himself bitterly. Sarah did not love him. His actions had long since crushed any chance at happiness they might have had. Now, in this time of peril, she might tolerate him as an ally. But that was the most he could expect.

She moaned and opened her eyes as they entered her bedroom. He felt her body stiffen as she recognized him. "What happened? Did I faint?" she asked in a tense whisper.

"You did. But it's all right. I talked Dooley into letting me put you to bed for a while. You need rest." Donovan battled the urge to lower his head and devour the tempting softness of her mouth. She was so soft and light, so vulnerable in his arms that it was all he could do to keep from crushing her.

Aching with frustration, he masked his feelings with anger. "You're the damnedest woman I ever knew, Sarah Parker!" he growled in her ear. "How the hell did you get yourself into such a mess?"

"I might ask you the same question," she retorted coldly. "I was doing fine until you let Cherokee sneak up from behind and crack you over the head! And now you dredge up this crazy scheme about the claim transfers! I was hoping Dooley would take those two monsters and leave once the bullet was out of his leg! Now we may never get rid of them!"

"Sarah—" Donovan had glimpsed a movement in the dim shadows of the hallway. Spade, he suspected, or even Cherokee. He might have guessed someone would be watching.

"And you!" she sputtered, ignoring his efforts to warn her. "Dooley hates you! He'll never leave you alive! And he's singled out Katy—"

"Be still, Sarah!" He wrenched her face upward and smothered her words with his mouth. His kiss was rough and angry, charged with desperate fear. For the first instant she went rigid in his arms. Then, as if she'd suddenly realized they had an audience, her hand caught the back of his neck. Her thin fingers combed through his hair as she pulled him down to her in a response so passionate that it sent a surge of hot, tight shock waves rocketing into Donovan's loins.

Sarah was playacting, that was all, he reminded himself as the darkness sparked dizzyingly around him. But he had to admit she was good at it. So damned good that when he dipped into the moist honey of her mouth, her lightly flicking tongue tip lit fireworks in his head. He pressed deeper into the sweetness, demanding more and more.

Somewhere in his head a voice shrilled its reminder that time was running out. Fifteen minutes, Dooley had said, and by now, at least a third of that would be gone. Marshaling his wits, Donovan swung Sarah toward the bed. Whoever was spying on them was going to get one hell of a performance.

Sarah struggled to keep her senses as Donovan swept Marie's gowns to the floor, his momentum carrying her with him onto the rumpled coverlet. Someone was watching them, she realized muzzily, and Donovan was putting on a theatrical performance to rival her own. But merciful heaven, didn't he realize what he was doing to her? Didn't he realize that whenever he touched her, her brain stopped working and her heart took over? They had to talk, had to make plans—but even now, with danger lurking all around them, her pulse was a whirlwind, her body a quivering pool of desire.

She struggled on the bed, pinned against the warm, hard length of him. "Let me go, you fool!" she muttered in his ear.

Donovan faked a lusty laugh. "Oh-ho, so that's your game tonight, is it, Miss Lydia Taggart?" he boomed loudly enough to be heard by any eavesdropper. "Well, it's a game two can play as well as one!" He heaved his body on top of her so vigorously that the bed shook. Sarah grunted her outrage as his elbows and knees caught his weight just short of crushing her.

"You're overdoing it!" she whispered. "Why couldn't you have just left well enough alone? If you hadn't interfered, Dooley and those unsavory friends of his could be on their way out of here by now!"

"Listen to me, Sarah." His lips nuzzled a tingling path to her ear. "We've got to keep Dooley here in the saloon until we can get the children to safety. Otherwise, there's too much danger of his taking one or more of them along."

She stiffened against him, fighting the virile power of his nearness as she willed herself to think. Donovan was right. With the children as hostages, Dooley could hold off an army. Even if he ran, there was no way he would leave them all behind.

"All right," she conceded with a sigh. "We can't afford to be working at cross-purposes. What's the plan?"

"You heard it downstairs. That's all there is. Stall him any way we can until some weak spot opens up."

He found her mouth again and kissed her lingeringly, sucking and nibbling at her lips, teasing with his tongue until Sarah whimpered with the exquisite torment. Stirred by her body's own heat, she strained against him, only to gasp as her seething hips encountered the long, rock-hard ridge of his aroused manhood.

"Sarah—" He groaned as she moved along the sensitive swelling, driven by deep burnings that would not let her keep still. "Blast it, woman, don't you know what you're doing to me?" He thrust himself against her through the unyielding layers of their clothes, his pressure igniting fountains of shimmering sparks between her thighs. She ached to surrender, to abandon herself in Donovan's arms. But eyes were watching them, Sarah reminded herself. Dangerous eyes. This could not go on.

Her hand pushed against his chest, the subtle gesture reawakening them both to the peril.

With a moan of reluctance, Donovan eased off her and rolled onto his side. "You're right. This isn't the time or the place," he rasped in her ear. "But promise me something." He curved his body, tugging her back against him so that they lay like two spoons. "Promise me that if we get out of this mess alive, you and I can pick this up where we left off."

Sarah closed her eyes against the pain. Once his words would have made her heart sing. Now they only made it ache. In this time of peril, with so many lives at stake, neither of them had the right to think about the future.

"I could promise," she whispered. "But we can't let ourselves want each other too much, Donovan. We can't cling to life for the sake of what might be. We have to think of the children first. If need be, we . . . have to be willing to die for them."

"I understand." He mouthed the sentiment as if he were only half-convinced of its truth. Sarah closed her eyes as he cradled her for a last lingering moment, his arms gentle now, his heart strong and steady against her back.

"Donovan—" She nestled closer against his chest. "What about those claim transfers? Do they really exist?"

"I don't know." The velvety strength of his mouth nuzzled her cheek. "It makes sense that they might. Smitty struck me as the sort who would have taken claims as payment. If we can locate them—"

"Yes! We could use them to bargain for the children!"

"That's a long shot, love. But even if no papers turn up, at least the search might buy us some time."

"Donovan, I'm scared." Her thin fingers trembled through the worn fabric of his shirtsleeve. "And I can't let myself be scared now. This is one time when I have to be strong."

His arms tightened around her. "You are strong, Sarah. You're one of the strongest people I've ever known. But it's all right to be scared, too. For a little while . . ."

The words trailed off as he kissed her, turning her toward him again and lowering his head to the warm softness of her mouth. Sarah's response was as natural as if they had loved each other all their lives. Her petal-silk lips parted at his touch, eager and sweet. Her arm slid around the back of his neck. Her fingers tangled in his hair, pulling him down to her.

Aching with tenderness, Donovan explored the honeyed moistness of her lower lip, his tongue gliding over the satiny inner surface, stroking, tasting. She whimpered in his arms, her whole body straining upward as she opened herself to him.

The time. Curse the time...

Sensing the danger, Donovan pulled reluctantly away from the heaven of her clinging lips. "I love you, Sarah," he whispered close to her ear. "I love *you*, Sarah Parker, and not some phantom from the past. Whatever happens, promise me you'll remember that."

Sarah did not speak, and Donovan realized he had said too much. Warm as her physical response had been, the old hurts still lurked below her sweetly passionate surface. She was not ready to give her full trust, let alone her love.

He eased her out of his arms and turned to pull the curtain over the shattered window. Below, in the street, he glimpsed the knot of townspeople keeping vigil outside the saloon. It would be an easy thing to pass Sarah out the window and lower her to safety. But she would have no part of it, he knew. Not as long as the children were in danger.

And in any case, how would she fare at the mercy of a vindictive town? Sarah could die out there in the street.

"I'll be all right," she whispered as he turned back toward the bed. "Leave me now. Be careful."

He leaned down and brushed a kiss across her mouth. "No heroics, now. Try to get some sleep."

"No promises." She pushed him gently away from her. As Donovan strode from the room, the last thing he saw was her face. He held the memory, burning it into his mind as he moved into the now-empty hallway.

Simeon Dooley was sitting up, fidgeting impatiently as Donovan came down into the saloon. "It's about time, Cole," he muttered. "You were pushin' your luck up there."

"You said fifteen minutes." Donovan crouched at the edge of the mattress, where the two of them could talk without being overheard by Zoe. "Anyhow, the timing couldn't have been better. I said I had a business proposition for you, but there's a part of it I'd rather not have Lydia hear."

"This damn well better be good!" Dooley growled, leaning closer. "I could shoot you dead right now and not lose a wink of sleep over it!"

"How good it is depends on how fast we can find those claim transfers," Donovan said, feeling his way now. "Whatever happens, I'm prepared to ride out of here with you, either as your partner or as your prisoner."

"You're not makin' sense."

"Either way, you're going to need me. Don't just think about tonight. Think about tomorrow and the day after. Children won't last on the run. Push them too hard, and they'll get sick and die on you. As for those two buzzards you're riding with—"

"Spade an' Cherokee will do anything I tell 'em to."

"But for how long?" Donovan pressed Dooley. "They're jailbait, those two. Spade's a hotheaded fool, and Cherokee's wanted in a half-dozen states. Sooner or later, they'll only get you in trouble. If you're smart, you'll split up the loot and part company now."

"And where does that leave me?" Dooley's eyes narrowed suspiciously. "All alone with a bunged-up leg!"

"Not alone. You'd have me. Like I say, you need me, Dooley."

"Yeah, an' you're full o' hogwash! Help me up, Cole. I gotta go."

Dooley reeked of sweat, blood and liquor. Donovan writhed with inner frustration as he heaved the big man to his feet and helped him to a brass spittoon behind the bar. In his three years as a sheriff, he had come to rely on his gun and his fists to get him out of bad spots. He was a lightning draw, a crack marksman and could hold his own in any fight. Even now, he reflected darkly, it would be an easy matter to overpower the injured Dooley, grab the rifle and blaze his way upstairs to take on Spade and Cherokee. But he knew better than to try. Here, in this wretched backwater saloon, his hands were tied. He was playing a new game with brand-new rules and the highest stakes he had ever known.

His gaze drifted over the dimly lit saloon—the flickering lamps, the scattered tables and broken glass, the dark stain on the floor where the hapless young deputy had died. He thought of the children, huddled fearfully in the upstairs room. He thought of Sarah, ill, exhausted and infinitely precious. Whatever the cost, he would save them, Donovan vowed. Whatever the price, it was one he would willingly pay.

He would pay with his honor. With his life.

"Just think about it," he said, starting again with Dooley. "You can spend the rest of your days running from the law, or you can go straight while you're still ahead. Find some quiet little town in Mexico, or Canada, maybe, and settle down in style. Get yourself some rich land and a good-looking woman. Hell, you could even run for mayor!"

Dooley had sunk into silence, ruminating, perhaps, on the picture Donovan was painting in his mind. "I still don't see where you fit in!" he grumbled.

"Look, you'll be wanted for robbery and murder, and you're going to have to lay low. You'll need a front man with a decent reputation to register those claim transfers and collect the money."

"You could do that much on your own. What the hell do you need me for?"

Donovan forced a bitter chuckle. "Dooley, old friend, what I need from you is my life—and the lives of those youngsters and womenfolk up there, who've never done you a lick of hurt."

"And once they was safe, you'd double-cross me in a minute. Hell, Cole, you must think I'm stupid or somethin'! I wouldn't trust you any further'n I could spit!"

"How far can you trust Spade . . . or Cherokee?"

As he spoke, Donovan felt a cold chill creeping up his spine. The hair on the back of his neck lifted and bristled like a wolf's, a sure sign of danger. His gun hand jerked instinctively, then paused, quivering as he remembered he was unarmed.

Dooley's alcohol-glazed eyes had shifted toward the stairs. Donovan turned slowly to see Cherokee gliding down into the saloon, his motion as silent as a reptile's. How long had Cherokee been listening? How much had he heard, this shadowy killer who never spoke, whose dark ferret face never betrayed a flicker of emotion?

Donovan's jaw muscles clenched as Cherokee drifted to the bar and poured himself a glass of Smitty's cheap whiskey. His spirit seethed with silent rage as he thought of the children, of Faye's kind heart and Zoe's courage, and of Sarah who would gladly offer her life to save them all. He thought of the anguished parents who waited outside in the dark street, and of Varina, huddled with her young ones in that miserable little cabin.

There had to be a way out of this horror. A hidden answer, a key he had overlooked. Somehow, he had to find it.

Easing to his feet, he ambled slowly over to where Zoe sat like a mahogany statue, still supporting MacIntyre's head in her lap. MacIntyre's round, homely face was the color of cement, but his breathing had lost the awful bubbling sound Donovan had noticed earlier.

"How's he doing?" he asked gently.

"Resting." Zoe's amber eyes were as fierce as a hawk's. "Bleeding's stopped, and he's been moaning some, but he hasn't come around yet."

"When he does—"

"Don't worry. When he does, I'll make sure he knows 'bout Miz—Miz Lydia."

"Good girl." Donovan gave her shoulder an awkward squeeze, hoping he didn't appear patronizing. "You look like you could use some rest. Want me to spell you?"

"No." Her tight black curls jerked as she shook her head. "But you could bring down a couple of pillows. He breathes easier with his head propped."

"I could haul down another mattress. Or better yet, we could try to get him to bed."

"No. Miz Sa—Miz Lydia says he's got to lie right here on the floor and not move, else he'll start that wound bleeding again. That's why I need to be here—to hold him still in case he wakes up."

"Stay, then. I'll get some pillows. And Zoe—"

Her eyes flashed.

"If anybody tries to bother you, call me."

At her silent nod, Donovan turned and strode deliberately up the stairs. No one tried to stop him as he disappeared onto the landing, swung down the hallway and caught up two cushions and a blanket from the bed in the nearest room. Tucking them under one arm, he paused, then slipped more cautiously past the door.

The rose-shaded lamp had nearly burned out, casting the corridor in a bloodred ghostly light that flickered eerily off the walls. Donovan's shadow flared and shrank as he edged toward the room where the children had been taken with Faye and George.

Spade was slumped in a chair, his legs braced across the doorway. For an instant Donovan thought he might have fallen asleep, and his pulse leapt. But then the gunman stirred, shifting the pistol that lay across his lap as he resettled his boots against the frame.

Donovan froze, his mind churning. Spade had not seen him. It might be possible to take him from behind and—

But what was he thinking? There were too many innocent lives involved in such a risk. A wild shot could hit one of the children. Or the sound of a scuffle could summon the murderous Cherokee upstairs in a flash, and there would be terrible reprisals.

As he hesitated, Spade turned and saw him. His fat, dullish face smiled in the red darkness as he raised the pistol and thumbed back the hammer.

Donovan backed off slowly, hands open to show that he meant no harm. Spade's crooked teeth glinted as he replaced the gun on his lap. His odd, high-pitched giggle echoed off the walls.

Sweating lightly, Donovan slipped into Sarah's room. She was fast asleep on the bed, her face camelia pale in the faint light, as clean boned as a small boy's below the thatch of tousled hair. Her outflung arms were bare and painfully thin, but where the light fell across her body, the low-cut gown revealed the still-seductive swell of her breasts.

Donovan's throat tightened at the sight of her. Sarah didn't deserve to be here, he reminded himself. It was his own accursed meddling that had brought her to this. That she had risen above the danger with so much grace and courage was a tribute to the woman she was, and had always been.

Sarah had struggled to build a life for herself here in Miner's Gulch, a life of caring for others. In his blind pride, he had snatched that life away from her. Whatever else the future held, he carried a sacred obligation to restore what he had destroyed.

Aching with tenderness, Donovan stood beside the bed and gazed down at her beautiful, sleeping face. "I'm going to get you out of here, Sarah," he vowed in an emotion-choked whisper. "Whatever I have to do, whatever it costs me, I'm going to give you back your life."

Sarah stirred in the darkness, whimpered softly and settled back into slumber. Fumbling at the foot of the bed, Donovan found the folded satin comforter that lay there and spread it lightly over her, from her bare shoulders to her slippered toes. Gently his hands worked the emerald satin shoes from her feet and placed them side by side on the carpet.

"Sleep, love," he whispered. "Sleep and be safe."

He bent close to brush a kiss on her rumpled curls, then turned and walked softly from the room.

Chapter Fourteen

"*No!*"

Sarah writhed on the bed as the nightmare swept over her. Flames leaping in the darkness. The splintering door. Rough hands bruising her flesh, jerking her screaming body downward over the hard, sharp edge of each wooden step, then dragging her by the wrists through the cold muddy slime of the alley. MacIntyre's livid face. The nauseating stench of molten tar...

The dream had tortured her so many times that it had taken on a familiar pattern. But this time it was more than a dream. Every detail was etched to razor-sharp clarity. Sarah could observe all that was going on, almost as if she were watching herself in a play. And yet it was happening *to* her. The jarring physical agony was real. The gut-wrenching fear was real. The rage and loathing that emanated from the little group of men burned to the core of her soul.

"*No, please—*"

They were dragging her toward the fire now, almost wrenching her arms from their sockets as they swung her in a sickening arc to crumple in a rain puddle at MacIntyre's feet.

MacIntyre's boots were caked with mud and with manure from the livery stable, and for one horrible instant, Sarah was afraid he would trample on her face. Instead, his

brutish fist seized the knot of her hair, ripping it upward
with a force that threatened to twist her head from her
body. A knife blade flashed in the firelight. Sarah
screamed, again and again....

Here the nightmare had always faded, leaving her sweat
soaked and gasping in the darkness. This time, however, the
dream did not stop. Like a runaway train, it plunged ahead
to crash with shattering force through the protective bar-
riers of Sarah's memory.

She felt the knife hacking away her hair, lock by lock,
releasing her weight as it slashed each taut strand. Rough
fingers clawed at her muddy shirtwaist, snapping the buttons from their anchoring threads, yanking at the sleeves
until there was nothing left of them. Hands—she did not
even know whose—clutched her breasts through the thin
muslin chemise, fondling and squeezing as she screamed.

Other hands ripped away her skirt, her petticoats. Fingers probed, jabbed and clutched between her thighs. The
air reeked with lust and seethed with the odor of boiling tar
as she kicked, struggled and pleaded. She heard Mac-
Intyre swearing as he stirred the sooty kettle. She glimpsed
someone's blackened fingers fumbling with a belt buckle....

"No—for the love of heaven—"

A shot, then—yes, she remembered clearly now—the
shot, ringing out in the darkness. The whinny of a horse
and the jingle of a harness. A wagon thundering up the
street, and a voice—

Donovan's voice.

Sarah stirred in her sleep. A sweet peace settled over her
as, in the dream, he caught her up and lifted her in his
strong arms. Yes—how could she not have known it was
Donovan who'd saved her? She remembered all of it now—
how his gentle hands had undressed her, bathing her
bruised and muddy limbs, tucking her tenderly into the
bed. She remembered how his arms had cradled her in the

steam tent, how his body had warmed her when she shivered with fever in the cold night.

How could she have forgotten?

She lay still now, drifting silkily between sleep and wakefulness as the memory sang inside her. She had felt so alone, forsaken by everyone except the women above Smitty's saloon. But it was all right now. Donovan had been there. He had cared for her with loving tenderness, and no matter what happened now—

"Miss Sarah!"

The tiny voice, piping in Sarah's ear, awakened her like a shot. Her eyes blinked open to see Katy standing next to the bed, tugging anxiously at a corner of the coverlet.

Sarah's heart froze with sudden fear.

"What is it?" she whispered, reaching out to pull the little girl onto the bed beside her.

"I'm scared, Miss Sarah!" Katy burrowed into the hollow of Sarah's arms, her body trembling like a baby rabbit's. "It's dark, and I don't like it here. I don't like those bad men. And I don't like the way you're acting. It isn't nice!"

"Oh, Katy!" Tears welled in Sarah's eyes as she pressed her cheek to the soft tangle of curls. "I'm scared, too, sweetheart," she whispered. "But we all have to be brave until we can get you and the others out of here."

"Then why don't you be nice to us?" Katy pushed away to gaze up at Sarah with round, clear eyes. "Don't you like us anymore?"

"Of course I do. It's just that for now, I have to pretend to be someone else, someone who can't be nice to you. Do you think you can—" Sarah broke off as the full implication of Katy's presence dawned in her sleep-dulled mind. "Katy! How did you get out of the room? Where are the other children?"

"Asleep. Everybody was asleep but me. I crawled under Mr. Spade's legs and came looking for you." Katy blinked in the darkness like a little owl. "What's the matter, Miss Sarah?"

"Shh! I've got to figure out a way to get you out of here!" Sarah's mind lurched to a frantic gallop. The stairs, if the back door was unlocked and unguarded—but no, Cherokee would have seen to it that no one could escape that way. She would have to think of something else.

The window—yes, there would be people outside in the street. She could use a sheet to lower Katy down to them, then go back for as many of the others as she could smuggle out before Spade awakened.

Cold fear gripped her throat as she considered what might happen if she were caught. Dooley would take reprisals—on her, certainly, maybe even on Faye, Zoe or George, as well.

Or on the remaining children.

Or on Donovan.

For the space of a breath Sarah almost lost heart. But no, as Donovan's niece, Katy was in more danger than any of the others. Surely Donovan would choose to take the risk.

"Go over by the window, Katy," she whispered into the danger-charged darkness. "Wait and be still."

As the little girl tiptoed to the far corner of the room, Sarah flung back the coverlet and began stripping the top sheet from the bed. She moved with speed and stealth, her heart pounding so violently that she was almost afraid someone might hear it. Her hands folded the sheet cornerwise, stretching it to achieve the most length. Then she knotted one end into a child-size sling.

Behind the threadbare velvet curtain the window was broken, its sash and frame shattered in Sarah's effort to warn the children away from the saloon. Her fingers groped along the edge, feeling for shards of broken glass that could cut Katy as she scrambled through.

In the street below, people milled in small, tense clusters or slumped dejectedly on the stoops of nearby buildings. Katy would be all right, Sarah reassured herself. The second-floor window was not dangerously high. Someone would surely see the little girl and assist her the rest of the way to the ground.

"Come on," Sarah whispered to Katy. "I'll help you into the sling, then I'll lower you out the window. Here, let's make sure it's going to work. That's a good girl!"

Katy submitted bravely to the sling. When Sarah hefted her off the floor in it, she dangled in midair with a confident little smile. But climbing out the window was an entirely different matter. When Sarah tried to lift her over the sill, Katy grabbed her neck and clung for dear life.

"I can't do it, Miss Sarah! It's too far! I'll fall!"

"*Try*, Katy!" Sarah whispered frantically. "All you have to do is hold tight to the sheet! Do that, and I promise you'll be fine! Let go of me, now...that's my brave girl!"

By now people in the street had spotted the movement in the window. Sarah's heart sank as a voice bawled out of the darkness.

"Look! Somebody's up there! They're tryin' to get out!"

Katy's arms locked around Sarah's neck as the noisy crowd swarmed beneath them. "I'm scared," she whispered, pressing her face into the hollow of Sarah's neck. "What if nobody catches me?"

"You'll be all right, love," Sarah whispered. "Please believe me. All you have to do is—"

"Hold it right there, Miz Lyddie!"

Spade stood outlined in the bedroom doorway, his pistol cocked and leveled. Sick with fear now, Sarah gathered Katy tight against her. There might still be a chance to fling the child out the window. But it was only a chance, and the dangers were fearful. If no one caught her, Katy could be badly hurt, even killed. And if Spade chose to fire his pistol... No, Sarah concluded, the risks were too great. She could move fast, but not fast enough to outmaneuver a bullet that might hit Katy.

"'Pears to me you think more of them kids than you let on," Spade drawled nasally.

"Let her go, Spade!" Sarah whispered, clasping Katy close. "Let them all go! I'll give you money, gold, anything." Rash promises, from one who had nothing to give, Sarah knew. But she had reached the edge of desperation.

Spade probed a nostril with his index finger. "Uh-huh. An' Dooley'd shoot me dead for sure. C'mon." He stepped to one side of the doorway and motioned with the pistol barrel for her to follow. "Looks like I got to keep you corralled with the others."

Still carrying Katy, Sarah let him usher her down the hall into Faye's room, where three of the children—the boys— lay tangled on the bed like a litter of sleeping pups. George had stretched out on the rug with a spare pillow and blanket. Faye, drawn and haggard in the darkness, sat in her carved cherrywood rocker with little Molly Sue Gordon sprawled in slumber across her lap. Her eyes met Sarah's in anguished sympathy, but she did not speak.

Sarah found a space at the side of the bed and settled herself cross-legged on the floor. Katy had begun to cry softly as the fear settled in, pooling wet tears along the hollow of Sarah's collarbone. Sarah cradled the little girl close, crooning a whispered lullaby as she savored the sweetness of a child in her arms. Dear, spunky little Katy. The daughter of her truest friend. The precious niece of the man she would love forever.

To save Katy and the others, she would give her life without hesitation.

As the small, sob-racked body relaxed in sleep, Sarah closed her eyes and, for the first time since waking, allowed herself to think about Donovan.

He had said he loved her—loved *her*, and not the laughing ghost of Lydia Taggart. Once his words would have made her heart soar. Now she could only reflect that he had spoken them too late. The odds that they would both come through this ordeal alive were too grim to contemplate. Her dream of happiness would die, as her dreams always died.

It was part of her punishment, the price she paid for her wickedness.

They had no promise of a future, she and Donovan. Their only time was the bleak and dangerous present, their only happiness the few morsels they could snatch here and now from the jaws of darkness.

Katy was sleeping soundly by now. Her russet head lolled in the curve of Sarah's shoulder. Her warm breath was as sweet as new hay, as innocent as springtime.

Outside, it had begun to storm again. Rain battered the roof overhead as Sarah leaned against the side of the bed and tried to make herself comfortable. She would not sleep again, she knew. Time was too short. Life was too dear.

Donovan had been playing five-card stud with Dooley and Cherokee when the commotion started in the street outside. Acting on reflex, he'd bolted out of his chair, only to be halted by the sound of Dooley cocking his lever-action Spencer.

"Siddown, Cole, you ain't goin' nowhere." The big man kept the rifle leveled at Donovan until he resumed his seat, then nodded brusquely at Cherokee. "Go on upstairs and make sure everything's under control. We'll hold the game."

Dooley fiddled with his cards as the half-breed glided up the stairs. "I've learned not to ask Cherokee what's goin' on," he said. "Sneaky little bastard can't tell me nothin' nohow. Can't even write it down, 'cause he don't know how to write, and he don't like makin' signs with his hands."

"Have you thought any more about what I said?" Donovan asked, pressing the subject while he had the chance.

"About them claims? Hell, I don't know. It sounds pretty damned complicated to me. Safest thing would be for me to ride outa here soon as them fool townies deliver the horses and vittles, with a couple of them kids tied across the saddle 'case anybody gets too close."

Donovan leaned back in his chair, struggling to appear detached and uncaring. "Like I say, the kids are liable to die on you. I won't."

"And kids won't shoot me in the back or turn me over to the law. No dice there, Cole. But..." He chewed his lower lip while Donovan held his breath. "I don't suppose it'd hurt to look around for them claim papers. If you find 'em, maybe we can deal. If not, there ain't no sense even talkin' about it."

"I'll need Lydia to help me look."

"Fine. Get her. But we finish the game first. I don't want my quiet friend gettin' suspicious."

Donovan glanced up to see Cherokee moving back down the stairs. He picked up his cards again, pretending to peruse his hand as the half-breed slid back into his chair.

"Everything all right up there?" Dooley asked him.

Cherokee nodded, his face as expressionless as a hatter's dummy. One brown finger nudged two chips to the center of the table. From outside, a roll of thunder echoed through the thin plank walls of the saloon.

"Damned rain," Dooley muttered. "Leastwise, it oughta quiet down them fools in the street. Maybe slow up the posse, too. But the mud'll make for hard goin' and easy trackin' when we ride outa here." He glanced impatiently from the clock to the door. "Hells bells, them supplies ought to be here by now! What happened to that damn fool whore we sent outside?"

Only the rain answered him, its rhythmic dirge drumming through the windowless walls. The dampness that seeped through the cracks was gloomy and cold. Donovan suppressed a shiver as he watched Cherokee shuffle the cards. The dark gunman's movements were swifter than sight, his small, thin hands wasting no motion. His eyes were as bland and unblinking as a snake's. Where were his vulnerable spots? Donovan wondered. Every man had at least one—an unsteady hand, a bad eye, a temper that eclipsed good judgment. But apart from Cherokee's lack of speech, no weakness showed itself.

Fathoming Dooley was easier. He was a bully, given to excesses of rage and intemperance. A man who craved acceptance, even from his enemies. There had to be a way to play one man off the other, Donovan calculated. With the women and children as hostages and no weapon of his own, it was his only chance of beating them.

"I fold," he said, laying down what might have been a decent hand, had he chosen to play it. "You two can fight it out for the winnings. I'm going upstairs and check on Lydia and the youngsters."

Moving deliberately, he slid his chair away from the table. Cherokee's hand flashed for his holster, but Dooley stopped him with a glance.

"No tricks, Major," he growled. "One false move, and Spade'll put the first bullet through that little redheaded niece of yours."

"No tricks," Donovan muttered, knowing full well that Dooley spoke the truth. He turned away from the table and would have headed upstairs if a knock on the front door of the saloon had not broken the silence, riveting the men at the table.

At a nod from Dooley, Cherokee drew his pistol and cat-footed across the room to unlatch the door. It cracked open to reveal a rain-soaked Greta shivering on the open porch.

Donovan stared at her in dismay as she stumbled inside, water puddling off her clothes, her yellow hair dripping in strings around her plump, rouged face. Greta could have stayed away and saved herself. How could she be fool enough to risk her life coming back?

"I told Herr Satterlee you needed supplies," she said in a tired, toneless voice. "Everything you asked for will be on the porch in an hour, along with three saddled horses from the livery stable. Nobody will try to stop you. They only want the children safe."

Dooley's breath rasped tautly in his throat. "What the hell took 'em so long?"

Greta's head drooped wearily as she slumped into a chair. "Herr Satterlee would not give up the supplies until the people paid for them. It took all this time to collect the money. Herr Satterlee...has no children." Her voice broke. She stared dejectedly at the floor.

Donovan gulped back his disgust. He'd had his own problems with the mercenary little storekeeper, but this tale was beyond imagining. "What are you doing here, Greta?" he asked gently. "You didn't have to come back, you know."

Greta raised her head to give Donovan a ragged smile. "And where else was I to go, *jawohl?* This is my home. This is where my friends are. I don't belong out there."

Donovan swallowed the hardness in his throat. "Come on, Greta," he murmured. "I'll help you upstairs so you can get into some dry clothes. We don't need another patient on our hands."

He circled the woman's shivering shoulders with his arm and drew her dampness against his side. Neither Dooley nor Cherokee made a move to stop them as they mounted the stairs. Why hadn't someone taken Greta in? he wondered. What was wrong with the people in this town? Why would Sarah battle so hard to stay in such a place? Why would Varina refuse to leave?

"Is everybody all right in here?" Greta whispered as they reached the landing and turned the corner into the mauvered darkness of the hallway.

"No worse off than when you left. What was causing all that commotion outside a while ago?"

"*Donnerwetter!* You don't know?"

Donovan's tight-lipped silence answered her question.

"It was Miss Sarah! She had one of the children—the little girl with red hair. She was trying to lower her out of the window. *Ach!* Some *dumkopf* outside started shouting, and—"

"What happened to them?" Donovan felt his heart slam.

"I don't know. They disappeared inside. We didn't see them again." Greta paused outside her bedroom door, cast him a look of tragic futility, then vanished inside. When Donovan checked the adjoining room where he had left Sarah sleeping, he found it empty, the knotted sheet lying crumpled on the floor.

"Damn!" Donovan's stomach knotted with dismay. For Sarah to take such a chance—

His thoughts scattered like blown straw at the sight of Spade, lounging feet-up in the doorway of Faye's room down the hall. Spade glanced up, saw him and grinned.

"Hey, Cole, your galfriend tried a pretty dumb trick. She shoulda knowed better. Shoulda knowed I'd catch her."

Donovan's teeth clenched as he bit back a surge of fury that would have sent him lunging at the pudgy gunman's throat. "So help me, you bastard, if you've so much as touched her—"

Spade hawked and spat on the floor. "Hell, I ain't laid a hand on the woman. Not that she didn't offer to let me, mind you. Offered right nice, she did. But my taste runs to gals with some meat on their bones. Don't know if I could of even got it up with a skinny one like her."

Donovan groaned, wrenched by near-physical agony at the thought of Sarah's offering herself to a man like Spade for the sake of the children. The urge to seize her shoulders and shake her till she whimpered for mercy faded, however, as he looked into the bedroom and saw her. She was seated on the floor, her head bent like a tender Madonna's over the slumbering Katy. Her eyes lifted as he stepped into full view. In their silver-shadowed depths, he read anguish, frustration and—unbelievably—love.

He tore himself away from her luminous gaze. "Dooley wants her downstairs," he told Spade.

"Shucks, how do I know you ain't lyin'?"

"Go and ask him."

Spade chewed his thumbnail as the realization sank in that checking with Dooley would leave his charges unguarded. "Take 'er," he grunted. "You know what'll happen if you're aimin' to cross me."

"I know." Donovan waited while Sarah settled the sleeping Katy across the foot of the bed. Then he stepped back into the hallway, emotions churning as she slipped out the door to join him. He was sick with fear for her and desperately angry at the risk she'd taken. But when she was beside him, when he looked into her beautiful, tired face, he could think only of how much he wanted her.

He did not trust himself to speak. Not yet. But as they moved back down the hallway toward the stairs, he caught her elbow and swung her into Zoe's empty bedroom, his arms trapping her against the near wall.

"Donovan—" Her eyes were wide gray pools, their surfaces vibrating with uncertainty. "I know what you're—"

Donovan's hard mouth blocked her words. His lips ground onto hers with a fury that exploded like nitroglycerin, torching blazes of wildfire in his veins. His arms jerked her to him, crushing her fragile flesh to his belly.

For the space of a heartbeat Sarah quivered rigidly against his burning length. Then her hands flashed into motion, fingers gripping his neck as she pulled him down to her. Her lips molded to his heat. The moisture of her swollen mouth mingled with his own as her tongue thrust deep for his suckle, velvet rough, tremblingly eager in its seeking. The taste of her was wild honey and moon musk to his reeling senses.

"We—we mustn't—" she whispered. But the words were smoke, spiraling to air in the rising heat of her response. She wanted him, too. Every breath, every move of her supple body told him so.

Groaning with the heaviness of desire, Donovan slid his hand downward to clasp the cleft moons of her buttocks through the ripple of green silk. As he pressed her hard against his achingly aroused shaft, her gasp melted to a crescendo of tiny whimpers. Her fingers clawed his hair as he thrust his weight against her, pinning her writhing hips to the wall. Hunger-wild, she butted and twisted, feeding the flames of their urgency. Reason shrilled that they had no time, no place of safety. They had only what they could steal from each perilous moment.

"I want you, Sarah," he breathed in a frenzy of need. "Heaven help me—"

"Heaven help us both," she murmured, drawing away to catch her breath. Her eyes were large and soft in the darkness. Donovan recognized the glimmer of tears. He gathered her close again, with exquisite tenderness this time, forcing his passion back to a warm simmer.

"I love you, Sarah Parker," he said softly.

"And I love you," she whispered, muffling the words against his chest. "I've always loved you, Donovan. But I can't let myself want more than this. Our own lives matter so little right now. Our own happiness—"

"Hush." His kisses were gentle now, urgent, seeking nibbles that grazed her forehead, her eyes, her cheeks. "We'll take this one step at a time, love. Right now, what we need to do is go downstairs and spend some time looking for those claim papers. We'll stall where and when we can, keep our eyes open, and maybe, somehow, we'll discover a way out of this mess. Whatever happens, Sarah, I promise you—"

"No!" She sealed his lips with a determined forefinger. "No promises!" she declared fiercely. "One step at a time, that's what you said. That has to be the only way for us. Otherwise, I'll never be able to bear it!"

"All right, no promises." He brushed a lingering kiss across her darkly swollen lips. He could make no promises to Sarah, but he could make them to himself. He would have a life with this woman, Donovan vowed. He would give her a home, sire their children with his love, care for her, protect her, grow old with her. Somehow, so help him, he would find a way to make it all possible.

The creak of a floorboard startled them apart. It would be Spade, most likely, checking on what they were up to, Donovan calculated. Or Greta moving about inside her room. In any case, he and Sarah could not stay here. Dooley would be waiting for them downstairs.

"Come on." He guided her into the corridor. His hand, resting on the small of her back, felt the coiled-spring tension of the muscles that rimmed her spine. Her skin was cold to the touch, her face serene except for the resolute thrust of her chin.

As they descended the stairs Donovan's thoughts darted back to Richmond. The old bitterness had waned from the memory now, tempered by a fresh understanding. As he had battled for his beliefs, Sarah had fought for hers—her beauty, her skill as an actress, and her coolheaded courage her only weapons.

What kind of bravery had it taken to face the enemy day after day, unarmed and vulnerable? he asked himself. What kind of fortitude, to wear the carefree mask of Lydia Taggart in the face of danger and heartache? What kind of strength, to bear up under the awful aloneness she must have felt?

Donovan's hand tightened protectively around her waist. His lovely, fearless Sarah. In all his life, he had never known a woman to equal her.

A curious peace crept over his spirit as they reached the bottom of the staircase. For an instant Donovan was puzzled. Then, as his understanding fell into place, he realized that for him, the terrible war between North and South was over at last. He had come to the end of it with Sarah in his arms. Whatever battles remained to be fought, the two of them would fight side by side, as one.

Simeon Dooley glanced up from his card game. "Well, get on with it, then," he growled with a cautious glance at Cherokee, who was glowering at his hand. "No tricks, now."

"Tricks? Us? Why, Corporal, I can't believe you'd suspect us of anything like that!" Sarah was back in character now, her smile brassy, her laughter coarse and careless. But the game she played was more dangerous than ever. Donovan thanked his stars that the mute half-breed could not tell Dooley what had happened upstairs with Katy.

"We may have a lot of looking to do," Donovan cautioned.

Dooley shrugged and glanced at the pendulum clock on the wall. "It's five minutes till two. I'll give you till first light. Then, providin' them supplies and horses are here, we're ridin' out—regardless of what you find. Got that, Cole?"

Donovan nodded, his eyes on Cherokee. The man was listening intently, his narrowed gaze fixed on Dooley. Clearly he was puzzled about what was going on. At least Donovan hoped he was.

"Come on, Lydia, darlin'." He circled Sarah's shoulders with his arm. "Let's start by checking your office again. With luck, we may not have to look any further than that." The conspiratorial glance he cast at Dooley could have been read by a blind man. "We'll let you know the minute we find anything."

Donovan paused to gauge Cherokee's reaction. The gunman's thin, dark face could have been chiseled from mahogany. It took Sarah to make a difference. When she turned at the doorway to Smitty's office and shot Dooley a hoydenish flicker of a wink, Cherokee's jaw muscles twitched perceptibly. Yes, the seed had been planted and was beginning to sprout.

Half-afraid Sarah would overplay her hand, Donovan stepped inside the office, jerked her after him and closed the door.

Sarah's head spun as Donovan caught her in his arms. Things were moving too fast. She could not grasp them all.

She clung to him as she struggled for her physical, mental and emotional bearings.

His kiss was quick and hard. "That wink was a good touch, but don't overdo it, love," he whispered. "You'll have the big bruiser in your lap! Next thing you know, he'll be riding out of here with you slung across the front of his saddle!"

Sarah blinked up at him, then exploded. "Donovan, what in heaven's name are we supposed to be doing? I've been trying to follow your signals, but it's like fumbling my way through a maze!"

He guided her toward Smitty's cluttered rolltop desk. "One step at a time, isn't that what we agreed on? We've got till first light—that's about four hours—to find a way out of this mess. Otherwise, Dooley plans to leave and take some of the children along as insurance. Let's start by going through our late friend Smitty's paperwork."

They began with the desk and its contents. The miserly Smitty had possessed the hoarding instincts of a pack rat. Bills, receipts, notes, invoices and orders were stuffed haphazardly into every available cranny. There was no easy way to get through it all, and time was already running out.

"What difference does it make if we *do* find anything?" Sarah dumped the contents of one pigeonhole in her lap and began pawing frantically through them. "Why should Dooley bargain when he could take the claims and the children, too?"

"It's not that simple, love." Donovan was shuffling through a drawer he had yanked out of the desk. When he spoke, it was almost in a whisper. "The claims, if they exist, should have been signed over to the Crimson Belle, or to Smitty himself, whatever the poor old devil's real name was. If we can convince Dooley the papers are worthless without you or me to file them at the land office—"

"Is that really true?" Sarah's whirling mind struggled to grasp Donovan's strategy.

His only reply was a maddening shrug. "What does it matter whether it's true or not, as long as we can get Dooley to believe it?"

"And if we don't find any claims at all?"

Donovan's eyes softened for an instant. His hand reached across the desk to give her shoulder a slow caress that sent a thrill coursing through her body. "Then, my dearest Sarah, we'll just have to work with whatever we *can* find," he murmured mysteriously.

She studied him, fighting her way through clouds of perplexity. "Back there in the saloon, when I winked at Dooley, it was Cherokee's response you were watching."

"You're a very observant lady." A hint of a smile twitched the left corner of his mouth, and Sarah realized, for the first time, what a dangerous game Donovan was playing. Enemy against enemy. Cherokee against Dooley. And neither man would hesitate to kill him. The sudden awareness of it left her breathless with fear.

"Try the next drawer," she said in a voice that could be heard clearly through the closed door. "If we can just lay our hands on those papers, you and I and the corporal could be very wealthy partners indeed."

The look he flashed her blended gratitude and warning. She could not afford to overplay her part, Sarah reminded herself. Cherokee was no fool. He would recognize an obvious deception. For now, she would be better off to follow Donovan's lead and take her cues from him.

Sarah bent over the contents of the top drawer with a new sense of purpose. They worked together now, she and Donovan, the intimacy of danger shimmering like fox fire between them. Any accidental touch, any meeting of their eyes set off bursts of love inside her. Her awareness of Donovan, and of the bond they shared, was as exquisite as pain.

If the next few hours were all fate held for them, she would accept each moment as a gift. She would savor every breath and heartbeat. She would fill her senses with the

sight of his face and the sound of his voice. She would hold
the scent of him, the feel and taste of him in her memory
for as long as time would allow.

His eyes met hers over a sheaf of papers. "I love you,
Donovan," she whispered.

"And I love you." His fingers reached out to stroke her
cheek. "Don't be afraid, sweetheart. Someday, we'll be
telling our grandchildren about this night." His palm
cupped her chin, tilting her face toward him. "And if I have
anything to say about it, we'll be telling them together."

Sarah dropped her gaze, unable to accept the freshet of
joy that swelled her heart. She had spent her life paying for
real or imagined sins. Punishment she accepted as her due.
But happiness? Happiness that glowed inside her like a
dancing rainbow? No, that was something that happened
to people who deserved it. Not to her. Never to her.

"No promises, remember?" she murmured. "That was
what we said—"

"It was what *you* said." His thumb grazed her jaw as his
hand slipped achingly along the curve of her throat to rest
on her bare shoulder. Sarah could feel her flesh trembling
against the warmth of his work-roughened palm.

"I've never believed in looking too far ahead," she
whispered.

"But I'm not made that way." His voice rasped with
emotion. "I've never had the patience to bide my time and
wait for things to come about."

"Donovan—"

"No, I have to say it. I want you for my wife, Sarah. I
want to spend the rest of my days loving you and caring for
you and building our future together. Whatever else this
hellish night brings, I'm not turning that dream loose."

Sarah stared at the papers in her lap, biting back tears.
This couldn't really be happening, she told herself. Not to
wicked Sarah Jane Parker. This was only a new kind of
heavenly punishment—to dangle everything she'd ever

wanted right in front of her nose, then jerk it away the instant she reached out.

"Please," she whispered, her hands clenching so tightly that she could feel her nails cutting into her palms. "It's too much, Donovan. First we've got to find those papers, if they exist. And we've got to get the children out—"

"Sarah, what are you afraid of?" His fingers massaged her shoulder with gentle insistence. He would demand an answer, she knew, before he let her go.

Her hand reached up to rest on his, drawing strength from the power of tendons and sinews, from the warmth of his skin. "I'm afraid of wanting you too much," she whispered. "I'm afraid that if I start thinking about our future, it will all be taken away, that I'll lose you."

"Why?" he asked softly. "What does wanting have to do with losing? There's no connection."

"Not in your mind." She glanced up at him with a bitter smile. "But you have to understand that I've never been truly happy, not in the way I could be with you. Over the years, I've come to accept the fact that I don't deserve happiness, that I'll never have it. To reach for it now..." A shudder passed through Sarah's body. "Don't you see? It would only be tempting fate."

He captured her hand and raised it to his lips. Sarah felt the rough stubble of his unshaven whiskers as he brushed his mouth to her palm. "Blast it, Sarah—"

"Please," she pleaded, pulling her hand away as if she was fearful of hurting him. "Let's just look for the papers now. Maybe later, when, if, we get through this—"

"All right. We'll do it your way." He turned back toward the desk with a bleak resolve that left Sarah empty and aching. She stared down at her clenched hands, groping for sensible reasons. What else could she have done? she asked herself. With so many lives at stake, how could she think of her own happiness?

As she bent to shuffling through the jumble of papers, Sarah felt a jabbing sense of regret. Donovan Cole was a proud man, too proud to open his heart on a whim. What if she had wounded him too deeply?

What if she had already lost him?

After fifteen minutes of sifting through the entire desk, even dumping out the drawers and inspecting the inner framework, they had found no claim papers.

"But we've found no cash, either," Sarah noted. "There's got to be someplace we haven't looked—a safe, a box under the floor, even a hollow wall—where Smitty would have kept his valuables." She rose from her chair to move restlessly about the office, tapping on the plaster, tilting the picture frames, rumpling the rugs. Nothing.

"What about storage?" Donovan had shoved the desk aside, revealing plain, rough floorboards, securely nailed. "There was no liquor in the cool room where I stashed the bodies. Where else would—"

"Liquor—the wine cellar!" Sarah froze as the memory slammed home. Greta had mentioned how Smitty had locked up the three women the night of the tar and feathers. The wine cellar—that could be the key to everything!

Donovan blinked his disbelief. He stamped the floor lightly with his boot. The sound was dull and solid, with no hollowness to it. "There's no cellar under here. Where could it be?"

"I'm not sure. But the girls would know. I'll need to go back out there and ask one of them."

"We'll both go." Donovan's hand caught the small of her back and steered her toward the door. "I don't like leaving those three galoots alone too long, anyway. You find out about the cellar. I'll visit with our friend Dooley for a few minutes."

They came out from behind the bar to a scene much like the one they had left, except that Spade and Cherokee had traded watch on the children. Spade sat alone at one table wolfing down a bowl of beans and some bread from the kitchen, interspersing bites with gulps of whiskey. Dooley dozed at another table, his hat over his eyes. One hand lay on his saddlebags, the other on his rifle. Donovan hesitated, then slipped into the chair across from him.

Zoe sat with MacIntyre, supporting the wounded man's head and shoulders in her lap. She shivered in her thin silk wrapper, while he lay bundled in a quilt that someone had brought. She had not left his side, Sarah realized as she walked quietly over and laid a hand on the dark woman's shoulder.

"How is he, Zoe?" she asked softly.

"Hard to say." Zoe's amber eyes swam with weariness. "Sometimes I almost think he can hear when I talk to him. He stirs and moans like he's comin' around. Once he even opened his eyes. But he—he didn't act like he knew me." She forced a weary smile. "It's gonna take time, I guess."

"I could get Faye or Greta to sit with him if you like. That way, you could get some rest."

Zoe shook her head. "No. I'll stay. It's all I've got to do." Her honey-molasses voice lowered to a whisper. "But I wish I was somewhere away from Mr. Spade. I don't like that ugly little man. Don't like the way he talks, or the way he looks at me."

"Dooley told him to leave you alone."

"Dooley can't watch him all the time."

Sarah glanced back at Spade, then spoke cautiously. "Zoe, I need to get into Smitty's wine cellar. Where's the entrance?"

Zoe stared at the floor. "Closet off the kitchen. Trap-door's hid under some crates. Take a lamp."

"What's down there?"

"Not much. Bottles. Shelves."

"No safe? Nothing that might have money or papers in it?"

"Not that I ever saw." Zoe's words trailed off as she smoothed MacIntyre's thinning hair back from his face. Her strong, dark hands were gentle, her expression sad and tender.

She loves him, Sarah realized, jolted by the sudden awareness. *All this time he's been her customer, and she loves him!*

"I'm sorry for what he done to you, Miss Sarah," Zoe murmured. "It was a bad thing, I know. But he's not really a bad man. It's just that he's got so much hurtin' inside him. Sometimes it makes him do hurtful things."

Zoe looked up into Sarah's eyes, her full mahogany lips parted, as if she was waiting for something. Gazing into her anguished face, Sarah felt the events of that awful night welling up inside her again—the screams, the clutching hands, the tar pot scorching on the flames...

Let it go, Sarah Parker, a voice whispered inside her. *The past is behind you. Set it free....*

No—against all reason she clung to the memory, to the pain and the anger. She had been brutally wronged. She deserved recompense. She deserved justice.

Let it go....

She gazed down into Zoe's eyes, into amber-flecked depths that swirled with tears. Little by little she willed her stubborn mind to release the thing that had happened. Little by little, she felt the heaviness lifting from her spirit as the memory rose on tar black wings. The lamplight formed iridescent circles as her vision blurred. A single drop of moisture trickled down her cheek.

"It's all right," she whispered, one hand tightening on Zoe's shoulder through the threadbare silk. "Tell him—if and when you can. Tell him it's all right."

Sarah turned away swiftly, fearful of breaking under the strain of her own emotion. A glance around the saloon told her that little had changed. Spade was still bent over his beans and bread. Dooley was still slumped in his chair, asleep. Broken glass was strewn around the bar, and there was a hideous red-brown stain on the floor where the panic-stricken deputy had died.

The situation was as dismal as ever, Sarah realized. But the simple act of forgiving MacIntyre had changed something inside her. The black weight of hopelessness was gone. For the first time she felt ready to think about something beyond this night—and ready to fight for it.

Donovan had risen from his place at Dooley's table. Sarah gave him a subtle nod, then strode toward the kitchen. She heard his footsteps behind her, felt the electric tension of his presence as they moved through the door. Her senses tingled.

Strange as it seemed, she had never felt more alive.

Chapter Fifteen

The trapdoor yawned into darkness. Sarah hovered anxiously at Donovan's side as he thrust the lantern into the murk. "What do you see?" she whispered.

"Not much. Shelves and bottles—isn't that what Zoe told you to expect?"

"Can we go down? Maybe there's more."

"The ladder's right here." He was already moving downward, balancing the lantern with one hand as his feet groped for the rungs. Seconds later, she heard his boots scrape bottom, followed by a metallic clink as he hung the lamp on a nail. "Watch your step," he cautioned as Sarah struggled with her skirts and high-heeled slippers. "Here—"

She gasped as his strong hands caught her waist from behind, lifted her off her feet and swung her to the floor. Time stood still as his grip lingered, the pressure of his fingertips all but searing Sarah through her corset. For the space of a heartbeat, she dared to hope that his arms might slip around her, that he might gather her close in the flickering darkness, then lean down to let his lips graze the curve of her bare shoulder while his hands curled upward to toy with her breasts until she ached with sweet, hot urges.

But no, she knew what to expect. Out of her own senseless fear, she had pushed aside his proposal and wounded his pride. Donovan's behavior, she realized gloomily, would be as proper as a deacon's. They would spend what might be their last time alone together in polite posturings, avoiding so much as an intimate meeting of their eyes.

How could she have been such a fool? How could she have believed she was unworthy of love, that it would be snatched away if she had the effrontery to reach out for it? Everyone, even a man like MacIntyre, was entitled to love. Even wicked, worldly Sarah Jane Parker had the right to claim love when she found it. She knew that now.

What if she had learned her lesson too late?

Sarah's heart fluttered and sank as Donovan backed away from her to survey the cellar. It was no more than a half-dozen paces across, its earthen walls braced with mining timbers and lined with crude shelves. The shelves held crated bottles of Smitty's rotgut whiskey and a few odd jugs of muscatel. That, and dust.

"But there's got to be something more!" Her fingers flew urgently over every surface she could reach, groping for some hidden flaw that might indicate a cache. "Where would Smitty have kept his important papers—and his money?"

Donovan responded with a shrug and an impatient sigh. "Judging from the condition of his desk, Smitty could've used his important papers for wiping his boots. As for money, anyone who knew where it was could have grabbed it after he was shot. One of the girls, maybe."

She turned on him, snapping under her own strain. "No, not Faye or Greta or Zoe! None of them had the chance! And even if they did, I can't believe any of them would do a thing like that!"

"Then you're as starry-eyed as my sister, and just as damned mule stubborn!" he retorted coldly.

"I take any comparison with Varina as a compliment!" Sarah flared. "Even from the likes of you!"

Suddenly they were glowering at each other, nose to nose almost, like two bristling wolves. The silence quivered with unvoiced fury as they stood dramatically frozen, each waiting for the other to make the next move.

Donovan's eyes shot jasper sparks as the long night of tension, frustration and fear tore at his patience. He would explode, Sarah thought. They would both explode, and they would tear each other to pieces.

She waited, braced for the onslaught of his rage. To her astonishment, it did not come. He was holding it in with an effort so agonizing that, as the seconds ticked by, it became more and more ludicrous.

It was Sarah who finally broke. She felt the release bubbling from deep inside her, rising like springwater to emerge as a half-suppressed giggle.

Donovan's mouth twitched once, twice, and then, as the blessed wave of laughter swept over them both, he caught her in his arms and crushed her against him. Clasped together, their bodies shook until the tears came.

"I'm—sorry," Sarah gasped when she was finally able to speak. "You looked so...funny—"

His kisses, swift, hungry, desperate little nibbles, fell like warm rain on her wet face. "Sarah...blast it, love, is this what our life together's going to be—you and me, always at loggerheads?"

She clung to him, reassured by the strong, steady beat of his heart against hers. "It may be that we'll argue," she whispered, knowing full well the promise his question, and her answer, implied. "Oh, but think what wonderful times we'll have making up!"

"I love you, Sarah," he whispered, his lips tousling her boyish curls. "Whatever happens upstairs, in that hellish place, promise me you won't forget it."

"I promise." Sarah's voice was raw with the pain of her tight throat. As she strained against him, burning the memory of his size, strength and perfect form into her own flesh, she felt the shaft of his desire rise hard and urgent against her belly.

His face warmed with the awareness of what he could not hide. "We . . . ought to be getting back," he murmured.

"Just a little longer." She pressed closer, savoring the exquisite torture. Above them, in the saloon, a nightmare of fear and danger awaited their return. But here, in this moment, was heaven. "Hold me, Donovan," she whispered. "Don't let me go."

His arms tightened around her. For the space of a long breath they stood perfectly still, their desire a pulsing flame that welded her body to his in the darkness. Sarah closed her eyes in contentment, knowing she was his, that he was hers for as long as they lived.

For as long as they lived.

With a sigh of reluctance, he released her. "There's nothing here, love," he muttered huskily. "We may as well get back upstairs."

Sarah nodded sadly, knowing he was right. There were other places to search—the storerooms, the kitchen and Smitty's own quarters. And there were desperate acts to be accomplished before first light. She turned away from him, then suddenly froze.

"Donovan, look at the floor!"

He caught the lantern off the nail and lowered it to where she was pointing. "I don't see—"

"There! Those curved scrape-lines at the base of that shelf! They've almost been wiped out by footprints, but if you look closely—"

Donovan crouched closer to run his fingertips over the hard-packed earth. A long, low whistle slid past his lips as he realized what Sarah had found. "I'll be damned!" he muttered. "A movable shelf!"

Setting the lantern on the floor, he stood up, hefted the supporting corner of the shelf and pulled it outward. It yielded to his strength, grinding from a pivot point at its far end to an opening about two feet wide. Behind it lay a round hole that widened into what looked like a low, dark, down-sloping tunnel.

"Stay behind me," Donovan ordered as he stooped into the entrance, thrusting the lantern into the darkness. Sarah crept along after him. She had expected the tunnel to be shrouded in cobwebs, but the passageway was surprisingly clear. Smitty—for she could think of no one else who might have built and used it—must have come down here fairly often.

Ahead of her, Donovan uttered a grunt of disbelief. Seconds later, he straightened and stepped full height into a whitewashed room.

"What on earth—?" Sarah blinked as the lamplight danced off the glaring walls. The well-finished chamber was half as large as any of the bedrooms upstairs. Boxes of canned food were stacked along one wall, along with jugs of water and a necessity. A brass bed, covered with a faded patchwork quilt, filled one corner. Next to it stood a battered leather-bound trunk.

"I'd say our friend Smitty had some enemies," Donovan muttered, gazing around the room. "That, or he was on the run from the law and needed a place where he could disappear in a hurry. Look, there's even an air shaft!" He pointed to a hole in the ceiling where a nickel-size opening wafted a thin draft of fresh air. "The old boy could have lasted for weeks down here."

Sarah reached up to test the air trickle with a moistened fingertip. "This air is too cool to be coming from inside the saloon," she mused. "I'd say the shaft comes up somewhere out back, maybe under the spruces where nobody would notice it."

"And where there'd be some protection from the snow." Donovan scowled pensively at the ceiling. "The cellar would be right below the kitchen. But this room isn't under the saloon at all. I wonder if it's possible—"

"The children!" Sarah clutched his arm. "If we could just get them down here, they could hide until Dooley left, or until someone could dig them out."

"Maybe." Donovan's shoulders sagged in frustration. "But getting them down here, away from Dooley and his watchdogs, that would be the problem, love. Once you got that far, you'd be doing better to put them right outside."

Sarah sank dejectedly onto the bed, knowing he was right. She had hoped this secret room might hold the key to their deliverance. But there *was* no key, she realized at last. There was no magic solution waiting to be discovered, no miracle that would snatch them all to safety in the nick of time. She and Donovan could depend on nothing but their own resources. Nothing but their trust in each other. And if worse came to worst, even that might not be enough.

The battered old trunk sat like a nightstand beside the bed. On its curved top lay an unlit candle, a small paring knife, some matches, a box of cheroots and an empty glass. Donovan used the knife to pry up the unlocked hasp while Sarah cleared the other objects onto the floor. The hinges creaked as the dusty lid swung upward. A faded pair of trousers and a dusty white shirt lay folded on top. Underneath them . . .

Sarah stared. Donovan swore under his breath.

The chest was filled to the brim with money—bills and coins, tossed in haphazardly with no attempt to count or order them. Hundreds, even thousands of dollars, Sarah estimated. Smitty's hoardings over the years of his miserly life.

"Damnation!" Donovan muttered.

Sarah squeezed his shoulder, sharing his ironic disappointment. Money would be of little use in bargaining for the children. The outlaws could simply take the cash by force, and the little ones, as well.

"Maybe there's something nearer the bottom." Sarah began scooping out the cash and piling it on the floor, but the contents were the all same. Defeated, she slumped back onto her heels. "I don't understand it," she muttered. "There's got to be something here we can use!"

But Donovan had lost interest in the chest. He was fumbling with the bedclothes, lifting each corner of the mattress.

"Smitty had everything he needed down here," he replied in answer to Sarah's puzzled glance. "Food, water, light, money—what's missing? What haven't we found?"

He answered his own question by pulling a small, sinister-looking pocket revolver from under one of the pillows. A quick spin of the cylinder proved it to be loaded.

Sarah felt her knees go watery at the sight of the weapon in his hand. More people would die before sunup, she realized with a sickening certainty. Fate, luck and skill would determine who perished and who survived, but even the thought of the children, or the women, or Donovan—

"Are you all right?" He reached down to cup her chin with his free hand. His eyes searched her face, their depths dark with concern and love.

"Forgive me," she murmured, gazing up at him. "Seeing that gun in your hand, and thinking about what could happen ... I'm frightened, that's all. I love you so much, and I'm so afraid—"

"Come here, Sarah." He laid the pistol on a corner of the chest and drew her up off her knees, into his arms. She burrowed her face against his shirt, filling her senses with his warmth, his strength and the rich, masculine woodsmoke aroma of his clothes.

"I'm afraid, too, love," he whispered, his throat moving against her hair. "What we've found is too good to lose." His arms tightened fiercely around her. "But I promise you, somehow, some way—"

"You can't promise, Donovan. You can't know what will happen. None of us can."

Sarah raised her face for his kiss. His lips closed on hers with a tenderness that stirred aching whorls of need inside her. She slid her arms around his neck, her breasts straining against his beating heart. She clung to the moment, knowing it was not enough...knowing what they both wanted.

His mouth was wild honey on hers, his kiss as poignant as autumn moonlight. Sarah closed her eyes, savoring the sweet-salt taste of his tongue, the delicate roughness of its probing tip. A luminous throb rose from the dark center of her body. She nestled closer to him, feeling it surge until it shook her like the waves of a turbulent sea.

Donovan.

She had loved him from the moment of their first meeting, Sarah realized. She had loved him through the perilous days of Richmond and through their long years of separation. She had loved him that night at Varina's cabin when he'd stripped her mask away, and later, when his kiss had shattered her pretense once and for all.

She remembered those times now with a bittersweetness that clutched at her heart. If she had known it was all she might have of him, that their love would be not so much a destination as a journey...

But enough of regrets. If tonight was all that remained to them, Sarah resolved, she would live every moment to its fullest.

His arousal swelled hot and hard against her pelvis as his kiss probed deeper. She trembled in his arms as the pressure ignited a pulse of tiny flamebursts inside her. Dampness slicked her thighs as her body moistened to welcome his thrust. But as he hesitated, Sarah knew that even now he would not force her beyond her wishes. He was waiting in agony for a word, a signal of her own desire.

She pulled a little away from him, her lips swollen, her chest jerking with emotion. His eyes burned into hers in a moment of naked understanding. Never again could there be anything but the purest truth between them.

"We don't have much time." His voice was raw with urgency.

Her finger touched his cheek to linger for a heartbeat at the corner of his strong, sensual mouth. "Make love to me, Donovan," she whispered. "Here. Now."

"Sarah," he moaned low in his throat as he arched her onto the waiting bed. "Sarah, my darling."

She pulled him down to her, blurring the words with her mouth. Their lips teased and nibbled, tongues blending like flames in a yearning dance that sent ripples of molten heat cascading through Sarah's body. She felt his hand sliding over her thighs, her hips, his exquisite touch a licking fire through the fabric of her gown.

Her breath stopped as his fingers worked the low-cut bodice off her shoulders to expose the silken moons of her breasts. The texture of his callused palm was ecstasy on her skin. She gave herself up to its sweetness as he cupped her, stroking and kneading until she began to moan. Her hips shifted beneath him, pressing against his hardness in a frenzy of need.

Hand pausing, he leaned above her in the lamplight. His eyes were dark with love, his breath a harsh rasp in his chest as he gazed down at her face. "My beautiful Sarah," he whispered. "You don't know how long I've wanted you, or how much."

"More..." She arched her breast to his hand again, but instead of doing her bidding, he bent his head to capture one tingling nipple in his mouth. His rough-tipped tongue moved with exquisite slowness, circling the puckered ring of the aureole, sucking, laving the exquisitely sensitive tip until a crescendo of aching tugs erupted downward through Sarah's body. Her hips arched upward in a frantic quest for the fulfillment that only he could give her.

"Please..." she begged. "Please, Donovan..." One hand found his belt and tugged at the buckle. There would be no time to fully undress, she knew, but their clothing seemed to melt away in the driving heat of their desire. His hand found the parting of her legs. With a sure touch his fingers moved upward to tangle the fevered nest of curls, to stroke and caress the desire-moistened folds....

Sarah's mouth went slack as he touched her. For a long moment she lay still, her eyes closed as the exquisite sensations rippled over her. Then she stirred in his arms. Her fingers tugged wantonly at his buttons, frantic to free him from his confining clothes. Spurred by her impatience, he finished the job himself, only to groan as her hand closed around the smooth, hard shaft of his manhood.

"Sarah, I don't want to hurt you...."

"I love you, Donovan." She opened to him like a flower. She felt his touch, his probing as he readied her. Then her mouth opened in a little cry of joy as he thrust into her damp, pulsing center. Her hands clenched on his buttocks, holding him, pulling him deep.

Heaven.

Sarah's head fell back with an ecstatic whimper as he began to move in long, urgent strokes. Unbidden, she met each quivering thrust with her own, arching to him until their bodies moved as one. Little by little the singing began inside her, a trembling life paean that flowed from the core of pleasure, through every nerve, fiber and cell, until she felt as if her whole being were made of exquisitely throbbing light. It was as if Donovan had become part of her, and she part of him.

It was as if their souls had joined.

She felt his gasping breath against her shoulder as the rapture took them both. Her hands raked his hair, fingers clasping and quivering as the mounting waves of ecstasy swept over them.

"Sarah—" He rasped her name as his body shuddered against her. "Sarah, love—"

Her breath stopped as his seed burst into her. She felt her womb clench like a warm, wet fist, again... again...

And then there was only stillness. Stillness and love.

They rearranged their clothing in silence, both painfully aware of the fleeting time. Donovan ached with tenderness as he watched Sarah pull up her stockings and smooth her skirt over her petticoats. They had stolen a few brief moments for themselves, but the dangerous night would spare them no more. It was time to get back upstairs, to face what had to be faced.

He took the small revolver from the corner of the chest and slipped it into his pocket. The paring knife he handed to Sarah, watching as she slipped it into her bodice. Her gray eyes were huge in the flickering lamplight.

"Let's go," he muttered, taking up the lantern. Sarah nodded, her lips pressed tightly together. The love between them was strong and sure, but this was no time for sentiment, or for promises that could not be kept. Both of them knew it.

They passed into the cellar and she took the lantern, holding it while he pushed the shelf over the opening. Donovan felt her fragile strength beside him. He felt the warmth of her love as he moved up the ladder behind her. If only he could leave her in the secret room, to wait safely until the danger was over.

But Sarah, he knew, would not hear of it. She would fight at his side.

His thoughts dissolved at the sound of a scream from the saloon—a woman's throaty voice, vibrating with terror.

"It's Zoe!" Sarah sprinted across the kitchen, leaving Donovan to conceal the trapdoor and shut the closet. He saw her burst into the saloon, only to freeze in the doorway, thunderstruck by what she saw.

"What the devil!" Donovan had caught up with her now. He stared past her shoulder into a nightmare scene from hell.

MacIntyre had awakened. He was lying on his back, head straining upward, eyes bulging with enraged effort. His single, massive, iron-muscled hand was clenched in a stranglehold around Spade's throat.

Zoe cowered against a corner of the piano, clutching her torn dressing gown against her breasts, her mouth agape in a silent echo of her scream. It was easy enough to guess what had happened. With Dooley dozing, Spade had seized the chance to make another pass at her. Now the gunman's body jerked spasmodically as MacIntyre's immense fingers crushed his windpipe like a garrote.

Spade was dying, Donovan realized numbly as he gripped Sarah's arm and jerked her against his shoulder. That, or he was already dead, and MacIntyre's rage was too maniacal to recognize a stopping point.

For an instant, Donovan's gaze flashed to Simeon Dooley. What he saw chilled his flesh to the bone. Dooley was sitting back in his chair, fingers toying idly with the trigger of his rifle as he watched Spade die. Clearly, he had no intention of rescuing his slow-witted cohort. Spade had outlived his usefulness. His death would remove an inconvenience and leave more robbery loot for the two survivors.

Spade's body slumped to the floor as MacIntyre let go. The gunman lay limp as a rag doll, his head skewed grotesquely on his twisted neck, his eyes already glassing over with death. MacIntyre had fallen back onto his pillow. His eyes were closed, his forehead beaded with sweat. Zoe crouched beside him now, her sensual mahogany face gray with shock as she cradled him in her arms.

Only now did Dooley raise the rifle to his shoulder and lever back the hammer.

"No!" Sarah's cry ripped the air as she tore free of Donovan and flashed across the room. Her outthrust arm caught the barrel, jarring the muzzle to one side.

Donovan moved.

"Leggo, you hell-bitch!" Dooley snarled as Sarah clung desperately to the barrel.

"No!" she muttered as he whipped her back and forth like a rat. "I won't let you—"

Her words ended in a painful gasp as Dooley's big left hand crashed into her cheek, knocking her into a sprawl on the floor. Dooley swung the rifle, taking aim at Sarah now.

But he was not fast enough. In a flash, Donovan had reached him and jammed the barrel of Smitty's pistol against the outlaw's temple.

"Slow and easy, if you want to live, Corporal," he said. "Lay the rifle on the floor."

The sweaty stink of fear rose from Dooley's body as he lowered the Spencer with his right hand. "Son-of-a-bitchin' lawman," he growled, "I should've let Cherokee kill you right off!"

"Shut up and drop it." Donovan jabbed the cold muzzle into his flesh and thumbed back the hammer. Only then did he remember Cherokee upstairs with the children. A silent prayer moved his lips as he realized what a fearful gamble he had taken in saving Sarah. "Let the gun go, Dooley," he ordered. "Put both hands on the table where I can see them."

The rifle thumped against the floor as Dooley obeyed. Donovan used his foot to scoot the weapon toward Sarah. "Pick it up," he ordered her softly. "Do you know how to use it?"

Sarah nodded. Her face was white as she bent to pick up the weapon.

"Now, I want you to hold it on our friend, here, while I get Zoe and MacIntyre outside," Donovan said. "If the murdering bastard moves, shoot to kill. Can you do it?"

Sarah leveled the cocked rifle at Dooley's chest, her mouth set in a determined line. She would be all right, Donovan reminded himself as he eased off the pistol's hammer and tucked the small gun into the back of his belt. As Lydia Taggart, she had faced years of danger with a brave heart and a cool head. He knew he could depend on her now.

Dooley's face widened into a desperate grin as Donovan moved along the bar. "Why, Miss Lydia! How could you hurt me—a pretty little thing like you? I thought we were friends."

Sarah's shoulders stiffened as she gripped the rifle. "We might be friends under the right circumstances, Corporal, but when you threaten people I care about, it ends right there. If you think I wouldn't shoot you in the blink of an eye—"

Dooley's grin froze and faded as Sarah's finger tensed on the trigger. Yes, she would be all right, Donovan concluded as he turned away to help Zoe shift the groaning MacIntyre onto the quilt and drag him toward the front door. There was always a chance the motion might reopen MacIntyre's wound, but in any case he would be safer outside, where someone could get him to his house.

Zoe carried the foot end of the blanket. Her sultry features mirrored her concern as she leaned over MacIntyre, unmindful of her torn, disheveled dressing gown. Signaling a halt at the threshold, Donovan took an abandoned coat from the rack and placed it gently around her shoulders. When she passed through the front door, Zoe would be entering a world almost as hostile as the one she had left. He could only hope she would find welcome and sanctuary.

As he slid back the bolt and cracked open the door, Donovan glimpsed the flare of torches in the street. The storm had ended and a large crowd had assembled to keep vigil. The supplies Dooley had demanded were piled on the stoop, covered with a wet tarpaulin. Three horses, saddled and bridled, drooped along the hitching rail, their manes and tails still shedding rainwater.

The crowd edged closer as someone noticed the opening door. "Somebody come and help these people!" Donovan shouted above the mutter of voices. There was an agonizing pause, as if no one dared get within range of a possible bullet. Then, suddenly there were hands, lifting MacIntyre in the quilt, hands ushering Zoe out of harm's way. The two of them would be safe, Donovan reassured himself as he swiftly bolted the door and turned his attention back to the drama inside the saloon.

Sarah stood steadfast, still covering Dooley with the Spencer. But her face was ragged with fatigue, her eyes bloodshot in the flickering lamplight. She had long since reached the end of her physical strength and was running on sheer willpower. If he could not bring this ordeal to a swift end, Donovan knew, she would shatter under the strain.

With Smitty's pistol still tucked in the back of his belt, he strode to her side and carefully disengaged the rifle from her hands. "Get back out of the way, love," he murmured. "I'll take over from here."

She yielded the long gun with a small breath of relief. Almost as an afterthought, Donovan gave her a furtive nudge as she passed behind him. The motion brushed the butt of the pistol against her forearm. She hesitated, then, guessing at what he wanted, slipped the weapon out of his belt.

"That's it," he muttered, his eyes riveted on Dooley. "You've got exactly the right idea." He gave her a few seconds to hide the pistol in the folds of her skirt. Then, as she moved toward the far side of the saloon, he stepped closer to the big man and jammed the rifle muzzle against his rough-whiskered throat.

"So that's your game!" he declared in a loud voice, gambling that Cherokee would be listening. "Pretty clever of you, Dooley, letting that poor devil MacIntyre get rid of Spade for you. Now, who're you counting on to kill off Cherokee, so you can have all the loot to yourself? Are you waiting for *me* to do the job?"

"Shut up, Cole!" Dooley growled. "An' if you know what's good for them kids upstairs, you'll put down that gun!"

"Listen, you double-crossing bastard, I've got your plan all figured out!" Donovan plunged ahead, starkly aware of the prickling danger sense that raised the hair on the back of his neck. "You'll kill off Spade and Cherokee and get away clean. Then when the claims are transferred, you'll get rid of me, too. I've a mind not to take you on as a partner after all, not unless you change your tune."

"You found the papers?" Dooley's eyes narrowed greedily.

"We found more than papers. You can be a rich man for life if you make the right choice, Dooley. Get your slit-mouthed friend out of the way, and we'll talk."

"You're full o' hogwash, Cole!" Dooley smirked up at him. "And you might as well lay that rifle down. You ain't gonna shoot nobody."

The danger sense was unmistakable now. It clawed at Donovan's nerve ends, screaming like a cougar in his head. He heard Sarah's horrified gasp, and he knew that he had carried his bluff as far as he dared.

Dooley's sneer widened into a grin. "Turn around, Cole. Put the gun on the table. Then look behind you."

Donovan lowered the rifle, moving now with exquisite caution. He knew exactly what he would see. Even so, as he turned, the sight that met his gaze tore at his heart.

Cherokee crouched partway down the staircase. Clutched against his side, white with terror, was Katy.

The rage that welled up in Donovan's chest was white-hot, dizzying in its fury. Katy's eyes were saucers of fear in her wan little face. Through the lamplit glare, they pleaded silently for help and comfort. But there was nothing he dared do. The cold iron barrel of Cherokee's Colt lay black against her russet curls, its deadly muzzle resting like a viper's head along the pale curve of her cheek.

Donovan forced his tight throat to form words. "Let her go, Cherokee," he rasped. "You've gunned down a lot of men, I know. But I'll wager you've never had a child on your conscience—a pretty little girl who'll grow up to be a fine woman one day."

He paused for breath, heart pounding with fear and frustration. If his words had pierced Cherokee's silent wall, it didn't show in his face. The dark features were as impassive as stone.

"Look at her," he pleaded, risking more boldness. "Then look at Spade, lying there with his neck crushed. Dooley let it happen, Cherokee. He watched Spade die without lifting a finger to save him. And he'd do the same for you—"

"Shut up, Cole!" Dooley had picked up the Spencer, and he jammed the barrel hard against Donovan's spine. "I shoulda killed you first thing! And when I'm through with you, by damn, I will!"

Donovan could see Sarah out of the corner of his eye. She was crouched on the edge of a chair, frozen in mid-motion. He remembered the pistol and wondered what she'd done with it.

"Go ahead, then," he said. "Let the others go and take me with you. The horses and supplies are waiting outside. No one in the street will raise a hand to stop you. They only want the children back."

"No. I have a better idea." It was Sarah who spoke. She was on her feet now, trembling like an aspen in a strong wind. "Take me with you instead. A woman hostage would give you more bargaining power against a posse. And you could keep me prisoner. You could hole up somewhere and hold me for ransom until you got word that Donovan had filed the claim transfers."

Donovan cursed under his breath. He wanted Sarah out of this. He wanted her safe. Why couldn't the maddening woman have kept still and left things to him?

Dooley scowled, his eyes darting to Cherokee, who had not moved a muscle except to tighten his grip on Katy. Dooley had tried to conceal all mention of the claims from the silent half-breed. But now everything was out in the open.

"For all your fancy talk, I haven't seen one piece of paperwork on them claims!" Dooley snarled, turning back to Sarah. "Are they real, or have you been bullin' me all along?"

Sarah's thin, bare shoulders quivered above the wilted green silk. "They're real," she said doggedly. "And I'm sure I can find them, if you'll just give me a little more time."

"Time!" Dooley exploded. "Hell, you've had most of the night! Time's runnin' out!" He glanced at Donovan and spat on the floor. "I'll give you one hour to come up with them claims! While you look, I'm keepin' your friend the major right here. Bring me the papers and we'll talk. Otherwise, Cole's a dead man, and I promise you it won't be pretty!"

Chapter Sixteen

"Tie him tight, Lydia, honey. No tricks now, or I shoot the both of you."

Sarah's fingers shook as she knotted the rope that bound Donovan to the chair. Neither of them spoke—there was little to be said, with Dooley smirking at them down the barrel of his rifle. But she could feel the tension in the taut cords of Donovan's wrists. She could feel the helpless rage in every rise and fall of his chest. He was afraid for her, Sarah knew. And she was even more afraid for him. Her offer to produce the claim papers had been pure bluff. Now, if she could not deliver them, Donovan would pay with his life.

Dooley had ordered Donovan to drag Spade's body to the cool room. That accomplished, Cherokee had been allowed to take Katy upstairs again. The last sight of the little girl's tear-streaked face had wrenched Sarah's heart, and she could only imagine what it had done to Donovan.

"Please—" She'd turned on Dooley in desperation. "Just let the children go. We've got money—you can have it all!"

He had only scratched his flat nose and grinned at her helplessness. "You make the offer sound right temptin', honey," he drawled. "But money can't hold off a posse. Kids can. Just finish tyin' up your boyfriend and bring me them minin' claims. That is, if you really got 'em."

"I've got them," she'd lied. "I remember the box where I put them now. It should be in the upstairs storeroom." She had circled Donovan's body with the ropes, leaving them as loose as she dared. His eyes looked straight ahead now, betraying nothing.

"Tighter, honey." Dooley jabbed at her ribs with the rifle's cold steel muzzle. "Don't leave him no wigglin' room. You do, and I'll know it."

"Do as he says." Donovan's voice was low and taut. Sarah tightened the ropes, weighing the chance she was about to take.

"Just a little more back here." She edged around behind him, to a position where his body shielded her from Dooley's sight. As she tested the knot that bound his wrists, one hand darted to her bodice. Praying that Dooley would not notice, she pulled out the small kitchen knife and slipped it into Donovan's sleeve. A subtle twitch of Donovan's wrist told her he knew what she had done.

A fine beading of sweat chilled Sarah's face and arms as she stepped away from him. "I'm finished," she declared. "Check the knots if you like, Corporal."

"No need!" Dooley snorted his amusement. "If the major gets loose, I'll just plug a bullet through him!"

Sarah bit back the urge to tell the man what an evil monster he was. "I'll be going to look for those claim papers now," she said. "If you so much as touch him—"

He grinned at her implied threat. "Why, ain't you the feisty one, Miss Lydia Taggart! You oughta be lickin' my boots for not killin' you both right here! Now, get on with you! Either find them claims or quit yappin' about 'em!"

Sarah cast him a contemptuous glance and stalked toward the staircase. She could feel Donovan's gaze on her, but she did not look back. She did not dare. A single meeting of their eyes would be enough to shatter her.

She should have kept still, she thought as she mounted the stairs. She should have left matters to Donovan. Instead, her blind desperation to save his life had left him in helpless peril.

Smitty's pistol, which she'd managed to tuck beneath a garter, lay cold against her thigh. The small firearm was her only hope, but how could she use it? If she ambushed Cherokee, Dooley would kill Donovan. And shooting Dooley would unleash Cherokee on the women and children.

Reeling with exhaustion, she reached the landing and paused to collect her thoughts. Find the mining claims—no other step made sense. But she did not even know whether the claims existed. And if they did, her task loomed as hopeless as finding the needle in the proverbial haystack. Smitty's office, the cellar and the secret room had already been ransacked. She could only guess at where to look next.

The storeroom lay at the far end of the hall. To reach it, she would have to pass the room where Cherokee guarded his prisoners. Squaring her shoulders, she strode down the narrow corridor. In the bloodred light, she could see the outlaw seated with his crossed legs spanning the doorway. His hat brim was tilted over his eyes, and he appeared to be dozing, but Sarah knew better. He would be fully awake and well aware of her approach.

Her footsteps slowed as an idea took root in her mind. It was a wild scheme, born of desperation and not likely to work. But if ever there was a time for risks, it was now.

She came abreast of the door and paused in the opening. Cherokee did not raise his head, but a barely perceptible twitch of his gun hand told Sarah he knew she was there. He was waiting like a coiled snake, waiting for the slightest excuse to strike.

Leaning cautiously past him in the doorway, she peered into the darkened room. All five of the children sprawled sleepily on the bed. Freckle-faced Isaac, Eli, Harold, Molly Sue, who was sucking her thumb, and brave little Katy. Sarah's gaze lingered lovingly on each small face. She would save them, she vowed. Whatever the cost, she would save them all.

George, the wounded piano player, stirred restlessly on the rug next to the bed. Greta huddled in a corner, snoring in puffy little breaths. But Faye was wide-awake. She sat upright in her rocker, her fatigue-glazed eyes staring into the darkness.

"Faye!" Sarah stage-whispered across the distance.

Faye's gaze shifted.

"Faye, I need to talk to you! There's something I have to find!"

Faye eased out of the chair and crept closer to the doorway where Sarah stood. Cherokee had not moved, but Sarah knew he was listening. She leaned past him, to speak close to Faye's ear.

"How much do you know about Smitty's business?"

Faye's husky shoulders lifted in a shrug.

"I'm looking for the mining claims...." Sarah's eyes pleaded for understanding. "You know, all those worthless claims he took as payment years ago, when the town was going bust?"

Faye hesitated foggily. "Oh," she said at last. "*Them* claims."

"Donovan says the claims are going to be valuable again now that the new smelter's opened up in Central City." Sarah paused, then threw caution to the winds. "When we find them, Dooley says he'll take us on as partners. We can use the robbery loot to set ourselves up in Mexico. Then, when the time's right, we can sell the claims for cash. We'll be rich!"

Again Faye hesitated. One eyelid twitched in the red darkness. Had it been a wink, Sarah wondered, or only a nervous tic?

"How 'bout me?" she asked plaintively. "How 'bout Greta and Zoe and George?"

"We...can talk about it after we find the claims," Sarah hedged, still uncertain of how much Faye understood.

"And how 'bout him?" She glanced down at Cherokee. Sarah saw the cords tense in the gunman's wrist. Yes, Faye knew and she was playing along. Sarah could have hugged her.

She dropped her voice to a conspiratorial whisper. "Not him. Dooley wants to make a fresh start. He figures Cherokee'll draw too much trouble. I suppose we'll have to buy him off—that, or get rid of him somehow."

"How 'bout cuttin' me in for sure if I help you find them claims?" Faye's rough voice exuded an innocence that was almost childlike.

"You know where they are?"

"Maybe. Any way you look at it, two heads is better 'n one."

"Shh!" Sarah cautioned. "All right. Come on, then."

Lifting her skirts, Faye negotiated her way over Cherokee's pointed Mexican boots. Sarah was afraid the outlaw might try to stop her, but he kept up his own pretense of dozing, hat cocked over his eyes, as the two women crept down the hall. They stopped long enough to borrow a lamp from Greta's chamber and light a match to the wick. Then they hurried on toward the storeroom.

The room was closed but not locked. They slipped inside and shut the door behind them. The lamplight flickered on a ceiling-high mountain of old furniture, sacks and boxes.

Sarah gazed upward, racked by hopelessness as she faced the truth.

She would never find the mining claims. Even with Faye's help, it would take hours, maybe days to sift through the contents of this one room. Even if they were to empty every box and scrutinize every paper, the effort would be wasted. The claims did not exist. She had bluffed and lost. Time would run out. Donovan would die, and her heart would die with him.

Sarah ripped open the drawer of a dusty desk, dumped its contents on the floor and began pawing furiously through them. She could not give up. No matter how black things looked, no matter how hopeless . . .

Her whole body had begun to shake. With growing despair, she jerked out a second drawer, then a third.

She was reaching for the fourth drawer when she felt Faye's hand on her shoulder.

The blade lay thin and cold beneath the fabric of Donovan's sleeve. The small kitchen knife was not particularly sharp, he knew. But if he could position it just right . . .

"Sit still, Major, you're makin' me nervous." Dooley leered at him from across the table. "You don't want to make me nervous. I might get jumpy enough to shoot you." His laughter echoed eerily off the walls. "Your girlfriend's been gone quite a while, now, eh, Cole? Probably lit out while she had the chance. I coulda told you she'd do it. All that bull about them claim papers—"

"Shut up, Dooley," Donovan snapped. "It's bad enough sitting here waiting to get shot. I shouldn't have to listen to you, too."

Laughter again, punctuated by an alcoholic hiccup. The big man had been swilling whiskey all night, and the effects were finally beginning to show. His speech was slurred, his eyes glassy as he leaned sideways in his chair. The hope that he might pass out fluttered in Donovan's heart, then swiftly vanished. Simeon Dooley had the endurance of a grizzly bear.

"Your bottle's empty," Donovan said. "Untie me, and I'll go get you another one."

"Sure, and then you'll come back and play me a hand of poker, too. What time is it, Cole? Seems to me your hour should be about up."

"Twenty minutes to go." Donovan glanced at the clock and thought of Sarah. He knew she would not return with the papers—there were no papers to find. But she had the pistol. He could only hope she would have the sense to rescue the hostages and get out while there was still time. His own life would be a small price to pay for nine others.

Willing his shoulders and torso to keep still, he worked the knife lower along his wrist. "So, Dooley, how do you plan to kill me?" he asked mockingly. "Describe it to me. Give me every bloody little detail...."

Sarah stared, transfixed, as Faye worked the rolled sheaf of papers from the depths of her ample bodice.

"I ... don't understand," she murmured.

"There ain't many secrets in a place like this, child. Zoe heard you talkin' about the minin' claims. She told Greta, and Greta told me, so we all knowed you was lookin' for 'em." Faye unrolled the papers, curving them backward to flatten them. "When Cherokee took that little gal downstairs, I grabbed these out from under the mattress, where they been hid all these years."

Thunderstruck, Sarah riffled through the yellowed pages. Mining claims. Fifteen or twenty of them at least, all legally witnessed and signed over to Faye Margaret Swenson.

"Smitty never took claims for payment," Faye explained. "He said they wasn't worth the paper they was printed on, and we wasn't to take 'em, neither. But me, I felt sorry for some o' them ol' boys. They was lonesome and down on their luck, and if one of 'em offered me a claim for a roll in the sack, hell, I took it. 'Course, I always made sure the signin's was witnessed so's they'd be legal...."

Sarah's knees had gone weak. "Faye, do you have any idea what these claims might be worth?" she whispered.

"Don't reckon it matters much, since I'm givin' 'em to you. If you can use 'em to buy them poor young'uns out of here, that's good enough for me. 'Course, they'll have to be signed and witnessed again...."

Sarah blinked away tears as she riffled through the papers. "Faye, you're so...wait! There's no reason we have to use all of these! Keep a few for yourself. Here—choose the ones you want to take back!"

"Let me see..." Faye scowled at the claims, her frowsy vermilion hair sticking out around her jowled face. "I reckon one's enough for me. This 'un came from Jorgen Bertelson. I always did have a special yen for that big, black mustache o' his an' the way it tickled." She separated the paper from the others, rolled it to the diameter of a cheroot and thrust it back into her generous cleavage. "You take the rest. Come on, we better be gettin' back."

Sarah followed Faye out of the storage room, her heart pounding frantically as she clutched the papers. Would Dooley keep his word and let Donovan go? What if he'd given up on her? What if she was already too late?

By the time she passed Faye's room, Sarah was all but running. Her tear-blinded eyes did not even see the shadow that moved in the doorway.

Not until the thin, iron fingers closed around her upper arm, jerking her around like a lash, did she realize what was happening.

She stared into the anthracite slits of Cherokee's eyes and felt the chilly muzzle of the Colt against her ribs.

At first Sarah did not know what he wanted. Then, as he shoved her along the corridor, she realized he was taking her downstairs with the claim papers. The bit of playacting with Faye must have worked. Too well, perhaps.

She caught a glimpse of Faye, watching in horror from the doorway. "The children!" Sarah gasped. "Faye, get the children out the—"

Her words ended in a little cry as Cherokee's hand cracked the side of her head. The blow sent her reeling against the wall. He caught her wrist and, with brutal force, whipped her back against him. She could feel his white-hot rage as he jammed the gun into her ribs. He no longer cared about guarding the hostages—that was clear enough. His silent fury was focused elsewhere now. At Dooley. At Donovan. At her.

If he had his way, Sarah realized, he would kill them all.

Donovan strained desperately against the ropes that bound his arms and wrists. The scuffling noises overhead told him there was trouble, and every instinct screamed that Sarah was involved. Sarah and Cherokee.

He had managed to work the knife down as far as the ropes without dropping it. With Dooley watching, however, he could make only the smallest movements. The blade had cut through a few outer fibers, but the thin, tough hemp still held.

His fists clenched at the sound of something striking a wall. A rampaging Cherokee, he knew, could be as savage as a wounded mountain lion, and if he'd gotten his hands on Sarah . . .

Donovan sawed frantically against the blade, heedless now of what Dooley thought or did. The rough rope strands chewed into his flesh, sliming his hands with blood.

"Damn it, Cole—" Dooley had been distracted by the noise. Now he glared at Donovan and raised the rifle.

"Cut me loose, Dooley!" Donovan rasped. "Lord, don't you know what's happening up there? We've got to—"

The words strangled in Donovan's throat as Cherokee appeared at the top of the stairs. Clutched in the crook of his arm, his Colt thrust hard against her temple, was Sarah.

Donovan's heart broke as he looked at her. She hung limp with fear against Cherokee's side, her left cheek purpled by a swelling bruise. Her eyes were wild with terror.

In one thin, white hand, she clutched a sheaf of yellowed papers. Donovan swallowed hard at the sight of them. Mining claims. Somehow she had found them. And Cherokee knew it.

Donovan had been baiting the half-breed all night, hoping to turn him against Dooley. The ruse appeared to have worked, except that he had not counted on being tied up at the critical moment. And worst of all, he had not planned on endangering Sarah.

As Cherokee kicked and shoved her down the stairs, Donovan wrenched violently at his bonds. The knife, so tenuously held, suddenly slipped loose from his blood-slicked fingers and clattered to the floor.

Donovan stopped breathing.

Dooley had not noticed. Nor had Cherokee. But Sarah's stricken eyes darted to him, and he knew she had seen it fall. He flung his strength against the constricting ropes, straining to break them with his raw wrists, but the stubborn strands held.

In desperation, he thrust his weight to the right, rocking the chair until it toppled sideways. He did his best to cushion the noise with his own flesh. All the same, he was surprised when Dooley did not even glance in his direction. The big man's eyes were fixed on Cherokee, his gun hand resting nervously on the trigger of the rifle.

Donovan's fingers groped the floor for the knife and found it. Working the blade into position, he began to hack furiously at the ropes. But even as he struggled, his eyes were fixed on the drama unfolding in the circle of lamplight.

Cherokee and Sarah had reached the bottom of the stairs. With savage roughness, he shoved her toward Dooley's table and flung her violently against the edge. She struck with a cry of pain, the claim papers scattering as she clawed the edge for balance.

Simeon Dooley had glimpsed the murderous expression in Cherokee's eyes. His shaking hands caught up the rifle, cocked and aimed.

But he was not fast enough for Cherokee. The Colt barked once, twice, three times as the big outlaw sagged in his chair, then toppled forward with his face on the table.

Donovan felt the ropes separate, freeing his hands. "Get down, Sarah!" he ordered, struggling to reach her. "Get me the gun!"

He had meant the pocket pistol, the one she'd taken off him earlier. But he suddenly realized she had grabbed Dooley's rifle and was swinging the barrel toward Cherokee. Donovan saw him turn, saw his thumb catch the hammer of the Colt—

Both shots went wild as Donovan upended the table between them. Seizing Sarah by the waist, he spun her out of the line of fire, wrenching the rifle out of her hands. "Get back, damn it!" he rasped. "Leave the bastard to me!"

As Sarah disappeared somewhere behind him, Donovan noticed that one of the bullets had shattered the oil reservoir of a lamp. Tongues of fire were licking up one of the walls toward the ceiling. Minutes from now, the whole rickety building would be ablaze.

"Get out of here, Sarah!" he bellowed as Cherokee's first bullet whined past his head. "Get out now!"

She flashed past the periphery of his vision, headed for the stairway.

"Damn it, Sarah, *get out!*"

"The children—I have to make sure—" Her voice faded as she pounded upstairs. Cursing under his breath, Donovan ducked behind the overturned table and swung his full attention back to Cherokee.

The outlaw had retreated behind the fortress of the bar, where he crouched, waiting for an opportunity to shoot. He had pumped three bullets into Dooley and missed Donovan with a fourth. That would give him no more than two shots, unless he was taking advantage of the chance to reload right now.

Sweat trickled down Donovan's face as he gripped Dooley's rifle, wondering how many bullets *he* had left. There was no time to check without leaving himself open to Cherokee's fire. All he could do was plan to shoot as if each round were his last.

Glancing up, he saw a tide of flame sweeping across the ceiling. The smell of smoke and burning timber singed his nostrils. For an instant his thoughts flashed to Sarah. She would be gone by now, she and the others, all safely outside by way of the back stairs. The fight was between himself and Cherokee now. And it would not end, Donovan knew, until one of them was dead.

The upstairs rooms were empty. Sarah's shoulders sagged in relief as she gazed down the back stairs toward the smashed-open doorway. They were all safe—Faye, Greta, George and the five children. All she had to do was follow them, and she would be safe, too.

The corridor was already filling up with smoke. It curled between the floorboards, black and bitter where the heat scorched the rotting wool of the carpet. Seconds from now, Sarah knew, the back stairs would be ablaze, cutting off her escape. She had to get out now, before it was too late.

But her feet would not move. Something was holding her back, and suddenly she knew what it was. Donovan. Downstairs with no help at all, fighting for his life.

She could not leave him.

Holding her breath against the strangling smoke, Sarah wheeled and plunged back down the hall. Her motion jarred the cool weight of Smitty's little pocket pistol against her leg. She reached the landing, red eyed and gasping, only to hear a shot ring out from below, then another. The gun...yes, she would need it. Heart lurching with fear, she tore at her skirt and jerked the weapon free.

The smoke was thinner here because the fire was working its way from the far side of the saloon. But the blaze was spreading fast, racing up the walls and along the crossbeams. The tinder-dry boards crackled as they burst into flame. Sarah stifled a spasm of coughing as she crept down the first few steps, the pistol clutched in her hand.

Through the smoky red haze, she could see what was happening in the saloon below. Cherokee cowered behind the bar, protected from gunfire by its thick structure. Donovan's position was much more vulnerable. He was crouched with the rifle in the middle of the floor, shielded only by the meager thickness of the overturned table. Pushing the table before him, he was inching his way toward the end of the bar, but Cherokee had every advantage. He could wait for Donovan to come to him, then choose the best moment to shoot.

And the outlaw could wait for something else, Sarah realized to her sudden horror. The fiery ceiling above Donovan's head was starting to buckle. Seconds from now, it would collapse in an avalanche of flaming death. From his more protected spot, Cherokee would be left with the chance of escaping through the kitchen.

Sarah stifled the urge to call out a warning. The distraction could catch Donovan off guard, leaving him open to Cherokee's deadly aim. The pistol—she felt its sinister weight in her hand, and suddenly she knew there was only one thing she could do.

From her perch on the stairs, she had a clear view of the space behind the bar. Wiping her smoke-burned eyes, she cocked the tiny gun, gripped it with both hands and aimed it at the dark, crouching figure of Cherokee. A prayer moved her lips as she squeezed the trigger....

The shot was no more than a pop amid the roar of the flames. Donovan did not even appear to have heard it. But she saw the half-breed jump and glance nervously around, as if the bullet had struck close by. Willing herself to move fast, Sarah cocked and aimed again. Even if she couldn't hit Cherokee, she could drive him out of his shelter.

Closing her eyes against the blinding smoke, she squeezed the trigger. This time, when she looked, Sarah realized she'd managed to hit him. He was clutching his shoulder, his gaze darting frantically around the saloon as Donovan crept closer.

The ceiling was a sea of flame. Its stifling heat seared Sarah's lungs as she fired again. And now Cherokee was turning. His eyes widened as he spotted her on the steps. Her heart strangled her throat as she realized she had no place to go. The top floor of the saloon had become a torch. Any second the ceiling would collapse, and with it, the stairway.

Cherokee's eyes narrowed to slits as he aimed the Colt. In desperation, Sarah dived. Her body struck a few steps below to roll over and over in a blur of motion. She heard two shots, heard the unearthly scream that ripped from Cherokee's throat as he staggered and fell.

She glanced up at the ceiling. It was sagging lower, the timbers shrieking as they gave way.

For the space of a heartbeat she glimpsed Donovan through the smoke. She heard him shout her name, and then the whole world became a roaring inferno as the charred joists gave way and the second floor of the saloon collapsed into the first.

Protected by the wall, Sarah crawled along the floor. Her breath came in coughing gasps as the smoke filled her lungs. Donovan could not reach her, she knew. He could no longer see or hear her. Not even if he was still alive.

Her groping fingers found the entrance to the kitchen. Knowing the back kitchen door was her only chance of escape, she plunged inside. But even here the ceiling had caved in and a wall of blazing timber cut off her exit. Flames ringed her on all sides, blistering her skin, sucking away her breath. Sarah felt her mind spinning, her senses darkening.

Donovan . . . her mind whispered. *I love you, Donovan. . . .*

Donovan awakened with a jolt.

"Sarah—" He struggled against the arms that pinned him to the ground. "I've got to go back! I've got to get her—"

"Lie still, Mr. Cole." It was Watson, the town's barber, undertaker and occasional doctor, who leaned over him.

"You've been unconscious for an hour. The fire's burned itself out."

"Sarah—"

"She's gone, son." Sam Cahill's rotund face, streaked with soot and perspiration, thrust into Donovan's vision. "When we heard you shouting, we broke down the front door and managed to drag you outside before the whole saloon went up in flames. You were out of your head, fought us like a wild man till you lost consciousness. But there was no sign of Sarah. Maybe when we clear away the rubble, we'll find some trace of—"

"No!" Donovan wrenched himself to a sitting position, his head reeling. Sarah couldn't be gone. Not when they had just found each other. Not when they had their whole lives ahead of them!

His head dropped to his blistered hands as the awful reality crashed in on him. He had seen Sarah inside the saloon just before the ceiling caved in. She had come back to help him. Her courage in distracting Cherokee had probably saved his life. But afterward, as the burning structure collapsed, he had not been able to reach her. He had shouted her name as she vanished behind a solid wall of fire, and that was when the townspeople had smashed the front door and dragged him outside.

Donovan's body heaved with anguish. With all his heart, he wished that he could have died with her.

His beautiful, brave, passionate Sarah.

A soft hand on his shoulder stirred him back to awareness. He looked up to see Mattie Ormes, with little Isaac clasped in her arms. "I'm sorry," she whispered. "I was terrible to Sarah, and she saved my boy. I'll never be able to repay her."

"And she saved our Molly Sue." Tom Gordon had shouldered his way through the crowd. "We were wrong to judge her for her past. I'm sorry."

"Sarah Parker was an angel!" It was Eudora Cahill who spoke up now. "Whatever she might have done before, she was the best thing that ever happened to this town!"

Donovan sat in the mud, disconsolate as the people of Miner's Gulch milled around him. Staring dazedly toward the saloon, he could see that the fire had indeed burned itself out. The place was nothing but a heap of glowing, blackened timbers. No one could have survived such an inferno.

Many people were still carrying buckets. The brigades had managed to save the other buildings along the main street. Even Amos Satterlee's store had been spared, its exterior soaked down by water from the pails. Satterlee himself, however, was nowhere to be seen.

Something new had happened in Miner's Gulch tonight, Donovan realized. For the first time in recent memory, the scattered, apathetic citizens had pulled together for the good of their community. He sensed a new pride in the way they held their heads, a new unity in the way they spoke to one another. There was hope, after all, for this backward little town that Sarah had loved so much. That hope had been her final gift.

The eastern sky was pale with dawn. As the first sun ray brushed the mountains, the birds burst into a chorus of song. Donovan listened to the joyous sound, remembering Sarah. Remembering her beauty and the splendor of her defiant spirit. Remembering her warmth. Remembering the unbridled sweetness of the love they had shared in the secret room...

The secret room.

Suddenly he was on his feet, stumbling through the crowd. The odds were long, so long that he was a fool even to hope. But he had to find out. He had to know for sure.

"Sarah!" He was running down what used to be the alley, rounding the smoldering corner where the black-charred trunks of the spruce trees rose stark against the morning sky.

"Sarah!" He was kicking aside the rubble, searching wildly for the tiny opening where the air vent surfaced, shouting her name again and again. People had stopped in their tracks to stare at him.

A sound—had he imagined it? Donovan froze, straining his ears. Yes, there it was again, faint through the blanketing earth. Her voice. Sarah's voice, calling to him.

His gaze swung back toward the watching crowd. "Come on!" he shouted, clawing at the mud. "She's down here! She's alive!"

From all directions people came running. With picks. With shovels. With willing hands. They swarmed around Donovan and began to dig. Wet earth flew as the sun rose over the peaks to herald a glorious new day.

Epilogue

A year of seasons had come and gone. It was spring once more in Miner's Gulch. A time of renewing life.

In the creek bottom where the willows hung pale with catkins, red-winged blackbirds called and scolded, their colors flashing against the water. Mountain streams gurgled with the sound of melting snow. Graceful Vs of migrating geese etched the wide blue dome of the sky.

Sunlight blanketed the land with gold. It sparked points of diamond fire on the snow-crested peaks and stirred wild bees to wakefulness in their hollows. It glittered through a glass prism that hung in a bedroom window, casting rainbows on the wide bed where Sarah lay damp, exhausted and happy beyond words.

Varina leaned over her, her face wreathed in smiles. "Here she is, Sarah. Here's your little girl," she whispered, placing the tiny, squirming bundle in Sarah's arms. "Just look at her! Isn't she beautiful?"

"Oh!" Sarah's heart burst as she gathered her baby close. Her eyes examined the crinkled rosebud face, the perfect hands with their exquisite little fingernails. "And wouldn't you know it?" she said with a laugh. "Red hair!"

"She's a Cole, all right!" Varina grinned as she tidied the room. "And she'll probably be just as stubborn as the rest of us!"

"Donovan—he's got to see her! Find him, Varina!"

"That won't be hard. He's right outside, pacing a hole in the carpet." Varina opened the bedroom door so abruptly that her brother almost tumbled across the threshold. Recovering, he crossed the room in three long strides to gather Sarah in his arms.

"She's...beautiful," he whispered huskily, gazing at his daughter. "What shall we call her?"

Sarah kissed the spot where his chestnut hair curled in front of his ear. "I've been playing with names for months." She laughed softly. "But as soon as I saw her red hair, I knew what her name had to be. Varina Faye Cole. Do you like it?"

"I like it." He made himself comfortable on the bed beside her as Varina wisely tiptoed from the room. "She's going to be the prettiest girl in Colorado."

"And the smartest." Sarah snuggled against his shoulder and closed her eyes, basking in the most perfect bliss she had ever known. The life she had all but lost was so good now, every part of it, that sometimes she wondered if it was all a dream.

Even the town was doing well. The gold ore, while not an El Dorado, had made many citizens, including Varina, comfortably well-off. Donovan had bought out MacIntyre's livery stable and gone into the freighting business, employing a fleet of wagons to haul ore from the mines to the smelter in Central City. The enterprise was prospering, and Donovan's cheerful manner told Sarah her husband was more than content.

She could only wish as much for MacIntyre and Zoe. They had taken her share of Smitty's cash and left together for California to start a new life. Sarah remembered them often, but reason told her, sadly, that she would never hear from them again.

Amos Satterlee, too, was gone. The Cahills had purchased his store and planned to build a new bank alongside it, on the site of the burned saloon.

A smile flickered across Sarah's lips as she thought about Faye. The single claim she'd saved had yielded a vein of pure gold. Faye Margaret Swenson was now the wealthiest person in town. With Greta and George as her partners, she had bought the vacant hotel, renovated it inside and out, and was now doing a thriving business.

The baby stirred and whimpered in Sarah's arms. She brushed her lips over its velvety head, feeling the tenderness in Donovan's gaze. "So, what are you thinking?" she whispered in his ear.

"That you're wonderful. That our daughter is wonderful. And that I'm the luckiest man alive."

"Mmm..." She nuzzled his whiskers. "I'm thinking about your sister. I wish she'd say yes to Jamie Trenoweth. I'd like seeing them as happy as we are."

"Oh, she will, I think, sooner or later. Jamie's a fine man, and her children adore him. But you know Varina. She has her own way of doing things."

Sarah smoothed the baby's russet hair. "And do you think our little Varina will be like her?" she asked with a smile.

Donovan's arms tightened around his wife and child. "Time will tell, love," he whispered. "Time will tell."

* * * * *

BRIDE'S BAY RESORT

UNLOCK THE DOOR TO GREAT ROMANCE AT BRIDE'S BAY RESORT

Join Harlequin's new across-the-lines series, set in an exclusive hotel on an island off the coast of South Carolina.

Seven of your favorite authors will bring you exciting stories about fascinating heroes and heroines discovering love at Bride's Bay Resort.

Look for these fabulous stories coming to a store near you beginning in January 1996.

Harlequin American Romance #613 in January
Matchmaking Baby by Cathy Gillen Thacker

Harlequin Presents #1794 in February
Indiscretions by Robyn Donald

Harlequin Intrigue #362 in March
Love and Lies by Dawn Stewardson

Harlequin Romance #3404 in April
Make Believe Engagement by Day Leclaire

Harlequin Temptation #588 in May
Stranger in the Night by Roseanne Williams

Harlequin Superromance #695 in June
Married to a Stranger by Connie Bennett

Harlequin Historicals #324 in July
Dulcie's Gift by Ruth Langan

Visit Bride's Bay Resort each month wherever Harlequin books are sold.

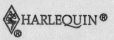

HARLEQUIN®

Harlequin Historicals is very pleased to announce a new
Western series from award-winning author Ruth Langan
starting in February—The Jewels of Texas

DIAMOND February 1996
PEARL August 1996
JADE January 1997
RUBY June 1997

Don't miss this exciting new series about four sisters as wild and
vibrant as the untamed land they're fighting to protect!

Harlequin® Historical

Coming in February from Harlequin Historicals

The next book in Suzanne Barclay's dramatic
Lion series—

LION'S LEGACY

"…fast paced, action packed historical romance…4 1/2 stars."
—*Affaire de Coeur*

"…absolutely captivating!"
The Medieval Chronicle

Whatever you do. Don't miss it!